Three-times Golden Heart □0476830
learned to pack her suitcas
learned to read. Born to a r
lived in the United States, Puerto Rico, Portugal and
Brazil. In addition to travelling, Tina loves to cuddle
with her pug, Alex, spend time with her family, and
hit the trails on her horse. Learn more about Tina
from her website, or 'friend' her on Facebook.

**Juliette Hyland** began crafting heroes and heroines
in high school. She lives in Ohio, USA, with her
Prince Charming, who has patiently listened to
many rants regarding characters who fail to follow
the outline. When not working on fun and flirty
happily-ever-afters, Juliette can be found spending
time with her beautiful daughters, giant dogs, or
sewing uneven stitches with her sewing machine.

# STARTING OVER WITH THE SINGLE DAD

TINA BECKETT

# REAWAKENED AT THE SOUTH POLE

JULIETTE HYLAND

**MILLS & BOON**

First Published in Great Britain 2021
by Mills & Boon, an imprint of HarperCollins*Publishers* Ltd,
1 London Bridge Street, London, SE1 9GF

www.harpercollins.co.uk

HarperCollins*Publishers*
1st Floor, Watermarque Building,
Ringsend Road, Dublin 4, Ireland

Starting Over with the Single Dad © 2021 by Tina Beckett

Reawakened at the South Pole © 2021 by Juliette Hyland

ISBN: 978-0-263-29776-8

09/21

**MIX**
Paper from
responsible sources
FSC™ C007454

This book is produced from independently certified FSC™ paper
to ensure responsible forest management.
For more information visit www.harpercollins.co.uk/green.

Printed and bound in Spain
by CPI, Barcelona

# STARTING OVER WITH THE SINGLE DAD

## TINA BECKETT

**MILLS & BOON**

To my husband.
I'm so glad that chance brought us together.

# PROLOGUE

*Fifteen years ago*

THE KISS CAME out of nowhere. And Lord, it was so incredibly heady. Decadent, even. Her lips clung to his warm mouth in desperation, her heart pounding in her chest. And Mysti North couldn't get enough.

She'd never dreamed her goodbye news would get this kind of a reaction from her childhood friend. But things had changed between them recently, and she couldn't stay in town with the way things were now.

The rain pounded down on the car and thunder cracked around them, but it couldn't reach inside and stop what was happening.

Mysti's arms slid around his neck, and a tiny sound emerged from her throat before she could stop it. Jesse's reaction was immediate. He pulled her even closer, tongue edging forward to meet hers and tangle with it. Her world changed colors for several heart-stopping seconds.

The boy next door had morphed into a hunky high school quarterback four years ago, and suddenly girls had flocked around him. Including her best friend, Kandid. And Kandid was everything Mysti wasn't. Beautiful, poised, a cheerleader and confident in her own feminine powers of attraction, she'd set her sights on Jesse almost immediately after Mysti had confided in her friend about her own crush on him, and of course she'd emerged the victor. He and Kandid had been dating for several months now, her friend regaling Mysti with stories of their intimate talks about the future. Which included children.

Mysti had never even dreamed she might have a chance with him herself. Until this very moment.

Jesse had had to stop the car when the rain turned torrential, the weather reports of flash floods holding true as water rushed across the small bridge that led into their hometown. He'd said he didn't dare cross that line and risk the consequences.

But he had dared to cross another kind of line—by kissing her. And it had brought the smoldering spark of hope inside her blazing back to life.

He'd offered to give her a ride home from the last game of their high school careers to save her mom from making the trip in the rain. And as she'd thrown her clarinet into the back seat, she'd decided that this was her chance to say a private goodbye to him. In person. Without the crowd that normally revolved around him. She'd already talked to a local army recruiter about her options and they, at least, seemed eager to have her.

So when he'd pulled over, she'd turned to him, clutching her hands in her lap and willing herself to make this final break. To give herself permission to walk away from her role of standing on the sidelines with the rest of Jesse's adoring public and find out what life held for her outside this town. Life without Jesse.

What she hadn't expected was the look that had crossed his face when she'd told him about her decision to join the army. "You're leaving Forgotten Point?"

"I am. I don't think this town holds much in the way of a future for me."

Especially not when all she could foresee was Jesse marrying Kandid and then forever having to meet him with a band on his finger that marked him as someone else's. Her friend's husband. But, God, how could she move away and leave him behind? He'd been a constant in her childhood, and to imagine him with anyone else hurt her beyond all imagining…

Except she'd never even dreamed of him staring at her like he had after she'd told him of her decision. But when he'd suddenly reached for her, she'd responded immediately, all of her repressed feelings flaring to life in an instant. She could call that recruiter and tell him she was no longer interested, couldn't she?

His fingers toyed with top button on her white shirt, and she sensed more than felt his hesitation. As if he were contemplating what going any further than this might mean.

*Do it, Jesse. Please! Choose* me.

Just then something seared the backs of her eyelids and she jerked them open, finding that another car had pulled up beside them, blue lights flashing. Jesse reeled back in his seat, shock and horror clearly written across his face.

Had he forgotten who he was kissing? Had he pictured Kandid sitting here with him, instead of her?

She recognized one of the town's patrol cars. The door opened and out stepped Andy McGee, a flashlight in his hand. He came around to Jesse's window and used the torch to tap on it, rain streaming over the plastic that covered his hat and plopping onto his rainproof slicker. Jesse's eyes closed for a second before he seemed to straighten in his seat.

As he rolled down his window, bile crawled up Mysti's throat, and she waited for the lecture she was sure was coming. All she wanted to do right now was get out of this car and run into her bedroom. So much for hoping that Jesse had finally understood he was supposed to be with her, rather than Kandid.

"You kids aren't thinking of drivin' 'cross that bridge, now, are you?"

"No sir. I was just waiting for the rain to slow."

Andy leaned down farther to peer in at Mysti, and she wrapped her arms around her middle, suddenly freezing cold, although it had to be close to eighty degrees outside. Her eyes met Andy's for a second before skipping away again.

"Your folks know where you are, Mysti?"

"Yes, sir. Jess was just giving me a ride home. Then the rain struck and…"

"Got it." He tapped the side of the car. "It's dangerous sitting here like this, and the rain is only just starting to let up. I'll lead you back to Forgotten Point another way and get you home safe."

Home. She suddenly realized this was not her home. Not anymore.

"Okay, thanks."

Jesse waited until Andy got back into his vehicle, and then turned and pulled out behind the patrol car.

He glanced at her quickly, the appalled look in his eyes making her cringe inside. "Damn it, Myst. I am so sorry. Your friendship means more to me than anything. My dad…hell, I hope you know I would never even think of—"

"Don't say it." She forced herself to stop him as an almost overwhelming pain burst through her. Jesse's dad had cheated on his mom over and over, then abandoned his family, leaving his son to do his best to hold things together. The fact that he could even think he was anything like that horrible man…

She forced herself to continue, the shakiness of her words making her close her eyes briefly to try to pull herself together. "You are *nothing* like your father, Jess. Let's just pretend none of this ever happened, okay?"

Easier said than done. She had a feeling she was going to relive this kiss for many years to come. It had been good. So very good. The kind of kiss she'd dreamed of happening between her and Jesse. Had often prayed for. But not like this. Not with the feelings of guilt it would carry with it. As much as she'd hated that Kandid was dating Jesse, her friend couldn't help who she fell in love with. Everyone loved Jesse.

Everyone…including Mysti.

But no more. She wasn't going to sit around this small town and let her sadness fester until she became a bitter shell of a person. If she could do some good in this world she was going to take the opportunity. And right now, the army seemed like the perfect place to do that.

Her stomach clenched hard as she braced herself for what she knew was coming as they wound their way through country roads that led into Forgotten Point. Jesse didn't say anything else until he pulled up in front of Mysti's house.

She didn't want him to try to apologize again, so she yanked on the door handle, and the mechanism made a snapping sound that jarred her to the core. Then, before she opened the door, she heaved down a breath and prayed for the courage to make this final break. Turning to look at him, his haunted gaze made her throat ache with unshed tears.

"Bye, Jess."

She forced a finality into those two words that she didn't want to contemplate. Didn't want to accept.

But right here, right now, she was drawing her own line in the sand. Jesse belonged to someone else. He was on one side of that line, and she was on the other.

He wasn't, and nor would he ever be…hers.

# CHAPTER ONE

*Present day*

MYSTI TOOK ONE last look at the gray building as she tossed her duffel bag into the taxi and climbed in after it. After six months of getting counseling for what was deemed PTSD, she'd finally graduated back to real life. She guessed she should have bought an actual suitcase as her time in the military came to an end, but who knew where life would take her next. For right now, though, she was going home. A place she'd always sworn she'd never go back to.

But a long time had passed since she'd made that vow. And what she'd endured in Joronha made the silliness of her first crush and her first-ever kiss seem like something out of a romantic comedy. Except none of it had been funny, and she hadn't gotten her happy ending. Just the ending.

So why go back to Forgotten Point?

Because she needed to. At least for this next phase of her life. She required the stable routine that Forgotten Point had always managed to give her. She smiled. She'd once been so contemptuous of that stability. The lack of surprises. She'd wanted so badly to do things that were reckless...see the bigger world outside her small town. Well, the first of those two wishes had happened in the front seat of Jesse Grove's car. And the second had happened on a series of foreign battlefields. Neither of those experiences had turned out quite the way she'd envisioned they might. So right now, Forgotten Point, Kentucky, looked very attractive. And safe. Far from the trauma of exploding helicopters and lost friends. The offer to take over for a surgeon who was on maternity leave at a hospital on the other side of the bridge from Forgotten Point had come at the perfect time for Mysti. And the fact that it wasn't a "forever" job made it that much more attractive to her. She didn't know yet how she would feel about the town once she got home.

The taxi driver glanced in the rearview mirror. "Where to?"

She managed a smile that was a lot less shaky than it had been when she'd first landed back on American soil. "To the airport, please."

"You've got it."

As the cab pulled away from the building, she turned around and took one last look at it. So many years of her life had been spent following orders, she wasn't quite sure what to do now that she could choose for herself exactly where she went and how long she stayed.

Jesse would probably still be living in her hometown, although her mom had never once mentioned him during their texts. It was as if she'd known that her daughter had cared deeply about him and had somehow been hurt because of it, and hadn't wanted to add to that sorrow.

She shook her head and leaned back against the seat, closing her eyes. That part of her life was over. The last she'd heard—by means of Kandid's fancy hand-addressed wedding invitation—was that she and

Jesse had indeed gotten married. But Mysti had never RSVP'd, and she and Kandid had soon lost touch. The same way she'd purposely lost touch with all her other childhood friends. They were all reminders of what could have been.

Kandid and Jesse were probably still happily living their lives together.

Well, it was time that Mysti finally started living hers. Her mom was so excited that she was coming home. Mysti had asked her to keep it quiet for now. She needed a few days to get her bearings and hopefully find a temporary place to live before people started dropping off pies and coming over to welcome her back. She could stay with her mom, but really, she needed her own space to continue to heal from the trauma of losing her friend in the field a year ago.

And she needed to brace herself for the time when she would eventually run into Jesse and his wife. She wished she'd gotten more closure on that whole childhood crush thing. Because right now there was a rock in the pit of her belly that was the size of a boulder.

Hell, he might not even recognize her. She'd lost weight over the ensuing years due to the busy hours spent operating on injured soldiers and the trauma she'd endured at the end of her last tour. Her mom would fuss over her, and she'd gain everything back, and probably more in short order.

Well, there was time enough to think of all of that once she got on the ground and started work. Until then, she needed to do what her counselor had told her. Take one day at a time. Focus on moving forward a little bit each day.

Until the past year was a distant blur she could no longer see so clearly in her mind's eye.

\* \* \*

Jesse helped his patient sit upright on the table, noting her wince as she did so. She hadn't mentioned her previous L2 compression fracture as her reason for visiting today, but he could see it was still bothering her. "How's your back doing, Mrs. Evans?"

Gertrude Evans had been one of his teachers in high school. Now well into her seventies, she was retired and living alone at home, her husband having passed away last year.

"The pain is still there, but as long as I don't try to stay bent over for too long, we get by." Despite the arthritis pain that sometimes plagued her, she was surprisingly healthy. Healthy enough to still get out and tend to her animals and small farm with some help from her sons. The compression fracture had been the result of a fall from a ladder while adjusting a gutter on her house, which she'd insisted could happen to anyone. And she was right.

Although Jesse's real love was caring for elderly patients like Mrs. Evans, he was glad that med school had required him to specialize in internal medicine before he went on to his fellowship in geriatric medicine.

When his grandmother had been struck down by a mystery illness, there'd been no one at the hospital who'd specialized in geriatrics. Oh, her medical care had been above reproach, but it had been hard to get to the root of the problem, since her early dementia had made it hard for her to sort her symptoms in the order they'd appeared.

Jesse had already been in medical school by that time, and had planned to specialize in orthopedics. His grandmother's illness had made him switch tracks. And he'd had no regrets about that decision. But the truth was that the hospital wouldn't have hired him on as a geriatrics specialist alone. This wasn't Florida or one of the other retirement meccas.

"Well, you let me know if it starts getting worse and we'll come up with some other treatment options for you."

"Thank you, Jesse, but I suspect I'll just work through it myself in time. Everything else looks good?"

"Yes. Your lab results came back just fine."

Gertie slid from the table with an ease that would put some forty-year-olds to shame. "How's your girl doing? I haven't heard about her in a while."

He stiffened for a second before he realized she was talking about his daughter. "She's just fine. Starting third grade this fall."

"They grow up so fast." She crammed her feet into footwear that made him smile. People swore those hole-riddled plastic shoes were incredibly comfortable, but somehow they seemed incongruous on someone like Gertie. Then again, she never had been one to follow the crowd, even as a teacher, which had made her very popular with her students.

"That they do." He glanced at the planner on his phone. "I want to check on your back again to make sure it's not getting worse. We'll set your next appointment for six months out, but call if you notice something before then."

"I will, thanks."

He walked her out to the reception area and said goodbye before ducking out into the hallway. The medical office building was housed in an annex of the Serenity Regional Medical Center itself. It made it convenient when it came to doing rounds of patients he had at the hospital, especially during inclement weather, or on days like today when he was going to pop into the cafeteria for a quick bite to eat.

The double doors that connected his wing with the hospital opened with a whisper of sound, and he went through them, his mind running through all the things he needed to do before he picked up Sally from school this afternoon.

He spied Tom, the hospital administrator, across the lobby talking to someone. Jesse gave him a short wave, but Tom gestured for him to come over. He did, his smile instinctively including the other person who'd turned around to see who Tom was motioning to. Jesse stopped in his tracks.

Surely that wasn't…

He swallowed.

Damn.

Her hair was different, which was why he hadn't recognized her from behind, but it was definitely her. Mysti North. A ghost from his past.

His distant past. He had to remind himself of that fact as his feet began moving again. What the hell was she doing here?

She'd sworn she was shaking the dust of Forgotten Point off her feet and never coming back. The last he'd heard from her mom several years ago was that Mysti had qualified as a military doctor and was being stationed somewhere in the Middle East.

Mysti looked just as shocked as he was as Tom made the introductions.

She nodded. "Yes. We've met."

Jesse stared at her. Her voice was just the same. The slight rough huskiness hitting him in the gut, just like it had that night. But like her hair, the tone was different. Tighter. Chillier.

"Yes," he agreed. "We have. We were in high school together, but it's been, what? Fifteen years since you left?"

"Something like that." Her stiff smile as she glanced between him and Tom contained no warmth. Just a cool indifference that seemed so out of character with the person he'd once known.

"Great!" Tom said enthusiastically. "Are you in a hurry, Jesse?"

"No, I was actually just going to grab a bite to eat."

"Would you mind showing Dr. North around the hospital? The cafeteria would be a good place to start."

Dr. North. Oh, hell, Tom had used her title. Was she going to be working here? He should have known when his day started off as well as it had that there was bound to be a downside somewhere along the way.

What could he say? No, he didn't want to show her around? Didn't want her working here?

Both of those things were true. But if he said so, the next time he saw Tom, there would be some uncomfortable questions asked. Questions he'd rather not answer.

"Of course." He sent an inquiring glance to Mysti. "Have you eaten yet?"

"No, but I don't want to hold you up. Seriously."

She sounded just as reluctant to spend time with him as he felt.

"Nonsense," Tom said briskly. "I'm sure Jesse wouldn't have asked if he didn't want you to join him."

That just went to show that his hospital administrator didn't known him as well as he thought he did.

"Of course not." He forced another smile, feeling it shrink to match the reluctant vibes Mysti was giving off in waves. She obviously didn't want anything to do with him. Hell, he couldn't blame her.

He'd been dating Mysti's friend for a couple of months when that kiss in his car had happened. And although he and Kandid hadn't been serious about each other at the time, he'd still felt like he'd cheated on her. It just went to show that Jesse was indeed capable of acting exactly like his father, something he never would have dreamed possible before that night. So he'd failed as a boyfriend—and he hadn't done such a great job of being a husband, either.

"Well, I'll leave you two to it, then, since I have a meeting in about twenty minutes. Thanks, Jesse."

"Not a problem, Tom."

But it was, although he wasn't sure why. What had happened between them was a long time ago. They'd both moved on with their lives. He'd married Kandid, and Mysti had joined the military. They were past those juvenile hormones that came with being a teenager.

*Was this why you went into geriatrics? To remove the temptation of ever getting married again? You don't exactly meet many women your age...*

The words slithered through his head, winding around his brain cells in a way that made him frown. No, he'd gone into that branch of medicine because of his grandmother. He'd never cheated on Kandid in all their years of marriage. But his wife had made it clear that he didn't make the cut when it came to taking care of her emotional needs.

"The cafeteria is this way."

She fell into step beside him, keeping up with him with ease. His wife had been shorter than him by far, whereas Mysti was taller than Kandid, long-limbed and lithe and...

*No. Don't compare them.*

"I didn't realize you worked here, too, Jesse."

"I have hospital privileges, but technically, I don't work for Serenity Regional. I have a practice in the building attached to the hospital. And of course I'm called when the hospital gets a patient they need help with." He glanced at her, turning down the corridor where the cafeteria was. "I take it you're going to be working here, then?"

Her brows went up. "Is there any reason why I shouldn't? I was an army surgeon. We're doctors as well."

"I didn't mean that." Was it his imagination or was her level of defensiveness way above where it should have been? "I didn't realize you were out of the military."

"Yes. I'm out." The inflection behind the words was different than he'd expected. There was a flatness to the tone that went along with her stiff manner. Almost robotic, he would have said.

She was different. In so many ways. But maybe that would work to his benefit. There was no hint that any past attraction from that night in his car had lingered until now.

And on his side?

That hard thud of his gut when he'd seen her said otherwise. But it was manageable, just like the rest of his life. Maybe he should have enlisted as well. He'd found that being regimented helped him stay grounded and comfortable—the impulsiveness from his youth firmly quashed. He was pretty sure that aspect of his nature was good and dead by now. But the side effect of that particular medicine was that he'd ended up being just as regimented at home. He'd never found the switch to turn it off. A point that had caused terrible friction between him and Kandid.

"Well, here it is." He turned into the hospital's small but busy cafeteria. "I can't claim that it's up to gourmet standards, but it does what it needs to do."

The first hint of a genuine smile appeared on her face. "I wouldn't know what to do with it if it were gourmet, so that suits me fine."

Of course. She'd been in the military. She was used to food that was plain and ungarnished.

They got their plates, with Jesse opting for a BLT and fries. Mysti picked up a yogurt and fruit.

She was still very beautiful. Her strawberry blond hair was quite a bit longer than it had been during high school. The shining waves were caught up in a long ponytail that bobbed between her shoulder blades. The freckles across her cheeks and nose were still in evidence, although in school, she'd tried to cover them with makeup. It looked like those days were long gone. There were slight shadows under her eyes that hadn't been there when he'd known her before, either.

They found a small table against a wall and sat down. Mysti wasted no time peeling the top off her yogurt and dipping her spoon into the container. She slid it into her mouth, eyes closing briefly as if savoring the taste.

His head buzzed, and he had a hard time pulling his eyes away from the look of pleasure on her face. Taking a deep breath, he met her gaze, deciding to spear the topic he'd been avoiding. "So what brings you back to Forgotten Point? Or are you? Back, that is."

Maybe she was living on the other side of Serenity in Doak's Cove or even farther out.

Her spoon froze halfway to her mouth before continuing on its path. She finished the movement, the silence lingering while she swallowed.

Just when he thought she wasn't going to answer the

question, she shrugged one shoulder. "I am. At least for the next three months. I'm taking Sara Severs's place here while she's on maternity leave. And...well, it seemed like returning home for a while was the logical place to come after leaving the army."

He felt like a jerk for asking the question. But her answer confirmed that her move back wasn't permanent. He should have known it wouldn't be. Felt relieved, actually. She hadn't been able to get out of here fast enough after school, had she? But her mom was here, and it was a natural landing spot since it was someplace familiar with family and people she knew.

"And you, Jesse. You never left town?"

"No. I never did," he said flatly.

Her gaze dipped to his left hand. "How's Kandid? Did she ever become a teacher like she wanted to in high school?"

The bite of sandwich that he'd taken turned into a rock as it slid down his esophagus. He'd just assumed she'd already known all about Kandid's illness. That her mom would have given her the news. But Kandid herself had rarely mentioned Mysti over the years. He'd wondered if his wife had guessed what happened between him and her friend. But he'd never confessed, and he was pretty sure Mysti had never said anything to anyone, either. It could be they'd simply lost touch, just like he had with some of his old football buddies. Mysti hadn't been at their ten-year high school reunion either, and Jesse had been relieved beyond belief that there'd been no sign of her. Maybe she'd been stationed overseas and hadn't been able to get away.

That made him feel like a clod.

"I thought you knew," he said in a low voice.

Her head tilted. "Knew what?"

"Kandid died three years ago of breast cancer."

There was no sound for several long seconds. Then her voice came through. "Oh, Jess, I'm so sorry to hear that. I—I didn't know."

Her hand covered his, her expression the softest he'd seen it today. The effect of that look combined with her gentle touch sent a shiver of apprehension through him. What was it about this woman that still got to him so badly? Even after all these years.

"Thank you."

He and Kandid had had a good marriage for the first few years. But by the time Sally was born, they'd begun fighting almost nonstop. And then a year before Kandid's death she'd discovered she had stage IV cancer and the arguments had stopped as quickly as they'd started. Their last year together had been spent fighting the disease, rather than each other, and trying their best to make sure their daughter was spared the worst of the effects of the chemo Kandid had elected to try.

Sally had been only four when her mom had died, and it grieved him how quickly her mother's memories had faded. He kept Kandid's pictures scattered around the house as a way to keep her memory alive.

For Sally's benefit. And his own. Although that thought seemed so hypocritical now, especially sitting across from the one woman who could have derailed his relationship for good. All it would have taken was for Mysti to have made one phone call to Kandid telling her what had happened. And she would have had every right to tell on him. But she'd evidently kept her word and hadn't said anything, because Kandid had never even hinted that she knew.

And although he'd loved Kandid when he'd proposed to her—or at least thought he did at the time—

somewhere along the line, he'd finally admitted to himself that his rush to the altar had been partially to assuage his guilt over what had happened with Mysti. To prove to himself that he was as far from being like his father as he possibly could be. It hadn't been a good move for either himself or Kandid. Oh, it had seemed ridiculously romantic to her at the time that he couldn't wait to marry her. But his head hadn't been in the right place, and he'd walled off parts of himself that she should have had access to.

Yet despite his mistakes, something truly good had come of their union. Sally.

He wouldn't trade her for the world.

As if realizing she was still gripping his hand, Mysti sat back, letting her hands drop back into her lap.

"I'm surprised your mom didn't tell you," he said evenly.

"Mom always tried to protect me from things she thought might upset me." She stared at her plate. "But you can't always protect people from everything, can you?"

That was the truth. He would have given anything to have been able to shield Kandid from the horrible effects of chemo, would have given anything to protect his daughter from the loss of her mother. But life didn't always work that way. You had to play the cards you were dealt. Unlike a game, though, there was no discarding these cards or trading them for others that had better options.

He'd played them to the best of his ability, although it hadn't always been easy. He was actually grateful Mysti had left, although that had come with its own dose of guilt. Had that last push to leave been because of him? It wasn't like she'd tried to seduce him or anything. The fault in that kiss had been all his. He'd initiated it, and although she'd clung to him like she never wanted to let go, the blame was his alone.

"You're right. You can't." Like Kandid, Jesse hadn't been able to protect Mysti from his impulsive move.

Her chest rose as she sucked down a deep breath. "So you said you have an office in this building. What do you specialize in?"

The question surprised him. "Geriatrics, actually."

"Really? And you have enough patients to fill a practice?"

He bristled, and he wasn't sure why. "I'm also an internal medicine doctor." His jaw clenched and he tried again. "I see patients other than just those who are up there in years. But my main love is in helping patients who are often brushed aside or not heard the way they should be."

"Sorry, I wasn't trying to offend you. It just took me by surprise, that's all. I knew geriatrics was a specialty, but I've just never met anyone in that branch of medicine." She smiled. "Of course, that could be due to the fact that most soldiers don't use walkers."

Of course it was. If he had thought through her question for a minute, rather than reacting so quickly, he would have realized why she'd never met a geriatrician before.

"Hell, Mysti, I know you weren't trying to offend me. And you didn't. I've just had that same question tossed at me time and time again. And there aren't a ton of us around. If someone wants to go into geriatrics for the money, they've chosen poorly. But if they're in it because they want to help an increasingly vulnerable sector of our population, then I think it can be one of the most rewarding specialties out there."

"Yes. I can understand that. I think I went into surgery for the same reason. I felt I was helping soldiers who were at their most vulnerable. And it was hard, never knowing if someone was going to rally and live or just slip away."

He nodded. "Yes, that's it, exactly."

They looked at each other for a long minute, then Mysti piled her trash onto her tray. "Well, I'm sure you have patients to see this afternoon, so I won't hold you up."

"When do you start work?"

"Tomorrow, actually."

Tomorrow. Even though he had his own office, he ventured into the hospital almost daily due to patients of his who'd been admitted or for administrative reasons. He would be running into her on a regular basis, more than likely, something he'd never in his worst nightmares imagined possible. Hell, it was just one more thing he had to deal with in an already hectic life.

But maybe...

His gaze dipped to her left hand, hoping to see some kind of sign that she was already involved with someone. Or better yet, married. Totally unavailable. But the all-important finger was bare.

That still didn't necessarily mean anything, though, and he certainly didn't want to come out and ask her if she was dating or in a committed relationship.

So he decided to leave things where they were. "You sure you don't want me to show you around?"

"I think I've seen all I need to see."

A hint of relief went through him. At least they would be able to cut this meeting short. And he might make it a point to eat somewhere other than the cafeteria from now on.

If he did that, he could hopefully mitigate any problems that came with seeing her on a regular basis while she was here.

At least that was his hope. But as he'd learned from hard experience, life didn't always hand you what you expected it to.

# CHAPTER TWO

MYSTI CAME IN the next day and found a full surgical schedule waiting for her, including one patient whose chart listed Jesse as his personal physician. Not what she needed today. Or any day, really. The shock of seeing him yesterday had thrown her for a loop, even though she'd known that was going to be part of the price of coming back home.

So much for thinking she could just cruise through the next three months with no speed bumps.

She'd hoped it would be a place where she could quietly heal. Instead it threatened to open up old wounds and reignite a guilt that had never entirely gone away.

The scars on her back pulled as she bent over to retrieve a piece of paper that had fallen out of her pocket. She glanced at it. Her mom's grocery list.

Somehow Mysti had thought she might spot Jesse or Kandid in front of the milk case in the town's small store and steer clear of them until she'd figured out how best to approach seeing them again. She'd half hoped she might not even recognize them after fifteen years and vice versa. But what she hadn't expected was to find that Kandid was no longer alive and that Jesse was a fixture at the hospital.

And she'd recognized him immediately. God, had

she ever. And it had brought back a whole host of emotions from a time in her life when she'd felt safe. Safe... except for that one moment when her emotions had gotten the best of her and she'd played with fire.

A good friend's fire.

Jesse hadn't been hers, no matter how much she might have wished it to be different. And there was no way she'd wanted to be the reason he'd broken it off with Kandid. Her decision to leave town had been the correct one. Because he'd gone on to marry his girlfriend. So she'd chalked up what had happened in the car to her long-simmering crush, and the romantic atmosphere created by the close space, the heart-to-heart talk and the storm. They'd been safe in their little cocoon, his voice lulling her into the mystical realm of fairy tales.

She should have known. Fairy tales had never been something that landed on her doorstep. Instead, she'd made choices that had proved devastating. If she hadn't kissed him that night, she might have changed her mind about enlisting. Might not have been accompanying an army friend whose unexpected pregnancy had needed to be kept hidden. Might not have been in the wrong place at the wrong time and had to watch her friend Laura die after triggering an IED and been caught in the blast herself.

Laura's secret had followed her to the grave. And Mysti would have given anything to be able to change the past and go to tell someone about the pregnancy instead of agreeing to her friend's request to stay silent. If she had, Laura might have been shipped home alive. Rather than in a box.

Every time she did surgery, that patchwork of scars on her own back—a stark reminder of what terrible things secrets could do—stretched and ached, not allowing her to forget what had happened and her own responsibility for it. Not that she ever could, even if she wanted to. And she didn't. It somehow seemed fitting that she hadn't come away from the event physically unscathed, no matter what the military psychiatrist had said.

She shook her head to clear it and headed toward the room where Jesse's patient was waiting for her. Seventy-year-old Larry Rogers had a bowel obstruction. The MRIs showed it was scar tissue from a past surgery that had encircled his intestines, slowly strangling a section of it. The surgery should be pretty straightforward.

She went into the exam room and swallowed, her heart sinking.

Straightforward. But not with Jesse standing in the room talking to her patient. Geriatrics. Of course. This had to be the patient who'd listed Jesse as his primary-care doctor. She shook her head, frustrated with herself for not remembering. Ugh!

He glanced up and saw her, never missing a beat in what he had been saying to the elderly man. Something about fishing.

Realizing she was frozen in place, she shoved herself forward, forcing her lips to curve in the semblance of a smile. She kept her eyes on her patient. "Hello, Mr. Rogers. I'll be performing your surgery this morning."

The man frowned. "What happened to that other woman? Did you scare her off?"

Her smile faltered, and it was a second before she could engage her tongue to answer him. "Other woman? Oh, you mean Dr. Severs. I'm taking her place while she's on maternity leave." A burst of relief went through her. Who else would the man have meant? Kandid?

Her gaze flitted to Jesse, and she saw his face had

transformed, white lines appearing at the sides of his mouth and a dark frown between his brows.

Had his thoughts gone where hers had? Surely not.

"Larry is worried about an upcoming fishing tournament. And how soon he'll be back on his feet," Jesse remarked.

"When is the tournament?" Looking at the man's face, she saw a sad expectancy in it. He didn't expect to survive this surgery. She'd seen the same look on gravely wounded soldiers' faces when the outcome was uncertain.

"In four weeks."

She did some quick calculations. Bowel obstruction surgery could carry up to a three-month recovery period, but since this wasn't a full obstruction and she was doing it laparoscopically, there was hope that by simply cutting through the fibrous scar tissue, it would free the intestines to start functioning normally again. Although anything could happen. She could get in there and find a situation that was more complicated than the MRI showed.

She touched his arm. "We'll see what we can do. Will you have someone in the boat with you? Or is this a solo competition?"

"No, we'll fish in pairs. I've always partnered with my son. I've fished this tournament for over thirty years."

A pang went through her. She remembered fishing in it with her dad. It was one of the things she'd missed while she'd been stationed in Joronha. And now her father was gone. There'd be no fishing with him ever again. So she could guess how important this tournament was for both Larry and his son.

She tilted her head. "If he can do most of the heavy

lifting, I don't see any reason why you wouldn't be able to go." The tournaments in Forgotten Point weren't fly-fishing, where his arm and abs would be in constant motion, aggravating his surgical site. "Maybe I'll even enter the tournament, so I can keep an eye on you."

Jesse's head whipped around to look at her, but he didn't say anything.

"Who would your partner be?" Mr. Rogers asked curiously.

The pang in her belly sharpened. "I'm sure I can find someone. I used to enter with my dad, but…" The rest of her sentence got caught in her throat.

"Which is why I don't want to miss this with my son. None of us knows how long we'll travel this earth."

Damn, she needed to derail this conversation quickly. "Well, you'll be traveling this earth for a while longer, I think. So let me get to work and see about getting those insides of yours free and working again."

For the first time since she'd entered the room, the older man smiled. "Let's get to it, then."

Their patient had already signed forms giving her permission to operate, and although those papers outlined the risks, she hoped everything would go smoothly.

Except why on earth had she said she might enter the tournament?

Because the look on his face had spoken volumes. And in some part of her, Mysti still felt she had some sort of penance to pay.

So much for all those months of therapy. Snap your fingers and you could regress all the way back to the beginning.

She finally forced herself to glance again at Jesse.

"Do you want me to let you know when the surgery is done?"

"Not necessary. I'll know. Because I'll be there."

Shock held her still for a moment. He was planning on coming into the operating room with her? There was no way she'd agree to that. As if he knew she was about to cry foul, though, he added, "I'll be in the observation room."

Okay, so that was almost worse than him being in the actual room with them. She was still getting her feet back on the ground. She was used to having back-to-back cases of trauma surgery, where she had to work as fast as she could to save lives. The space between patients here at the hospital seemed so huge. So organized.

"You don't have other patients to see?" she asked him slightly desperately.

"Not until this afternoon."

Didn't he trust her with his patient?

Hell, why should he? They didn't know each other. Not anymore.

Actually, they hadn't known each other back then, either, despite living next door to each other. Not properly. They'd only been kids.

It was on the tip of her tongue to bite out a sharp reply, but she didn't want Mr. Rogers wondering what was going on between them. Because nothing was.

"Okay. I guess I'll see you after the surgery, then."

Mr. Rogers smiled at her. "And I'll expect to see you in a boat in four weeks' time. I'll have you know my son and I have won the last two years."

"Then I'll have to see if I can give you some stiff competition this year, won't I?"

With that, she smiled one last time, hoping and praying that the glass to the observation room was one way and that she wouldn't see him up there. Serenity Regional wasn't a teaching hospital; it was a small local medical center that she remembered from her own childhood and adolescence. But she'd never actually thought she'd be on this side of the patient-doctor equation.

Was this where Kandid had died? Not a question she was ever going to ask anyone. And the sooner she got out of here and completed this surgery, the sooner she would be rid of Mr. Rogers's primary doctor, too.

At least for today. Suddenly the thought of three months working in such close proximity to Jesse seemed to stretch ahead of her like a never-ending road. All she could do was take it one day at a time, and hope like hell she made it through.

Mysti's glorious hair was nowhere in sight, having been ruthlessly stuffed into a surgical cap. But that didn't mean Jesse couldn't immediately pick her out of the team. Her high cheekbones and delicately arched brows were somehow burned into his memory. He immediately tried to call up Kandid's image and found it more than a little blurry after three years. Except it had been a hell of a lot longer than three years since he'd seen Mysti.

His gut clenched as guilt arced through his system, just as sharp today as it had been fifteen years ago. He flicked it away with an angry sweep of a mental broom. This was ridiculous.

It wasn't like he had sat around pining after Mysti for all these years. No, he'd lived his life with the knowledge that she was out of his life forever.

Except here she was, back again. For now.

Surgery was well under way. She'd said she expected it to take around an hour to free the intestines.

She made her first small incision and then another one after that. She was hoping everything could be done laparoscopically unless she ran into a complication. Her fingers fed the scope and her instruments through the incisions and like magic, the screen at the front of the room lit up, magnifying what was happening inside his patient's body. Her eyes were also focused on the screen and Jesse had the sensation that they were looking at this together, his mind running through the steps that would happen, even though he wasn't a surgeon. As long as Mr. Rogers remained stable and she didn't nick something other than the scar tissue while in there, she was right—it would be a fairly easy surgery.

Once she was past the muscle, the smooth, pale structure of his intestines came into view. Mysti had already mapped out the location of the adhesion, which was fortunately not all the way at the bottom of the stack. She moved the scope farther in and the problem area immediately came into sight. The squeezed section of intestine was red and angry-looking. The tissue encircling it was thankfully not so thin that it had actually cut through the organ. Instead it was thick and fibrous-looking.

"I'm at the area of adhesion. Going to cut through both sides and pull the tissue out to keep it from wrapping back around."

She skillfully moved the other instruments, using one to grip and cut and then held it while she moved to the other side and snipped that as well. Her glance went toward where he sat, but there was no way she could see him from her side since the glass was actually made like a mirror. He was glad. Something about her eyes meeting his still had this incredibly weird effect on him.

And the fact that she was willing to go out on a boat and fish near her patient just to make sure he was okay? That sounded like something *he* would do. Jesse tended to show he cared for someone in practical ways. Kandid had had a hard time understanding that. And it had been partly to blame for the rift that grew between them. That in itself was probably responsible for what had happened later in their marriage. The funny thing was in the end it hadn't been him who'd been unfaithful. It had been Kandid.

He turned his mind back to the tournament.

Who would Mysti pair up with? He blinked. Did she even have access to a boat?

A thought swirled in his head, which he discarded before taking it right back up again. It wouldn't hurt to ask what her plans were. If she'd just been saying she'd go fishing without really meaning it, Larry would be horribly disappointed. Maybe Jesse could take Sally out on the lake and fish nearby for the same reason that Mysti had said she was going. He hadn't been out on the lake in ages. Larry was right. None of them knew how long they'd get to travel on this earth. And Sally was growing up far too quickly. Life had been kind of in limbo since Kandid had passed away. They'd bought the boat to use as a family, but Kandid had been diagnosed with cancer soon afterward so it was virtually new. Maybe it was high time he got it out of the storage area and checked if it still floated.

He might not have been the ideal husband, but he was determined to be a good dad. The kind of dad he hadn't had when he was a kid.

When his head cleared a little, he glanced down to

see that Mysti had completed Larry's surgery and was saying something out of range of the microphone to the anesthesiologist. That was his signal to get moving and head down toward the recovery room. She couldn't see him anyway, so any kind of congratulatory signal would be hidden behind the one-way glass.

Soon he was in one of the rooms, and Larry's gurney arrived a minute or so later. His patient was already awake, although he was pretty groggy. Jesse moved toward the bed just as Mysti came into the room. She'd already stripped off her PPE, except for her hat and booties.

Jesse smiled at her. "Congratulations. It looked like everything went well."

"So you were in there, watching."

"Of course." Did she not think he'd keep his word?

Her eyes moved to take in Larry as well. "Hi. I found that pesky scar tissue that was causing the problem. You should start feeling better very soon, once the soreness from the procedure wears off."

Larry struggled to focus. "I'll be okay?"

"More than okay." Mysti squeezed his arm, leaning over the bed. "I'm thinking you're definitely going to make your fishing tournament in four weeks' time."

"Good." The man's voice was slightly raspy from being intubated. "You're still coming, right?"

"I'll be there… Somehow." Her voice had lowered so that Jesse could barely hear her last word.

Was she already regretting making Larry that promise? Or maybe he'd been right, and she didn't have a boat.

Something that was easy enough to find out. "Larry, I'll be back to check on you this afternoon before I leave, okay?"

The man gave him a weak thumbs-up sign.

Jesse then turned to Mysti. "Could I see you outside for a minute?" He held open the door.

Her eyes widened before she nodded and walked through it. "Sure. I have about a half hour before my next surgery."

"How many more do you have scheduled today?" He frowned. Hopefully Serenity Regional wouldn't work her into the ground on her first day.

*She's a big girl, Jess. She can handle herself.*

"Just one. I know my limits." She gave a half shrug and a smile. "Most of the time, anyway."

Was she saying he didn't know his? Like on that stormy night fifteen years ago when he'd stepped over a line he never should have crossed?

That was one conversation he wasn't planning on having. Now or ever. So he steered back to the topic at hand. "Larry really looks forward to those fishing tournaments."

She frowned. "I know he does. I grew up here, too, remember?"

Tension wound in his skull. "Except you haven't been home in years. So it's hard for you to know just how important this is for him, specifically." He hadn't seen her once since that day they'd gotten caught in the storm.

Her chin went up. "I'm aware of how often I came home. My parents regularly used their vacation time to come and see me, whenever I wasn't stationed outside the country." She paused. "I'm not sure what you're getting at, Jess."

Every time she said the informal, shortened version of his name like that, as she'd done when they were young, it elicited a muscular reaction in him. A tightening of abs that he hoped she couldn't see. He forged forward. "You told him you would come out on the water and keep an eye on him. He'll be expecting you to do just that, if nothing more than to have people around him."

Her eyes shut for a split second. "I know, and as soon as I said it I realized I shouldn't have. I was trying to make sure he was as stress-free as possible before surgery."

"So you lied." He thrust down a feeling of disappointment.

"No!" She looked down at her hands. "My dad and I used to go every year, too, before I enlisted. I just…it'll be hard to be out there alone. With all of those memories of how it used to be when I was with him."

He knew what she meant. But it had nothing to do with fishing. Jesse and his father had not been close and had never done things together like fishing tournaments. Or anything, really. His dad had been way too busy trying to prove his virility with anything that moved.

Hell. He hadn't brought her out here to go down these old roads yet again.

Before he could think of a response, though, she continued in a soft voice. "Besides, Mom sold the boat a couple of years ago to someone in Forgotten Point."

That's what he thought. "I have a boat."

"Oh, I couldn't borrow—"

"No, not borrow. But maybe we could go out and fish in that tournament together, so that you don't disappoint Larry. Like he said, it has to be done in pairs at least, so you can't fish alone. And it wouldn't be safe. I'm sure Sally would be ecstatic to come along, too."

Mysti visibly recoiled, her eyes wide with a look of horror. Was the thought of fishing with him that abhorrent? Hell, why wouldn't it be? He'd kissed her while still dating Kandid. Did he really expect her to let that go? To allow them to go back to being friends?

"I wouldn't want to intrude on you and your... friend."

"Friend? What friend?" He had no idea what she was talking about.

"This Sally person. Although after Kandid, I'm glad you've been able to find..."

Her voice faded away as if she didn't want to finish her thought. He realized in a second what she thought, and he laughed. A short sound that was born of relief, not mirth. Was that why she'd flinched? She thought he was involved with someone else. His laughter died a hard death. So she thought he was inviting her out on the lake while involved with someone else?

"Sally isn't a friend or a girlfriend, Myst." He swallowed a hard lump in his throat before pushing the next words out. "She's my daughter."

# CHAPTER THREE

FOR A SECOND or two no one said anything.

Jesse had a daughter? With Kandid? Her mom had never mentioned it. Then again, why would she feel the need to detail every birth in Forgotten Point? Especially when it had to do with Jesse. Neither her mom nor Kandid knew what had happened in that car between her and Jesse, but Mysti was pretty sure her mom had guessed something had gone on between them. It made her doubly glad she'd left town so soon afterward. If Kandid had ever found out...

Well, Jesse might not have his daughter.

"I—I'm sorry. I didn't know you had children."

"Child. One child. Sally. She was only four when Kandid passed away."

"I'm so sorry. I can't imagine how difficult that was." Her dad had died of a heart attack while she was in Joronha. At the time, there'd been few flights out and despite bending over backward, she hadn't been able to come home for the funeral. It had made what happened to Laura that much harder. Because her remains had been shipped home, and Mysti hadn't been able to be there for that funeral, either.

"It wasn't a fun time, that's for sure." He pulled his phone out and glanced at it. "I know you have your next surgery coming up. So about the fishing tournament? Will you come with Sally and me? Or should I just take your place as Larry's babysitter?" He said it with a smile as if trying to soften the question.

*So you lied?*

His earlier words whispered through her mind. Unfortunately, when it came to Jesse she'd lied about more than that one thing. She'd lied about her feelings for him back in that car. She hadn't lied about visiting the recruiter. But she'd lied about Forgotten Point making her feel claustrophobic. Had lied about itching to see the world and shaking the town's dust off her feet. But if she hadn't...

Suddenly she wanted to meet his daughter. Needed to see the child that he'd had with someone else. Maybe that would finally drive home the fact that he'd loved someone else back then. Loved that person enough to marry her and have a child with her. And since Sally would be...what...seven, now, it wasn't like Kandid had gotten pregnant while dating Jesse and had a rushed wedding. They'd *wanted* to get married. Had loved each other enough to commit to each other for life. And hopefully Jesse had proved to himself once and for all that he wasn't like his dad, since it sounded like he and Kandid had kept their vows, including 'til death do you part.

"Yes, I'll come. If you're sure Sally won't mind."

"No, she won't. I'd thought of selling my boat actually, too."

She understood that. Had understood her mom's reasons for not wanting to hold on to something that brought back painful memories of happier times. But maybe having a daughter helped Jesse with the pain of Kandid's loss.

"I'm glad you have her, Jess. Sally, that is." The soft

words came out of nowhere, but she wouldn't take them back, even if she could.

"Thank you. She's my whole world." He smiled and glanced at her. "Hey, do you have time for a coffee before your next case?"

Something about the way he was looking at her sent a shiver of remembrance over her. God, when he'd stared at her in the car that night, she'd been completely lost. Had forgotten about everything except for being there with him. And right now, her thoughts were shifting in that direction.

*No. Not again.*

She could not afford to be caught off guard again. Couldn't afford to let him get close only to have him pull back from her in horror like he'd done in that car.

Straightening her spine, she gave him a direct look. "I… If we could keep things on a professional level, I think the next three months will be easier on both of us."

Lord, he hadn't been asking her out on a date. Just coffee. But she'd made it sound like he was making a play for her, her own self-righteous little speech making her wince. "I'm sorry, Jesse, I didn't mean that the way it came out."

But it was too late. The softness in his face had disappeared. "It's okay. You're right—thanks for that piece of advice. It's not like we grew up next door to each other or anything." His head tilted. "What happened to you, Mysti, that a simple offer of coffee has you suddenly bristling with the need to remind me that you're getting out of Forgotten Point—again—just as soon as you can?"

A crushing sense of regret flattened her. He was right. They'd practically grown up together. So her comment about keeping things on a professional level had to have been a slap in the face. Little did he know that it had come out of a need to protect her heart. Out of the fear that she might find her feelings for him weren't quite so dead after all.

Well, good. Maybe it was better for him to think she was cold and unfeeling. He had no idea just how cold she could be.

"What happened to me, Jesse? Wow. That's rich coming from someone who's never stepped foot outside of their own little world." She was digging herself in deeper, but the words kept pouring out no matter how hard she tried to stop them. "I had to change in order to survive army life—to cope with what I saw on a daily basis. Soldiers who were little more than children came across my table one after the other. Some with missing limbs. Some who were too far gone to save. If I let myself feel too much, I couldn't have done my job."

She swallowed back what felt like a solid ball of emotion. "Once again, I am so sorry, Jess. You didn't deserve to have me unload on you like that. The transition from the military to civilian life has been harder than I expected, although that doesn't excuse it." She clasped her hands in front of her, fingers biting into each other. "You'll let me know about the tournament?"

"You sure you still want to go?"

His tone was tight and rough. Evidently she wasn't forgiven. Although why would he? She'd been a witch with a capital *B*.

"I want to help Larry, although I'll completely understand if you no longer want to let me on your boat."

"You're welcome to come. We'll just draw a line down the middle and each keep to our own sides."

She shot him a quick glance, not entirely sure if he

was joking or serious, but there was no way she was going to ask. "Thank you. I'll make sure to clear my schedule."

"I'll check on Larry this afternoon. I can just text you a report, if you're too busy to make it back to see him."

"That would be great. I'll try to check in on him, but it depends on how my day goes," she said.

He nodded, pausing for a second or two. "This must all seem incredibly boring after your army work."

It wasn't. But that didn't mean it was any easier. Maybe coming back to Forgotten Point had been a huge mistake.

"Right now, boring is good. Very good. Because it means people aren't dying." She glanced at the clean white walls and floors that were so different from her work in medical tents. At least gunfire couldn't easily penetrate these walls. When snatches of the more disturbing memories started infiltrating her head, she knew it was time to go. Before they had a chance to take over. Or before she snapped at Jesse again for no good reason whatsoever. "Let me know about Larry, okay? I do need to go."

"Yes, of course. Go. I'll see you later."

Yes, he would. And that was part of the problem. But like what she'd seen in Joronha, she would just have to somehow compartmentalize Jesse and not let him take over her thoughts.

And hopefully with the boundaries she'd just set for herself and for him, she'd be able to succeed in that goal.

The rest of her day was uneventful, thankfully. The surgery she'd had scheduled after Larry's was to clean out an infected pocket in someone's leg. It had taken all of thirty minutes. Found deep in the patient's thigh, the fact that it had become encapsulated had both helped and hurt treatment. While it had kept the infection from spreading to nearby tissues and from eroding the large blood vessel that it was pressed against, those things had provided challenges in not nicking said vessel. And it had also been why it had been hard for antibiotics to push into the cocoon of infection.

She was just finishing up her paperwork when one of the nurses told her someone was waiting for her at the information desk. Her muscles tensed instantly before she forced them to relax. It wasn't Jesse.

Not that she'd wanted it to be.

She glanced at her phone to see if she'd had any calls and saw that she'd missed two from her mom. A trickle of fear went through her. Heading for the elevator, she pressed the call button, hoping it was nothing serious.

Her mother answered immediately. "Hi, honey, I was just wondering if you're still up to going with me to pick up Brutus. I know you said you were getting off around five."

Oh, hell, she'd completely forgotten. Fortunately, she was done for the day.

"Are you downstairs? I'm headed there now."

"Yes, I thought I'd just come and wait since the vet is on this side of the bridge."

Brutus was her parents' dog. Well, he'd actually been her dad's pride and joy. And although her mother loved the Saint Bernard dearly, he was quite a chunker—especially if he had to be lifted into the car. Much like the patient she'd just had, Brutus had gotten himself speared by a branch he'd been tossing around. It had lodged, then broken off in the dog's left thigh. Trying to lift his bulk into the car to go to the vet's had taken both of them, with her mom inside guiding the front and Mysti lifting from the back, while trying to hurt the pup as little as possible.

"How's he doing?"

"They said he's sore. I'm sure someone at the office could help me get him into the car, if you're busy."

"Nope. I'm just finishing up. See you in a minute."

But by the time she stepped off the elevator five minutes later, she saw that her mom was not alone. Jesse was there talking to her.

She tensed, then relaxed. It was what people did here. They engaged in small talk. All the time. He wasn't telling her about their fishing plans. Not that they were plans. And even if he was, what did it matter? It wasn't like it was a date or anything.

Maybe she was afraid her mom would take it that way. After all, Jesse was an eligible widower. And her mom had always liked him when they were kids.

*It's not like we grew up next door to each other or anything.*

Those words were going to haunt her for a long time.

But they weren't kids anymore, and her mom had already made vague hints about the grandchildren she hoped to have one day. And since Mysti was an only child, nobody else but her could bestow that pleasure on her mother.

Mysti knew she did want children. She'd just never found anyone to "want" them with. Her glance strayed to Jesse before popping away in a rush.

She hurried over to them. "Hey."

Jesse nodded to her. "Hi. I was just getting ready to go check on Larry. I finished up later than I thought I would."

"Actually, I did make it up there. He's doing fine."

Her mom looked from one to the other. "Larry Rogers? Was his surgery today?"

Another thing about small towns was that everyone knew practically everything about the other folks who lived there. It was pretty amazing that her mom had never found out about her and Jesse's kiss all those years ago. But the only people who'd known they were in that car together were Mysti, Jesse and the officer who'd stopped to make sure they were okay. And he'd clearly had no clue about what he'd interrupted.

Thank God he'd come along when he had, though.

"It was." Even though it was her mom, she still needed to respect the HIPAA laws.

"I don't suppose you can tell me how he is other than what you just said to Jesse?" Her mom waved off the question. "I know. It's okay. I'm sure someone in town knows every detail of that surgery by now."

Mysti laughed. It was true. HIPAA was no match for the town's robust rumor mill. She glanced at Jesse. "Well, we're off to pick up Brutus from the vet. Our dog," she added, in case he didn't know who she was talking about.

"I've seen Brutus out in the front yard when I've driven by the house. Is he okay? Or is that protected under HIPAA, too?"

Mysti laughed, glad for the lighter atmosphere between them. "He's doing fine. He speared himself with part of a tree and had to have surgery, but it looks like they got him all fixed up."

"Do you need me to lend a hand?"

Mysti's "Oh, no!" was countered with, "Oh, could you?" by her mom. She shot her a glance, but her mother just smiled.

"You know how hard it was for us to hoist him in by ourselves when we drove to the vet."

"But we managed, right?" There was a hint of desperation behind the words, but if her mom heard it, she was clever enough to ignore it.

"Which vet is it?" Jesse asked.

Her mom answered. "Bowman's. Just before you go over the bridge into Forgotten Point."

Leave it to her mom to point out that it would be on Jesse's way home.

"Tell you what," Jesse said, "I'll follow you over in my car. That'll be just about the time I normally pick Sally up from the aftercare program at school. And since you told me Larry is doing okay, I'll take your word for it."

Mysti gave an internal sigh. "If you're sure."

"I am."

Like a little caravan, the three vehicles made the trek to the vet's office and walked in together. As soon as her mom spoke to the woman at the reception desk, the sound of howling came from somewhere in the back. Brutus must have heard her mom's voice.

The receptionist smiled. "Can you tell he's been waiting for you? Every time the bell on the door rings he howls, despite still being under the influence of anesthesia." She sized Jesse up. "Good thing you brought help. He's not the steadiest on his feet right now. I'll let them know you're here."

A few minutes later, the Saint Bernard, wearing a massive cone around his neck, came through the door, his nails clicking and bumping as he struggled to pull his handler forward.

Then he was at her mom's side whining and shaking his head, as if trying to rid himself of the protective contraption.

Jesse stepped forward and took the leash, giving the dog a pat on his shoulder.

The vet tech said, "His leg isn't bandaged because of where the wound was, so the cone needs to stay on for a few days to keep him from messing with his stitches. Can you bring him back in a week? His leg should be less sore by then, so he should be back to being able to jump in the car." She eyed the group. "So you won't need a sling and hoist to lift him into it."

Her mom nodded. "That will be good. My husband was always great with that." Her eyes moistened for a second before she cleared her throat, as if chasing the emotion away.

Mysti's heart clenched. She remembered her mom letting her know that her father had a new puppy and that he was going to be a whopper. She was sure neither of them had any idea that her mom would be managing Brutus alone someday. She glanced at Jesse. "Want me to take him?"

"Nope, we're fine, aren't we, boy?"

In answer, Brutus sat on the tile flooring whining, his tail thumping on the ground.

She couldn't help but smile. It hadn't taken long for Jesse to win the dog over. Then again, it hadn't taken him any time at all to win Mysti over, either. She'd always been a sucker for the man's smile and long dark eyelashes. That certainly hadn't changed. Although she really wished it had.

Her mom thanked the receptionist and waited as Jesse and Brutus went through the door and headed out to her car.

"Back seat, I'm assuming?" he called over his shoulder.

"Yes, please. Passenger side. I have a blanket laid out for him already." Her mom took out her keys and pressed the unlock button on the fob.

Mysti went to the door on the opposite side, so she could help guide him, but before she could even get in place, Jesse had his door opened and Brutus put his front feet on the seat.

"Okay, boy, here we go." Sliding one arm under the pup's belly and the other behind his back legs, he lifted the dog with seeming ease, making the heaving and ho-ing she and her mom had done earlier seem like a joke. Brutus didn't even whimper.

"They must have given him some pretty strong meds." Mysti couldn't help the slight waspishness in her voice. Why did he make everything he did look so effortless?

Like letting her walk away from him that night fif-teen years ago?

No, he'd done the right thing there. And Mysti had gone out of her way to make sure he was free to go back to Kandid by leaving town.

Ha! Had her motivations really been that selfless? Or had she not been able to stand the thought of seeing him with one of her closest friends?

Either way, she'd felt there had been no choice. At the time, anyway.

And now?

They'd both moved on with their lives. And Jesse had a daughter. So whatever romanticized feelings she might still have about that night were meaningless. He'd loved Kandid. Had married her and had a child with her. Crucially, he had also not even tried to talk Mysti out of leaving Forgotten Point.

So that was that. She needed to do what he had done and get on with her life.

After Laura had died from that IED blast, Mysti had used all kinds of coping mechanisms to help herself get through her grief. But none of it had erased the horror and tragedy of that day. Her counselor had warned her against trying to mask the pain with drugs, alcohol, or damaging relationships. He'd told her the best thing to do was to face the pain and acknowledge it. Then to move forward.

She was still a little shaky on the last part of that equation, but she was trying to learn.

"Okay, Mom, I'll see you at the house." She forced herself to add, "Thanks for the help, Jesse."

"Happy to do it. Are you sure you don't need me to help you get him back out again?"

"No, he can pretty much do a marine crawl and then slide out on his own."

With a wave, her mom got into the car and headed on her way.

Mysti hesitated for a minute, glancing at him. "Well, I'd better go so I can help her."

"Right. I'm sure I'll see you around at the hospital."

Unfortunately she was sure that was true. But outside of leaving Forgotten Point before her three months were up, that was inevitable. So she would do what her counselor had said and turn and face the pain and regret of that time and then move forward with her life.

She slid into her vehicle, and with a final wave she turned the key in the ignition. It clicked, but didn't start. Oh God, please no. She tried again, with the same result. The car didn't even try to turn over.

That's what she got for buying the first used car she

came across. But it wasn't a clunker, and she'd needed something quickly.

Why oh why did it have to die on her now? In front of Jesse?

Right on cue, he motioned for her to roll down her window. She did, glad the electrical system still worked. "It's okay. I'll just call Triple-A. I think it's just the battery."

"I'll take you to your mom's, if you don't mind making a pit stop by the school. It'll only take a minute or two."

"Thanks, Jesse. Sorry about this."

"Don't be. We all get stranded at some point or another."

Like they had all those years ago during that storm? The thought made her chest hurt.

"Well, thanks. I'll call my mom on the way and ask her to wait for us before trying to get Brutus out."

She collected her belongings and then climbed into Jesse's SUV, which of course started up immediately. Then she called her mom and left her a voice mail saying they were on their way.

Five minutes later they were in front of the school in the pickup lane. It was incongruous that the Jesse she'd known back in high school, football player, accomplished athlete and the guy every girl wanted to date, was now a father, doing ordinary father things.

But he'd also been widowed at a young age, had succeeded in getting through medical school with a wife and a child, whereas Mysti had been unencumbered by romantic ties when she'd been in school. If she had gotten married young, would she have gone through with any of her life goals?

She actually didn't think so. In the end, her leaving

had not only been the right thing for Jesse, it had been the right thing for her. For the first time, she could see that with clear eyes.

Her heart lightened a bit. Maybe it had taken coming home again to see that. So as hard as it had been to come face-to-face with her past, she'd done it. Had confronted it head-on and could now move forward. She mentally snipped one of the elastic cords that tied her to the past.

"So your daughter's name is Sally?"

"Yes." He seemed to scan the lines of kids and teachers who stood waiting in front of the school. "She looks a lot like Kandid."

Of course she did. Mysti's heart squeezed again as she wondered for a brief moment what her own daughter might have looked like if she'd had one.

She thanked God again for that officer stopping by their car all those years ago. Because if he hadn't... Well, life might have gotten a lot more complicated in ways she didn't want to think about. Her actions could have hurt a whole lot of people. Because as she'd learned, actions really did have consequences.

"I'm happy for you, Jess. Not for losing Kandid, obviously, but for the life you've made for yourself here."

"Despite not stepping foot outside of this town?" He coasted forward as the line in front of them shifted before glancing over at her with a smile that took the sting out of the words. "You never married."

"No. But it was a complicated time. Between medical school and being deployed, life was pretty busy." She shifted her left shoulder as remembered pain rippled through her back, the memory of searing-hot shrapnel slicing through her uniform and embedding itself into her skin and muscle.

The car ahead of them moved forward again, and then they were in front of the school and Jesse rolled down his window to tell them who his child was.

And then a little girl came over. An adorable little girl with dark pigtails and huge brown eyes. He was right. She looked like Kandid. But Mysti also saw Jesse in there as a dimple flashed in her cheek.

"Hi, Daddy!"

The happy greeting made Mysti's heart clench.

"Hi, Sal, good day?"

The girl giggled. "The best."

A teacher opened the back door. "Don't forget to tell your dad about mismatch day on Friday." The woman glanced over at Mysti and did a double take. "Mysti North! Long time no see. I didn't realize you were back in town."

The face clicked with a name. Anna. A friend she'd gone to school with. "I am. And of course my car broke down and Jesse was kind enough to give me a lift to my mom's house."

Anna closed the door after Sally got in. "Let me give you my number. Maybe we can go to dinner sometime and catch up. It's really good to see you."

"Thanks, that would be great." Mysti pulled in a deep breath, glad that maybe she could start forging some of those old connections again. She typed the number Anna recited into her phone. "I'll give you a call."

Anna nodded, then backed away from the car so they could pull away.

Looking into his rearview mirror, Jesse addressed his daughter. "So your day was the best?"

"Except for my spelling test, which I think I bombed."

Mysti couldn't suppress a smile as she turned to

study the girl. She remembered those days when her biggest fear was bombing a test.

"Sally, this is Mysti North. She's an old friend who just moved back to town."

"Oh, hi! I didn't know my dad had any friends."

Jesse laughed. "Wait a minute. I do have friends."

"Only guy friends, and they don't count. I think it's good for you to have girlfriends, too."

Girlfriends. Yikes!

Mysti's face heated. But it answered her question about any new women that might be in his life. Then again, he probably wouldn't parade just anyone in front of his daughter, unless the relationship was serious.

Wisely, Jesse changed the subject. "So how would you like to go out on the boat in a few weeks and take part in a fishing tournament?"

"Really? That would be cool." Sally seemed to think for a minute. "Would I have to touch worms?"

"Not unless you want to. Mysti will be joining us, if that's okay."

She could feel the child's dark eyes shift from her dad to her. "Yes. We have a really nice boat. But Dad says we don't have time to use it."

A muscle worked in Jesse's jaw. Thinking about how he'd used to boat when Kandid was still alive? Lord. Every time Jesse looked at his daughter, he probably saw his late wife. The ache in her chest grew to encompass the pain he must have gone through when Kandid died. Probably still went through. It had hurt Mysti horribly when Laura died. Not only because she was a close friend, but because of the senseless way in which it had happened.

"Well," Jesse said, glancing in the mirror again, "I'm trying to change that, okay?"

"Yay!" She glanced at Mysti. "Do I have to call you Mrs. North?"

She swallowed. How did you explain to a child that it wasn't *Mrs.*? She turned to Jesse. "Are you okay with her calling me Mysti?"

"That's up to you."

Turning back to the girl, she said. "How about it? Want to just call me Mysti?"

"Misty...is that like fog?"

She laughed. "Something like that."

"I like that name." The child peered closer. "Your eyes are pretty."

"Thank you." She liked his daughter. She was sweet and curious, but not afraid to ask questions or assert her opinion on things.

And if she'd thought Mysti's eyes were ugly, would she still think that?

Jesse turned onto one of the side streets that led to her mom's house. In another minute or two they were there. "Thanks again for the ride." She glanced at Sally. "And it was very nice meeting you."

"I'm glad you're coming to fish with us. And that dad finally has a girlfriend."

Out of the corner of her eye, she saw Jesse roll his eyes, which made her laugh again.

"I'm just a friend." But despite her words, for the first time since Jesse had offered to go fishing with her, Mysti was actually glad she'd agreed.

He asked her if she needed help getting her car, but she shook her head. "We'll get Brutus settled and then my mom can run me back to the vet's office."

"And you're sure you don't need help lifting him out of the car."

"Yes, I'm sure." Her mom was already getting out

of her car and opening the door. "And I'd better go or she'll try to do it all on her own. Thanks again, Jess. And I'll see you later, Sally."

With that, she exited the vehicle, and without looking behind her, she headed toward her mom and Brutus.

# CHAPTER FOUR

SALLY HAD TALKED nonstop about the fishing trip—and
his new "girlfriend," Mysti—ever since she'd found
out they would be going. It had taken forever to explain
to his daughter the difference between a girl who was
a friend and a girlfriend and why Mysti was only the
former. It had also sent a warning flare up in his head,
and he realized how easily his daughter could attach
herself to a mother figure. It was one reason he'd never
really dated. Oh, he'd had a couple of quick encounters
after being asked out for drinks. But it had felt wrong,
knowing his mom was watching his daughter while
he rolled around in someone else's bed. So it had been
a year since he'd gone out with anyone, for drinks or
anything else.

He would not see his daughter hurt. By anyone.

Even if Kandid had lived, he wondered if their marriage would have lasted. It seemed like the longer they
were together, the further apart they had grown. And as
much as he tried to tell himself that it was inevitable for
couples to find other interests that held their attention
as the years went by, he'd sensed something else was
going on. Especially when she constantly complained
about him being emotionally unavailable.

He'd found out exactly what she meant by that after

she'd gotten her diagnosis, confessing that she'd cheated on him with a coworker. She'd cried and promised it was over.

At least she'd confessed. Which was more than what he'd done about Mysti. He'd never told Kandid about that, and it had eaten at him for years. The truth was, he'd felt nothing but relief that he wasn't the only one who'd fallen to temptation. And that worried him on another level entirely. Shouldn't he have been furious with his wife for cheating on him? Angry with the man she'd been with?

Instead he'd found she was right in her assessment of his emotions, or lack thereof. Because he'd felt a complete detachment over her announcement that had startled him, made him realize he'd just been going through the motions with her for years, maybe even since they'd gotten married. Guilt over his own actions with Mysti, perhaps?

He shook his head to clear his thoughts. It didn't matter now. They hadn't divorced, and Kandid had died. The condolences had been hard to get through at the funeral, because he'd felt like such a hypocrite. To the outside world they'd seemed like the perfect couple: high school sweethearts who had lived out their vows until the very end. A fairy tale. Except that's all it had been. Make-believe.

The cell phone on his desk buzzed. He glanced at the readout and frowned. It was the hospital. He'd just been getting ready to leave the office. His mom had Sally for the night after his daughter pleaded that they wanted to watch movies and eat popcorn, since it was a Friday night.

"Dr. Grove here."

"This is Reggie Worth. I'm a nurse in the trauma

unit. We have a patient down here who's been involved in a car accident. Her daughter just arrived and says she's a patient of yours."

"Who is it?"

"Helen Hastings."

He'd just seen Helen two hours ago for a routine checkup. She must have had the accident on her way home. "I'll be right down."

Helen was in good health except for osteoporosis. And if she'd been in a traffic accident...

His receptionist promised to lock up the office, so he made his way down to the main hospital. Unlike his office, which had finished seeing patients for the day, Serenity Regional never closed, never slept. It saw patients at all hours of the day and night.

He took the elevator to the second floor and headed to the nurse's desk. "Helen Hastings?"

The nurse glanced at her computer screen. "Room three. The surgeon is with her now."

"Thanks."

Surgeon. So the injuries weren't minor. Hell.

Helen's daughter Dorothy was in the hallway.

"How is she?" he asked.

"I don't know. She's broken several bones and may have internal bleeding."

He squeezed her arm. "I'll check on her."

Pushing through the door, he found Mysti leaning over the bed, palpating Helen's stomach.

He should have known she'd be there.

"What have you got?" he asked.

If she was surprised to see him, she didn't show it. "She was unconscious when she arrived, but from the feel of her belly we've got a possible ruptured spleen. I'm taking her into surgery. She has fractures to both of her femurs and to her left tibia, but those are going to have to wait. Anything on her chart I need to know about?"

"She has osteoporosis, but as far as allergies go, no. It should be on her chart with the hospital."

"It is, but since they said you're her primary care physician, I wanted to double-check."

Two nurses came in and got the IV cords adjusted and then unlocked the bed so they could wheel it down the hallway to the surgical area.

Mysti threw him a glance. "I need to scrub in. If I can get her stable, orthopedics will come in and set the bones."

"Go. I'll sit with her daughter."

In a small town like this, he knew almost everyone, was friends with most of the people who lived there. It made it hard to be completely impartial, and Dorothy had been friends with his mother for many years.

"I'll let you know."

Odds were, Mysti knew the family as well, but she was in surgeon's mode and anxious to see to her patient.

He went back into the hallway and asked Dorothy to join him in the waiting room, checking to see if she wanted a cup of coffee or some water.

"No, nothing right now. What's happening?"

"They're taking her straight into surgery. They think her spleen ruptured in the accident."

"Oh God." Once they got to the waiting room, Dorothy shared what she knew. "They said Mom was going across the bridge and suddenly veered off the side of the road. She'd evidently gone to the grocery store, since there were bags of food in the car. They don't know if she was trying to avoid an animal or if some kind of medical event happened. She hit a tree." She pressed a hand over her mouth. "The car is totaled and Mom…"

"She's in good hands. Dr. North has worked many trauma cases."

"She was in the army, wasn't she? Your mom talked to mine about her."

He tensed before he realized it was likely just normal chitchat. "Yes. And like I said, she dealt with many trauma cases there on a regular basis. She knows exactly what to do."

He actually had no idea how good a surgeon Mysti was, other than what he'd seen her do for Larry. But she'd been cool and calm that whole time, so he had no reason to think this would be any different.

"Please let me get you a coffee, Dorothy. They're likely to be in there a while." He should probably call his mom and tell her about Helen, but she was watching Sally right now, and he didn't want to worry her. He'd call her as soon as this was over.

"Thank you. Just some creamer, if they have some."

"I'll be right back." Jesse got up from his seat and headed to the doctor's lounge down the hallway. Fortunately the pot of coffee in there looked fairly fresh. There was a carton of creamer in the door of the fridge.

A ruptured spleen was a medical emergency. It also meant they'd probably have to remove the organ. Helen was in her late seventies, and if she pulled through the surgery her recovery would be a long and painful one. Especially with her thinning bones. But the lady also had a will of steel and if anyone could beat the odds, Helen would.

He fixed himself a cup to go with Dorothy's and headed back down the hallway. Handing her her coffee, he sat next to her again, listening as Dorothy shared stories of her mom and her childhood. Jesse knew that talking was sometimes the best thing to do during the long wait to hear news. He laughed when Dorothy shared some of the antics that she and his mother had gotten into when they were teenagers together.

"We were awful." Then she sobered. "I was sorry for what she went through."

He didn't have to ask to know she was talking about his father. After years of fooling around on his mother, he'd finally walked out on her, deciding to move in with his secretary, the ultimate cliché. They'd left town a month later, leaving his mom and teenage sons to pick up the pieces. None of them had spoken to him in many years. Nor had his father tried to contact him or his brother. Whether from shame or because he just didn't care, Jesse had no idea. And he had no intention of trying to find out.

"My mom had a lot of good friends to help her through things. Thank you for all you did for us."

He remembered the outpouring of love and support from people in the town. The entire community had rallied around them. It was one of the many things that kept him tied to Forgotten Point.

"Thanks for all you've done for my mom," Dorothy responded.

"She's a trouper."

"Yes, she is. I'm hoping that holds her in good stead. I'm not quite ready to…" Tears welled up in her eyes.

"I know. Let's just see where things stand when Mysti finishes with her," Jesse said gently.

Too late, he realized he'd used her first name instead of calling her Dr. North. But if Dorothy found it odd, she said nothing. Probably because they all knew one another from way back.

An hour later, Mysti came toward them. Dorothy popped out of her chair, a hopeful look in her eyes. "How is she?"

"Hanging in there. I had to remove her spleen, but there doesn't appear to be any head trauma, and there are no other areas of internal bleeding."

"Thank God."

"She's not out of the woods yet. She lost quite a bit of blood, but we're replacing that. She was stable enough after surgery that Dr. Burroughs is already in there setting the breaks in her legs. The tibia can just be casted, since the bones didn't actually separate."

"When can I see her?"

"Once Dr. Burroughs works his magic, we'll get her into a recovery room. You should be able to go in to see her then. She'll be in ICU for a couple of days just to have some additional care."

"Okay. Thank you so much," Dorothy said fervently.

"You're very welcome."

Jesse watched as Mysti drew her left shoulder in a bit as if relieving some kind of tension. Almost as if she were sore. Maybe from lifting Brutus a couple of days ago?

He decided he needed to call his mom, so she didn't hear about Helen's injuries from someone else. She was incredibly fond of Helen. He asked permission from Dorothy and then asked her, "Will you be okay here for a few minutes?"

"Yes. I need to call my daughters, anyway."

Jesse headed toward the hallway, motioning Mysti to follow him until they were out of earshot. "Are you all right? I noticed you rolling your shoulder."

Her eyes widened for a second before glancing away.

"I'm fine. I was just releasing tension from the surgery. It was a close call."

The answer was quick. Too quick, as if she'd had it ready as soon as he asked. But he couldn't very well challenge her without looking like a jerk. Besides, he remembered her talking about keeping their relationship on a professional footing. "Thank you for taking such good care of her."

"Of course. I remember Helen from my childhood. She was always great with all of us. And she gave out the best Halloween candy."

"Yes, she did." Remembering Mysti as a kid in various Halloween costumes made him smile. "I may have passed by her house more than once each year."

"You wouldn't have."

He laughed at the feigned outrage in her voice. "I did. Back then I tended to help myself to whatever I wanted."

As soon as the words were out of his mouth, regret speared through his gut. Candy wasn't the only thing he'd helped himself to in his lifetime. He'd once helped himself to the woman standing right in front of him.

"Well, it's a good thing you've grown up since then."

Had he? He looked intently at her face to see if there was any hidden meaning behind her words, if she'd thought the same as he had when he'd talked about helping himself to things. But if she did, she hid it well. There was nothing there except wry amusement.

"Yes, it is." He'd grown up enough to know that you didn't snatch at things that weren't yours. At least he damned well hoped he'd learned that lesson, even if his father never had.

"Can you call me if you hear anything more about Helen?"

"I will. I promise."

"Thanks, Mysti. I appreciate it."

"You're welcome. I'd better head back and see if they need me in the OR for anything else." She gave him a wave and off she went, back the way she'd come. Leaving Jesse standing there staring after her. And sure enough, she rolled that left shoulder a couple of times as she moved away from him.

Just relieving tension, like she'd said? Or was there something else going on?

If there was, it was obviously something she didn't want or need to share with him. And he had no right to push her for answers. Because unlike when he was a kid, he wasn't going to help himself to anything that didn't belong to him—including information.

Mysti met Anna for dinner a few days later. They caught each other up on what had happened in their lives. But whereas Anna shared freely, Mysti held back. There was no reason to tell her about what had happened in Joronha or the aftermath of it.

"I'm glad you came with Jesse to collect Sally the other day. Although I'm sure I would have heard from someone that you'd come home."

"In this town? Nah." She drew the word out in a way that held unmistakable subtext.

Anna scrunched her nose. "News does tend to make its way around Forgotten Point pretty quickly, doesn't it?"

"It does. If you don't want it shared, then you'd better keep it to yourself."

"Truer words were never spoken."

Mysti smiled, taking a spoonful of her soup and swallowing. It was one of the reasons she hadn't spoken about her injury to anyone. Even when she'd been rushed back to the medical tent, she'd refused to let them call her mother to let her know what had happened. She hadn't wanted anyone to know. She still didn't. So she still hadn't told her mom. The scars on her back were hers alone to bear. And they were nothing compared to dying, like Laura had.

When Jesse had noticed her using her shoulder to stretch the still-tight scar tissue back there, it had shocked her. The move, left over from her physical therapy days, had become such a habit that she didn't even notice herself doing it anymore. And no one else had ever questioned the reflexive act. Not even her mom.

So why had Jesse asked her about it?

She had no idea. But she wasn't going to assign any special meaning to his question. He was a geriatrics doctor and probably dealt with arthritis in his patients all the time. So maybe it was something he subconsciously looked for.

Yes, that was probably it. And although she didn't have problems with the joint at this point in her life, she could imagine she might. Someday.

Anyway, he seemed to have bought her explanation. And it was time she forgot about Jesse and focused on the conversation!

"So you're married now," she asked her old friend.

Anna nodded. "I am. And I have two boys. Would it be weird for me to take my phone out and show you pictures?"

"No, of course not."

It wasn't, but Mysti couldn't prevent a pang from going through her when she saw the smiling faces of Anna's husband and sons. "How old are the boys?"

"Seven and ten."

The younger one was the same age as Jess's daughter. The pang deepened.

Sally had probably brought Kandid so much joy. If she'd been Mysti's child, she would have…

But she wasn't Mysti's. She firmly pushed any other thoughts away.

Probably a lot of her high school friends had children in about that age range.

Even Laura had been well on her way to—

*Think about something else.*

"I don't recognize your husband. Is he from here? Although it's been fifteen years, so maybe he's changed."

With light sandy hair and a tall, athletic build, she could see what had attracted Anna to him.

"Nope, I met him in college, actually. University of Kentucky."

"And you came back to live in Forgotten Point?"

She grinned. "This town doesn't like to let go of anyone. And my husband loves it here. He grew up in the city. I kept expecting the small-town charm to wear off eventually, but so far, it hasn't. He's an architect, so he does a lot of his work from home, even though he has an office in Louisville. So he has an hour-and-a-half commute on days that he meets with clients."

"And he doesn't want to move closer to his office?"

"He says no. And I'm just as glad. Having my boys grow up in a house down the street from where I grew up is something I can't get anywhere else."

"No. It's not." Mysti hadn't regretted not having children earlier in her life, but now she couldn't seem to get away from constant reminders that she was thirty-three and there were no prospects for romance. No prospects of a baby daddy of any kind, actually. Not that she wanted to go the route of having a child with someone who wasn't part of her life.

But there were plenty of women who used sperm donors and went it on their own. Why hadn't she?

Maybe because too many soldiers had died on her operating table leaving loved ones—wives and children, brothers and sisters—behind. Could she in good conscience ask her mom to raise a child if something happened to her? Even if she chose the adoption route, it could happen. She felt like she had been away from Forgotten Point long enough that there was no friend close enough to ask to take on that responsibility. Maybe in a few years she'd settle down someplace. But not right now. And once she turned forty...

She shook her head, getting irritated with herself. It did no good to sit here and long for something she couldn't have!

"I used to think you and Jesse would make a cute couple," Anna commented.

*Oh, no. No, no, no.*

This was not a path she wanted to wander down. "Really? But Jesse only had eyes for Kandid. After all, he married her."

"Yes, he did. But without wandering into gossip, I don't think they had the happiest marriage. The summer before they tied the knot, he looked almost... I don't know. Sad."

Mysti hadn't even stopped to wonder if Jesse's marriage had been solid. She'd always assumed it had been, that whatever had transpired between them in his car that night had been a tiny blip on his radar. He'd talked about being like his dad. Maybe that's why he'd been sad. She'd tried to reassure Jesse that night that he was nothing like him, but maybe she should have tried harder.

"I wasn't here, so I wouldn't know about that. He definitely loves his daughter, though."

"Yes, he does." Anna lifted her wineglass. "Anyway, none of that matters. I'm just happy you're home."

Mysti forced a smile and nodded in agreement. "I am, too. Even if it's just for three months."

"Really? Are you leaving again?"

"Maybe. I haven't really let myself think beyond my temporary contract at the hospital."

Especially since she was already wondering if she'd done the right thing in coming back. If she'd thought she could come here and wipe away the ghosts that had followed her back to Washington from Joronha, she'd been wrong. They'd trailed along behind her, making the twinges in her back and shoulder more pronounced. Worse, in Forgotten Point, there were other kinds of ghosts to contend with, too. Memories of her dad, whom she hadn't gotten the chance to say goodbye to. And the memory of a certain kiss that she had never received closure on.

But right now, she was here. And all she could do was try to make the best of it. Until it was time for her to pack up and move. Again.

# CHAPTER FIVE

SUMMER ARRIVED IN a blaze of heat that wilted plants and people alike. Larry was coming back in for a checkup in about a half hour, and he'd wanted to kill two birds with one stone and have both Mysti and Jesse examine him together to give him the all clear to participate in the fishing tournament the following week. It was just as well, Jesse figured. This way he and Mysti could get some logistical things worked out for the tournament, such as a meeting place and time.

And it seemed like a better plan than meeting with her alone. Because when he did, his thoughts over-reached into other areas. Areas she herself had forbidden them to go.

So he texted Mysti to see if she was still going to be able to be there when Larry came to his office.

A few minutes later, his phone pinged.

Meet you at your office in a few.

The text was short and to the point. But then again, his had been, too. And his idea had been to meet at the exam room first, not at his office. So much for not being alone with her.

He cleared his desk off, not because he was afraid

someone would look through his paperwork, but because he didn't want it to look cluttered.

For Mysti?

Better not to answer that one.

A few minutes later, someone knocked on his door. "Come in."

Mysti poked her head around the corner. "I wasn't sure if you had another patient before Mr. Rogers."

"Nope, come on in. He's my next patient. He should be here any minute."

She slid into the room and sat in one of the chairs parked in front of his desk. She crossed her long legs, one slender limb swinging back and forth. He pulled his glance back up to her face just as she spoke. "Mom said Helen is doing okay?"

"Yes. I'm sure you've heard that she was released from the hospital yesterday and is in a skilled nursing facility. I'm supposed to go check on her tomorrow. But her prognosis is looking far better than it could have. Thanks to you."

"There were a lot of folks involved in her care, including you. Did they find out what happened?" She slid clasped hands over her knee.

"According to her daughter, a dog darted in front of her, and Helen swerved to miss it and couldn't regain control."

"It's kind of what I'd thought. She looked very capable of driving, despite her age."

A nurse stuck her head in the room. "Mr. Rogers is here in exam room two. Are you ready for him?"

"Yep. We're on our way."

They got up from their chairs, and he motioned for Mysti to precede him through the door.

When they arrived, Mr. Rogers was already sitting in one of the chairs.

"How are you feeling?" Mysti asked.

"Like a new man."

"No more belly pains?"

"None other than the scars from the incisions pulling every once in a while."

Mysti's shoulder moved in what looked like a half shrug. But it wasn't. It was the same movement she'd done on other occasions. Did she have a scar back there? From shoulder surgery, maybe? What had she called it the last time he'd asked? Oh, yes, shoulder tension caused by leaning over an operating table. But as far as he knew, she hadn't done surgery at all today.

"That's understandable," she said. "Do you mind if we examine you?"

"You make me sound a fish you're getting ready to gut."

Mysti gave a choked sound that she covered with a cough.

Jesse grinned. "Wrong venue, Larry. I think your mind is already on the tournament."

"Just planning my victory speech."

"I bet Mysti will give you a run for your money." He motioned to her to go ahead and start the exam.

"This is your medical practice," she said. "Why don't you do the honors?"

"But you're his surgeon," he insisted with a smile.

Larry's eyes swung from one to the other. "Hell, you sound like an old married couple. I hope you don't plan to do that during the tournament or you'll scare all the fish away."

Mysti's shoulder twitched.

Damn it, this was ridiculous. "Why don't you hop up on the table, Larry?" Jesse suggested.

Larry used the steps beside the bed to climb up. "I take it I'll need to undo my trousers. Good thing I wore clean shorts."

This time Mysti made no move to cover her laugh. God. He'd loved that laugh when they were younger. It was one of the things that had knocked down his defenses in the car when they'd been thwarted from crossing into town by water crashing over the bridge. Low and throaty, there was something sexy and seductive in the sound. It made you want to know all her secrets, want to know what it might be like to...

"I do need to look at your belly, Mr. Rogers."

Her words brought him back to reality with a bump.

"Please call me Larry. Everyone else in this town does."

Larry undid his shirt and the front of his slacks. Mysti moved closer at the same time Jesse did, and they almost collided.

That delectable laugh came again. "You first."

Gritting his teeth, he pulled out his stethoscope and used it to check the man's heart and lungs, carefully listening for any signs of congestion. It was all clear. He quickly checked his throat and eyes and ears.

"All this for my belly?" Larry's voice carried a hint of irritation, but it was made up. He had a reputation for being irascible, but it was all just a cover. Inside the man was a marshmallow.

"It's hard enough to get you into my office. I have to do it while I've got you here. Good thing you had that bellyache."

Larry made a disgusted sound. "Next time you have

a part of your intestines squeezed by a…a…what was it called?"

"An adhesion." Mysti's voice was full of amusement.

"That's it." He looked up at Jesse. "If you get an adhesion, don't expect a shred of sympathy from me."

"Yes, sir." Jesse took a couple of steps back, giving her a mock bow. "He is all yours."

She moved forward, pulling out her own stethoscope as she listened to his abdomen. "Some good sounds coming out of there, Larry. You said it's still tender?"

"A little. More if I move the wrong way."

She coiled her stethoscope and slid it back in her pocket before using her fingertips to press on his belly around where the incisions were. At one point he winced. "Is it worse here?" she wanted to know.

"Yes."

"That's where I had to strip away the adhesion. There was probably some bruising. How are your bowel movements, back to normal?"

"I'm still taking that stool softener, but things are moving through, and I'm back to being hungry."

"Very good." She took a step back and held out her hand to help him up.

Uh-oh. That was a mistake. Jesse had been called out on more than one occasion for trying to aid the man. With anything.

Larry didn't snap at her, however, he simply ignored her hand and sat up on his own. Wow. He guessed there was a first time for everything.

"I'd say you're well on your way to being back to normal. You can ease off on the stool softeners unless you're starting to strain when you use the bathroom. But let me or Jesse know if that happens."

She'd used his first name and hadn't caught it. But

evidently neither had Larry, since he simply nodded. "So I'm cleared to go to the tournament?"

"I would say so. May the best fisherman win."

"That's all I wanted to hear. I'm still expecting you to be there, though."

"I will be. I don't have a boat, so Jesse…er, Dr. Grove has offered to let me be a passenger on his."

That time she'd caught it. But he kind of liked that she'd let his name slip out. It made something warm settle in his gut, sending out long tendrils that reached other parts of his body. He could remember another time she'd said his name, her husky whisper making him want to take things much, much further than they'd actually gone.

"You taking that girl of yours out there, too?"

"Yes, Sally is looking forward to it."

Larry got a speculative gleam in his eye that Jesse didn't like. Maybe talking Mysti into going with him had been a mistake. He certainly didn't want the town to start talking about the two of them, or for Sally to get an idea that wasn't true. An idea that would end up hurting her.

But he couldn't very well blurt out to Larry that they were just friends. For one thing, he wasn't sure that they were. For another, it would look like a denial of something no one had even mentioned. And he didn't want Mysti to feel awkward and decide not to go to the tournament with him and Sally.

Because he wanted her there with them. He wasn't sure why. Maybe just because it had been a long time since he'd done anything fun with a woman. And Sally would be there to chaperone.

Did he need a chaperone?

If he even had to ask that question, he evidently did.

And if he really thought about it, there would be a whole lake full of chaperones, wouldn't there?

Larry slid off the table. "Well, I know you're going in order to keep an eye on me, and to be honest, I appreciate it. But that doesn't mean I'm going to go easy on you. I still intend to win that tournament."

"I never had any doubt that you're going to give it all you have. You always do."

Jesse sent him out to the reception desk, but stayed in the exam room with Mysti. "So what do you really think? He'll be okay out there?"

"I think so. As long as he doesn't jump into the lake and start doing the breaststroke he should be fine."

"He'll be wearing a life jacket. We all have to."

"I know. I used to go out with my dad, remember?" She tilted her head. "You never did the tournament with your brother and dad when you were young?"

"My dad wasn't the fatherly type."

"Oh, Jess, of course. I'm so sorry."

It was something they'd talked about when they were in his car, before she confessed she was leaving and he'd kissed her. Jesse had poured his heart out to her about what his dad had done to his mother. But why should she remember? He'd been nothing to her.

"It was all a long time ago. I wouldn't expect you to remember everything I told you."

"No, I didn't mean that." She closed her eyes for a second before moving closer to touch his hand and look up into his face. "I actually remember everything we talked about that night. What I said about you doing the tournament with your dad was just something I threw out to make conversation. Because I was nervous."

About being alone with him? Hell, that was somehow even worse.

"If you're worried about me trying something with you, then don't. Like I said that was all a long time ago."

Her left shoulder slid forward then back.

"I'm not worried about you…"

His eyes narrowed as they looked down into hers. If she wasn't worried about him making a move on her, then what?

*I'm not worried about* you.

So she was worried about herself?

Her fingers were warm on his hand, where they still touched him. Her face was still tilted up toward his, like a beautiful flower to the sunshine.

His hand turned over and caught hers, using it to tug her forward. His other hand slid up her back until his fingers were buried in her silky hair. He stared at her for a long time, his innards warring with his brain. "So, according to Larry, we sound like an old married couple, do we?"

"Evidently."

His head moved closer until his mouth hovered over her tempting lips.

*But you're not married.*

And he'd been down this road once before, almost to his ruin. He'd found out the hard way he wasn't exactly marriage material, hadn't he?

His teeth clenched so hard a sharp twinge went through his jaw, running up until it hit his temple.

He pulled back, swallowing down a wash of bile. Mysti's eyes opened and she frowned before realization dawned. She jerked back, blinking hard, a tide of color rushing up her cheeks.

"Hell, Myst. I'm sorry. So sorry."

She held up her hand to stop him. "Don't. This…this

can't happen again. It was my fault this time, I know, but it still can't."

"I agree," he said stiffly.

She sucked down an audible breath, her teeth coming down on her lower lip. "I need to go. Thanks for letting me come examine Larry."

With that, she turned and opened the door, letting it close behind her. He didn't attempt to follow her. Even if he wanted to with every fiber of his being, what was he going to do? Catch her wrist and whirl her around in the waiting area of his office? In the busy hallway outside of it?

Besides, what more was there to say? She'd already said everything his brain had been chanting at him: this can't happen again.

She was right. It couldn't. And he was going to see to it that there was never an opportunity for it to. No matter how hard that might prove to be.

He'd wanted to kiss her. She'd seen it in Jesse's eyes. In the way his face, his mouth had been so close to hers. And the burn in her chest when he'd pulled away... It had hurt.

This time it hadn't taken a police officer to haul them apart. All it had taken was Jesse's good sense to kick in. He'd been stronger than her last time.

And he'd been stronger this time, too.

Hell, he had chosen Kandid over her, so why wouldn't he be?

What was it about him that she couldn't resist? An ages-old crush? The memory of their last kiss? She had no idea, other than the fact that he'd been her first real honest-to-goodness kiss. And the fact that no one else had ever measured up to it afterward. She would have said she'd built the event up in her mind to proportions that no one would be able to live up to, except she'd felt that exact same heady ache as he'd come closer to her just now. As he'd murmured about them being an old married couple.

In that moment, she'd desperately wanted that to be true. Wanted to be the old married couple Larry had called them.

Was the long-ago crush not dead after all, then? Even after all this time?

If not, then it was just a phantom ache, a remembered need that had faded away a long time ago, like those soldiers who lost limbs but then still continued to feel them years later.

So what was she going to do about it?

She could back out of the tournament, but then Larry would ask questions and might just get a little too close to the truth. And Jesse might also guess just how much he'd affected her. Because she hadn't been the one to pull away. He had. And that was the hardest pill of all to swallow.

No, she'd go on that tournament, and pretend to have a freaking fantastic time—although she'd never been that great an actor. If she could focus all her time and attention on Sally instead, maybe she could get through it. She'd concentrate on helping Jesse's daughter while he drove the boat or whatever else he needed to do. She could pack them a lunch and spend time putting everything out and then picking it back up. That should take up an hour or so.

Yes. She would just plan out her day next week. And all of it would revolve around things that had nothing to do with Jesse and that had everything to do with surviving until her contract was up.

# CHAPTER SIX

"WHAT CAN I do to help?"

Mysti's question came from the passenger seat as they waited in line at the boat launch of Lake Serenity. But Jesse noticed she didn't turn to look at him.

The huge man-made lake spanned the towns of Forgotten Point and Serenity, curving like an amoeba and forming smaller bodies of water that connected with the main part of it. Those nooks and crannies provided great hiding places for fish and made angling a very popular sport in both towns.

He made his answer matter-of-fact. He had to remember his daughter was in the back seat. So no discussing what had so nearly happened between them in the exam room. "Once we've checked in, you can help guide me into the water and hold the boat while I park."

"Okay. I did that plenty of times with my dad." This time she gave a small smile, glancing into the back seat. "Are you excited, Sally?"

"Yes, but…" She made a face. "Do I really have to wear a life vest? I know how to swim."

Jesse opened his mouth to give a stern answer, but Mysti beat him to it. "I'm a very good swimmer, and I'm going to wear one. We all have to. If there was an

Olympic swimmer out here, even he or she would have to wear one."

"Okay. As long as you're wearing one, too."

"I will. And I bet I can beat you in how fast I can put mine on."

Sally giggled, which made him frown. He wanted his daughter to be nice to her, but he hoped she didn't get attached to Mysti in some way. This was why he'd been so careful not to bring women home with him before. Not that there'd been more than a couple over the last three years. Maybe he should pull Mysti aside and talk to her about it.

After what had happened? What better way to say, "Hey, don't get the wrong idea about me leaning over you last week" than to ask her to back off from his daughter!

No. He was sure Mysti wouldn't want Sally clinging to her like a limpet, so she'd be careful. Especially since she wasn't even planning on sticking around for too long. What did she have left? Only two months of her three-month contract? She hadn't been able to get out of town fast enough after high school. And it didn't look like she was going to stay this time, either.

All the more reason for Sally not to grow to love her.

It was their turn. He registered the trio and then turned his vehicle around so the boat trailer was facing the water.

He finally glanced at the passenger seat. "Ready?"

"Can I go help Mysti?" asked Sally.

Jesse's foreboding grew a little stronger. "I need your help in the car, pumpkin. You can look out the back window and tell me how I'm doing." There was no need to tell her that the backup camera on his SUV would give him a pretty good idea of where they were.

"Okay."

Mysti jumped out of the car. In her faded blue shortalls and pink button-up shirt, she was cool and casual, a look he hadn't seen on her since high school. And those damned legs were still long and slender and more than one time he'd imagined what it might feel like to have them wrapped around...

*Not happening,* he told himself sternly.

She motioned him to back up, indicating when he was drifting too far to one side or the other. Right when he thought he might be getting in too deep, she held her hands up, forming a T that he took to mean stop. Putting the car in Park, he started to get out of the vehicle, but she came up to the window. "I'll crank the boat into the water. That way you won't have to leave Sally in the car by herself."

"Are you sure?"

"Yep. Like I said, I've done this with my dad hundreds of times."

Mysti had had a good father. One who'd loved her and her mom and had spent his whole life being true. That's the kind of father and husband Jesse had wanted to be. He just hadn't realized how hard it would become when you couldn't give your partner what they wanted. What they needed.

As bad as their marriage had become, he'd mourned Kandid's passing. Was glad that there was peace between them at the end. Holding her hand that last night was one of the hardest things he'd ever had to do, except for trying to explain to a four-year-old child why her mother was never coming home again.

He glanced in the backup camera to see that Mysti had already released the straps and was indeed cranking the boat down. When she switched to her left hand, he noticed she turned the winch's handle a couple of times before stopping briefly, putting her hand on her shoulder and rotating it.

It hurt. That was no "release of stress" movement. There was an actual problem with her shoulder. Why lie to him about it? Was she afraid of someone thinking she wasn't competent as a surgeon if they found out? He knew better. But why not seek out help for it? Unless it was something she already knew couldn't be fixed.

Just as he was preparing to get out of the car to help her, she'd switched back to her right hand, and the boat slid into the water with a whisper of sound. Then, holding the line at the front of the bow, she released the hook of the winch. Someone to the side stepped up and wound it back up. Then he was free to pull the trailer out of the water and go park. He had loaded all of their supplies onto the boat when they'd first arrived in the loading area, including their life vests. He reminded himself to put Sally's on her before she actually stepped onto the boat. Then they got out of the car and made their way over to Mysti.

He hadn't seen Larry yet, but the plan was to meet at a specific section of the lake. Except he hadn't thought to ask which boat launch the other man would be using.

Mysti had already donned her vest and was in the boat, organizing some of the supplies. Although Kandid had claimed to love the water, she'd seemed fearful of being on it and concerned for Sally's safety, which was one reason they hadn't used the boat much. That and the fact that their arguments had slowly grown worse again after their daughter's birth. Kandid certainly wouldn't have volunteered to launch the boat on her own.

Hell, the last thing he needed to do was keep comparing the two women.

"Thanks," he said, noting that his and Sally's vests were already lying on the dock, ready for them. Mysti had brought a picnic hamper as well, which had been pushed in front of one of the seats so it wouldn't go flying once they got under way.

For the first time since what happened in the exam room, his mood lifted and he found he was looking forward to being out there on the water with his daughter and Mysti. He hadn't taken a real day off in ages. Oh, he'd spent his free days with Sally or with his mom and Sally, but he hadn't been on an actual outing with his child in quite some time.

After getting their vests on, he helped his daughter onto the boat, then he got in, making sure everyone was in their seats before he started the engine. Then he slowly backed away from the dock to let the next person waiting in line into the launch area.

The tournament's goal was to see who'd caught the largest fish by the end of the day.

"Everyone ready?"

Mysti smiled. "Yep, I think we are, right, Sally?"

"Ready!"

His daughter and the surgeon were seated on one of the seats that had been folded flat to form a bench. Mysti's long legs were stretched out in front of her, her hair once again pulled into a practical high ponytail. He appreciated her looking after Sally. Once they found their spot it would be easier. He'd put up the canopy to provide some shade when things got too hot. The nice thing about the bowrider was they could sit or fish from the seating area at the front of the boat. Sally had wanted to sit up there right off, but Mysti had insisted it was safer in the back until they'd reached the fishing area.

He inched up the speed, and the bow lifted a bit as they headed for a spot on the far side of the lake. Within ten minutes they'd pulled into one of the outcroppings that so far no one had claimed. The benefits of getting on the lake fairly early.

"What are we using as bait?" Mysti asked.

"I brought minnows, worms and artificial lures, so take your pick."

"Nice."

He steered into a likely spot, then threw over the anchor, making sure it was on the bottom before turning the boat's engine off.

"I haven't been on the water in so long," she murmured. "This is nice. Thanks for offering to go with me. I might have wound up in a rowboat otherwise."

He smiled. "It would have taken you a little longer to get here."

"Just a little."

As he was getting the large canopy in place, Sally went with Mysti to explore the front of the boat, where the U-shaped seats could hold several people. "Do you water-ski off this boat as well?"

"I haven't, but it's powerful enough that we could. Why? Do you ski?"

"I used to. But I haven't done it in a long time."

"We'll have to come again when there are fewer boaters on the lake." The words were out before he could stop them. Mysti's face turned toward him, a slight frown between her brows.

Of course she wouldn't want to come water-skiing with him. That whole "keeping things on professional footing" thing rearing its head again.

And those few moments in the exam room? She'd

seemed pretty receptive when he'd leaned forward to kiss her.

Before he could think of a reason for offering to take her out on the water again, she said, "Actually, I think my skis are still at my mom's house."

So she wanted to come?

Warmth unfurled in his gut that he couldn't seem to get rid of. But thankfully Sally's attention was on the water over the side of the boat. She hadn't heard the invitation. Well, if he did bring Mysti back out here, he was going to leave Sally at his mom's house.

He might be stupid enough to go out on another outing with her, but he wasn't going to involve his daughter in his foolishness. And when Mysti steadied Sally with a hand, when the little girl leaned out a bit too far, he knew he was right in worrying. The surgeon seemed wholly focused on Sally, barely throwing him a periodic glance.

She didn't have children of her own, so he'd half expected her to feel awkward having Sally with them, but she was clearly a natural with kids, shifting forward to listen carefully to something the child said and responding with a smile.

He didn't want her to be a natural with kids. Right?

Right. The last thing he needed right now was complicated.

They'd just set their hooks—Mysti had baited Sally's before he'd even finished his own—when a bass boat slid by. Larry and his son. Jesse gave a wave, knowing some fishermen liked silence while they fished. Mysti cocked her head and gave a thumbs-up sign to the man in the next boat. Larry nodded and returned the sign.

Was there anything this woman couldn't do? He was beginning to think not.

Giving a sigh, he settled into one of the white bench seats at the front of the boat with its other two occupants and prayed the day went by quickly.

So far, her plan had worked. She'd been able to concentrate mainly on Sally while keeping her gaze averted from Jesse's tanned limbs as he stood at the helm in khaki shorts and the boat shoes that provided traction on the deck. Her choice of sandals was probably a mistake, but the sun was so nice today that she couldn't resist trying to get a few rays.

And now that he was seated not fifteen feet away from where she was? Well, it was harder than it had been a few minutes ago.

She'd baited her hook with one of the minnows in the bait bucket and Sally's had a worm. Might as well see what was biting. "What'll you have?" she asked in a low voice to Jesse, whose line hadn't yet been cast.

"What do you suggest?"

The smooth way he said that made her glance his way.

*Stop it, Mysti. He's talking about bait, nothing else.*

"I don't know yet. Maybe try one of the artificial lures? I already have live baits on ours."

"Fake it is."

Sally was tugging at her life jacket. "It's hot."

"Do you want to go in the shade, Sally? I'll watch your hook." Her gaze swung to Jesse. "Did you bring sunscreen for her? I have some I can put on her, if not."

"I brought some." He dropped his rigged line into the water. "Mind watching that while I put some on her?"

Was there a slight emphasis on the word *I*? Okay, well, maybe fixing her attention on Sally looked like bossiness to him. Or maybe he just didn't like someone else taking care of his child. She could understand either of those options. But if she couldn't pay attention to Sally, then what could she pay attention to?

Her gaze went back to Jesse yet again.

No. She had to find something to do. Something that didn't involve staring at the hunky doctor with starstruck eyes.

She wasn't starstruck.

He was just dangerous to her self-control as he'd proved on more than one occasion.

Jesse spread a thick layer of sun protection on his daughter, working it under the straps of her life vest, then turned to her with the bottle still in his hand. "Need any?"

"No, I put some on before I left the house." Thank God for that. Besides, she hadn't even worn a bathing suit, because there was no way she was going to prance around the boat in it. And she didn't want him to see her scars. It was also why she didn't wear sleeveless shirts or sundresses. The puckered mark covered her shoulder blade and the top of her shoulder. He'd already noticed her habit of stretching the skin using movements of her shoulder. She didn't want to give him anything else to think about.

Pulling out an electronic device, he settled Sally in a chair in the shade of the tarp before turning back to Mysti. "Feel free to come into the shade if you get too hot."

"Thanks, but the sun feels wonderful. I think I'll just stay here for a bit."

Admonishing Sally to not get out of the chair without calling to one of them, he moved to the bow to join her. "I see that you brought some lunch, too. I actually brought enough for all of us."

That made her laugh. "So did I. What did you bring?"

"Sandwiches and chips. You?"

"Fried chicken, potato salad and some watermelon. I have ice packs in there to keep everything cool."

He smiled. "I can see who's going to be the most popular one on this trip."

"We could always ask Larry and his son to join us."

They glanced over at the other boat. It looked like the two men were very serious about their fishing. Neither was talking, and they were sitting on opposite ends of their boat.

"Did your dad fish like that?" Jesse asked curiously.

"Um, no. We were probably the bane of the tournament. We were always laughing about something."

"That sounds like the opposite of being a bane."

"No. Because fishermen like quiet. Even Larry warned us about carrying on near him."

Jesse's lips pursed. "I thought he was talking along the lines of people horsing around, throwing each other into the lake, that kind of thing."

"I think that might get us a permanent banishment from the tournament. Besides, when I was a kid, I'd never heard of brain-eating amoebas back then."

"I haven't heard of a case coming out of Lake Serenity."

She gave a shrug that was only half-joking. "It's been a very warm summer, so far. So no, I don't plan on jumping into the water anytime soon."

Jesse kicked his shoes off and propped his feet up on the cushions next to her hip. A warm sensation sloshed through her at how close to her they were. His feet were only a couple of shades or so lighter than his legs, and the image of him padding around his house barefoot lodged in her brain. The warmth grew and she forced herself to look at the poles that were sitting in holders on the bow of the boat. The tips flickered with the movement of the water, but so far there were no bites.

"I can't tell you the last time I took a real day off." He glanced toward where Sally was sitting, her face bent over the electronic device she held in her hand. "I probably shouldn't let her play with that tablet, but she normally has to do homework or chores before getting screen time, so this is a break for her as well."

"Yeah, it's been a while since I've been out on a boat. When I was deployed I saw a whole lot of sand, but there was no water in sight."

"It was hard."

She didn't want to ruin his day with tales of what it was like having to be constantly on your guard, so she simply said, "Yes. It was hard."

He leaned forward. "Thank you for your service, Myst. I knew you were going to sign up, but I was surprised when your mom said you'd qualified to be a doctor, too."

"They paid for my medical degree. It seemed a small price to pay at the time."

In the end, while she hadn't paid with her life, she'd seen plenty who had. And she realized the price wasn't small at all. Not for her, and especially not for the families of those who had made the ultimate sacrifice.

"It's a price not many are willing to pay."

"Someday, I hope there's no need for anyone to. It's made me realize how valuable the job is that we as doctors do. We patch up broken people. Or at least we try. And at least we're not the people who cause them to break in the first place."

"Yes."

The word was drawn out in a way that made her wonder if he was thinking about his wife and how it had been impossible to patch her up. Sometimes all their efforts were in vain. But it didn't stop them from trying.

She sighed, glancing across the water at the other boat. "We do what we can, right?"

"And we celebrate the times when it's enough to give someone another chance. Like Larry."

Silence fell over their boat for a few minutes. With the warmth of the sun beating down on her, she found her head jerking. What the hell? She shouldn't be tired.

Well, she hadn't exactly gotten a good night's sleep last night. The thought of being out here, like a little family, had hit her hard. Because they weren't a family and never would be.

"Why don't you stretch out and take a nap?"

She shook her head. "We've only just gotten here."

"You've had a major move to contend with over the last few weeks and you've started a new job. You said it had been forever since you'd been out on the water. How about the last time you got to sleep in the sun?"

"But what about Sally?"

"She'll be fine. I've been taking care of her on my own for the last three years. And shockingly, she's still alive."

"I didn't mean that...but..."

Maybe taking a nap would be a good thing. No need to make small talk with Jesse. No need to keep glancing over at him and imagining impossible scenarios.

No need to think. About anything.

So she nodded. "Maybe just for fifteen minutes then."

He set his feet on the ground. "Stretch out. I can change the angle of the awning to catch the shade."

"No need. I like the sun."

So Mysti did as he suggested and lay across the cushions where his legs had just been. There was a weird kind of intimacy in the act that she didn't want to explore.

And the cushions were surprisingly comfortable. "You won't steal whatever latches onto my pole, will you?"

"Isn't there a saying in the fishing world? Whoever lands it claims it?"

She giggled. "No, that is definitely not a saying."

"Okay. You'll just have to trust me, then."

"Promise you'll wake me up if you get a bite."

He stood, smiling down at her. "I don't think there'll be any sleeping through that, since the poles are behind you. Get some rest. I promise I'll wake you if anything important happens."

With that, she threw her arm over her face and closed her eyes, letting the gentle rocking of the boat and the clean smell of the lake lull her into a sense of contentment. It might not be real. And it might only be for a little while. But for the first time in a very long time, she felt…at peace.

"Mysti, wake up!" His urgent voice penetrated the lovely fog that had come over her, and she came to with a weird sense of confusion. It took her a minute to realize she was still on Jesse's boat and his hands were shaking her shoulder. The sun was warm and lovely and she didn't really want to wake up.

"What is it?" Her eyes opened and the second she saw the look on his face she sat straight up. "Is it Sally?"

"No. But something's wrong with Larry, and I need your help with him."

# CHAPTER SEVEN

SHE LEAPED TO her feet, all semblance of sleep shaken off in an instant. Turning to look at the other boat, she realized Larry was slumped in his seat, his son standing over him trying to get a response.

He could have been asleep, just like she'd been, but she knew deep down he wasn't.

Why had she given him the all clear to come out here? It must have been too soon.

Sally was seated back on the bench seat on the side of the boat and Jesse had already hauled in the anchor. "We're going over to him."

He started the boat and began slowly motoring toward the other vessel. "I don't want to swamp them."

"I'll call it in."

Dialing 911, she waited for an operator to come on the line, then quickly relayed what was happening.

"Stay with Sally," he called.

He'd tossed the line to Larry's son and asked him to secure it to his boat. The man quickly did, then Jesse leaped into the vessel carrying his doctor's bag. Thank God he'd thought to bring it, because she sure hadn't brought hers. What kind of army medic left without taking a medical kit?

The kind that had retired from the military. She

needed to assemble a new one once she got home. But right now, she was grateful that Jesse was here, ready to take on whatever was happening with Larry.

Between Jesse and Larry's son, they managed to get the older man stretched out on the bottom of the boat, where Jesse performed a quick examination. He checked the man's pulse, then peeled apart one of his eyes, gazing into it. "Reactive," he yelled.

Mysti relayed the message back to the dispatcher on the line.

Then he pulled out his stethoscope and listened to the man's heart. When his head came up, she saw it in his face. "I need to get him to shore. Right now. Can you manage my boat?"

"Go. I'll get everything in and follow you. An ambulance is en route to the place where we launched." She glanced back to see that Sally was slumped in her chair asleep, just like she'd been.

"Are you sure?"

"Yes. Just go!"

He looked at Larry's son and nodded. Without any further word, the man started the outboard motor and took off toward shore.

It wasn't Larry's recent surgery; it had to be a heart attack or a stroke. There'd been something in Jesse's face when he'd looked up at her.

Reeling in the lines as quickly as she could, she discarded the bait into the water. Then laying everything on the floor of the boat, she stuffed her feet back into her sandals, then woke Sally up, strapping her into the seat and telling her to hold on. "Where's my dad?"

"He's helping the people who were in the next boat."

"Are they sick?"

"One of them is. Your dad is helping them get to

shore. We're going to meet them there." She looked at the girl. "Ready?"

"Yes."

Mysti started the boat, grateful that he'd left the key in the ignition. Then she turned the wheel and pushed up the throttle and headed back to shore.

Jesse was dimly aware of another boat approaching the shore. It had to be Mysti and Sally. But still he kept working, giving chest compressions on the dock, where Larry Rogers's heart had faltered and then stopped beating.

In the background he heard an approaching siren, even as Mysti helped Sally out of the boat, keeping the child halfway behind her to shield his daughter's view of what was happening. "Can I help?"

"Ambulance is almost here. Just take her somewhere else, please."

He hadn't stopped CPR, and Mysti could only thank God that they'd kept their word and were out on the lake beside the other boat.

*Even that isn't always enough.*

The words whispered through her head. How many times had people died despite the large number of medical personnel who were working in the tents? Plenty. So proximity didn't always equal life.

But it did equal hope. Because he was at least getting expert attention and a chance. Even if it wasn't a large one.

Why now? His heart had checked out great before surgery. But then again, Mysti had known patients who passed their treadmill stress test and then died weeks later of massive heart attacks or strokes. Problems didn't always show up ahead of time.

Like IEDs?

Or almost-kisses that blindsided you?

Or the sudden desire to have a child of your own?

Was that last one because of Sally's recent comments that she was glad her dad finally had a "girl" friend? God, she hoped not. Because she would be here for two more months and that was it. There was not much chance that she would become Jesse's real girlfriend in that period of time. Or any other amount of time, for that matter. His almost-kiss had shown her that.

Sally's fingers gripped her hand with a strength Mysti didn't expect. She'd left the boat tied to the dock next to the one where Larry's was. There was still one more open dock, just in case other people needed to come in.

"Let's go see if they have something to drink at the check-in desk."

Sally glanced up. "Is that man going to be okay?"

She wondered how much this child had seen, having a doctor as a father. "I hope so, sweetheart."

An ambulance pulled into the entrance to the lake and someone waved them over to the scene going on behind her. She made it to the folding table. "Do you have anything she could drink?"

"We have some water and juice." The woman was sympathetic. She bet everyone already knew what had happened and to whom. It was the way both of these little towns worked.

"Do you have orange juice?" Sally's voice came from beside her.

"We have apple juice, will that work?"

The child nodded. "Thank you."

"Anything for you?" the woman asked Mysti.

"Actually, I'll have the same, please."

"Coming right up."

Two bottles were produced, the ice still clinging to their sides.

Mysti thanked the woman and then made her way over to a small bench, careful to keep their backs to whatever was happening behind them. She opened Sally's bottle and handed it to her before twisting the top on her own drink and tipping it up to her mouth, drinking thirstily.

She couldn't believe she'd actually fallen asleep on his boat. But then again, she'd been exhausted. She didn't even remember much about what had transpired before that point, although she did remember the warmth of the sun on her face and laughing about Jesse's threat to steal any fish she hooked on her line.

The apple juice was cold going down, the welcome splash in her belly helping to cool her down. "Good?" she asked Sally.

"Yes. I like apple juice, too."

"So do I."

She chanced a glance behind her and saw them loading Larry into the back of the EMS unit. Jesse was nowhere to be seen. She wasn't sure if he was riding in the back of the rig or if he had just handed Larry over to the EMTs. It wouldn't matter, except she'd just realized she didn't have keys to his car. Maybe it was on the key ring with his boat keys.

But none of that was important right now. She had no idea what was going on with Larry, but at the moment, all she could do was pray and hope for the best.

Jesse saw them sitting at the bench over by the information desk. They were facing away from him. He watched as Mysti leaned over to say something to his daughter, his chest contracting.

The scene was a little too familiar. Like something out of the not-so-long-ago past that hadn't quite blurred completely away.

It had to be what he'd just gone through. The paramedics had managed to get Larry's heart started again, but as their eyes had met, they'd confirmed his sense that the situation wasn't good. He wasn't even sure the older man was going to survive at this point. And that look in Larry's son's eyes...

Devastation.

What he'd felt when Kandid had died, even though he hadn't loved her anymore, if indeed he ever truly had.

What he'd felt when Mysti had said she was leaving Forgotten Point to join the army, and never coming back.

As if sensing someone was behind her, the woman in question turned slightly, eyes widening when she saw him. "How is he?"

"He's hanging on, but..."

What could he say? He couldn't very well say the man probably wasn't going to make it in front of his young daughter. Right now she deserved to have a world that was happy and carefree. Sally had been too young to fully understand what had happened to her mother, but that wouldn't always be the case. A time was coming all too soon when she would realize things were not always beautiful. That people left and never came back, whether it was from dying or by virtue of moving away.

Except Mysti had come back. But only for a while.

Jesse wasn't sure right now how he really felt about that. It had been so much easier when he couldn't see her right in front of him, when there was no hope of her return.

And now that there was?

Well, she was a reminder of what he'd almost done in behaving exactly like his father. That night had shaken his world. He never wanted to feel that unsure of himself ever again.

Jesse was realistic enough to know that Mysti had the power to make him feel exactly like that all over again. Just by her presence.

Except there was no longer the possibility of cheating on Kandid, because she was no longer alive. And if Mysti had been here when he and his wife had been going through their marital problems? Would he have turned to Mysti for comfort?

God, he hoped he would have done the right thing. The honorable thing.

But there was no way of knowing for sure. Because Mysti had not been in town during that time. And even without her presence he had failed Kandid as a husband.

"Daddy, Mysti bought me apple juice."

"I can see that." He looked at the surgeon and mouthed *thank you*.

She nodded in response. "I left your boat tied to the dock. I wasn't sure what else to do with it."

"Yeah, sorry for leaving you with all of that. I didn't want to try to transfer Larry over to our boat in the condition he was in."

"Of course. You did what had to be done. And Sally and I were fine. We still had the picnic baskets on the boat if we got stranded for a bit."

"Do you want to go back out onto the water? Or are we done for the day?"

"I think we're done, if that's okay. I'd be too worried

about Larry to enjoy myself." She twisted her lips to the side. "Besides, I already dumped the bait. I didn't figure we would be going back out."

"I guess that's that. Good call, though, on the bait."

He glanced at his daughter. "You want to go with me to get the truck so we can load the boat?"

"I want to stay with Mysti."

He frowned, but said, "Do you want to sit here for a while or go over to the dock?"

"I'll go over with you. I'll help winch the boat back onto the trailer," Mysti offered.

He took a step closer and touched her hand. "Thanks for your help today."

"I didn't actually help. Unless you call snoring in the front of the boat 'help.'"

He couldn't contain a quick laugh. "I wasn't going to say anything but…"

She nudged him with her elbow. "Very funny. I need to go check on Larry. After doing his surgery and thinking he was going to be okay… Then this. Can you drop me off at the hospital on your way?"

"We can both go. Let me put in a quick call to my mom and ask her to watch Sally."

"You don't have to. He's my patient."

"No, Myst. He's *our* patient. And he's a friend."

She nodded. "You're right. He belongs to both of us."

The way she said that made a spark flare to life in his gut. He could imagine her saying that about a child. Their child. Watching her with Sally had been…

He squared his jaw. But they weren't talking about a baby or a child or anything else. It meant nothing. Mysti had walked away once before. From him. From the town. And she was poised to do it all over again. Just like his father had. It all seemed tied up together somehow, the strings all wrapped and tangled into a jumbled mess. And he'd be damned if he could sort it all out. Not now. Maybe not ever.

They pulled the boat out of the water, and he called his mom.

"Of course I'll watch my little darling. Why don't you let her stay the night again?"

His mom was too good to him. "Because I don't want to take advantage of you. She just spent the night not long ago."

"If getting to play with my only grandchild is being taken advantage of, then you should do it more often. You know she's going to want to stay over. Is that really a battle you want to fight?"

"No. It's not. Okay, thank you. Do you still have some of her things there?"

"Pajamas? Check. Clothes for the morning? Check. I'll just keep her clothes from today and wash them for next time she stays with me."

With that settled, they made a quick trip to unhook the trailer at his house. He could move it back to storage tomorrow. And then he got to his mom's house only to find Sally was asleep in the back seat. While Mysti got the door, he carefully lifted her out of the car and walked up toward his mom's old farmhouse. She was already at the front door, waiting for him.

"Oh, poor sweet darling. Bring her through here to the couch. She can take a little nap."

He hesitated. He loved his daughter so much, and leaving her anywhere was always so hard. Maybe it was because of Larry and Kandid, but the realization that life was so fragile was never far from his mind. It probably made him more protective of his child than he needed to be. Even leaving her with Mysti on that boat had taken every ounce of his willpower.

There was no way he was going to let anything—or anyone—hurt her. It was why he'd never contacted his dad. Why his father had never met his grandchild.

And being around Mysti? A person who had had no problems walking away from the town and her life here before? Well, today they'd been together out of necessity. But letting her into his daughter's life on a regular basis would be a major risk, even if they just stayed friends and never dated. He wasn't sure he was willing to chance it, no matter how much Sally enjoyed her company.

"I can always pick her up when I'm done at the hospital, Mom."

"No, let her stay." Her eyes when she looked up said so much. "Please."

"Okay."

She smiled and turned her attention to Mysti. "It's so good to see you again, Mysti. Jesse said you've only been back a few weeks."

"Yes, I…er…was discharged from the military and so I decided to take a little time to come home and get my bearings."

"I hope you're back for good."

Mysti bit her lip. "My contract at the hospital is only for three months. I haven't really thought yet about what happens after that. I wanted to see how everything felt. How working in a hospital felt."

She was only saying what Jesse already knew. She hadn't come home with the intention of staying. Had just come home to see how she did in a small hospital before moving on to something bigger and better.

And with her skills those opportunities would be a dime a dozen.

After today, he was going to be extremely careful about letting Sally anywhere near her.

And himself?

Well, using her words, he was going to "see how everything felt." He wasn't a child. He was able to hold himself apart emotionally without letting anyone get too close. Hadn't Kandid always called him an expert at that?

His mom replied, "Well, we hope you'll decide stay here in Forgotten Point, don't we, Jesse?"

Hell, it was like the universe had read his mind. "I think that's Mysti's decision to make, Mom."

"Well, of course it is. But I can hope, can't I?"

Mysti took her hand. "Thank you for that. It's been good being home and seeing people I once knew."

"People you still know, dear. Time doesn't change that."

But it did. He could see it in Mysti's eyes, in the way her shoulder inched forward. Time changed a lot, and they both knew it. She wasn't the shy girl he'd once known. She and Kandid had been opposites, with her friend taking the lead in most things. Maybe it's what had drawn him to Mysti that night. She had a way of listening—really listening—that had gotten to him. He'd shared more about his father with her than he had with anyone else. And then finding out she was leaving town… Well, it was no wonder his emotions had gotten the best of him.

But they had both changed. Had learned their place in life. And that place wasn't with each other.

"Well, we need to go, Mom. We have a patient to see."

As if Mysti had suddenly realized where she was,

she let go of his mother's hand and took a step back. She glanced at him. "No word on Larry yet?"

"No, I checked for texts, but so far nothing."

Saying their goodbyes, they headed out the door and got back into the car. "Sorry about my mom. She doesn't always have the best filter."

"It's fine. It's nice to know I'm wanted." Her words were soft. Pensive. And there was something behind them that made him swallow. "It was hard that last year of high school, and things didn't always... Never mind."

Had she not felt wanted back then? Hell, he hoped he hadn't added to any stress. But he couldn't change what had happened in the past—he could only affect the present. "Well, you're wanted now. I hope you know that."

"Thank you." She turned to look out the window. "I hope he's okay."

"I hope so, too."

Ten minutes later they were back over the bridge and pulling into the parking lot of the hospital. They both got out of the car, and he and Mysti hurried toward the main entrance. "He'll probably be in the cardiac unit."

"Let's stop at the main desk and check to be sure."

She glanced at the waiting room. "I don't see his son."

Could he have been transported to one of the bigger hospitals? Serenity Regional was equipped for most things—it even had a trauma center—but there were times when more specialized care was called for.

Jesse asked at the desk. "Larry Rogers was brought in here about an hour ago. I'm his primary care physician."

"The heart attack victim from the fishing tournament?" She didn't even check her screen. A flicker of warning went through him.

"Yes."

She shook her head. "I'm very sorry. He didn't make it out of the ER."

They were too late. He'd had a bad feeling about it even as he worked on Larry at the boat launch. "Is his son still here?"

"No. He was pretty distraught. Said he had family to notify."

Larry's wife had died ten years ago, and his son—their only child—had never married. There were no grandchildren. No one to share his grief with except for extended family.

"He'd seemed fine at his checkup appointment last week." Mysti's voice came from beside him. She looked…stricken.

"Yes, he did. But we can't always predict when someone will throw a clot. Or stroke out. All we can do is give them the best care we can."

"It's just never enough. Never."

He didn't think she was necessarily talking about Larry.

"Let's go somewhere and get some lunch. Neither of us has eaten, and I could use a strong cup of coffee."

Mysti nodded, her hand going to her left shoulder and rubbing at it for a second. He didn't think she was even aware she was doing it. Much like she wasn't aware of when she was working it as if trying to find a more comfortable position for it.

"I'll call Larry's son later and see if there's anything I can do." His chest squeezed at the thought. He wished there'd been something more that he could have done at the scene. But being on the lake had made everything take longer. If they could have gotten him to the hospital sooner… If he could have kept doing CPR unin-

terrupted instead of having to get on and off boats…
None of those regrets were going to bring the old man
back, though.

"I wasn't even here when my dad passed away. And
there wasn't time for me to come home afterward,"
Mysti murmured.

Hell, he hadn't gone to her dad's funeral, either. In
fact, he'd kind of avoided Mysti's mom since Mysti left.
So had Kandid, come to think of it, and she'd been one
of Mysti's closest friends back in school.

"That couldn't have been easy for you."

"No. None of it was easy."

Again there seemed to be more behind the words
than simple grief. His chest squeezed.

"Come on, let's go into Serenity and find a place
to eat."

"Okay." She looked up. "You know you did everything you could for Larry, right?"

"There were delays when every second counted. Getting to him. Getting him to shore. Getting him out of
the boat."

She touched his hand. "Hey, there are always delays. You can't imagine the delays I've seen. Sometimes it makes a difference. Sometimes it doesn't. But
like you said, we just do the best we can. And pray that
it's enough."

# CHAPTER EIGHT

THEY ATE FISH and chips out of plastic baskets at a place in Serenity. Mysti didn't remember this place being here when she was a kid; then again, the neighboring town had changed more than Forgotten Point had.

"You okay?"

She wasn't. But what could she say? "Why wouldn't I be?"

"Is this your first loss since being back here?"

Was it? She'd had so many losses over the years. Her dad. So many soldiers. Laura… Now Larry. The list seemed to stretch endlessly.

And some losses didn't include death. She'd lost Jesse as a neighbor and Kandid as a friend. Kandid, the one person she'd confided in about her crush on Jesse the last year of high school. Kandid, who'd always had her choice of guys. She could have had anyone. And she'd chosen Jesse. Despite knowing that Mysti cared about him. That had been the worst thing about it. There'd been no apology from her friend. No explanation.

She'd made sure to invite Mysti to the wedding, although Kandid had to know there was no way in hell that she would have come. Life in California was busy. Or that would have been her excuse. The reality was she'd run as far away from Forgotten Point as she could get without falling into the ocean. And later, after she'd qualified, and once she was posted overseas, even the ocean hadn't stopped her.

She'd never heard from Kandid or Jesse again. And she'd never asked her mom for information about either of them—or anyone else, either. And as for Jesse's question just now?

She told him the truth. "Yes, it's the first loss of a patient since I've been back."

After all, Jesse had been lost to her for a long time. And even if her crush wasn't quite dead yet, he'd made his choice perfectly clear. He'd chosen Kandid. And Mysti didn't think she could bear to be a poor replacement for the love of his life. Anna must have been wrong about Jesse's marriage not being a happy one. After three years, he wasn't even dating anyone else.

"You told me I'd done all I could. So did you. You made sure his last weeks were comfortable ones. He would have died sooner if he hadn't had the surgery—would have spent each of those days in agony. The fact that he passed away doing something he loved so much isn't necessarily a bad thing. And from what Larry Jr. said, his dad simply slumped over in his seat. He hadn't complained of chest pain and had felt great that morning. Sometimes it just happens, and there's nothing anyone can do to stop it."

Like Laura's death?

But that was so very different. She hadn't simply slipped into a painless death like Larry had. She'd been blown to pieces by a bomb set by people with the express purpose of killing other people. Mysti would never understand it. She'd never had to lift her gun to shoot at anyone. Her job was to save people. Killing went against her very nature.

But there were so many people she hadn't been able to save.

"I know. And I'm glad we were there to save his son from having to second-guess himself. Medical care was only a boat away." She looked at him. "It's good that we went together."

She had thought about backing out, but if she had then there would have been no one to take Jesse's daughter and boat back to the dock while Jesse worked on Larry. And even if they had somehow managed to transfer Larry to the other boat, it would have used up even more time.

"Yes, it was. I never thanked you for getting Sally back safely and taking care of her."

"You did. You probably just don't remember it."

If only it were that easy to forget other things, too. She took out a hush puppy and popped it into her mouth, chewing it. They weren't exactly in the seafood capital of the world, but there were things she'd missed about these two small towns.

"I'll have to take you back out on the boat on a regular day to make up for today. You did me a favor, and I really appreciate it."

"There's no need to pay me back."

"What if it's not about paying you back?"

She blinked. Was he asking her out on a date?

Before she could say anything, he went on. "My mom is afraid of the water—she can't swim, and I haven't taken Sally out by myself. Mainly because of how busy life is and the amount of work it takes to get things together to go out on the lake. But also, I don't like the thought of Sally sitting in a chair while I'm navigating and unable to make sure she's safe."

"Oh." So he wanted her as a babysitter? As soon as that thought struck her, another one came on its heels. What did it matter why he'd asked her to go? She liked Sally, liked being around a child when for years she'd only associated with adults. She'd almost forgotten the joy that came with kids' laughter and questions. "Sure. I can watch her if you want."

"I'm not asking you in order to have someone to look after her. Except for what happened with Larry, I really enjoyed being out on the boat today. I actually haven't just gotten away from the house for much of anything in a few years."

Since Kandid's death. He hadn't said the words, but she heard them beneath all of the other things he'd said. Sometimes you did just have to get away from the memories, as she'd found out from leaving Forgotten Point. As she'd found out in leaving the military. It sounded like Jesse hadn't had a chance to do any of that. And if she could help him at all…

"That sounds like fun. I miss being out on the water, too."

"We could even take a pair of water skis. You said you used to ski, if I remember right. That your mom might still have yours?"

"I did. But I don't even know if I could get up now."

"Well, you'd have to be better than I'd be. It wasn't something I did as a child."

She couldn't imagine there being much of anything that Jesse Grove couldn't do.

"You could always learn."

"We'll see." He leaned back and pushed his plate away. "So you'll go?"

"Yes. I'd love to."

He pulled out his phone and flipped through a few screens. "I don't have anything next Saturday."

"That should work. Unless there's an emergency, most of my surgeries are scheduled during the week."

"Sally will be thrilled."

And Jesse. Was he thrilled?

Maybe. But if so, it wasn't because of her. It was because he'd be able to take his daughter out on the water without worry. And get a little bit of a break himself.

He glanced outside. "Looks like it's just as well that we're not still out there. It's getting dark."

"I saw that they were predicting some rain for this afternoon, but not until later. What time is the tournament on until?"

"Five. It's about fifteen minutes until then. They're supposed to announce the winner, so everyone should be back in with their catches by now. I'm sure they'll have the weigh station inside the community center if the weather turns bad."

Suddenly, she wanted to be there. Wanted to make a suggestion to the people running the tournament. "Wouldn't it be good if they named this tournament after someone who was there almost every year without fail? Who even came weeks after having major surgery?"

Jesse's head tilted. "If you're thinking what I think you are, I like it. It's always just been called the Forgotten Point Fish-Off." He glanced at her plate. "We'll have to leave now, though, if we're going to catch the committee there."

"I'm done."

After gathering their baskets and empty drink cups, they discarded them in the trash.

* * *

The rain held off as they drove over to the landing, and there were some patches of blue that made him wonder if it was going to rain at all.

Pulling into the dirt entrance, Mysti said, "Jesse, look."

He glanced over at the landing, where there were still a couple of stragglers pulling their boats out of the water. And still moored at the edge was a familiar bass boat, bobbing in the water with no sign of its owner. "Larry's boat. His son must not have come over to get it yet."

His gut shifted. He could imagine that was the last thing on Larry Jr.'s mind. Losing his father over the course of an hour had probably rocked his world. And like Mysti had said of her own father, Larry and his son had participated in this tournament for years. Many years.

"I think I'll see if I can get in touch with someone. Maybe afterward we can pull it out and take it home for them."

"It's going to be hard for his son to deal with that. It was the last time he was with his dad."

They parked and got out of the car, heading over to the fish weighing station, which was still active, despite the darkening clouds. Next to it was a large dais housing some chairs with some microphones at the front. There was a large building behind it, where he assumed everyone would retreat to if it started pouring.

A large whiteboard was propped up and a series of numbers was written on it, going up to fifty.

"I didn't realize there were that many entries. I thought maybe numbers would have dropped off over the years."

Fifty was the maximum number of boats allowed out on the lake during the tournament for safety's sake. "Does it always max out?"

She gave him a look before murmuring, "That's right, you didn't participate in it as a kid."

Well, he had gone out on a friend's boat during it one time. It was the first time he'd realized that not all families were like his, with a father who rarely came home and a mother who spent a lot of time crying. Her life had changed for the better when his father finally walked out. It had been hard. Really hard for a year or two while they got their bearings and while his mom found a better job, but they'd managed to keep the house. Their father hadn't even fought for custody rights, he'd simply dropped out of their lives, leaving town for parts unknown. And his mom hadn't sued for child support. Jesse hadn't asked at the time, because he knew nothing about divorce settlements or how things were done. But he imagined his mom hadn't wanted to face her ex ever again. They'd never talked about it since. Jesse steered clear of any mention of his father. And his mom didn't bring it up, either.

"I didn't. But I think this might be something that Sally and I could do every year."

Something shifted in her face.

"What?"

"Nothing." Her gaze traveled the group. "I think I see Earl Norman. He used to head up the tournament. I'm not sure he's still doing it. But surely he'll know who is, if not."

They walked over, and the man glanced up from his sheet of paper. "Sorry to interrupt," Mysti said. "Do you have a minute?"

"Mysti North. I remembered seeing your name on

the list of entries. Glad you're back at it. We sure do miss your daddy."

"Thanks. So do I." She paused. "You know that Larry Rogers died today."

"I heard. I couldn't believe it. We used to say that Larry was one of the founding members of the tournament."

She nodded. "I don't remember that far back, but I believe it. Any chance you can bring up an idea to whoever is on the committee?"

"What kind of idea?"

"About making this a memorial tournament in honor of someone who supported it with all his heart."

Earl's pencil stilled on the paper. "Larry?"

She nodded. "Something like the Larry Rogers Memorial Fish-Off. Maybe we could even start a fund helping less advantaged kids take part in the tournament. Ones whose families can't afford their own boats. Or ask for people to take one of those children on their boats and let them experience the tournament first-hand."

"I like that idea. Like sponsoring a kid?"

"Yes. It wouldn't change the number of boats allowed out on the lake, it would just be a chance for kids who want to be out there to have an opportunity to participate. The sponsoring entry could provide the extra bait and bring a spare rod with them. So the cost to the committee would be minimal."

Earl nodded. "Honestly, that's a great idea. We've been kicking around something similar for years. Maybe Larry's death will finally get things moving again." He glanced around. "I think the whole committee is here, so I'll flag them down and talk to them. It wouldn't be a bad idea to announce some sort of resolution today, so we can prepare for next year's tournament."

Jesse had to hand it to Mysti. He couldn't imagine the girl he'd once known coming in here and taking the bull by the horns. But the Mysti of today?

Yes. It seemed she would. He found he liked that. Really liked the confident woman she'd become. He'd thought she was cold that first day in the hospital. She wasn't. She just knew what she wanted and wasn't afraid to go after it.

"Thank you," she said.

Earl looked at Jesse. "Good to see you and your daughter out there, too, Jesse. Your first time?"

"It's the first time I've brought a boat out myself. But I actually came with a friend one year as a kid. They kind of did for me what Mysti is suggesting now. I still remember that trip out and catching my first fish."

Mysti's head cocked as she looked over at him, but she didn't say anything. Nor did she push Earl to use that information in his pitch. And Jesse appreciated that.

A lot.

Earl closed his pad and stood. "I'll round up a few people and see what they think. I'm not sure we can get it done by the end of the afternoon, but we can try."

"Thank you."

Earl headed off toward the scoreboard, which was probably where most of the other committee members were.

"That was a really good idea, Mysti. I think Larry Jr. will be grateful."

"Thank you." She glanced over at the crowd of people sitting in folding chairs that had been woven among the trees. "Can you stay for a while?"

"Yep. I'm anxious to see what size catch is going to win."

They went over to see what was going on, finding two chairs toward the back. So far entry number fifteen had the biggest fish with a ten-pound largemouth bass.

"How big was the fish you caught that day?"

Her question took him by surprise. He'd assumed she wasn't going to mention what he'd said. Or that maybe she already knew somehow.

"Four pounds. Not nearly big enough to win."

"But big enough for you to remember. We were your neighbors. We should have invited you to come with us."

"It's okay, you had no way of knowing." That day had changed so much for him. Had made him want to be better than his own father. Had made him want to be like the dad who'd taken him out in his boat and acted like it was something he did every day. And maybe he did. Or maybe the whole town had known what kind of home he grew up in. "And yes, that fish had been big enough for me to remember."

"I hope there are lots of kids in the future who have a great experience like that to look back on."

It wasn't just that day on the water that had been a wakeup call for him. Today had been, too. Seeing the exhilaration on his daughter's face when the bow of their boat had lifted had made him realize how little leisure time he actually had with her. She was already seven. In ten years she'd be graduating from high school and probably leaving for college. He wanted to give her a life like Mysti had had with memories that were cherished long after he was gone.

And he had Mysti to thank for that for making him realize it. As much as he considered that kiss all those years ago to be a mistake, maybe it could finally bring about something good.

"I don't know that I ever fully apologized to you for what I did all those years ago."

Her shocked face swung around to look at him. "Sorry?"

"For what happened in the car."

"We were both just kids, Jess. There was no need to apologize."

"I was dating Kandid. There was a need. I was just embarrassed that I behaved like that. But I am sincerely sorry. I hope that wasn't why you left Forgotten Point."

"Nope. It wasn't because of the kiss." She sighed. "And if anyone should apologize, it should be me. Kandid was my friend. It felt like such a betrayal of her at the time."

"I know what you mean. Is that why you didn't stay in touch with her? Didn't come to the wedding?"

"Maybe." She shut her eyes. "It was so long ago. And neither of us seems to be particularly scarred by the experience. You went on to have a great marriage, and you now have a beautiful daughter. So all is well."

His marriage hadn't been great at all. But maybe those cracks hadn't been as evident to everyone in town as they were to him. And why admit to Mysti now that there had been serious problems between him and Kandid? For one thing, it wouldn't change anything; it was all water under the bridge. For another, Kandid was dead. He'd never needed to make any hard decisions about divorcing her, and he certainly didn't want Sally to know how angry he and her mom had been at each other. So, no. He wasn't going to disabuse Mysti of the notion that he'd had a perfect marriage.

"Yes, all is well."

A cheer went up over the crowd and he looked up to see that entry number thirty-one had just taken the lead with a fish that was a little over ten pounds.

"So what was your biggest fish?" He asked the question without looking at her.

"I don't remember the exact weight. But it was probably around five pounds. I remember needing my dad's help to reel it in. To me it seemed massive, and I honestly didn't care that it didn't win. It was just fun being out there. Being with my dad."

"So if the committee doesn't take up the idea, what would you think of having a competing tournament instead using Larry's name and that idea of taking more kids out on the water?" He looked at her, trying to feel out her response.

"Do you think they won't vote to do it?"

"I'm hoping they will. But I'm sitting here thinking what action I should take in the event that they don't, and I'm convinced it's the right thing to do."

"I know. My mind is whirling with the possibilities. Maybe a fund could be started to buy a fishing pole for every kid who doesn't have one but wants one. Or even putting the entry fees toward something bigger, like a bass boat that we could lend to families who would like one but couldn't afford to buy or even hire one for day." There was a sparkle in her eyes that he liked.

"I'm pretty sure some boat manufacturers would like to get in on something like that."

They looked at each other and for a second or two he couldn't look away, watching as something in her gaze changed, her pupils enlarging until they seemed huge.

Another cheer pulled his attention back to the board. They watched over the course of the next half hour as the numbers slowly crept up and more and more numbers had weights beside them. His and Mysti's number was blank as were some others, one of them being Larry's boat, of course.

Then all the fish had been weighed and the winning fish, a twelve-pound largemouth bass, was held up by the person who'd caught it. He'd won a fishing pole and fuel for his boat for a year.

Then Earl got up on the makeshift platform. "I'd like to call up the members of this year's tournament committee. Most of these folks have served for a long time and have put in a lot of hard work to make this event happen each and every year. The committee stocks the lake with fish with the help of a nearby hatchery, releasing two fish for every one caught at the tournament."

Applause went up as people made their way onto the platform. It looked like there were about twenty people on the committee.

"We have one other item of business before we finish. Some of you may not know this yet, but we lost one of our own today. A man who looked forward to the fish-off every year."

Murmurs went through the crowd, and Earl held up his hands to quiet them down. "A suggestion was made—a great one, I might add—that we dedicate the future fish-offs to his memory and that we add a component of making it possible for disadvantaged kids to participate. How would we do that? By asking every boat that enters to consider taking on an extra passenger. We would collect names of kids who want to come, and those who are willing would draw a name, making sure they have a pole, bait and tackle, and a life vest available for that person. We'll be brainstorming more ways to give back to the community in conjunction with the fish-off. The committee was unanimous in favor of the idea, but I also want to hear from you." He waited for a beat or two. "How many of you would like to see this happen? Give us a show of hands."

Jesse swore every hand in the area went up. He searched the crowd and couldn't spot one person who wasn't in agreement.

Earl nodded, throwing a smile toward him and Mysti. "We have Mysti North and Jesse Grove to thank for the suggestion. Would you two please stand?"

Oh, hell. That was not what he'd wanted. But people had turned and were motioning for them to stand up. So they did, as the crowd clapped and gave whistles. Mysti rolled her shoulder back a time or two, so he wasn't the only one uncomfortable with the attention.

He also noticed two women look at each other and then lean forward to whisper something, smiling and nodding. Great. He was pretty sure that was going to be the start of some unfounded rumors about him and Mysti. But he could deal with a few rumors if it meant that Larry would have his Memorial Day each year.

He sat down as Earl's voice came back over the microphone. "So from today on, our annual tournament will be known as the Larry Rogers Memorial Fish-Off. Thank you all for helping to make this happen."

# CHAPTER NINE

"WE DID IT," Mysti said as the first big drop of rain hit her in the forehead. She couldn't believe the committee had gotten it done that quickly. She hoped Larry's son was happy with the idea. But why wouldn't he be? Maybe they should have run it by him first, but she was pretty sure that the man would agree that his dad deserved this honor.

More drops came down as people started scrambling to get their things together to head to their cars before the bottom dropped out of the sky.

"You did it, actually. But right now I think we should make our way back to the truck before we get completely soaked."

"I agree."

Too late—the drops turned torrential within a matter of seconds. Jesse grabbed her hand and took off at a run toward the parking area where his truck was buried among those of the other participants. Her foot slid on a wet rock and if Jesse hadn't had a hold of her, she would have gone down. As it was, her hand jerked out of his. He slowed his pace, wrapping an arm around her waist to make sure he didn't lose her again.

They ducked between other folks who were just as

anxious to get to their vehicles, but even with the crowd, they made it less than five minutes later.

He'd evidently used his fob to unlock the doors, because he grabbed the passenger one and yanked it open.

She hesitated. "I'll get your seat wet."

"You'll get it even more wet if you don't get in. The rain is driving straight in."

So she slid onto the leather seat, which was cool against her moist skin.

A minute later, Jesse was in his own seat.

Reaching over her, he pulled open his glove box and pulled out a couple napkins, handing her a few. She used them to mop her face, hands and legs. She shoved stray strands of hair out of her eyes, very glad she'd pulled it back in a ponytail today.

Then the absurdity of the situation hit her, and she started laughing.

"What's so funny?"

She shook her head, trying to figure out how to tell him. "Just that we were all out there on the lake today, with the possibility of falling into the water at some time, but all it took was a little rain to make everyone take off running."

He chuckled. "You're right. We were both getting spray from the boat earlier when we were moving toward our spot and no one thought anything of it."

"Nope."

"So what is it about rain that brings on such hysteria?"

She had no idea. What she did know was that sometimes it caused people to behave in ways they might not ordinarily behave.

The memory of them locked in each other's arms in a storm very much like this one came back to her.

How could she remember it so vividly? Yet she could. The feel of his lips. The heat coming off his body. The smell of skin washed by clean water.

She swallowed, jerking when the car next to them started its engine and pulled out of its space. It hadn't taken long for people to clear out. She chanced a glance at Jesse to find him with his hands gripping the wheel, staring straight ahead.

"Jess?"

When he turned to look at her, she saw it. She wasn't the only one who remembered that night so vividly.

"This is just like…"

"I know."

Mysti wasn't sure whether she reached out first or he did, but suddenly his hands were on her shoulders urging her toward him. Since her body was already in motion, she collided with his chest, laughing as he grunted at the impact.

Her laughter was soon swallowed when his mouth came down on hers, kissing her, his tongue thrusting home as if remembering how little time they'd had that night.

She was just as desperate to kiss him, too. Most of the cars had already pulled out of the parking lot, and she was pretty sure no one who was left was interested in what they were doing. They were just trying to get into their own vehicles.

Her hands found his neck, one of the spots he'd missed when he'd dried himself with the napkin, the hair at his nape cold and wet. This kiss was even better than their youthful foray, maybe because both of them were older and had lived lives that could be both happy and tragic.

This time, there was nothing tragic about having his

arms around her. It was heady. Magical. And she never wanted it to stop.

He lifted his head far too soon, and her mind screamed a protest. "Come home with me. Just for tonight," he urged hoarsely.

Go home with him?

Her brain was foggy with desire, and she didn't think she could say no, even if she wanted to. Because she didn't want to. She had dreamed about what being with him might be like long after she'd left town. And unlike last time, there was no guilt...no one standing between them.

That last phrase brought with it a whisper of caution, but she ignored it. Tuned it out.

"Yes."

He stared at her dazedly as if he couldn't believe what he was hearing. Then his head came down again, and he kissed her deeply, his mouth moving over hers as if he couldn't get enough of the taste of her. Fingers trailed down her neck, the feathery touch sending shivers over her skin as they slid over her shoulder and down her side, just grazing the edge of her breast. "We need to go. Or we won't make it out of the car. And if a police car comes up this time, we might not be found just kissing."

Her nipples puckered instantly. She wanted him so desperately. In the car. In his house. Wherever she could get him. After all this time this need for him was still as sharp as it had been fifteen years ago. Maybe even more, since she now knew how fragile and temporary life could be.

All thoughts of the tournament were forgotten as Jesse navigated the streets in the rain, his palm resting on her upper thigh, thumb brushing over the skin just beneath her shortalls and sending a shudder through her that had nothing to do with being chilled from the rain.

Unlike all those years ago, the bridge didn't have water sluicing over it, and they crossed it with ease. There was nothing blocking the path to what they wanted. At least for tonight.

It was okay, right? Just this one time. He had clarified that for her, so she didn't have to worry about there being any hint of commitment in play here, because she didn't think she could do that. Not with him. Not knowing he'd chosen someone else over her once upon a time, to be his wife and the mother of his child. She didn't know why that mattered, and she didn't have the brainpower right now to sort out whether that was teenage Mysti talking or adult Mysti.

But one night?

Oh, Lord, that she could do. That she *wanted* to do. It would put to rest once and for all those wild imaginings of what being with him might be like. Maybe she'd be sorely disappointed.

But somehow she didn't think so. Anyone who kissed the way he did, who made her react like he did, wasn't going to be anything short of mind-blowing in bed. Beyond her wildest dreams.

She reached out and wrapped her arms around his, leaning her head against the warmth of his shoulder. Just for today she could pretend that he'd chosen her. Because on this particular day, he had.

That would have to be enough. She'd make sure it was enough. And then they had next Saturday together, back out on the lake.

*No, don't think beyond today.*

"Almost there, Myst. I hope to hell I can make it out of this car."

She giggled, his meaning obvious. "Would it be that bad if you couldn't? There's always the garage."

He didn't say anything for a second, and she could have sworn he stiffened before his lips came down to kiss her temple. "The garage is full of…stuff, so unless you want the whole neighborhood to see you straddling me in the car…"

Heavens. It might be her this time who had trouble getting out. His palm slid higher on her thigh, pushing her shorts up. His fingertips slid beneath them, reaching the elastic of her panties.

"Although I might like that." His voice was low. Husky with desire. "You…straddling me."

She gulped. There was no "might" about it. She wanted to straddle him. Steering wheel at her back. Horn going off with each pump of her hips. "You're making me crazy, Jess."

"Ditto, Myst." His index finger drew another line around the edge of her panties, just as he pulled into a driveway and stopped. One hand cupped her face and turned it toward him, while the other one remained where it was. Then with a sudden movement he pushed underneath her panties, never breaking eye contact. She gasped as the heat of his palm hit her bare skin. He leaned forward, his cheek sliding against hers, stubble adding a delicious sense of friction until he was at her ear. "I can't wait to be. Right. Here."

As he said the words, his thumb edged farther down until he found the core of her.

The sensation took her by storm, and she couldn't stop herself from lifting her hips and pushing into the pressure.

"Yes," he murmured. "Just like that."

He teased her, sliding over her, going even lower,

until she wondered if she was going to be able to keep from exploding right here.

Then he withdrew, and the sound of the automatic locks cracked like thunder in the interior of the vehicle. "We need to get out now, before I really do shock my neighbors." He opened his door and climbed out of the car, as she tried to do the same, but her legs were like rubber, shaky and weak when she stood.

His arm went around her waist like at the boat launch, and he walked with her up to the front door of the house, using his key to unlock it and push it open. Then they were inside, and Jesse shoved the door shut with one foot and pivoted her, taking her lips in a smoldering kiss that pushed her into the strong wooden surface behind her.

Fingers undid the fasteners on her bib shortalls and the top of it fell down around her waist, only the side buttons keeping the garment from sliding down completely.

One hand went beneath her shirt, sliding up her torso until he reached her bra. He didn't take it off, but palmed her breast, the stiff peak craving pressure that it didn't get. She arched into him, but his hand was already gone, smoothing down her side until he reached the middle of her back. Her bra went slack two seconds later. Then he returned and this time, he gave her what she wanted, squeezing her nipple between his thumb and forefinger. Her eyes shuddered closed as waves of pleasure crashed through her.

All too soon, he released her, backing up a step and swinging her up into his arms. "Not here. I want you in my bed."

*You...straddling me.*

His growled words came back to her. And suddenly

she knew that's why he wanted her there. He wanted to fulfill a personal fantasy.

Well, that was okay, because her fantasies of him had included every possible angle and position. So she didn't care how he wanted her. She would take him however she could get him.

He entered a room that contained a huge bed.

Kandid's bed? Something in her recoiled at that thought before she threw the undesirable mental picture into a compartment in her brain and firmly locked the door. Did it really matter?

Not right now.

Holding her suspended over the mattress for a second or two, he finally dropped her onto it, and she squealed as she hit the soft surface. Then he stood over her, watching her. "You are so beautiful, Myst."

He turned and reached into a side drawer and took out a package. Condoms. Of course.

Something else withered inside her.

*Stop it, Mysti. Would you rather him not have them?*

No, of course not. Besides, the package was new; he'd had to rip open the top before he could withdraw a cellophane packet. She relaxed.

He tossed it on the bed beside her and then hauled his polo shirt over his head in a move that rivaled that of any movie hero, revealing a strong tanned chest and muscular abs. Whoa. That wasn't from a gym. Not with the tan that went along with that six-pack. He must do hard work in the sunshine on his time off.

What kind of work?

Yard work? Log splitting? Did it matter? No. As long as he got on this bed with her. Right. Now.

She reached for him, but he must have misread her

signal because he leaned down and gripped her hands, hauling her into a sitting position instead.

"What's wrong?"

He smiled, the flash of teeth giving a hint of cunning. "Nothing. Nothing at all." He tugged her to her feet, then unbuttoned her pink top, pushing it off her shoulders.

Damn! Her scars. She'd totally forgotten about them. And Lord, she didn't want him seeing them. Not now. Maybe not ever.

She was tempted to snatch her shirt back on, except he would question the move. And she'd be forced to explain.

She didn't want to explain. She just wanted him inside her.

*Distract him.*

So she undid the side of her shortalls and let them fall. Her bra was next. All she was left in were her lacy peach underwear.

At his intake of breath, she smiled. Yes. She could control how this went down. Could control what he saw or didn't see.

Mysti reached for the button of his khaki shorts and pulled the tab on his zipper, drawing the act out for as long as possible. Gripping the waistband, she tugged them down, watching as he kicked his way out of them. "Did I hear you mention the word *straddle* a little while ago?"

"Hell," he groaned.

She grinned. "Somehow I don't think this will be hell. More like heaven."

Taking his hands, she turned him until his back was to the bed. Then she pushed. Down he went, falling onto the bed with a lot more grace than she had a few minutes ago.

She thought she'd feel more self-conscious being nearly naked in front of him, but his very obvious re-action to her body gave her a courage that surprised her. "So who do you think should go first? You or me? Or should we make it happen together?"

He didn't ask her what she meant. Instead he went along with her. "Together. Definitely."

The wordplay was seductive. As exciting as any physical touch. Maybe more. Because it hinted at what was to come, without spelling it out.

"Okay. Together."

They both peeled down their underwear at the same time and tossed them aside. Jesse was hard and erect and mouthwateringly proportioned. And he would soon be all hers.

At least for an hour or two.

She climbed on top of him, her knees on either side of his thighs, stopping just short of where he jutted in wait. Her body was already a smoldering mass of need.

She wanted to touch him so badly. So she did. Slowly exploring him, amazed at the silky texture of skin that was so very warm in her hands. She pumped him once, twice, three times, watching his face as she did, fasci-nated by the tightening of muscles and the way his hips jerked up into her grip from time to time.

He allowed her to continue for another minute or two before grabbing her hands and pulling them free. "Enough, Myst."

The words were half croaked as he reached beside him and tore open the condom, rolling it over himself.

"Now," he murmured. "Come here."

She obliged, lifting her hips until she was poised

over him. She was already wet and ready, and she slid down over him in one smooth motion, taking all of him.

"Jess…" She was full. So full. Full of him. Full of heat. Full of the need to take them both over the edge. She leaned over to kiss him, but when his hands went to her back in an effort to touch her, she stiffened, then gripped them and carried them up by his head. "Let me do all the work. Just this time."

This time she kissed him, leaving him buried inside her while she remained inert and still. Except for her mouth, which was busy loving him, using her tongue and teeth to show him how much she wanted him. How much she needed him.

Then she started to move, undulating her hips in slow, easy motions that stoked the flame in her belly, urging her to go faster. Somehow she forced herself to maintain her even pace, wanting to draw this out for as long as possible. Never wanting this feeling to end.

He was all she'd dreamed of and more. And far from finally laying her curiosity to rest, she could think of so many other things they could do together. So many opportunities to learn about what he liked. What he didn't.

Unless she was mistaken, he really liked what she was doing.

When his hands came up to grip her hips this time, she didn't stop him. She was quickly moving beyond caring what he did and didn't see right now. Because her senses were wholly tuned in to what was happening in one small part of her body. Angling her a bit farther up, Jesse wrapped an arm around her waist, tilting her until her breasts were within reach of his lips. Then he pulled her into his mouth and the sudden suction on her tender flesh drew a moan from her that went on and on. One of his hands went between her shoulder blades and pressed her closer, and she barely noticed a pause as his fingertips moved over her, then retreated.

"Mysti, I need you." His hips surged forward as she came down on him, and realizing what he wanted, she began to move even faster.

His mouth came up and took hers again, kissing her with a desperation that she felt to her core.

Sitting up, she increased her pace further, her forearms braced on the taut muscles of his chest. Pleasure was winding around her with every thrust of her hips, tightening with each second that passed. His hand slid between them and he found her, sending a reflexive shudder through her, the sensation indescribably wonderful.

Higher and higher she went, her body no longer propelled by her will but by primal instinct. Her eyes closed, all of her focus turning inward as she reached for some distant goal. And then it wasn't distant, but rushing toward her at lightning speed. And when it reached her…

She exploded in a series of convulsions that balled her hands into fists and rolled her eyes in their sockets. From a distance she heard his loud groan, feeling him moving with a speed that seemed superhuman.

And then he joined her in pleasure, Jesse's pace slowing gradually until it was a languorous slide that was pure enjoyment. Her fists released and she relaxed against his chest, her head just beneath his chin.

"That was…" She couldn't finish the sentence, because there were no words that could do justice to what had just happened.

"Yes. I know. For me, too."

She nuzzled him, her lips touching the underside of his jaw before coming up to tease him with kisses across his cheek, planting one last one on his chin. Then she laid her head back down.

His fingertips trailed across her lower back, the sensation half tickly, half soothing, and she allowed her eyes to drift shut, enjoying his ministrations. His touch swirled higher, and she sighed.

"You're going to make me go to sleep."

"No. Not quite yet," he growled.

Not yet? Did he mean he wanted her again?

He chuckled as if reading her mind. Then his fingers paused at her shoulder like they had done earlier, and with a rush of awareness she realized where he was. When she tried to pull away from his touch, he held her still, his fingers still exploring.

"What is this?" He sat up, and he leaned to the side as if he was going to look, but she stopped him, shaking her head as swift tears came to her eyes.

"No, Jesse. Don't. Please don't."

# CHAPTER TEN

THERE WAS SOMETHING in her shaky plea that held him frozen for a second or two.

"Let me. Please."

Mysti's chin went up, but this time she didn't stop him from angling her sideways so he could look. His jaw clenched, all the memories of what they'd just shared obliterated when a series of thick angry scars came into view. Scars that riddled her left shoulder blade and sprayed in an arc that coated a good part of her back on that side. Most of it, though, was on the shoulder that he'd seen her roll more than once.

He repeated his earlier question. "What is this?"

For several seconds there was silence, then she said, "I was hit by shrapnel from an IED."

Words were stuck in his throat for several long seconds.

"Damn. Did I hurt you? When we were…"

"No. I don't notice it for the most part."

He didn't think that was quite the truth. "Did this happen when you were in Joronha?"

"Yes. A good friend of mine was killed by it. I survived because I was farther away from it when it blew." Her eyes closed. "And her…her body blocked some of the blast."

Shock and horror washed over him at her words.

"I'm so sorry. Why didn't you say something to me before?"

"Why?" She shifted around to face him. "What could you have said or done? Or maybe you wouldn't have wanted to make love to me if you'd known how bad it was."

"No." He took hold of her shoulders, trying to keep his own emotions under wraps. He could not even imagine what she had gone through. What she had endured afterward. "Nothing could have stopped what happened between us. It's been building for a long time."

She gave him a slight smile. "Yes. It has."

He separated himself from her, then tugging her with him, he moved until he was leaning against the headboard, with Mysti resting on his chest. "Do you want to tell me about it?"

She shrugged, and he wondered for a minute if that meant no. But then she started talking.

"Like I said earlier, Laura was a friend of mine. She was in my squad. I found out about a year into our deployment there that she'd become pregnant. If her commander had found out, she'd have been shipped straight home. So she hid it until she could decide what she wanted to do, asking me not to tell anyone. She said the father was a soldier she'd hooked up with over the period of a few months, but that it had never been serious." She sighed. "I don't know who it was. But I kept my promise and held on to her secret. I told no one. Not her commander. Not her other friends. Not even her parents after she died. I didn't want anything tarnishing her service record, not that it should have mattered. You're the first person I've ever shared that secret with." She pulled down an audible breath. "Anyway, we were on the way to see a local midwife we'd heard about to see how far along she was."

Her breathing quickened, and she plucked at the bedspread beside her. "We didn't make it that far. We were walking over ground we assumed had been cleared. I was ahead of her and she was following a small distance behind. I thought she was walking in my footsteps. Then something behind me exploded and before I could turn around, I was knocked off my feet by the blast, and felt a searing pain in my back that I immediately recognized from treating so many other soldiers.

"Someone had planted an IED. When I could finally sit up, I saw blood on the ground where I'd fallen and when I looked back…" She gave a visible swallow. "I couldn't even recognize what was left of her. I remember yelling her name, then everything went black."

"God. I'm so sorry, Myst."

"They said I woke up in the field hospital screaming, although the details of the first several weeks after being hit are pretty foggy. They evidently spent quite a bit of time picking pieces of metal out of me.

"After I healed, I couldn't work. Couldn't sleep. I was a mess. I kept thinking if I'd forced her to tell someone she was pregnant, we wouldn't have been sneaking away to see that midwife, wouldn't have been breaking the rules about going out in singles or pairs." Her eyes closed for several seconds, then reopened, revealing deep green wells of pain. "They ended up shipping me back to the States to go through counseling for what they said was PTSD."

"That's when you decided to get out of the military."

"Yes. I decided I was enough of a mess that I wouldn't be very effective back out on the field. Not in a month. Not in six months. So I decided to get out. I had a medical discharge, and they forgave the rest of the service time I had left for my medical degree. I thought home—Forgotten Point—might be a place of healing, which is why I applied for that three-month position at Serenity Regional."

"And has it been a place of healing?"

"I think so. At least until Larry died." She shook her head. "I treated so many wounded soldiers. I'd get them patched up and they would do well. I thought they would get better. Except some of them didn't. Some of them died from unforeseen complications. An aneurysm. A blood clot. One committed suicide a month after he was declared fit for duty."

"Hell. Did Larry bring back those memories for you?"

Her face crumpled. "We'd declared him fit, Jess. Then he died."

His arm tightened around her, a wave of compassion swamping him and threatening to pull him under. Hell, he'd had no idea she'd even suffered an injury, much less carried the guilt of her friend's accident, or of other soldiers' deaths, along with her. And although his medical specialty brought death with it on a regular basis, it was more the natural order of things. Elderly patients passed away. But to see young men and women suffer and die from something as senseless as a conflict between nations… It was hard to fathom how anyone dealt with it. And being a medical professional in that setting had to be traumatic for all of them.

"Larry *was* fit, Mysti. As fit as anyone could have guessed at the time. You can't always predict blood clots. Or heart rhythm episodes. Or even if you'll be hit by a car walking across the street. He was incredibly happy to be at that tournament. And he got help almost immediately. We were both on the scene."

"I know. I don't really know why it's hitting me as hard as it is."

"I can understand that." He paused, asking a question he hadn't realized had been forming. "You said being home has helped in some ways. Does that mean you're going to stay in Forgotten Point after the three months are up?"

A couple of beats passed. "I actually haven't decided yet. I thought I'd give myself this time to see how I fit here." She smiled. "So ask me again in another month or so."

His heart froze in his chest. She hadn't exactly said no to staying. But she hadn't said yes, either. Wasn't this why he'd decided not to let Sally be around her too much? And now he'd had her in his bed. Had asked her to go back out on the boat next weekend. What had he been thinking?

He decided to ignore his misgivings. She hadn't said she was leaving. Just said she needed to see if she fit here. What if she did? What then? Could he risk it?

His fingers teased the silky skin of her arm, feeling her snuggle closer as he did. Why did he need to think a month or two ahead? Why couldn't he simply enjoy her being back? Enjoy getting to know her again? He had a feeling she hadn't told anyone else about her wounds except maybe her mother.

"Does your mom know what happened to you?"

She immediately tensed. "No. And please don't tell her. I just haven't been ready to say anything. To anyone."

So she'd chosen to share that information with him first? He thrust down the pleasure. Not really. Only because he'd felt the skin back there and had wanted to see what it was. She'd actually tried to stop him at first. But once he'd seen it, she'd shared her story as if relieved to have someone finally know about it.

He was glad it was him. No matter what the reason.

"Thank you for telling me. It'll go no further."

"Thanks." Her stiff muscles loosened back up, her fingers coming up to touch his face. "You've got stubble coming up."

He smiled. "Does it bother you?"

"No. I like it. Loved feeling it scrape across my cheek earlier."

His fingers encircled her wrist, and he drew her palm to his lips, kissing the center of it. "I'm glad."

"I really like Sally. She's a sweet girl."

He forced himself not to react to the words. "Thank you. I'll admit, I'm pretty partial to her myself."

"As you should be." Her index finger traced his lips. "I'm glad I told you about what happened. It's like a weight has been lifted. More than with the counselors and treatment programs, even, since I opted not to disclose Laura's pregnancy. They couldn't really help me with my guilt, as they didn't understand the cause of it. But knowing you think I'm not a monster for keeping it a secret helps."

"Never. You're a kind, compassionate woman who suffered a horrific loss and a terrible injury. But thank God you're still here. I'm not sure I can imagine a world without Mysti North in it."

It was true. Jesse couldn't imagine Mysti not being somewhere. He'd grieved Kandid's death, but not the way a husband should have. He'd grieved more that Sally wouldn't grow up with her mother. Grieved that he hadn't always been able to love his wife the way he should have. In the end, he hadn't cheated on her, but he also hadn't been a stellar example of what love and marriage should look like. Maybe that's why Kandid had looked elsewhere for comfort.

And worse, maybe he'd never really gotten over a certain kiss in a storm. Whether his difficulty expressing emotions with Kandid had been due to guilt or because that kiss had triggered some deeper emotion in him, he wasn't sure. And exploring that in depth would only bring him more pain. More guilt. Maybe that's why he still hadn't been able to part with the bulk of Kandid's stuff. It was stored in the garage. His thought was that he could let Sally look through it when she got older and pick out what she wanted to keep, and then he'd get rid of the rest.

Really? Was that the real reason?

That was something else he wasn't going to examine right now with another woman in his arms. A woman who...

He gulped. Did he love her?

Too soon. Way too soon. Mysti hadn't even committed to staying in Forgotten Point yet.

He could wait. Let her get her footing over these three months. And if she did that and wanted to stay?

Well, then they might just have to sit down and have a long talk.

But for right now, he was going to do his best to live in the present. To enjoy the here and now with her.

He half rolled onto his side, one leg sliding between hers. Looking down at her, with her flushed face, her mussed hair, and eyes that were bright and alive, parts of him began to come back to life, nudging at her thigh.

Her eyes widened as if realizing what was happening. "Dr. Grove, you appear to have a growing problem."

"Problem?" He chuckled. "Where you see a problem, I see an opportunity."

"Oh, I'm not complaining. And I kind of liked that straddle thing."

His flesh reacted with even more enthusiasm. "Yes, I liked that, too. But this time I think I'd like to be the driver." He rolled the rest of the way on top of her, supporting most of his weight on his elbows. "And I mean that both figuratively and literally."

When she arched against him, he couldn't hold back a low groan.

"I really like the sound of that." She grinned up at him. "Both figuratively. And literally."

Jesse hesitated before picking up the phone several days later. But he'd promised himself he would not let what had happened that night change who they were at work. They were colleagues. Professionals. Doctors often called on each other to run things by them. And this was important.

So he turned his cell phone over and found her number.

Mysti picked up on the third ring. "Hi, Jess."

Of course she knew who it was. She would have entered his number into her phone. But she could delete it just as easily on her way out of town.

Where the hell had that thought come from?

"Hey. How busy is your schedule?"

"It's not packed. What's up?"

Jesse pulled the file closer. "I have a seventy-four-year-old patient who's down in the ER right now with a compound fracture to her radius. I'm about to head over there."

"Okay. Do you want me to take a look?"

"Do you mind? I would say this is normal, but the attending says she's insisting she slipped in the shower, and when she went to catch herself on the wall, she heard a sharp snap and the next thing she knew the bone was protruding from her forearm."

"Osteoporotic?"

"No, that's what worries me. She had a compression fracture to her L2 vertebra a while back after a fall from a ladder. At the time it seemed like a normal injury, but I ordered a bone density test just to be sure I wasn't missing something. There was some expected loss of bone mass but not enough to classify it as osteoporosis or even osteopenia." Osteopenia was a precursor to more serious loss of bone mass and would have given him cause to keep a closer eye on it.

"Snapping that bone would have taken quite a bit of pressure, then. Unless she actually fell with all of her weight on it…"

"I know."

"What's the patient's name?"

"Gertrude Evans."

"Wait." There was a pause. "As in Mrs. Evans who taught us at Forgotten Point High?"

"Yep. Can you meet me in the ER? She's being admitted and the attending… Well, let's just say he's not the most patient doc on the planet."

Jesse didn't like talking about his colleagues like that, but he also tended to be protective of his patients and wanted them with doctors who were good at handling the intricacies of emotion that sometimes came with aging. Mrs. Evans could be direct and would not take well to someone talking down to her like she was a child.

"Got it. I'm on my way there now."

While his receptionist phoned some of his afternoon patients to see if they could shuffle his appointments around, he headed down the hallway toward the main building. By the time he got to Mrs. Evans's room, he found Mysti already there talking to her. There was no sign of Eric Porter, the attending physician.

Mysti turned to him, trying to hide a smile. "She said she already fired the last guy."

"Yes, I did." His patient was holding her arm, which was already covered with a layer of sterile gauze to keep it clean. Despite her obvious pain, there was still fire in her eyes. "He didn't understand the meaning of 'Talk to me like I can understand.'"

The same plastic shoes she'd worn to his office over a month ago were on the ground next to the exam bed. There were a couple of spots of blood on them this time. Something about that made his gut tighten. "Tell me what happened. I know you already told Dr. Porter, but I want to hear the story."

Something about standing beside Mysti as Gertrude Evans explained what had happened felt good and right. He'd expected to feel some sort of awkwardness between them, but it was as if they'd reverted back to a time in the past when they'd been good friends, something he hadn't felt since that kiss in his car fifteen years ago. It was as if everything that had been turned on its head back then had been righted by the night they'd spent together.

"So you started to fall, your arm hit the grab bar on the way down and then you caught yourself with that same arm."

She nodded.

So either Porter had been in a hurry and hadn't gotten her story straight, or she'd been minimizing what had happened out of fear someone would want to take her farm away from her. He could see how that kind of fall could have resulted in the injury. Striking the arm hard enough against the bar could have fractured the bone, then catching herself could have pushed it through the skin. When he glanced at Mysti, she nodded as if reading his thoughts.

But he still wanted to check something out.

"You remember that MRI you had with your compression fracture? I'd like to repeat that with your arm."

"Okay. What are you looking for?"

"I'm not as worried as I was when Dr. Porter first called me, but I'd like to rule out a lesion on the bone causing the fracture."

"In other words, cancer."

Mrs. Evans had never liked things to be wrapped in pretty boxes. She wanted the ugly truth no matter what it was. "Yes. I just want to make sure nothing weakened your radius and made it more likely to fracture."

She eyed Mysti. "And you'll be the one fixing my arm?"

"I'm a surgeon, so I could in a pinch. But I think I'd like to see you with someone who specializes in orthopedics. I'm simply here to keep Dr. Grove in line." She smiled at the woman, who laughed.

"I always said he needed someone to do that."

Jesse read something behind the older woman's words that he hoped Mysti didn't hear. But if she did, she didn't show it, just kept on smiling.

"I'll get your MRI set up and see how soon we can get that arm fixed." He called the order in, and thankfully they were going to be able to get her in almost immediately.

Five minutes later, Gertrude was being wheeled out of the room and headed for the elevator.

Mysti and Jesse followed her out.

"Sorry for calling you over. What I heard over the phone didn't sound quite as clear-cut as Gertrude explained it."

"No reason to be sorry, and I agree with you. I also agree with getting an MRI just to be sure there's no underlying cause for that bone to be weakened. Care if I sit with you as she gets her scan? I always did like Mrs. Evans as a teacher."

"So did I. And I could certainly use some good news on this case."

He didn't have to say he was referring to Larry. The quick feel of her hand squeezing his before letting go told him she understood how he felt, because she felt the same.

The MRI didn't take long, and since he'd asked for the scans to be read immediately so they knew how to proceed on the surgical repair, the radiologist met them there.

The group peered at the slides as they came off the computer, with Deke Phillips frowning as he studied each one. "I'll give them a closer look after I finish my day, but I'm not seeing any obvious problem areas in that bone or in her other arm. If there's a lesion, I'm just not spotting it. So I say go ahead with surgery and get the break repaired."

They stood and shook hands. "Thanks, I appreciate you coming down."

Deke laughed. "Not a problem. I had her in school. So I know better than to do a sloppy job. She'd call me out on it."

Yes, she would. He imagined there were quite a few folks in Forgotten Point who'd had Mrs. Evans as an English teacher. And Deke was right. He would be called out, in exactly the same way she'd called out Dr. Porter.

They gave her the news together, letting her know that the orthopedic surgeon was already scrubbing up to repair her arm.

"Is he any good?"

"I'd say you'd give him an A if he were in your class."

Gertrude reached out and grabbed Mysti's hand with her good one. "I'm going to hold you to keeping this one in line. He needs it."

With that, she was wheeled away yet again, leaving Jesse and Mysti staring after her.

When they looked at each other, they both burst out laughing. "She is too funny." Mysti scrubbed a palm under one of her eyes to blot the tears. "You were right, you know. We did need some good news. And I think we just got it."

"Yes," he murmured. "I think we just did."

# CHAPTER ELEVEN

MYSTI WAS EXCITED about their boating trip today. Even though they'd seen each other at work, a full week had passed since she'd spent the night with him. And although they hadn't slept together since then or talked about what had happened, she remembered with a shiver how he'd reached for her again and again in the middle of the night. He had fixed her a delicious breakfast before driving her home the next day. And he'd been friendly ever since, with a hint of almost flirty banter between them at the hospital when no one was around.

The case with Gertrude Evans had seemed to solidify that easy rapport. And boy, she could get used to this.

It was what she'd once dreamed about having with him. The fact that he'd married Kandid was something she couldn't go back and change, and she certainly didn't want to ask him about it. He'd obviously loved her deeply or he wouldn't have married her.

But widowed people did remarry. And she was pretty sure none of those people thought their new partner was second best or somehow less than the spouse who'd died. It was just different. Maybe it was the same way parents could love more than one child.

Who'd said anything about love?

Not her. She was just going to keep things loose and

easy. She was still sorting out how she felt about returning to Forgotten Point. But she had to admit, she was feeling better and better about being here.

And she was looking forward to being with him. To getting to know Sally a little better. She'd finally gotten to see what being with Jesse in a more intimate setting was like.

It had been wonderful and amazing. And when he'd turned her onto her stomach and traced her scars, he'd brought her to tears, loving her as he kissed those marks one at a time. It had made her feel wholly accepted. Wholly cared about. Wholly…

Nope. She was going to stop right there.

She glanced at her watch. He was due to pick her up in just a few minutes. She quickly pulled on her bathing suit, the first time she'd worn one since her injury. She turned around to look at the scarring in the mirror. Her strap covered part of it up, but the scooped back showed off more than she would have wanted, once upon a time. But it would just be her and Sally and Jess. And if his daughter asked what had happened to her, she would simply respond that she'd gotten hurt.

She slid on shorts and a loose gauzy top that was long enough to act as a cover-up for her suit if they ended up using an inner tube or skis. But she didn't care about any of that. She just wanted to be with him. They could have gone cycling for all she cared. But Jesse had said he wanted to start using his boat more, for Sally's sake. And for his.

She shoved her feet into sandals and tucked a pair of water shoes into her tote bag in case they ended up getting out and wading in some shallows.

Her phone rang, and she glanced at the readout. It was her mom.

"Hi, how did Brutus's appointment go?"

Their vet was open on Saturday mornings, and her mother had wanted the Saint Bernard scheduled for a recheck. "It went fine. I told you I wouldn't need help. He jumped in and out of the car like a champ."

"Great." She'd been a little worried about that, but her mother had insisted on taking the dog on her own, especially once she'd heard that Mysti had plans for today.

"I'm so glad you're going out. Jesse's seemed kind of sad ever since Kandid's death."

She tried not to think of all the pictures of Kandid that had been scattered throughout his house when she was over there. There weren't any in the bedroom. But the living room had more than enough framed snapshots to make up for that. The pictures had made her tense when she saw happy smiling faces in all of them, but of course Jesse wouldn't throw those away—or even put them in storage. He'd loved Kandid. And she was Sally's mom.

Mysti frowned. "I'm sure he was. She was his wife for quite a while, Mom."

"I know that. But people do fall in love again."

*Please don't ruin this.*

The fact that she herself had just thought the exact same thing didn't help. Those pictures meant nothing. Right? Not even the one of Jesse gazing lovingly at Kandid while she held a baby Sally in her arms.

"You didn't," she pointed out.

Her mom laughed. "I know. But your dad and I had been married for almost forty years."

"I don't think there's a time limit on love." Her voice came out a little harsher than she meant for it to. "Sorry. I just don't want you making a big deal over this. Jess and I are friends. We've been friends since we were kids."

"Yes. I know."

The way her mother said it confirmed some of her suspicions about what her mom knew or didn't know about her feelings for Jesse all those years ago. At least she prayed that was what this was about. She hoped to hell she wasn't giving off some kind of weird pheromones that told her mom she had her sights set on Jesse. Because she didn't want to do that. Didn't want to rush into anything. Especially not after everything they'd both been through in their lives. Jesse had Kandid's death to recover from. And she had Laura's and her own injuries to get over. Maybe she was just grabbing at life a little too fast.

Her doorbell rang at that second, thankfully.

"Mom, I have to go. They're here for me."

"Okay, have fun. And forget everything I said. I'm just being a hopeless romantic."

Mysti sighed, sorry that she'd snapped. "I know you are. It's one of the many things I love about you. And I'm glad Brutus's appointment went well. I'll call you when I get home. And I'll have my cell phone on me if you need me for anything."

"Go. I'll be fine. But I promise to call if there are any problems."

"Thanks. Talk to you tonight."

With that she hung up and grabbed her tote bag, hurrying to the door. She wondered if she should have packed a lunch. But they hadn't gotten a chance to eat the last one, because of Larry, and they hadn't talked about how long they'd be out on the water. Maybe he didn't mean for this to be an all-day excursion.

Pulling open the door, she smiled when she saw Jesse

there holding his daughter's hand. He'd done an admirable job putting Sally's hair into two neat pigtails, pink ribbons tied in a bow on each side.

"Hi," she said, giving him a nervous smile.

"Hi, yourself. I think I'm a few minutes early, so if you need more time…"

"Nope, I'm ready." She stepped out, closing the door on her little rental cottage. It sat at the back of a local farmer's property. He'd originally built it to house his adult children and grandkids, but even the grandkids were now grown up. So Mysti's mom had talked him into letting her rent it for as long as she was here. She was pretty sure the farmer was just glad to have someone in it to keep it clean. And fortunately, it had come fully furnished, which was a huge help. Even if it hadn't, Mysti was used to soldiers' quarters and tent housing. So this was like a luxury hotel in comparison.

"How's Gertrude doing? Have you heard?"

"She's great. Doing too much with her arm in a sling, but that's Gertrude."

A sense of relief went through her. "I'm so glad."

She then smiled and stooped to look Jesse's daughter in the eye. "Hi, Sally. Are you ready to get back on the boat?"

"Yes! Dad said I might be able to sit with him on a tube."

"A tube?"

Jesse glanced at her. "I brought some skis and some water things, but I told her maybe. I didn't promise. I didn't want to commit you to driving the boat if you didn't want to."

"I think that sounds like fun. I'd be happy to, especially since I forgot to ask my mom about my skis. Anyway, I can go nice and slow."

He reached and gave her hand a squeeze as she stood back up. "Thanks. So can I."

They shared a look that made her smile.

If Sally noticed the exchange or the quick touch, she didn't say anything. But it sent an unexpected burst of warmth through Mysti. She was glad things weren't weird between them, but was also kind of weirded out that they weren't. Her mouth twitched. So by using *weird* twice in a sentence, did it act like a double negative, meaning things really *were* weird?

*Ugh. Too much thinking. Again.*

She walked toward the car, Jesse and Sally behind her. The boat and trailer were already hooked up to his truck, so they wouldn't have to stop and do that. When something brushed the skin of her left shoulder, she flinched before realizing it was Jesse.

"Sorry. I was just going to say, I like your blouse."

The white cover-up was scooped in the back like her swimsuit and probably still revealed some of her scars when she moved. She hadn't checked, but was glad that it didn't bother him.

It certainly hadn't seemed to last week.

"It's okay. It just startled me." She opened the back door for Sally and waited for her to climb in. "I didn't pack a lunch. I wasn't sure what your plans were."

"No plans. And I packed one again this time. I seem to remember you had cold fried chicken on the menu, so I brought that."

"I love it."

She leaned into the truck and got Sally buckled in, tweaking her nose as she did, causing the child to laugh.

More warmth bubbled inside her. This little girl was absolutely precious.

She realized it might seem like she was taking over

with Sally, but Jesse didn't seem to mind. In fact, he smiled at her when she closed the door. "I hope it was okay for me to buckle her in."

"Yes. It was more than okay."

She swallowed down an unexpected rush of emotion, moving away to get into the front passenger seat.

Twenty minutes later, they were back across the bridge and at the landing they'd used for the fishing tournament. The place looked oddly abandoned, with only three boat trailers parked in the lot. A week ago, Larry was out there fishing and planning on taking home that trophy for the third time in a row.

How things changed in such a short space of time. What had he said in that exam room?

*None of us knows how long we'll travel this earth.*

Larry certainly hadn't known. Neither had Laura. Or Kandid, for that matter.

So shouldn't she try to make the most of every moment?

Yes. She should. And part of that was allowing herself to enjoy today for what it was. There was no need to worry about what tomorrow might bring or the next day. Sometimes it was better to live in the here and now.

And for today, at least, she meant to do just that.

The sound of screaming eclipsed the rumble of the boat motor and Jesse turned quickly to look before smiling broadly. Sally and Mysti were huddled together on a towable tube he'd purchased just for the occasion. In his mind, it reminded him of a small inflatable boat and seemed safer than an inner tube, which had no bottom to it.

Mysti's arms were around Sally, despite the bulk of both of their life jackets, and from what he could tell, his daughter was having the time of her life. He'd already taken his turn with her while Mysti steered the boat, and she'd insisted that she wanted to ride with Mysti next. A momentary flash of worry had been quickly quashed.

Today was a day for fun. Not worrying. If this had been one of Sally's friends, he wouldn't be sitting here stymied by the idea of her getting too attached or anything else.

Maybe he should be more worried about *him* getting too attached to her.

Because from everything he sensed inside himself, that was more than just a possibility. It was already a reality. But Mysti seemed happy in Forgotten Point, despite her earlier words about not being sure if she'd extend her stay after her three months were up. He hadn't felt in her that frantic need to leave that she'd had the day of their high school kiss and afterward.

He waved, then turned back to navigating the boat. It had been quiet on the lake today, probably because of how busy it had been last week. And since Sally was here and there were no plans for her to spend the night at his mom's house, there would be no sleepovers or anything else with Mysti. So it took away some of that pressure. Not that there wasn't part of him that wanted her. Had badly wanted her all week.

*Not going to think about it.*

Not going to think about how right it looked for his daughter to be held by a woman other than Kandid. He made a wide turn so that they could go over the boat's wake, not that there was much of one at this slow rate of speed. But that was his daughter back there, and he wasn't taking any chances, no matter how much she yelled for him to "make waves."

He'd made enough waves already with what had happened with Mysti last weekend. But those waves had been wild and wonderful, and he hadn't given a thought to speed. He'd wanted to go as fast as he could. Until he couldn't go any more. It had been the night of a lifetime.

He rolled his eyes. And there he went again. Thinking.

Changing directions and circling to the left, he gave Sally another small wake, then he throttled down and slowed to a stop. He didn't want her or Mysti getting seasick by keeping them out there for too long. It had already been twenty minutes, and his grumbling stomach told him it was about time to take a lunch break.

Letting the boat drift toward the center of the lake, he slowly reeled in the tube until they were within reach of the teak swim platform at the back of the boat. Jesse held the rope while Mysti handed Sally over, setting her on the platform. He put her in the boat and told her to go sit down, then he held out a hand for Mysti. She took it and stepped onto the platform, passing a little too close to him. On purpose?

Her saucy smile said yes, and he grabbed her hand and tugged it until she was flush against him. "Sorry. Looks like you tripped." He grinned at her and then let her go.

"More like I was tripped by a certain someone."

She stepped onto the boat, walking toward the seat next to Sally while he hauled the float inside and lashed it to the aft side so it wouldn't blow away. "I'm going to move toward shore and set the anchor. I don't know if anyone else is hungry, but I am."

"Me! Me!" Sally raised her hand, her pink nose reminding him that he'd probably better reapply her sunscreen.

They set up the canopy for shade, and Jesse flipped

up the little tables that were attached to each of the seats. He then passed out plates and containers of food.

"I am going to be so spoiled," Mysti remarked. "You haven't let me do anything today."

"You've made my daughter happy. That's huge."

"We had fun, didn't we, Sally?"

"Yes! I want Mysti to always come on all of our trips!"

His insides tightened before he forced them to release. "We'll have to see what happens."

Mysti nodded as if thanking him for pulling her out of the fire. That worried him a bit. He wasn't going to pressure her or force her to make decisions she wasn't ready to make, but he did need to think about Sally. As much as he'd thought about Mysti being like any of Sally's other friends, it wasn't exactly true.

But it was still early days. If Mysti disappeared out of their lives right now, Sally wouldn't really suffer. Because there hadn't been a big emotional investment made in her.

Except by him.

But he was a grown-up. He'd handled her leaving once before. He could handle it again.

Maybe he could think of a way to put some feelers out. She'd definitely been flirting with him earlier. Of course, he had been just as guilty of playing games.

But a time was coming when he was going to want something a little more substantial than games.

He sat down across from them and ate, while Sally talked about school and her friends. And she commented on how much she liked her teacher.

"I'm glad you like her," Mysti said. "Ms. Lewis and I went to high school together."

"She said you did. She's really nice. She lets us pet frogs."

Mysti laughed. "She had a bearded dragon as a pet when we were in school. I helped her feed it."

"She has one of those now, too. He's our class mascot. His name is Snuffles and we help take care of him."

"Wow," she said. "I guess some things never change."

Jesse tensed again at that before deciding he was reading too much into her words. It wasn't a warning from fate. She was just talking about a friend and her lizard.

And he could say the same of kissing her again in the rain. Some things never did change. Or maybe they did. Because watching his daughter laughing with Mysti had done his heart good. He and Kandid had rarely laughed with their daughter. Oh, they each did in their own way, but when they were all together, there'd often been an underlying tension that was hard to overcome.

He'd asked himself a question the other night, and maybe it was time to own the truth. He loved Mysti.

Maybe he always had and just hadn't realized it. Hadn't let himself admit it. Even in school.

But by admitting it now, wasn't he setting himself up for heartache all over again? Maybe. Probably. But at least he wouldn't always wonder what would have happened if he'd told her the truth about how he felt. Not in the past. But right now.

Maybe he would. He'd give it a little more time. He could ask her out on an actual date. One where they dressed up and went out to dinner and where they talked like they had after they'd made love. She'd shared stuff with him that she said she'd never told anyone else. That had to count for something, didn't it?

He really hoped so.

Mysti got up from her seat and picked up the trash from their lunch, disposing of it in the trash bag they'd brought with them. She gave him a smile, the sides of her nose crinkling in a way he remembered fondly. And he didn't think she'd rolled her shoulder one single time today.

He caught at her hand, releasing it when she turned toward him. He still needed to be careful about displays of affection around Sally. "How is it?" He nodded in the direction of her injuries.

"Hmm… I don't think it's bothered me at all today. Maybe it's from all the stretching on the float."

"I'm glad."

"Yeah. Me, too." She smiled, touching the back of his hand with her index finger and letting it slide against his skin for a second. "Thanks for inviting me."

"I'm really glad you could come."

She pulled in a deep breath and let it out with what sounded like sincere contentment. "So am I."

They stayed on the boat another hour or so before Sally started to get restless. "Ready to call it a day?" Jesse asked.

He didn't want to. He could stay out here forever, but they were going to have to go in sometime.

"I guess we should. Besides, I told my mom I would call her when I got in."

Mysti didn't sound any more anxious to go than he did. And that made him happy.

They made their way back to the boat launch and winched it out of the water. "Do you mind stopping by the house to drop off the boat first? Turning around on your narrow lane was a little challenging this morning."

"That's a great idea."

All too soon they were in front of his house. He

unhitched the boat. "Anyone need to make a bath-room break?"

"It probably wouldn't be a bad idea." She unstrapped the float from inside the boat. "Where do you want this?" she asked as he gathered up the picnic stuff and life jackets.

"We'll just dump all of it in the garage. I'll rinse them off tomorrow."

They walked toward the house with their arms loaded with stuff. And he unlocked the front door for Sally, so she could go to the restroom.

He set all the stuff on the ground. "I'll go around and open the garage door for you."

"Sounds good. I'll wait here."

Mysti smiled to herself as she waited for Jesse. Today had been…wonderful. And it just went to prove that the pictures in his house were just reminders. Remnants of the past that didn't hold a real place in his heart any-more. A part of her felt like he'd proved that today.

God, when he'd pulled her to him on that swim plat-form, she'd thought her heart was going to burst. It was like a dream. One she never wanted to wake up from.

This was the same Jesse she'd wanted back in high school. The one who made little comments only the two of them would understand. The one who kissed her until she was breathless. The one who…loved her.

She swallowed. Could he ever?

She'd been devastated once before; could she risk her heart again? This time with a more mature Jesse? Maybe one who realized love wasn't all about looks or popularity, but about two people who genuinely liked each other.

She heard a sound from inside the garage, and the

door slowly rolled up, the click-click-click of the mechanism seeming to echo the ticking of her heart.

She picked up the float while Jesse came and grabbed an armful of the other stuff. As he came nearer he kissed her softly on the lips. She smiled. "Where's Sally?"

"Somewhere she can't see."

"Mmm… In that case…" She leaned forward and kissed him a bit harder. "Okay, back to work. Where do you want this exactly?"

"Just in the middle of the floor. It's kind of cluttered in there right now."

"That's okay."

She ducked inside, letting her eyes adjust to the light. Then she glanced around as she found a place to set the float. Jesse dumped one load, then went out for another.

Something on the wall caught her attention, and her heart lurched. There was a cheerleading skirt and shirt in a clear garment bag hanging on a hook. And there were clothes racks. With dresses. And shoes. And sparkly formals.

Kandid's stuff. He hadn't gotten rid of it.

Everywhere she looked she saw more of it. A dressing table. A tall vase. Knickknacks. She turned toward the wall on the other side of the space and a strange pressure built in her head. There was a large portrait of Jesse, Kandid and a much younger Sally sitting on a painter's easel. It looked similar to one she'd seen inside the house.

But this was so much more than some pictures on the wall in the living room.

It looked like a shrine. A shrine to Jesse's dead wife.

Nausea gathered in her stomach, frothing around the edges and threatening to find the nearest exit. Jesse came back inside and somehow…from somewhere within the depths of her, she managed to dredge up a semblance of a smile. "I'll just wait outside."

"Do you need to use the restroom?"

"Nope. I'll be home in just a few minutes. Thanks though."

She went outside and waited by the car.

How was she going to pretend that everything was normal all that way? Because those "few minutes" were going to take forever. No one kept all their loved one's things for that many years unless they were finding it impossible to let them go. Look at her mom, who refused to date or even look at another man, because she was still so desperately in love with her husband. She hadn't thought that was weird, so why would it be weird for Jesse to hold on to Kandid?

Mysti closed her eyes, trying to keep the pain at bay. He'd made love to her as if she'd meant something.

But then again, he'd kissed her in high school as if she'd meant something, too. That had proved to be a lie, because he'd gone ahead and married Kandid.

Was sleeping with her just as much of a lie? She pressed her hand to her mouth to hold in a low, tortured cry as a thought erupted from somewhere inside her. Had she simply been a placeholder for Kandid while she'd been in his bed?

The evidence in that garage said so. Said he'd just needed someone to let off some steam with. And all that flirting on the boat?

Why would it be anything different? If he was ready to move on, he would have donated Kandid's things— or at least her clothes—to charity, wouldn't he? She couldn't bear to go inside the house right now and see all of those other pictures again.

Sally and Jesse came back out. "Sally wants to know if you want to get ice cream on the way?"

The nausea returned full force. "Oh, honey, I'm sorry but I can't. I promised my mom I would check on Brutus and see how he's doing. I think I told you about how he got hurt."

Jesse tilted his head. "You sure?"

"Yes. If you'll drop me off, you two can go. I'm beat. And like I said, I promised my mom I'd call. But thanks for today. I had so much fun."

It was true; she had. But God, she wished he'd never opened up that garage door.

And if he hadn't? And she'd slept with him again, confessed that she loved him, like she'd been toying with? How big of a fool would that have made her?

Kandid was dead, and she wasn't coming back. But Mysti couldn't—she *wouldn't*—compete with a ghost. Yes, widowers married again, but they didn't usually choose someone from their past. Someone they'd already passed over once in favor of their late spouse.

What was she going to say if he asked her out again? If he pulled her toward him?

Oh God. She was going to have to leave town again. She couldn't stay here. Not after this.

Her only consolation was that her job wasn't permanent and that she'd already told Jesse she wasn't sure if she was staying afterward. So if she told him that she'd gotten a job offer somewhere else and had decided to take it?

That would be a lie.

Except that technically, it wouldn't. She'd already spoken to a friend from Doctors Without Borders right before coming back to Forgotten Point. He'd told her to call him if she ever decided to do something different with her life. Something that would do a lot of good in a lot of different places instead of just one. He'd give her a job immediately. She'd wondered if coming back here was a mistake. And it looked like she'd just gotten her answer. It was.

Because there was no way she could bear it if Jesse told her the truth: that he was still in love with Kandid and that was never going to change.

Somehow she got in the truck and made the appropriate small talk as they drove to her house. A million thoughts and plans were racing through her head. And they all centered on escape. Escape from this car. Escape from this situation. Escape from Forgotten Point.

But her ideas were slowly crystallizing into something solid. Something she could hang on to until she was able to leave.

First, she was going to call her friend and see if he'd been serious about his offer. If that didn't pan out, she was going to give the hospital whatever notice they required and live off her savings until she could actually find something else. She had no doubt that she'd be able to by the time her notice was up. Trauma surgeons with her experience weren't exactly a dime a dozen. How much trauma work had she actually seen in this small hospital, anyway? Besides the trauma to her heart, that was.

They pulled into her narrow gravel lane and drove the rest of the distance to the cottage in silence. She'd given up trying to talk during the last couple of minutes. Jesse had glanced at her a couple of times, frowning slightly, but didn't ask any questions. For which she was more grateful than he would ever know. He stopped in front of the house, and she was out of her seat belt in a flash, hand on the release for the door. "Thank you again for everything. It was fun."

"I'll walk you up."

"No need. You go and get Sally some ice cream. I bet she sleeps well tonight."

"I'm sure she'll sleep better than I will. See you Monday?"

His attempt at humor made her heart ache. "Of course. Well, I'll let you go." She got out of the car and pulled in a deep cleansing breath that she hoped would hold her in good stead. At least until she got into the house. Closed the door. And cried her eyes out.

## CHAPTER TWELVE

A KNOCK ON his office door sounded Tuesday morning. He smiled. That was probably Mysti. He'd tried calling her several times, but the call kept going to voice mail. And he hadn't seen her at work at all yesterday, but then again, he'd been slammed with patients.

She'd seemed to be acting so oddly when he'd taken her home, but he'd finally chalked that up to his own paranoia. Because she hadn't acted strange while they were out on the water earlier. She'd been playful, and they'd even sneaked in little touches here and there.

"Come in."

The door opened. It wasn't Mysti, though. It was the hospital administrator. He blinked.

"Hi, Tom. What can I do for you?"

"I'm not sure." His words rolled out slowly. "Have you heard anything about Dr. North wanting to move out of the area? HR just contacted me saying they'd gotten a call from Doctors Without Borders asking for job and character references. And she's taken today and tomorrow as personal days."

It took him a minute to process what he was hearing. Then he pushed his chair back in a daze, an ugly feeling of déjà vu pressing at his midsection.

"She what?"

Tom shrugged. "She hasn't formally given notice yet, but I think I see the writing on the wall. She still has quite a bit of time on her contract left. Any idea what's going on?"

"No. Sorry."

Except he did. She was heading out of town, just like that. Just like she'd done the last time. She hadn't given him any notice that time, either, just said she was leaving. And that was that. He hadn't seen her again after that night in the car.

So why had she acted the way she had on the boat? All soft and smiley, warm and affectionate. She'd won his daughter's heart over already. Sally had asked about her all weekend long.

Damn her! It was one thing to play with his heart. It was another thing altogether to toy with his daughter's affections like that.

Tom shrugged. "Okay, well, if you hear of anything, let me know, will you? We'd like to fix whatever is wrong if possible. I'd hate to lose her. She's excellent with her patients and a damn good surgeon, from what I'm told."

"Yes. She's both of those things."

But what she wasn't…was honest.

*Wait a minute. She played it straight when you asked her if she was staying. She told you she wasn't sure.*

But he'd sure as hell thought she'd at least work out her contract.

After what she'd been through, though, could he blame her? Maybe it was too hard to face the people she'd known before her military days. Maybe after telling him what she'd been through, she'd decided she couldn't play twenty questions with every friend and old acquaintance who asked about her scars. To relive that pain over and over and over. Even he had made a big deal about them, going as far as touching the ones on her shoulder as they'd headed to the lake.

Maybe going where everyone was a stranger was preferable.

"I'll let you know if she says anything to me."

Otherwise, he was keeping his mouth shut. He wasn't going to spread gossip about Mysti or anyone.

And if she'd wanted him to know she was leaving, surely she would have told him. So was she just planning to ghost him?

*Why not?* A terrible voice in his head jeered. *It's exactly what she did last time.*

*Go after her. Ask her.*

He didn't think so. He'd tried to call her already, and she hadn't responded. Now he knew why. He wasn't going to track her down and beg to know what was going on. If she'd wanted him to know, she would have returned his calls. Maybe she'd just realized that she couldn't handle a relationship. Not now. Not with him.

If that were the case, he needed to respect that decision.

So what was he going to tell Sally?

The truth. That Mysti had decided to change jobs and had to move. Far away.

Where he would probably never see her again.

His throat squeezed tight.

His daughter would be sad for a little while, but she'd get over it, especially with school and all the other activities she had. And him?

He didn't rebound as easily these days.

Jesse barely noticed Tom letting himself out of his office. Instead he squared up his jaw and picked up his next patient's file. It was the only thing he could do. No matter how he felt, his personal life had no business intruding during office hours. His patients deserved all his skill and attention.

And that's exactly what they were going to get.

Jesse lasted a whole three days. And last night, he'd stayed awake unable to sleep, playing back what had happened on that trip last weekend over and over in his mind. It made no sense. But he was damned if he was going to spend night after night torturing himself with whatever he'd done wrong this time.

He'd said he wouldn't beg her to stay, and he wouldn't. But what he could do was go see her face-to-face and ask her why she'd decided to contact Doctors Without Borders without telling him. Why she still hadn't been back to work since their day out.

Was he going to go to her house and admit he'd listened to what boiled down to as gossip?

Well, it wasn't exactly gossip if Tom had said the nonprofit had already contacted the hospital about her.

But maybe this time, Jesse could at least gain some closure. Closure that he hadn't gotten last time because of his own crazy feelings about kissing her. His fear of repeating his dad's mistakes had held him back from pursuing Mysti that time. He hadn't sought her or Kandid out to try to explain things.

But he hadn't cheated on his wife, damn it. He hadn't been happy with her, but he suspected she hadn't been happy, either. Even after discovering she'd cheated on him, he'd stayed in the marriage because of her illness. Because of their daughter. And he wasn't sorry he had. Because there, at least, he'd had closure. He'd been able to say goodbye.

What he was sorry for, though, was not tracking

down Mysti and talking through with her what had happened. He'd cared about her back then. Had probably even loved her, although he hadn't realized it.

Was he going to make that same mistake this time? Let her walk away without a word? Or was he going to do one of the hardest things he'd ever done in his life and go to her and admit that he loved her?

If she didn't feel the same way, that would be that. But he'd at least have the peace of knowing he'd tried.

Larry's example of living life to the fullest because "none of us knows how long we'll travel this earth" had stuck in his head ever since they'd sat out on that lake together in the tournament. Larry had given them a thumbs-up sign that day. He'd been happy. Had done what he loved doing. Until the very end.

Jesse had the chance now to do exactly that. And this time, he wasn't going to let the opportunity pass him by while he sat in his office and did nothing.

He was done with his patients today, so he closed the files he'd been working on and slid them into the top drawer of his desk. Then he closed out his computer and called his mom, asking her if she could pick up Sally from school. If she could keep her for the night.

"Of course, you know I love having my grandbaby with me. Is everything okay?"

"Yes. I just need to spend some time with a friend."

He hung up and left the hospital, getting in his car and driving to a place he hoped might hold the answers he was looking for.

It didn't take him long to get to her house. Her car was parked out front. The crops in the fields surrounding the house had turned it into a little green oasis. There were marigolds planted in the small bed out front, and the window boxes boasted their own greenery. This didn't look like a house that was about to be abandoned.

He rang the bell and waited. No phone calls this time. If she was leaving, she was going to have to tell him to his face.

The door swung open, and she stood there for a second before her head tilted and she frowned. "Jess?"

"Can we talk?"

She licked her lips, but nodded and stepped aside. "I— It's good that you're here, because I actually need to tell you something."

Here it came. She was going to tell him she was leaving—going overseas again, this time with Doctors Without Borders.

Forever.

Because if he lost her this time, he knew in his heart of hearts he would never have another chance with her. So he was going down the hard road. Not the easy road. Not this time.

He moved through the doorway, and the first thing he saw were boxes. Moving boxes. None of them were taped shut, but most of them had stuff in them. "So it's true. You're leaving. Tom said HR had gotten a request for your employment information."

"This has been a difficult decision." Her eyes shut for a second before opening. She looked agonized. "Let's sit down."

"No. I'd rather have this out right here. I'm done wasting time. So just tell me clear and plain. Yes or no. Are you leaving?"

"I was going to."

"Was? Does that mean you've changed your mind?"

She sighed heavily. "That depends."

That was not the answer he'd expected. "On what, exactly?"

"On your answer to a question."

He had no idea what she was talking about. But it

sounded like he had indeed done something wrong on that outing. He just had no damn idea what. "Okay. What's your question?"

She bit her lip. "I really do need to sit down for this."

Leading the way over to a small love seat, she motioned for him to sit. He did. But instead of going over to the chair across from it, she actually sat down beside him, turning toward him. "Are you still in love with Kandid?"

"What?" he asked incredulously. He leaned back against the back cushion trying to read her face. "What does Kandid have to do with whether or not you leave?"

"Everything." Her chin wobbled for a second before going still. "Kandid has everything to do with it. I saw it all, you know, in your garage."

His garage?

His head spun for a few seconds, and suddenly he realized exactly what this was about. Why she'd changed so suddenly at the end of their day together.

Hell, looking at it through her eyes...

"This is all because of Kandid's things still being out there."

She nodded. "After that night at your house, I thought that...well, I thought you might be able to move forward."

Mysti rolled her shoulder, and he wanted to stop her. To touch her and ease the way. Because he knew exactly what that nervous gesture meant. She was struggling with something and wasn't sure of the outcome. He wanted to grab her and tell her everything was going to be okay. But right now, he couldn't promise her that, because he still wasn't sure it would be.

"I care deeply about you, Mysti. That garage..." How could he explain it so that she would understand?

"You care about me. But you don't love me." Before he could even respond to that, she went on. "You chose Kandid over me that night in your car, and I'm honestly not sure I can—or even if I want to—compete with that. I need it to be *me* that you see when you take me to bed. *Me* that you see when I'm holding Sally. Kandid's gone, and I'm so sorry you lost her. But I can't be her replacement. I *won't* be her replacement."

He reached for her hand and held it tightly. "God, Mysti, that has never even crossed my mind, and I'm sorry if I ever made you feel that way. That night in the car…" He tried to sort through his chaotic memories of that time. "I was dating Kandid, but that kiss of ours just blew me away. And the thought that came immediately on its heels stunned me—I wondered if that was how my father felt when he kissed women who weren't his wife. It just about killed me."

"I told you the truth back then. You're nothing like him."

"Maybe, but at the time, that fear consumed me until I couldn't think straight. It kept me from coming after you. Kept me from contacting you after you left town."

He went on. "I made such a mess out of things back then. I made a mess with Kandid, too. I was not a good husband to her. I didn't cheat. But I held back from her emotionally. I think I finally know why." He took her face in his hands. "It was because of you. And I think that is why I held on to all of Kandid's things—guilt."

If Mysti could confess the secret about her friend who'd died, he could confess his own secret. "I kept them all because I felt guilty. A couple of years into my marriage, I realized I didn't love Kandid the way I should. But I was determined to prove to myself that—unlike my father—I fulfilled my commitments no matter what the cost. And I did. But in doing so I made us both miserable. And then Sally came along and later, Kandid got sick… Well, I told myself I was keeping that stuff so that someday our daughter could look through it and choose what she wanted. But that wasn't it. I hadn't made Kandid happy in our marriage, and I was ashamed. That is the awful truth of it."

Mysti stared at him as the silence grew from a few seconds to a full minute.

"Oh, Jesse. I'm so sorry. I just assumed you couldn't bear to let her go. But *my* sad truth is something I realized just this morning. I can't bear to let *you* go."

His eyes widened as he gazed at her. Had she really just said that? "You can't bear to let me go?"

"No. And I decided something else, just now. I'm not leaving Forgotten Point again, even if you don't feel the same way about me."

A strange thumping began in his chest. "And what is it you feel?"

She leaned her cheek into his palm. "I feel love. I love you, Jess."

He sat there frozen for a second before snatching her to him, squeezing her against his chest as he tried to contain the emotions that were tearing through him. "You've just said the words I thought I'd never hear."

"So…you…you…"

"Yes. I love you. I think I loved you in the car all of those years ago. I was just too immature to realize it. And too cowardly to stop and think things through."

Her lips pressed against his throat. "Hmm…that kiss was a funny thing, because I definitely had a crush on you back then. What I feel now is no crush, though. It's the real thing."

Hope poured over him in a cleansing stream that

washed away old regrets. That made everything seem brand-new.

"I promise you, mine is the real thing, too. So what are we going to do about it?"

She pulled back and looked into his face. "Oh, no! What time is it? Do we need to go get Sally from school?"

*We?* Had she just said *we*? He couldn't believe how much he loved the sound of that.

"My mom is picking her up, actually. Sally's going to spend the night with her. Because I wasn't sure how long this was going to take."

"As promising as that last part sounds, I'm a little disappointed we can't tell her that she was right."

He cocked his head. "Right about what?"

"That her dad finally has a girlfriend." She said it in a singsong voice that had laughter flowing through every note.

Oh, how he loved this woman.

"I think she's going to be very happy to hear that." He kissed her mouth. "And so am I. So I have a girlfriend, do I? I was kind of hoping for a little more than that."

"You were? What kind of things were you hoping for?"

He brushed the hair back from her face. "I think it might take me a while to list them all. A long while, in fact. Interested in some company tonight?"

"Definitely." She smiled and rubbed her fingers across his jaw. "Stubble. I love it. Love feeling this at the end of your workday."

"I'm glad, because I think you're stuck with it. And with me." He leaned down to kiss her again. "What do you suggest we do with ourselves tonight?"

She made a humming sound in her throat. "I think I know the perfect thing. The thing that will set our union in stone."

He liked the sound of that. So did his body. It began to think through all kinds of scenarios. "I'm listening."

"The one big thing I need you to do for me…" She trailed her fingertip down his chest and swirled a big circle around one of his nipples. "That would make my whole world come alive…"

"Yes?" The word came out in hoarse expectation.

"Is help me unpack all of these boxes." She laughed at the expression he must have made. "But only after we go and figure out who'll be in the driver's seat tonight."

# EPILOGUE

"ARE YOU SURE we should be out here?"

Mysti smiled and linked her fingers through his. "I told you. I'm fine." She leaned her head against his shoulder. "But I have to tell you, you're driving like an old grandpa right now."

"Ow." He pressed his hand to his chest as if her words had found their mark.

Glancing back at where Sally was lounging on a cushion in her life vest, the little girl chortled. "Mimi called you a grandpa."

Her throat swelled with so much love, she couldn't speak for several seconds. They'd decided on what Sally would call her at a family meeting the day before they got married. And every time the little girl called her Mimi, she wanted to grab her and hug her until she squealed.

"That's right, I did. And if he keeps going this slowly it'll take us all day to get to our fishing spot."

The first annual Larry Rogers Memorial Fish-Off was already a roaring success. Larry's son had cut the ribbon on the bronze statue of a man in his boat, fishing line cast in the water. A tribute to the man who'd loved to be out on this lake.

Jesse growled. "I'm not taking any chances with either of my girls. Nor the new little one you have growing inside you."

"The obstetrician gave us a green light to be out here."

His brows went up. "'As long as you don't do anything crazy.' Don't forget that part."

"Not much chance of that, is there?" She popped him with her hip. "Move over. I'm driving."

"Um… No. You got to drive last night."

The pointed reference to their passionate lovemaking the night before made her laugh. "Only because you were driving like a grandpa then, too."

"Oh, ho. We'll have to see about that, Mysti." But he stepped out of the way and motioned toward the wheel. "I'm warning you, though. You have precious cargo on board."

Suddenly she couldn't see through a rush of tears. Yes, she did. Sally and Jesse were definitely precious cargo. As was the baby that was due this winter. They almost didn't make it to this point. Had almost let go of everything that mattered.

But they hadn't. They'd stayed and fought for each other, fought for the chance to bond into a new family. One built on all the right things: love. Commitment. Sacrifice.

Mysti had stayed on at the hospital when the doctor on maternity leave decided against returning. And she wasn't sure yet what she was going to do when her own baby came. Jesse had suggested they form a new practice, saying it was the perfect partnership.

She couldn't agree more.

And although Jesse said he regretted not going after her all those years ago, maybe he'd been right not to. They'd both grown into two mature adults who were ready to love each other in a way they might not have been able to back then.

So she held out her hand to him, maintaining the boat at the speed he'd originally set. When Jesse gripped her fingers and moved closer, kissing her left shoulder, where those scars lay hidden beneath her shirt, she sighed.

"Precious cargo. I love that. We all are, though, aren't we?" As she looked at her family, her next words were a vow that she hoped Larry could somehow hear. "For as long as we travel this earth."

\* \* \* \* \*

# REAWAKENED AT
# THE SOUTH POLE

JULIETTE HYLAND

**MILLS & BOON**

For Mom.

Thanks for all the encouragement and love.

And for always looking the other way
when I stole the Harlequin novels off your closet shelf.

# PROLOGUE

BOUNCING BEFORE HER twin brother's dorm room, Helena Mathews worried her heart might escape her chest at any moment. But she wasn't sure if it was from excitement or fear.

*Probably both.*

As of this afternoon, she was officially a nursing major. She swallowed as she tried to force herself to raise her hand. Knocking on a door shouldn't be this hard!

Owen would understand why she had to change degrees. Would understand that focusing on emergency medicine was her passion. And help her find a way to explain to her parents why it wasn't dangerous—at least not really.

They'd been born early, like most twins. But unlike her brother's, Helena's lungs hadn't been fully developed. She'd spent the first three months of her life in the NICU. After she'd contracted a lung infection, her parents had been told to prepare for the worst. But Helena had rallied. Though until her teens, any time she got a cold, it tended to go into her lungs. And then she'd spend at least a few days in the hospital.

But she hadn't spent a night in the hospital in years. She'd always been on the tiny side, something she wanted to attribute to genetics, but her parents believed it was because of her rough start. For her entire childhood, and even now, they'd kept her sheltered—worried over every cough and sniffle.

Helena had begged them to let her live on campus at the University of Chicago, even though it was less than twenty minutes from their home. They'd allowed it, but she suspected that was only because Owen was in the prelaw program here.

And because she'd chosen a safe degree in art history.

Her mother had said on more than one occasion that museums were safe—no dangers there. And so Helena had selected the degree, even though it wasn't her passion.

To please her parents.

Except right now there was a heavy anatomy textbook cradled in her arms. She'd stopped by the campus bookstore and bought the text even though she wouldn't need it until next semester. The human body fascinated her. But she didn't want to study how others drew it—she wanted to heal it.

Tapping her book, she stared at the door. It would thrill most people that their child wanted to go into medicine.

But not her parents, at least not with her.

Helena pulled on her long braid. She'd never done anything to displease them. No matter what, she bent to their expectations. To keep them from worrying.

But she wanted more than the safe life her parents thought she should follow.

And she had an escape hatch. The scholarship she'd earned as the valedictorian of her high school would cover most of her school expenses, even if she changed her degree plan. She could chase her dream.

Her dream.

"Helena?" Carter Simpson's deep voice rumbled through her as he crossed his arms and leaned just slightly to the left. The famous Simpson lean. It was a habit his father developed in childhood, though the reasons were lost to memory, according to Dr. Simpson. And, as his mini-me, Carter had imitated it for as long as she'd known him. She'd teased him about the habit when they were younger, until she realized he didn't even know he was doing it.

His handsome face showed surprise as he pushed a hand through his silky dark hair.

How did she explain hovering in the hallway?

It shouldn't be that difficult. It was just Carter. He'd been in her house nearly every day since she and Owen had entered kindergarten with him. The boys had been inseparable and had occasionally let her tag along on their adventures, though they'd protected her from getting dirty and made sure she was never in danger. Not even a skinned knee.

Nothing that might add to her parents' worries.

The boys had elected to room together when they'd all received their acceptances to the University of Chicago. Carter had never been more than Owen's best friend to her—until they'd all headed to college in September.

Three months…ninety days. A blip in the timeline of their friendship, but everything had changed. At least for her.

She wasn't exactly sure why the shift had happened. Why studying with the boys now made her palms sweat and her heart race if Carter's knees brushed against hers. Why their morning coffee and breakfast talks, which her brother always skipped, were now the highlight of her day. Helena had gone to bed more nights than she wanted to admit thinking of the strong-jawed boy standing before her.

"Helena?" he repeated.

Her cheeks heated as she met his chocolate gaze. Of course her voice would disappear around him at the most awkward time.

"Owen is still at the library. I suspect he will be there until it closes. A big test in—" Carter shrugged "—in some law subject that I can't remember."

"Introduction to Political Theory." She'd helped Owen write up his study notes.

"Of course you know." Carter tapped her shoulder, then immediately pulled his hand back and stuck it in his pocket.

Did his fingers pulse with the need to touch her like hers did whenever she looked at him?

"Maybe I could use some of your helpful meddling," Carter teased, seemingly oblivious to the desire rolling through her.

"It wasn't meddling, just drafting up some note cards." Her energy deflated as she sighed. She'd wanted to tell her brother the good news.

And it was good news.

But she needed someone to celebrate with her to alleviate the anxiety that was poking all around her happiness bubble. She could already envision the worry in her parents' eyes.

There had to be a way to make them understand. To make them happy with her choice. Surely there was a way, even if her brain couldn't find it in this precise moment.

"I was just teasing, Helena." Carter's smile lit up her darkening spirits. "Hey, human anatomy. I have that textbook. Are you using it in one of your art classes?"

His voice was calm, a balm to the prickles running along her skin.

"I changed my major." The words popped out of her mouth, and she saw the shock radiate across his eyes before he stepped back and gestured for her to come into the small space.

She sat on the edge of Owen's bed and waited while Carter pulled his desk chair directly in front of her. There wasn't much space in the boys' dormitory room, and she was very aware of how close he was. *Very.*

"I'm a nursing student now. Or I will be when we get back from the holiday break in January. I just... I just want to be a nurse." Once the words slipped from her lips, Helena couldn't keep them buried. "I've wanted to be a nurse since I was a little girl. Probably all those times in the hospital."

She hadn't meant to say that, either. She'd told her mother that once, and she'd fretted over the viruses she might be exposed to. Worried she'd spend more time as a patient than as a nurse. Helena had recognized, even as a little girl, that expanding on that dream would only upset her parents. So she'd smiled and said something lost to the fog of memory. But her heart had never forgotten the desire to wear a stethoscope as her badge of honor.

"I remember us playing doctor's office when we were little. If I remember correctly, Owen always needed his leg put in a pretend cast because of some accident we'd dreamed up."

"And I always fixed it by giving him a shot." Helena laughed, enjoying the memory. Carter leaned closer, and flashes of heat erupted along her body that had nothing to do with the anxiety of talking to her parents.

His fingers reached for her, and Carter pulled the book from her lap. Setting it to the side, he gripped her hands. His touch was warm and soothing. Helena's heartbeat pounded in her ears as she tried to focus on something other than Carter's full lips. But it was hard when they were so close.

"Worried about telling your parents?"

"Am I that easy to read?" Helena's chuckle sounded nervous, and she pulled her hands back. She needed to focus on the problem at hand and not on what it might be like to kiss Carter Simpson. And that was easier to do when she wasn't touching him.

Though not by much.

"Not really." He sighed and crossed his arms.

It took all her control not to reach back out to him.

"But I know your parents pretty well, and I suspect this will be a shock to them."

"I want to be a nurse, but I don't want to disappoint them. I want them to be happy, too." She hated the whiny tone. If only there was a way to shake the worry from herself...without him seeing.

Carter slid from his chair, and the bed sank a bit as he sat beside her. He wrapped an arm around her and didn't protest when she laid her head against his shoulder.

God, he smelled delicious.

That was not a thought she should be having about her brother's best friend.

"They always worry..."

"But you are fine, healthy *and* you can't live a life that has no risks," Carter interrupted.

"Easy for you to say. You and your father have been discussing your medical career and how one day your name will be in those journals that cover every surface of his office. He is always proud of you." The man was constantly boasting about how great his son was.

Her throat closed as panic raced along her spine. She always pleased her parents, pleased everyone. She hated upsetting anyone. They'd spent a lifetime caring for her, protecting her, worrying about her. The medical bills had nearly bankrupted them, but they'd never complained.

"I owe them so much."

He squeezed her. "Only you get to live your life, Helena. There is nothing wrong with chasing your own dreams."

She wanted to believe him. "I've never upset them before. But I can do this." The phrase sounded a little hollow to her ears, but she was going to be a nurse. She'd taken the first tentative step, and she would not deviate.

An expression passed over Carter's face that she feared was doubt, but he smiled. The dimple on his right cheek sent more heat tumbling through her. Her fingers ached to run along the late-evening stubble, to see what might happen if she leaned closer.

*Get it together, Helena.*

She'd come looking for her brother, not for Carter. Though she was glad it was Carter who'd opened the door.

A tad too pleased...

"Maybe we'll be in the same anatomy lab next year." Helena sighed, shifting the topic away from her parents' expectations—at least for a moment. Though as his eyes dipped to her lips, she wasn't sure it was a safer topic.

"I'd like that. A lot."

*A lot.* Her heart melted at his soft voice, and she

raised her gaze to meet his. Heat burned in them. And her body felt heavy as she let her eyes wander to his lips.

"Helena." His fingers brushed along her jaw.

Need rushed through her as she realized he wanted to kiss her, too. Helena could feel it. "Carter—"

The door burst open, and they jumped apart.

"The library lost power." Owen dropped his backpack on the floor, oblivious to her presence or the tension radiating between Helena and his best friend.

Her brother shook his head. "Helena?" His eyes drifted from Carter to Helena, and then he kicked his backpack. "Sorry, I am just really stressing over my final tomorrow."

Helena patted Carter's hand, and then she grabbed her textbook and stood. "You should get some sleep, Owen. Your head is crammed with all the knowledge it can take." She hugged her twin and started for the door.

"Helena, didn't you come here to talk to Owen?" Carter's voice was tight.

She turned to find him so close their chests nearly touched. Her body wanted to lean into him. Wanted to pull him into the dorm hall and see if they could recapture the energy that had vibrated between them a few seconds ago. But it had passed—at least for now.

"It can wait. Owen has a big day tomorrow, and my stuff…" She motioned with her hands, hoping to make him understand. This time it was doubt and a touch of disappointment she saw hover in Carter's gaze. Her stomach dropped. But Owen had a lot going on, too. She'd burden him with this when his finals were over.

She dropped a chaste kiss along Carter's jaw and felt her eyes widen. She'd never done that, but Owen was too caught up in his own worries to notice the dynamic changing between his best friend and his sister. "I look forward to studying with you next semester," she whispered, careful to make sure the words were too quiet for her brother to hear.

"Me, too." His fingers reached for her, but he pulled them back just before they grazed hers.

"Are we still getting breakfast tomorrow?" Helena bit her lip as she studied him, hoping her hesitation tonight hadn't driven away whatever was blooming here.

"I wouldn't miss it." Carter's gaze lingered on her, and for just a moment she thought he might kiss her.

"Carter?" Owen's voice rang out.

"Good night, Helena."

Then the door closed. Helena hadn't accomplished her plan for the evening, but her soul felt lighter.

So much lighter.

# CHAPTER ONE

THE AIRMAN SITTING across from Helena looked a little green as the LC-130 aircraft shook around them. The flight from McMurdo Station to the Amundsen-Scott South Pole Station was hazardous at the best times of year, but this was the last flight of the season, and the winter winds were causing severe turbulence.

Crossing her arms, Helena offered the aircrew member a smile. She'd heard him bragging about how excited he was to get to go to the tip of the earth before they boarded—a last-minute replacement for an ill crew member. A few of the veteran Skibird members had tried to tell him the flight wasn't usually smooth sailing, but the bravado of youth and excitement of setting foot where so few did could overcome most things.

He gripped his stomach, and Helena leaned forward. "Breathe through your nose and out through your mouth. Real slow with me." She inhaled for a minute, then exhaled slowly through her mouth, pushing the air out with a heavy sigh. There wasn't much medically she could do for him, even if it was possible to leave the safety of her seat, but research showed changing breathing patterns helped air sickness.

He followed her patterns for a few minutes, and the

color in his face slowly returned. "How come you're not sick?" His bottom lip shook as he got the question out.

Gesturing toward the rest of the air crew, he continued, "They fly to the research station several times a week during the summer, but you're so…" His cheeks colored, but this time from embarrassment.

Helena raised her eyebrow as she looked at the airman, barely out of his teens. "So?"

He bit his lips, and Helena decided to save the airman any further embarrassment. There was no need to make him uncomfortable, particularly because she knew what he saw.

What everyone saw.

A petite blonde. Barely over five foot tall.

*Delicate. Ethereal. Breakable. Out of place.*

It had been the story of her life.

She'd been the tiny twin. The sick child and the pampered, sheltered family princess. Even after changing her degree and doing a medical combat tour, her parents still saw her as the weak one.

Particularly after the tour ended with her spending six months recuperating in her childhood bedroom.

Her mother's emails had always been filled with questions about her health. But they'd only gotten worse over the last two years. Her fingers dipped unwittingly to the base of her hip. She couldn't feel the giant scar through the layers of thermals, but her fingers knew exactly where it was. Even though she never let her eyes drop to it, she'd memorized the puckered skin. Knew how it looked. Knew what it made people think.

She'd nearly proved herself to them—until the accident.

Her parents boasted about Owen. He'd been expected to do all the important things. And he'd succeeded, far beyond even her parents' expectations. Graduating first in his class at law school, he was now a partner at one of the most prestigious law firms in Chicago. There had even been some discussion of him running for a local judgeship.

And Helena…

Helena was the slight beauty. The one who needed to be cared for. But she was not *just* the tiny, fragile baby her mother had fretted would never come home.

Not anymore.

"This isn't my first time in a tense situation in a C-130." Helena leaned her head against the cool metal that was the only thing keeping her safe from the frozen temps outside. She'd served a yearlong tour as a medical contractor in Iraq. During more than one supply run, the C-130s had had to take evasive measures from incoming rockets before landing. Turbulence didn't seem nearly as terrible.

And it was far from the worst thing she'd been through during her yearlong commitment. Her fingers traced the edge of the jagged scar that ran from the top of her left hip to just under the base of her rib cage on her right side…again.

She still didn't remember the accident, the flight to Germany or the weeks she'd spent in an infection haze as her colleagues worked to save her life.

The wound had taken her chance at having her own children. But Helena hadn't mourned that loss much. She enjoyed children, adored her nieces and nephews, but she'd never attached the feeling of family to genetic material. There were many children who needed a family that she could mother.

It shouldn't have mattered, but the accident, her long

recovery—and the scar—had torn her dreams of a happily-ever-after away.

It had been almost two years since Kevin had seen it and recoiled. He'd quipped that she'd never look normal again. That she was broken.

*Broken.*

Taking the job as a medical contractor had been his idea. A way to pad their résumés…except he'd never signed his contract. But Helena had made a commitment, and she'd followed through. What was a year apart if they were planning to build a life together? Kevin had agreed—probably too readily. But she had ignored that red flag.

And so many more.

He'd ended things two weeks after she'd gotten home, while she was still trying to recover her strength. He'd claimed it was just that they'd grown apart. But they'd spent the months she was gone discussing marriage, looking at houses online—pretty little row houses in Chicago. And he hadn't seemed to care when she'd told him she couldn't have children before she got home— then abruptly changed his tune.

The man who'd claimed to love her more than anything had tossed her aside when she no longer fit his described mold.

*Broken.*

That was the description her parents had used throughout her childhood as the reason she couldn't do all the fun things that she wanted. It hadn't been true then—but maybe it was now.

The flannel was soft between her thumbs as she traced the line she'd memorized at her hip. *Broken.* That was the label she was running from. The label that seemed destined to cling to her. No matter how hard she tried to please, to fix things, she never seemed to be enough just as she was.

"Where are you from?" The airman was rocking back and forth, but at least he no longer looked like he was going to lose his stomach.

"Chicago." The word was enough to send a wave of homesickness pulsing down her spine.

Helena had left the city a few weeks before coming here.

*Fled* was more accurate.

She'd told her parents that it was because her flights had been moved up, but mostly it was because she couldn't stand the sad looks her mother kept giving her as she prepared to winter over in the South Pole. She knew they loved her, but their attention was suffocating.

She bit the inside of her cheek as that thought raced through her. She was lucky. Her parents loved her. That was so much more than others had. But she wished her mother would put aside her worries. That her parents could see the woman her daughter had become. Celebrate it.

The last month at home had been torturous as her mother constantly reminded her that the last time she'd gone on an adventure she'd come home torn apart. Barely able to stand for more than a few minutes after the muscle loss from weeks in the hospital fighting the infection. It didn't matter that the car accident, a rollover, had had nothing to do with combat.

Another driver had lost control and the driver of her vehicle had overcorrected. An accident like those she treated in the ER in Chicago far too frequently. But the similarities were lost on her parents.

She was determined that this tour would not be that

way. When she went home this time, her family would accept her for who she was.

They had to.

She was excited to see the end of the earth, to set foot in a place almost no one did, but that didn't stop the longing for home. To put down roots in her own house. To build her own home. The outline of the city chased through her dreams.

But at home, she was Helena Mathews, broken beauty. And she wanted to be so much more. Needed to be more.

"We're landing in fifteen!"

The call over the radio sent a wave of excitement through her, mixed with a tiny piece of anxiety. She was going to winter over in the South Pole! This was the adventure of a lifetime, but it carried risks. Lots of them.

Which was why this was the perfect place to prove to herself that her scars were only surface level.

This was the last flight until October. In a few days, the temperatures would drop low enough to freeze the plane's fuel and hydraulic lines. Even now, as they unloaded the last supplies, the plane would keep running so the lines couldn't freeze.

Nearly nine months in the most uninhabitable region of the world with a support staff and researchers from around the world. If something happened, a rescue wasn't coming. She'd known all that when she volunteered. But as the replacement for the nurse practitioner who'd had to be evacuated following a medical emergency, she was hyperaware that she would not get the evac that had occurred two weeks ago.

Not that there was any reason for her to need one!

Helena was in excellent health and had a well-managed self-care routine. She was going to be fine.

And following this, her family would finally understand that her choices were right for her. That she was more than the sick child they'd worried over.

"Dr. Carter Simpson is a bit of a grouch. Just in case no one told you." The flight engineer sitting next to her crossed his arms as the plane shuddered again.

"So I heard." Keith, the director of polar medicine at the research center, had made it clear that her colleague was an excellent physician, but prickly. He'd wanted to make sure she understood the operating environment. But every nurse dealt with difficult physicians. One thing her upbringing had taught her was how to smooth over rough patches. "I'm sure Dr. Simpson and I will manage." Her tongue was dry as she forced the words out, but it wasn't because of a grumpy doctor.

*Carter Simpson.*

That name was a blast from her past. It was a common enough name. In fact, she'd worked with a Carter Simpson in the ER in Chicago and tracked another one down in his office in the physicians' office building. She'd gotten excited those times, too, hoping it might be him. It hadn't been, and there was little chance the Dr. Simpson at the South Pole was the boy she'd never forgotten.

Besides, the term *grouchy* did not apply to the Carter Simpson she knew…had known. The silly, laughing face of her brother's best friend danced before her eyes. He'd always worn a smile. Always had a joke to tell and a deep laugh that could send an entire room into happy chuckles. Her heart pounded as the memory of his chocolate eyes floated in front of her. He was welcoming and…

And then he'd disappeared.

After she'd told him about changing her major, they'd

hung out several times over the last week of finals. They'd never kissed, but the heat between them had been undeniable. He'd even asked her to meet him for coffee over break, though he'd never shown up to the café.

Not that it had surprised her, since Carter had stopped answering her and Owen's messages on Christmas Eve. And he hadn't returned to the university after the break, either; he'd emptied the room he'd shared with Owen of all his possessions and seemingly disappeared off the face of the earth. If she didn't have a bank of memories, she might have thought he was a figment of her imagination.

When his parents had separated, it had stunned Helena. Though if she was honest, she'd hardly ever seen his parents together. But kids rarely saw the adult problems around them. It was Carter's father who'd been at everything.

Helena had always been a little jealous that Carter had a parent who celebrated him and encouraged him to do so many things. After they'd put their home up for sale the day after Christmas, Helena had stopped by, trying to ease her brother's distress. And her own. Carter's father had said he didn't know where his son had gone.

*And didn't care to know.*

Those words still sent a shiver down Helena's spine. How could anyone not care where their child was? Her family could be suffocating, but she'd never wish that they weren't speaking. Just that they were speaking on different topics.

After her accident, and the end of her engagement, Helena had moved into her parents' home to finish her recovery. Painfully working through the physical therapy to rebuild the muscle she'd lost during her weeks in the hospital. And her parents had suggested that she change careers. Maybe something less physically demanding.

Helena had seen red. Even now, her chest heaved at the memory. That they thought she'd let the accident steal away the career she'd worked hard for and loved... it was like they didn't know her at all.

Still, she longed to return home, this time a full person. Not the injured daughter. Maybe settle down with her own place in Chicago. Perhaps even find someone to share her life...if she could find someone who wanted her, scars and all.

Helena closed her eyes as the LC-130's skis connected with the frozen runway. The skis of the plane slid along the runway before it finally came to a halt.

"All right, folks, I want to be air bound again as quickly as possible. Gear up!" the pilot called over the speaker.

Helena pulled on the heavy thermals over her looser thermal clothes and slid on thick boots, gloves, her neoprene face mask and goggles. She was virtually indistinguishable from the airmen next to her as the back of the LC-130 lowered.

The blast of cold whipped up through the hold, and Helena smiled under her mask. She was really here. Really, at the end of the world.

"Where is the welcome party?" The loadmaster's head tilted as he headed down the rear door.

Helena grabbed the small pack they had allowed her as a carry-on, mostly empty now that she had on her gear. Her hand patted the small med kit and mini chess set that she always traveled with. As long as she had those things, Helena could get through anything. The rest of her allotted goods were with the final cargo supplies. Packed tightly to ensure the most efficient load carry.

"What is going on?" Helena leaned close to the copilot as he stepped next to her, hoping he could hear her over the engine's and wind's competing roars.

His head tilted, but if his face shifted at all, it was lost beneath his layers of gear. "No way to know. There should have been a whole ground crew here to meet us. We need to get these goods off-loaded and…"

"There's been an accident!" The loadmaster's voice reverberated up the rear door. "We've got an overturned Arctic Truck, one occupant trapped!"

Helena gripped her pack as she took off. This wasn't how she'd planned to start the adventure, but it was why she was here.

"I sent you the résumé of Jennifer's replacement." Dr. Keith Hollenbreck's voice carried over the clinic's phone's speaker as Dr. Carter Simpson checked off the last item on his pharmacy inventory.

"I saw the email," Carter confirmed.

"Are you okay with the replacement?" Keith's voice wavered, but there was no way for Carter to determine if that was because the director of polar medicine was concerned about his reaction, or because the satellite connection was having issues.

Carter sent a brief glance toward the phone. "I haven't had a chance to look. With Jennifer gone, I've been busy." It was the truth, and he didn't have the time or inclination to assuage Keith's concern. No matter what he thought, the woman was on the last flight in.

The Center for Polar Medicine had high standards.

So she was qualified. And Carter never got close to his colleagues. To anyone.

Carter pulled up the inventory list for the items arriving on the last flight today. Not that it mattered if anything was missing. They were going to have to make do until October either way. But it was good to be organized.

"Seriously, Carter. You didn't even look at it."

Carter raised an eyebrow at Keith's tone, but he was grateful the director of the polar program couldn't see his expression. At least he'd found a replacement. There were not many medical professionals who were qualified to winter over in the most inhospitable environment on the planet. Particularly when there was no chance of rescue if things went terribly wrong.

As horrible as it was that Jennifer had slipped and broken her leg in three places, requiring surgery, at least there were flights to evacuate her. If it had happened a few weeks later, well, Carter was glad he didn't have to consider that option.

This was his third winter rotation at the South Pole; he and the new nurse would find their way just like he had with the others. And she'd learn he was a good worker but not interested in social engagements.

*Lone wolf, distant, prickly.* Those were just a few of the descriptors he'd heard whispered about him. And all true. Though those weren't labels he'd always worn. But after his family had thrown him away at eighteen it had broken his ability to trust for years. And later, his fiancée had shattered the repaired pieces when she'd had an affair with his friend.

Life was easier if you didn't get close to colleagues, to friends…to anyone.

"I figure whoever you sent is who I am wintering

with for nine months. We'll figure it out. Or we won't. Those are the only two options."

"That famous Carter optimism." Keith sighed loud enough for the phone to pick it up.

The sound didn't upset Carter. The optimism that had bubbled forth easily during his youth evaporated his freshman year in college. In fact, he could pinpoint the moment.

Freshman anatomy and physiology class—the lecture on blood typing in the final week before Christmas break. He hadn't known his blood type, but had assumed it was A or AB. He'd sent a copy of his birth certificate with many of his college applications, and his parents' blood types were both listed. His father had been AB and his mother A. Only O wasn't an option. Except…

There was no way to describe the emotions that had raced through him. And the fantastical scenarios he'd invented to avoid the obvious. His entire body had locked down when the results landed in his hands. Somehow, he'd made it through his final exams, grateful that everyone was so caught up in their exams that no one had noticed he was cracking.

Except Helena.

But he hadn't been able to find the words to voice his worries. His fears.

He'd packed his bags before his last class and gone home without saying goodbye to anyone. Without seeking her out.

That was a regret that still cut deep when he woke with the memory of her jade eyes staring at him.

If he'd known the last time he'd see her would be the *last* time…

Carter hadn't really expected the confrontation with

his parents to be explosive. Switched at birth, secret adoption… His imagination had refused to consider infidelity. Maybe that was why it had been such a shock when he'd blown up his family.

Apparently, his father had always suspected his mother had cheated on him. But Carter's question had laid bare more than one affair over the course of their union. They'd never been the picture of happiness. His mother had complained repeatedly that if they'd stayed in New York her acting career would have taken off. And his father had pointed out that acting wasn't a stable occupation, but his career had provided for their family.

Even with their occasional fight, they'd seemed content. At least through his childish eyes.

His question had exposed the web of lies his mother had weaved through her marriage. Carefully crafted stories that made it seem like she was helping when she was simply covering her tracks. She might have failed on the stage, but in their home her acting had covered a multitude of mistruths. The implosion had been epic.

And Carter had caused it all. His mother had said his father only cared about the image of the family. The perfect son with good grades and athletic abilities. She'd claimed that she'd never wanted to be a homemaker, never wanted the fairy tale that his father wanted to present. And without a career of her own, she'd felt trapped.

They'd never been close. He'd always felt like he was annoying her, like she wished he wasn't there. But he'd never thought it was because she *actually* wished he wasn't there.

The mask she'd worn of the contented homemaker had evaporated. The bitter and vengeful woman, angry at how her husband had cared more for his medical career than for her, emerged. And Carter had turned into her target.

She'd informed Carter that he was a mistake. That if it hadn't been for him, she could have continued to seek out the stage. At the very least she would have walked away from her marriage. But she had been terrified that her husband would demand a paternity test and cut her spousal support.

A suspicion her husband confirmed, though his options were limited since Illinois law didn't allow for the consideration of infidelity in divorce proceedings. Another thing that his father had screamed about.

Carter shuddered as the memory of the damage he'd caused rocked through him. His father had refused to look at him. After bragging to everyone about Carter's athletic and academic achievements for years, the man he'd always wanted to be proud of him pretended he didn't exist.

The pain wasn't as fresh now, but the image of his father pointedly looking away still haunted his dreams when he was suffering too much stress.

On Christmas Eve, his father had ordered him and his mother from *his* house. Carter's mother had refused to leave. But Carter had packed a bag.

He couldn't stay where the two people he thought loved him saw him as the person who'd destroyed their illusion. He was their child. Maybe not by blood on his father's side, but the man had raised him as his son. And his mother believed he was a mistake—the person who'd destroyed her chance at success and happiness.

Who said that to their child?

He'd been lucky. His academic scholarship transferred when he requested admittance to Boston University, and he'd worked odd jobs to make ends meet whenever necessary. It had taken a year longer than planned, but he'd earned his medical degree and worked in critical care in Boston for five years before applying for a position through the Center for Polar Medicine.

And he hadn't looked back. At least not too often.

He never talked about his family, or where he was from. But on lonely nights when he was lying in bed, he'd trace the Chicago skyline in his mind. *Home.*

And the faces of the few people he missed would pop through his mind. Owen Mathews—his best friend, the brother he'd never had. And Carter had left without even saying goodbye.

In the numb months following the breakup of his family, the family Carter destroyed, Owen had reached out multiple times. His texts shifted between concern, and as the unanswered messages grew, anger.

How did you tell someone that you'd destroyed your own family? That you no longer knew who you were? That you were rudderless after never doubting yourself?

By the time he'd been stable enough to reach out, that bridge felt too long to cross. He'd typed up emails, written letters, even started a few texts, but after years, why should Owen respond? And that fear of rejection was too much to handle. As long as he didn't reach out, he could still hope that maybe one day he would. Though in his heart, Carter knew he'd never work up the courage.

That fear didn't stop his longing. To find out if Owen had completed law school, if he was married. If he'd gotten what he wanted out of life.

If his sister was happy. If she'd had the courage to follow through with her nursing dreams.

Helena Mathews…the girl who still captured his dreams during the long, lonely winters.

What would she think about the man he'd become?

"Did you hear me?" Keith's voice ricocheted through Carter's mental wanderings.

Grateful for the distraction, Carter shook his head, trying to clear the image of Helena from his brain. "I was trying to focus on making sure we are prepared for the winter." The lie slipped from his lips as her jade eyes fell away in his mind.

*Focus.*

"You know—my job." Carter tried to make his voice more upbeat, to push away the touch of sadness that always tore through him when he thought of Owen—and his twin. "What is it you want to tell me about the new nurse practitioner?"

Carter frowned as he double-checked the bandages in the drawer. It seemed a little light. He'd had to use several to treat Jennifer's injury, and he'd ordered more that should be on the last flight in. But would it be enough?

Most of the problems he treated, other than viral and bacterial infections, were accident-related. Broken bones and lacerations were common over the long winter months—and his team was the only help that injured parties had between them and disaster. Carter had never had to use the morgue at the station, and he didn't plan to start now.

"The nurse practitioner has worked in multiple critical units, including with the Department of Defense. I was lucky that she was willing to come on such short notice. Helena Mathews should do well on the ice. Maybe you could be nice enough that she might want to do more than one winter."

"Helena Mathews? Nice…" Carter leaned over the desk.

It was a common enough name.

He hoped she'd gone into nursing, but the Helena he'd known would never land on the ice. Never get this far from home. But it didn't stop the small bead of hope pressing against the walls he'd built.

Her bright green eyes, long braid and beautiful smile flitted through his memory. She'd been so lovely. Though it wasn't her beauty that Carter missed—it was the intriguing mind behind it. Not that she'd shown it off much.

They'd played chess together a handful of times, and Carter had been stunned by the girl behind the pretty face. The glimpses of her sharp mind and playful wit. But her parents were always so concerned that she might slip away from them. She'd spent time in the hospital as a young child. He'd made her more than one get-well card, but by the time they'd reached junior high, she'd been healthy. And strong.

And she'd make an excellent nurse.

Assuming she'd ever worked up the courage to tell her parents that she wasn't going to reside behind some desk at a museum. Helena was a beauty, but she was also a pleaser. He'd never seen her go against her family's plans. She'd always played into her family's expectations, never wanting to upset them.

Except she'd changed her major without asking. Though he'd seen doubt hovering in her eyes the night she'd told him. Then she'd quickly hidden her feelings behind a smile.

At the time he'd been frustrated, desperately wishing she'd say what she wanted. In the solitary days after, he'd replayed that moment, remembering the hundreds of times over his life that his mother had done the same. Hiding her feelings, redirecting the conversations to cover the half-truths, or lies, she'd spoken. And he'd wondered if anyone was capable of just saying what they felt, of telling the truth.

The seed of doubt was tiny though and easy to ignore when he remembered the feel of Helena's head pressed against his shoulder. The soft scent of coconut shampoo. The shape of her lips as she looked at him. And the overwhelming urge to kiss her.

*If Owen hadn't interrupted us...*

Which was good. If he'd known the path his life would take less than two weeks later, he'd never have let the evening shift in such a way. Or maybe he would have kissed her so he didn't have to spend a lifetime dreaming of what might have been.

But Owen had barged in, and the moment had evaporated. And she'd chickened out on telling her brother about her big news. Put his needs in front of hers. He wished he could see it as an admirable trait.

But his mother had hidden so much behind a false smile. Never letting the world see how unhappy she was until Carter had pulled the cornerstone from the house of cards.

And how often had his ex-fiancée done the same before he discovered her and Brian together?

"Are you there, Carter?" Keith's question broke through the memories.

"Yep," Carter sighed, trying to push the loneliness that always stole through him when he thought of Owen

Mathews…or his amazing sister. "Just enjoying the quiet clinic before the new nurse gets here."

"I worry you spend too much time alone." Keith's voice crackled through the speaker, and Carter wished he'd hung up already.

*Better to be alone than broken by love.*

But Carter kept that thought to himself.

Love was a fantasy. It wrapped you in false promises. Got you to trust, only to be smashed against the walls of disappointment when people showed you who they truly were.

"Mayday! Mayday. We've got an accident next to the runway. Truck blown over by wind. One passenger trapped."

The radio crackled and adrenaline pumped through Carter's veins. He grabbed the mobile crash unit and swung it over his shoulder. The rest of the supplies were in the makeshift ambulance. "Gotta go, Keith! I promise to be nice to the nurse practitioner."

# CHAPTER TWO

As SHE STEPPED out of the back of the LC-130, her eyes widened as she took in the vast landscape before her. It would have been nice to orient herself to the area, or even to take in the expanse of the South Pole, but there wasn't time. The wind nearly tipped her over. She might be tiny, but nothing was going to keep her from her patient.

Snow drifted across the runway as Helena looked over the accident site. The truck was lying on the driver's side on the other side of the runway, but she could see the outline of the driver in the small passenger window. Or at least she thought she did.

The truck looked mostly undamaged, besides no longer sitting on four wheels. But she'd seen crashes that looked horrid and people walked away unscathed and others that had seemed minor that left permanent life-altering injuries. Until she could assess the patient, there was no way to tell.

The aircrew took off, running toward the scene, and she had to force herself to move slower despite the adrenaline pumping through her veins. Perhaps after more than half a year at the pole, she'd be as stable on the thick ice as they seemed to be, but even with heavy boots designed for the poles, her feet felt a little unstable. Falling and injuring herself would help no one, but she still wished she were moving a little faster.

A small crowd was gathering around the truck, and she could hear someone talking on a radio to the base station. If possible, righting the vehicle would be the best option for getting the victim out safely. But only if they knew the patient's condition.

Arriving at the scene, she pulled her med kit out of her carry-on. Then she turned to the loadmaster who'd made it to the accident before her. "Hold this." She passed him her bag without waiting for an answer and stepped to the truck.

"I'm Helena Mathews. The new nurse practitioner." She directed her attention to the person holding the radio in his hand. She didn't know anyone or what position they held, but the man with the radio seemed to be the most in control, at least at a glance. And she needed to check on the person in the car.

"Jeff Banks. I'm the director here. I've already radioed the clinic. Dr. Simpson is on the way." The voice was deep, but she could see concern wavering in the man's eyes behind his goggles.

This would be a unique way to meet her prickly colleague, but they'd have plenty of time to get acquainted after they'd handled the situation here. "All right. That is good. I am going to check on…" Helena paused. "Who is trapped?"

"Kelly Jenkins. She's a supply manager out here. The truck rolled twice, and we can't open the doors on this side."

Helena looked at the truck, trying to figure out the best way in. "Do you have something to break that back window?" It was far enough away from the driver's seat that any glass wouldn't hit her patient. The seal on the vehicle's heat would break, but she needed to see to Kelly's condition.

"I have a crowbar but that window is tiny." The man tilted his head, and she barely restrained a groan. They were wasting valuable time.

She kept a tight hold on her budding frustration. Jeff was worried about Kelly and also trying to protect Helena. It was admirable, and he didn't deserve to be snapped at. But she needed to see to Kelly, too.

"So am I!" Helena gestured to herself. "I can fit, and it's the best way to make sure Kelly is okay." This was not the first small place she'd climbed into. During her career there'd been several instances where her small size had allowed her to get into a position her other colleagues were too tall for.

She'd have to take the top layer of her gear off, but the truck would protect her from the elements long enough to get an idea of the situation. "So let's get moving. We need to know how she is, and the safest way to move her. That knowledge won't be any different when Dr. Simpson gets here."

The eyes behind the goggles traced her one more time before Jeff moved to the back of the vehicle and raised the crowbar. It took three swings, but eventually the glass gave way. At least it didn't shatter. But after he punched it out, there was still some glass left.

Jeff started raking the crowbar on the sides of the window, trying to clear the last of the sharp fragments, and then Helena heard Kelly moan. That decided it for her; glass or no glass, she was done wasting time.

Helena quickly stripped off her heaviest coat and neoprene face mask. The cold was an experience that she wasn't sure she could put into words. It reached into her bones as she made her way to the window. But there wasn't another choice—or at least there weren't any other good choices.

The coat was too heavy to let her through the window, and there were still pieces of glass on the edges. In a normal place she'd have kept the face mask on to protect herself from the glass, but she couldn't order a replacement and have it delivered to the South Pole. Better to risk cuts to her face than to have a face mask that was basically useless for the next nine months. Her goggles would protect her eyes, and time was of the essence.

She tossed the med kit into the truck. Dropping her feet through the window, Helena slid into the sideways vehicle. Pain ripped along her cheek, but there wasn't time to worry about any cuts she'd received. At least her face mask would be intact for the rest of the winter.

The heat from the vehicle raced through her as she grabbed the med kit and slowly made her way to the front. "Kelly?"

"Here." The response was soft, but at least she was conscious.

"I'm Helena," she offered as she did a quick visual assessment. Kelly was still strapped into the seat. A cut along the edge of her jaw was going to need stitches, but it was Kelly's glassy eyes that sent a needle of worry through Helena.

Concussion.

"Can you tell me anything?" Helena pressed her fingers to Kelly's shoulders looking for any tenderness. Kelly winced as Helena checked her left shoulder. Hopefully, just bruised, but she needed to brace it before they moved her.

"Truck hit a hole, flipped, turned off engine."

Helena gently patted the woman's hand. "That is

excellent information." It was good that the truck was off. It lessened any chance for an explosion from spilled gasoline, though Helena thought that was unlikely given that any spilled liquid would freeze on impact. Would the truck even start again? The LC-130's engines ran constantly on the runway to prevent a frozen line, but that was a worry for someone else.

"But can you tell me how you are feeling?"

Kelly's eyes floated open again. "Head hurts. And shoulder. Tongue feels weird."

"Can you stick your tongue out?"

The pink appendage Kelly stuck out showed no damage.

It was what Helena had expected. The feeling in Kelly's tongue was due to the concussion. A concussion would make you feel like your tongue could not form words, when it was your brain that was struggling. However, Helena had seen multiple patients bite through their tongues in car accidents, so it was something all trauma care professionals checked.

They needed a neck brace, a sling for Kelly's arm and a knife in case when they righted the truck Helena had to cut her from the seat belt. Grabbing a pack of sterile gauze from her pack, Helena quickly made a pressure bandage. "The cut on your jaw is going to need stitches. You likely have a concussion, and we need to X-ray your shoulder, Kelly."

Helena kept using the woman's name. Fatigue and confusion were common in concussed patients, and she'd found that they could pay better attention if you kept reinforcing that you were speaking to them—even if they were the only individuals in the room.

*Or the only ones in a rolled-over truck.*

The woman nodded, then let out a low moan.

"I need you to stay as still as possible for me, Kelly. We do not want to upset your head any more than necessary." Most people were familiar with concussions but didn't realize the severity of them. Even a mild concussion could leave a person groggy for weeks as the brain healed.

"What do you mean the new nurse practitioner is in there? And without a coat!" The growl echoed from the back of the vehicle. Or maybe Dr. Simpson's voice was deeper because of the mask covering his face? "I don't need two patients."

Nope! That was definitely a growl. Not the initial impression she'd planned to make with the grumpy resident physician. But the situation had demanded it. She'd find a way to smooth his ruffled feathers later.

"Kelly." Helena waited until Kelly's eyes met hers. "I am going to talk to Dr. Simpson. Let him know your condition. I'll be back in a moment." She didn't wait for her patient to respond, but she wanted her to know where she was going.

Sliding to the back seat, Helena braced herself against the cold. The heat that had been contained in the truck's closed container had evaporated with the open window, but the four walls of the vehicle still kept the inside at a reasonable temperature. At least for the South Pole.

"Can you pass me a neck brace, shoulder sling, scissors or knife for the seat belt, and my coat?" She directed the questions to the tall man standing near the broken window before her throat seized as recognition tore across her soul.

He wore a neoprene mask that was almost identical to the one she'd dumped with the loadmaster. He looked nearly the same as everyone else on the runway, but she'd recognize Carter Simpson's crossed-arm leaning posture anywhere.

Her breath caught in the back of her throat as Helena's eyes met his.

Dear God. He really was here.

There wasn't time to focus on that. Even if her brain could figure out the right reaction.

When he didn't immediately respond, Helena hit the side of the truck. "Carter, we are wasting time. Coat, neck brace, shoulder sling and scissors or a knife?" she repeated as she stared at him—unable to read any expression through his goggles.

Carter shook his shoulders and grabbed her coat from the person she'd handed it to earlier.

She saw shock register in the person's posture, clearly stunned at the uncomfortable exchange between the medical personnel.

Her coat was unceremoniously dumped through the window. At least someone had finished removing the last slivers of glass. She pulled it on, savoring the warmth it brought, and waited for the other supplies. "Kelly has a concussion, a deep cut along her jaw, probably from impact with the steering wheel. And her shoulder is tender. It may be from hitting the window, but I want it in a sling before we move her."

Carter nodded as he passed the neck brace and sling through the window. "They are going to try to right the vehicle. Hopefully, the door on the other side will open and we won't need a knife."

His voice halted as he bent next to the window and held up a switchblade. "This will rip through anything."

His gloved fingers closed over hers as he handed her the blade. And he didn't release it right away. "Be careful with it."

Was that normal concern? Or was he looking at her as the sheltered young woman she'd been? Raising her chin, she nodded. "No need to worry about me. I've handled many blades, Dr. Simpson. I'll be fine." Then she turned back to her patient without waiting to see his reaction.

The brace and sling went on quickly. Then Helena buckled herself into the passenger seat. "We're ready."

"Helena, get out of there." Carter's voice was tight.

She could hear the tension even through his face mask and several feet away. Why did he think she'd asked for the blade with the other equipment? There was no need to have it if she was out of the truck when they shifted it. Helena sent her eyes to the ceiling of the truck, annoyed that he hadn't understood the obvious. She would not leave Kelly alone.

"This way there is someone with her if necessary."

"She won't be alone. I'm coming in."

She heard a scuffle at the back of the truck and turned in her seat to meet Carter's gaze. His eyes were harder than she remembered. But the concern for her, for Kelly, was evident in the determination. But it had been a tight squeeze for Helena to shimmy through that window.

"Carter." She waited for his gaze to settle on her before she stated, "Stop wasting time!" How many times was she going to repeat that phrase today?

Helena was glad she couldn't catch the mumbled words from behind Carter's mask. But he didn't argue with her as he retreated from the window.

"Here we go, Kelly." Helena reached out her hand and held Kelly's tightly.

"Oh my!" Kelly let out a soft cry as the truck rocked with the effort to lift it.

"Just breathe." Helena squeezed her hand and closed her eyes as she felt the side of the vehicle lift. "Here we go." But the repeated muffled words were more for herself than Kelly. And went far deeper than the emergency they were currently in.

Carter Simpson was here. *Here.* At the end of the world.

They were going to be working together for nine months. Months and months with Carter. Working with Carter. Seeing him every day. Her stomach flopped as her heart did a flip. She wasn't sure which reaction was worse.

*Here we go.*

Helena Mathews put Kelly Jenkins's shoulder X-rays on the light box. Carter still couldn't believe his eyes. If it hadn't felt ridiculous, he'd have pinched himself. Not that it would do any good. This wasn't a dream.

She was truly here. At the Amundsen-Scott South Pole Station. The odds were astronomical. This was a situation that one saw in cheesy movies. Not actual life.

Time had been exceedingly kind to Helena. Her features were more refined now, but the beautiful young girl had transformed into a stunning woman. The long blond hair she'd worn in fancy braids was shorn close to her head in an adorable pixie cut. It was a cut that her parents—particularly her mother—probably would have hated, just like she probably disliked the small diamond stud in Helena's nose. But both seemed to suit the woman standing next to him.

And some things hadn't changed. Like her jade eyes or the full lips that barely stuck out in a pout. Kissable lips.

Carter shook himself as he stared at the light box.

He needed to pull his shaken core together. Seeing Helena was a shock, but it changed nothing. He wanted to believe the lie, but his heart hammered against his chest, denying that anything about this winter assignment would be the same.

For the first time since he'd ended his engagement, he felt like he was at a crossroads. In those broken moments he'd sworn he'd never step off the isolated path he'd chosen, and nothing was going to change that. Yes, Helena was here, but that didn't have to mean anything significant for him. She was just another medical professional wintering at the research station.

*Except...*

His brain cut that thought off before he allowed it to wander.

Crossing his arms, he studied the X-ray. It was Kelly's shoulder that mattered right now. Not the soft woman standing inches from him.

"I don't see any breaks, Carter."

His name on her lips sent a wave of unwelcome emotions through the darkened corners of his soul. Light poured into places that had been dormant for years. Home...it felt like home. Warm, welcoming, supportive. All the things he'd taken for granted. All the things he did not need.

*Home.*

What a ridiculous thought, but Carter couldn't shake the feeling rippling through him. He hadn't had a home since he'd discovered his mother's deception. For a brief period, he thought he'd found it with Laura. But that had been a hollow illusion, just like his parents' union.

So he'd convinced himself that he didn't need one.

And he didn't.

He'd done fine on his own. Graduated from med

school and created a career. If he occasionally missed Chicago and the people he'd known before he'd destroyed his family...that was just something he'd learned to deal with.

Helena's presence was a shock, but it had only activated a touch of nostalgia. Everyone got it if they reunited with someone from the past.

Someone he hadn't been able to push from his memory.

"That is quite a frown. Are you seeing something that I am not?"

Helena moved closer to him, and the soft scent of coconut invaded his nostrils. Nostalgia—except his heart seemed disinclined to accept his brain's statement.

*Focus!*

His gaze roamed the X-ray. She was right, there was no break. Which was good because the LC-130 had taken flight thirty minutes ago. Though his clinic was more than capable of treating a broken bone or two, he was glad that they didn't have to worry about that with Kelly.

"No break," he confirmed.

She turned her head, crinkles appearing at the edges of her eyes as she stared at him. "Soft tissue injuries will make her uncomfortable, but at least it isn't a SLAP tear. Since surgery is not a great option here."

"Not a great option" was an understatement. In the event of an emergency, he had the supplies necessary and contacts with experts around the globe to guide him. At the turn of the century, the resident physician had performed orthopedic surgery via a telemedicine link. It was groundbreaking, and Carter hoped he never had to do the same.

"True." Carter studied the X-ray again, though there

was nothing left to discover. But it felt safer than turning to the woman beside him. *Coward.*

Clearing his throat, he reached to turn off the light box. "We'll keep her comfortable here and monitor her under concussion protocol for at least the next twenty-four hours."

"Why the frown then?" Helena raised a brow as she took the X-ray. "Kelly is stable. And the mechanic even thinks he can get the truck functional again. Overall, today was a win."

Of course she'd notice the tension radiating through him. Helena had always read others and adjusted herself to make them comfortable. In fact, the girl had been consumed with making others happy, with fixing even minor inconveniences for everyone.

His mother and ex-fiancée had had that skill, though it had been used to facilitate their lies. He yearned to believe that it was simply part of what made Helena such a caring person. But each time he'd trusted those instincts, his world had shattered. It seemed like too big a risk...even if it was Helena Mathews standing before him.

Her tongue ran along her bottom lip, and Carter's heart hammered as his brain tried to find any words. He was always cordial with his work colleagues. But he didn't get close, and no one ever commented on his facial expressions. The easy smiles and laughter had died long ago.

Helena was here, and he had no idea how to process that, but staring at her mutely was the wrong answer.

Helena shook her head as she crossed her arms. "They warned me you were grumpy, but if our patient is going to be all right, once her concussion is under control, then there is no need for such deep worry lines. Unless you're concerned about the new nurse practitioner."

He felt his eyes widen.

He saw her shoulders shift, but Helena didn't back down. "Is that it? Are you upset it's me who walked off that plane?"

*No. Yes.* Both words rattled around his brain, only one syllable each—but impossible to choose between.

"It was a shock." That was an answer. Though it was surprisingly unsatisfying. How could Helena be here, and why were his insides refusing to stop their twirling?

An expression he couldn't read passed over her features before they slipped away. She offered him a small smile that stretched the bandage on her cheek. "We'll make it work, Carter. I've been told I am easy to work with. And I'll do whatever is needed to make this transition smooth. Anything you need fixed, you just set me on it."

She gave him a playful salute. She was trying to ease the tension of the meeting, but she meant her pledge to make this smooth. Still, there was an underlying worry in the back of her eyes. He was almost certain of it.

So Helena could still smile when she was unhappy or uncomfortable. He'd disliked her ability to close off her emotions, to make her family comfortable then... he hated it now. Why couldn't people just say what they meant? Why couldn't Helena just be herself?

She was a nurse, so that meant that she'd stepped out of the cocoon her parents had put her in. Surely she didn't still feel the need to please everyone. But could she strip that much of herself away?

He wanted to slap the questions out of his brain. They were colleagues, not young students lost in the thralls of first crushes away from home. Though part of him might always wonder what would have happened if he'd kissed her, or if he'd shown up for their date, or called, or…

He let those thoughts drift away. That door had shut over fifteen years ago. And some things were better left alone.

Searching for a safe topic, Carter started, "It will upset Kelly to miss the movie night, but with a concussion she wouldn't enjoy it much."

Her face lit up with a smile that time couldn't change. "*The Thing from Another World* and both versions of *The Thing*. Classic movies." Helena slid the X-ray onto the counter.

"You've read up on the traditions here?" Carter didn't know why that surprised him. Helena had always been smart and inquisitive—though she'd been a homebody. While he was pleasantly surprised she'd followed her nursing dreams, it stunned him she'd left Chicago. She and Owen had never talked of living anywhere else.

Owen. How was his former best friend? The question was on the tip of his tongue, but years of refusing to address the pain of the past wouldn't let it pass his lips.

"I read everything I could about this place." Helena crossed her arms as she let her gaze wander the clinic. "I've been fascinated by serving down here since a recruiter from the Center for Polar Medicine talked to a group of us when I was working in the Mercy emergency room. I figured they'd never contact me. But I updated my résumé after I completed my military contract position with the Department of Defense and indicated that I could do a quick fill. And now here I am."

*Medical contractor.* Carter's head spun as he tried to picture Helena serving a tour with the armed forces. In a war zone.

He'd had several colleagues who'd agreed to those contracts. The hazard pay helped pay off extraordinarily high med school debt. But you got hazard pay because it was dangerous. The idea of sheltered little Helena in such a place was unthinkable to him.

Who was this woman now?

Swallowing that question, too, Carter focused on the cut on Helena's cheek. She'd put a bandage on it, but there was blood seeping through it now.

Her first polar wound. Most people turned their ankle on the ice or bruised their tailbone falling outside. But Helena had gotten hers from crawling through a busted-up window without a coat.

He had to admit that he'd shifted from awe that the new nurse practitioner had sprung into action, and horror that she'd done it with no outer coat. He recognized that getting through the small window would have been difficult, but when Helena's head had popped into the back window, demanding a list of supplies for their patient—and then her coat—Carter had nearly lost his mind.

Helena Mathews had looked so tiny in that window. So out of place with blood coating her cheek. His entire body had frozen. Then she'd barked out the list of needs again.

"That cut needs at least a stitch or two, Helena."

Her fingers started toward her cheek before she caught them. Even with the bandage covering it, one could introduce bacteria. And that was never a good idea. Her lips turned down, and he saw her swallow whatever she was going to say.

Was she worried the stitches would leave a scar? If they did, it would be small. And easily covered with makeup when the wound healed. Still, he'd met many people while working in emergency rooms who'd panicked at the idea of any scar.

"All right." Helena sighed and hopped up on one of the treatment beds. "Then will you show me around the clinic? I spent far too much time searching for things when I was trying to help you treat Kelly."

"No." The word hung between them as Carter pulled the numbing gel from the counter. It was her first night at the South Pole. She should unpack her things and go to the movie night. It was a bonding experience for the whole crew. And she was going to need friends here... people besides him to keep her company.

Carter never participated, and eventually people had stopped asking for him to join them. He lived in the clinic and his small dorm room. He was... Happy was not an emotion that he was sure he'd felt in years—but he was content enough with his life. But Helena would want more. As she should.

Maybe if she was busy with others outside the clinic, that would keep her from prying too much into the reasons for his disappearance. Or trying to fix his aloofness.

The knowledge that Helena would spend her free time with others instead of him cut across his heart. He swallowed the discomfort. He shouldn't want her to spend all her time with him. That was a dangerous feeling. Carter didn't get close to anyone. But Helena Mathews was not just anyone.

"I am here to work, Carter." Helena's fingers tightened on the edge of the bed as he pulled the bandage from her cheek. But the tension radiating through her didn't seem to have anything to do with pain.

He gently rubbed the numbing gel along her cheek before he met her gaze. The sprinkles of gold hovering in the green depths still called to him after all these years. His tongue felt tight as he forced it to make words.

"It's your first night at the pole, Helena. You need to unpack." His breath felt trapped in his throat, but he forced the uncomfortable feeling away.

*And I need a night away from you to process the surprise.*

To put his emotions and the homesickness that her arrival drew forth back in the boxes he'd slammed shut so long ago.

"It's not like I brought much."

The challenge in her gaze sent a spark of fire down his spine. Carter walked through the world without succumbing to emotion. He never let himself get close enough to others that their words or looks, or lack thereof, mattered. But he didn't want Helena angry or frustrated with him. He wanted—

Well, Carter wasn't exactly sure what he wanted from his former best friend's sister. But he suspected chasing any of it wouldn't be good for his plans to remain aloof from everyone, always. Loneliness ached, but the pain of being tossed aside couldn't be described. He'd known it twice, and he didn't think he could survive hitting a triple.

And if Helena knew how he'd imploded the Simpson family… He didn't want to see the reaction play across her gorgeous features.

"Movie night is a tradition here. It will help you make friends since you arrived late. Kelly only needs one of us to monitor her. And I've spent two other winters here."

Though he'd never attended the movie night.

"First thing tomorrow you will walk me through the clinic and the expectations?" Helena raised her chin.

The question sounded almost like an order, and Carter barely caught the smile twitching at the edges of his lips and the joke tickling the back of his throat. It would be easy to slip into a lighthearted banter with Helena. The part of his soul that had been dormant for so many years seemed to crave it.

But Carter was a pro at wrestling that piece of himself.

"You have my word. Now, let's stitch you up." Carter quickly put three stitches in her cheek.

Setting the needle down, he ran a hand along her chin, hating and loving his gloved fingers that kept him from touching her skin. "Already injured less than twenty-four hours after landing. That may be a record. But it shouldn't be too terrible a scar. You'll still be mostly perfect."

He winked, then saw pain wash over her face. Carter blew out a breath. It would be a minor imperfection, barely noticeable. And she was a woman who'd climbed into a tipped truck less than ten minutes after arriving at the South Pole. Surely this wouldn't matter too much. Though people reacted to scars in a wide variety of ways.

After pulling off his gloves, Carter squeezed her hand. The connection sent vibrations of desire rumbling through him. She was gorgeous, and the tiny scar couldn't change that. "Seriously, Helena. It won't mar your pretty face too much, and you can always cover it with makeup."

"It won't be my first scar, Carter." Helena hopped off the table and grabbed the small bag that one of the LC-130 loadmasters had dropped off while they were treating Kelly. A shudder raced across her shoulder, but she didn't look at him as she headed for the door. "I'll see you tomorrow."

Then she was gone.

Carter blew out a breath as he gazed at the closed door. The clinic seemed duller without her.

*No.* It seemed exactly as it had the last two winters. Bright, clean and quiet. Just the way he liked his life.

*And lonely.*

# CHAPTER THREE

"I CAN GET THAT."

Carter reached for the box in Helena's arms, but she stepped back. In the three days they'd been working together, he'd carried nearly everything she'd picked up, even things that were light as a feather. He'd also taken most of the chores in the clinic and left her feeling like an ineffective employee, rather than a trusted colleague. A nuisance.

The few times she'd tried to strike up a conversation about anything other than the clinic, he'd given her a one-word answer. She loved nursing, but during a long shift, conversations always wandered to other things, to private lives and joys. It was only natural—except Carter was cocooned in a grumpy shell that she hadn't been able to penetrate.

What had happened over the last fifteen-plus years?

She knew that her arrival had shocked the man. His presence stunned her, too, and she hadn't mentioned it to Owen when she sent him an email telling him she'd arrived safely. It would thrill Owen to know he was here. But she had no answers for the dozens of questions her brother would ask.

The man standing before her now was not the Carter she'd cared about. Not the man she'd scoured medical journal articles and social media for. The one she still occasionally dreamed about when her subconscious was bent on tormenting her.

Physically, he still resembled the boy she'd known. Though the intervening years had chiseled the boyish features into a handsome man who was gorgeous, but aloof. His shoulders were broader now. And instead of the close-cropped hair he'd maintained throughout their childhood, it was now an unruly mass of dark curls that hovered near the top of his ears. It was adorable.

Was this how he treated everyone?

The loadmaster and polar medical director had warned her that Carter was grumpy, but he hadn't been overly testy with her. In fact, he'd barely acknowledged her at all—unless he was pulling something from her hands or taking over a simple task.

"This box hardly weighs a thing, Carter. I am more than capable of carting it around all day if necessary, and certainly across the fifteen feet needed." Helena purposefully stepped around a table to keep him from reaching for it again.

He pushed a hand through his hair as she passed him, but he didn't try to take the box again. Still, worry lines pressed into the corners of his eyes. She'd fled Chicago to avoid her family's worried stares, and she would not stand for them here. She simply couldn't.

"Is this how you acted with the other nurse practitioners stationed with you?" The question cut across the quiet clinic. She saw color rise along the base of his neck and knew she'd made him uncomfortable. The old Helena would have made a light joke, apologized for adding awkwardness to the conversation and flitted away. But she'd stopped being that girl when she'd broken with her family's expectations.

Mostly.

She would always try to make others happy. To make sure they knew their worth, but she was not going back into the sheltered shell her parents had constructed around her. Even if that made Carter a little uncomfortable.

Besides, the first step to getting him to break out of the ice he'd encased his soul in was forcing him to be a little uncomfortable. They could both stand the awkwardness if it helped fix the dynamic between them.

"No." He let out a soft sigh. "But they…"

Carter's voice died and ice poured through Helena's veins. Of course it wasn't how he'd acted with them. She swallowed the lump of pain pulling at the back of her throat.

He opened his mouth but shut it before whatever he planned to say escaped.

It didn't matter that he'd treated them differently.

She wished for just one second she could believe that lie. That the boy she'd never forgotten about might treat her as a competent colleague, rather than his childhood best friend's fragile twin sister, unable to carry a box across the room. After all, he'd encouraged her when she'd shown up at his door the day she'd changed her major. Said he was looking forward to being in classes with her.

*Nearly kissed her.*

Then he'd stood her up and disappeared.

But that was ancient history. Except the questions she wanted answered were bouncing around the back of her brain. Questions she knew the man now standing in front of her would have no interest in addressing.

"If we are going to work together for the next nine months, I need you to see me as something more than

Owen's delicate sister." She felt her lips tip down and forced her frown away.

The direction her first few days had taken was disappointing. But this was still the adventure of a lifetime. The chance to prove to her family, and herself, that she wasn't completely broken. And she wouldn't wallow.

At least that was one skill she'd picked up in her family's house. She was a pro at forcing herself to look on the bright side. It had been a requirement to survive in the household where everyone constantly worried and fretted if she even sighed loudly.

Besides, life was too short not to find the best in the day and in others. The accident that had nearly stolen her life and left the giant scar across her abdomen and hip had taught her that. Each day was a gift.

"Do you think I can do the job?" The question hovered in the room as she watched Carter run his hand along the base of his chin.

It was a motion he had always made when he was thinking. So there wasn't an easy answer.

That knowledge rubbed against her heart. Her résumé was impeccable. Maybe she hadn't wintered over in the South Pole twice already, but she'd worked through a war zone and in an emergency room nearly overrun in a pandemic. She was more than capable of the work required of her here.

Others had doubted her, but except for her parents and her ex-fiancé, she'd quashed their concerns with her hard work and bright demeanor. And it usually only took a few days.

She'd hoped Carter would look at her skills and just accept her—that she wouldn't have to prove anything here.

But what if she wasn't capable?

That insidious thought wormed its way through her brain as she mentally shook it off. She'd spent more than half a year recovering from the accident she'd been in during her deployment, painful months to rebuild her strength. And she was basically whole…mostly.

But the doubt echoing in his features ripped open a hole in her chest. What if she failed here? What if the scars really were more than surface level?

Tension rippled through her as she tried to push away the insecurity that had crept in since Kevin looked at her and walked away. She was strong. She was.

"I am not sure." Carter's voice was steely as his dark eyes met hers.

He'd always been honest—to a fault, some might say. No one ever had to guess what Carter thought of them. If you wanted to know, all you had to do was ask. He'd prided himself on that personality trait, said he'd learned it from his father.

Though privately Helena had believed he'd learned it in spite of his mother. The woman was beautiful and constantly doing good deeds—but only when it suited her. She'd been the queen of gossip and little white lies. And sometimes bigger ones.

Once she'd taken credit for a high school fundraiser after the debate team had raised nearly ten thousand dollars for an organization dedicated to researching childhood cancers. She might have been the parental helper, but it was Owen's and Carter's success. They'd organized the teams to ask every business in the area for sponsorship, then made sure that they emblazoned the businesses' names on the debate team's T-shirts for the year.

Helena had pointed it out, and Carter had agreed. But

then just shrugged and said he was used to his mother telling little lies.

How did you get used to that?

"Winter-over syndrome is real. I've seen—" Carter pulled at the back of his neck. "I've seen individuals I would never have thought fall victim to it. Most people spend months preparing to come here. You're a last-minute replacement."

She knew all about the seasonal stress disorder that affected researchers living at the polar research facilities. It caused a range of symptoms from irritability to absentmindedness to aggression. There was no known way to diagnose who might be more susceptible to developing the disorder, but she didn't have it at the moment. And carrying boxes would not cause it.

Gathering her patience, Helena tried to keep her tone level, unemotional. Not an easy task when she really wanted to scream that he was overreacting to a nonexistent crisis. That would not be helpful to prove herself to the aloof man before her. "I appreciate the honesty, but I am more than capable, Carter. I am not the girl you knew."

"Clearly."

She saw him flinch, and Helena knew he hadn't meant to let that slip from his lips. But it was better that she knew he was worried because of who she'd been. Even if it hurt.

"You are an excellent nurse, Helena. I do not doubt that. You wouldn't be here if you weren't." An emotion passed through his eyes that Helena thought was pain.

"Are you okay?" The question escaped before she had time to think it through. The label *grumpy* had clung to Carter for at least two winters, and she suspected far longer. It wasn't accurate, though. Carter wasn't grumpy—he was detached. Keeping her and everyone else at the base at a distance. And he was in pain. She was certain of it.

"Carter?" She stepped toward him, and he retreated. So now it was him putting distance between them. How were they supposed to overcome this?

"I need to see to something in my office." His neck was red, but he didn't offer any other comment before turning away.

Nodding, she started back toward the supply closet. He'd disappeared into his tiny office eight times over the last three days—another number she'd counted. If she asked him how he was or if she tried to start a conversation about anything other than work, he ran. She looked over her shoulder at the closed door before she entered the supply closet. He was so close, but so far away.

Rolling her shoulders, she looked at the well-stocked shelves. She'd been doing inventory for most of the day. It was nearly finished, but she wanted a few minutes to compose herself. To right the tumble of emotions clogging her chest. To figure out how she might reach the distant doc stationed with her.

She'd started this mission knowing that the person here was grumpy. She'd promised herself that it wouldn't matter. That she would do her best work, and if the grumpy physician wanted nothing to do with her outside the clinic, then she was still on an adventure.

But the person here was Carter.

*A very grumpy Carter.*

She couldn't just ignore him. She wouldn't. It might

take all winter, but she'd melt the thick layers of ice that Carter had encased himself in.

"Helena." A pained voice echoed from the clinic's entrance.

She moved quickly as Bodhi Larson leaned against the clinic's door. The tall man she'd met at the movie screening her first night at the station was pale and sweating. "Bodhi."

As she reached his side, he gripped his stomach. She grabbed a bucket just in time.

"Sorry."

"It's fine." Helena offered a smile. One didn't last long in the healing professions if body functions made you squeamish. "How long has this been going on?"

"Started this morning." Bodhi let out a groan as Helena led him to a bed.

"What's going on?" Carter asked as he moved toward them.

"I almost got sick on Helena's shoes." Their patient lay back in the bed, closed his eyes and groaned as he gripped his stomach again. "These stomach cramps feel like they are going to kill me."

"Any other symptoms?" Helena reached for the tablet they used to check a patient into the clinic. In most doctors' offices, the nurse practitioner saw patients, did diagnosis work for acute problems and could prescribe medications. She hadn't been to med school like Carter, but she could handle most of the issues they were likely to encounter this winter.

Bodhi gripped his belly again and cringed. "Stomach issues started this morning, cramps, diarrhea and vomiting. I swear I haven't felt like this since I was a kid—if then." He sucked in a deep breath and curled into the fetal position. "It feels like my insides are trying to escape my body."

Drawing the thermometer across his forehead, Helena let out a breath. "Normal. No fever." Carter nodded as she reached for the blood pressure cuff. "One nineteen over seventy-five."

"I think it's just a stomach bug. But I am going to keep you with us for the night. Just to be sure." Carter nodded to Bodhi before looking to Helena.

"Agreed." Helena returned her focus to the patient. "A stomach bug. Minor but uncomfortable to be sure!"

"This doesn't feel minor," their patient groaned.

She patted Bodhi's arm. "You've been ill all morning. Try taking a nap, then we'll get you a sports drink and see if you can sip it. Dehydration can worsen your stomach cramps."

Bodhi shook his head, "I don't know if I can drink anything, but I'm exhausted."

"Let's see how you feel after a nap." She reached over the bed and turned off the light above Bodhi. It didn't take much of the light out of the clinic, but it was the best she could do.

Carter met her gaze, nodded and then headed back to his office without saying anything else. It shouldn't sting. But it did.

She sat with Bodhi as he closed his eyes. She didn't know if he would get much rest, but he was displaying typical rotavirus symptoms. Uncomfortable, but only dangerous if you got seriously dehydrated. It took over half an hour, but eventually Bodhi's breaths lengthened, and his body relaxed.

Standing, she headed back to the supply closet. The last tasks took no additional time. Rolling her shoulders, she tried to work out a bit of the tension. It would be nice if she could pretend that the tightness was because of something innocuous. If only she could blame it on the accommodations at the station…

Her dorm was only large enough to house a twin bed, a desk and a closet that was barely big enough to contain the limited clothing she'd brought. It wasn't much, but it was fine. And the bed was comfortable enough— which meant the tight strings roping her body together were because of Carter.

"Ugh!" She wrapped her arms around herself. "He's your colleague for the next nine months. You'll make it work." There had to be a way to fix the distance Carter insisted on keeping between them.

"Helena?"

Carter's voice struck her back.

*Dear God.*

He had to have heard her, and now she had to turn and face him. And there was not enough time to gather the emotions racing through her. Part frustration, part something that she didn't want to put a name to. "I finished the supply check." Her voice wobbled, but she kept her chin raised as she faced him.

"That isn't what I wanted to talk about." Worry lines pinched in the corners of his eyes as he shook his head. At least he didn't seem inclined to bring up her private outburst.

"What do you need?" She was grateful her voice sounded even now, despite the heat tracing along her back.

"I owe you an apology."

Whatever she thought might pop out of his mouth, she still hadn't expected that. When he didn't say anything else, she swallowed the anxiety and straightened her shoulders. "For being standoffish since my arrival?

Or doubting my abilities? Or for standing me up and disappearing from my life? From Owen's?"

She'd worried about him. Panicked that his father hadn't been willing—or able—to tell her where he was. She'd drifted through days, unable to provide any comfort to Owen as their calls and texts went unanswered. Unable to fix anything and desperately worried about the man before her.

Who'd clearly managed to make his way in this life. He was a doctor, the thing he'd always wanted most. But brokenness coated him now, and as frustrated as she was by the years of silence, she ached to know what had happened to him.

To offer some form of comfort. To let him know that there were people who'd never forgotten him. Never stopped hoping that he might pop back into the life he'd vanished from.

"You are not the quiet, soft-spoken girl who always tried to please her parents that I knew." Carter's head tilted as his gaze held hers. "I'm glad."

It had cost her a lot to become the person she was now. Most of the scars grew inside her, though the fingers wrapped around her middle lay over a very physical one. But she hated the twist of longing that pulled at her as Carter's last words landed against her heart. He was the only person from her past, besides Owen, who'd acted happy that she'd changed.

"I'm sorry for the gruffness. And for saying I wasn't sure if you could make it here. I had one colleague who suffered from winter-over syndrome. He…" Carter sucked in a deep breath before continuing, "He was really strong, the last person I would have suspected would get anxiety from the environment here, but… well, it ended all right once we got him evacced."

He closed his eyes and rocked back on his heels. "I have also worked with others who have thrived here. I should have focused on those instances instead of the bad. But optimism is not a strength of mine."

"It used to be one of your strongest traits." The minute the words were out, Helena knew they were the wrong ones.

Opening his eyes, Carter pursed his lips, but his gaze raked over her. Through her.

"You're not the only one who isn't the same person."

Then he was gone. Leaving her alone with stacks of medical supplies and no answers. But Helena was going to get them. Carter was hurting. She didn't know why, but she could help him. She just needed to get past the shell he'd built around himself.

"Dr. Simpson!" The scream echoed from the clinic entrance, and Helena saw Olivia Rickson grip the side of a chair as she lost the contents of her stomach, too.

Carter made it to Olivia's side before Helena did, but his gaze captured hers as he led another patient to their second-to-last bed.

What was going on?

The alarm echoed on his nightstand, and Carter barely had the energy to push himself off the bed. His joints screamed as he stretched, and he tried to ignore the ache in his stomach as he pulled on his scrubs before heading for the clinic. He'd fallen into bed after his shift without grabbing dinner, exhaustion overwhelming any signal for sustenance.

His stomach twisted again, but Carter didn't feel overly hungry. Or hungry at all. It was just the stress of the last few days traveling through his body. He'd never had a winter-over that was so eventful—and today was the last day of the first week.

Reaching his fingers over his head, Carter pressed his palms into the ceiling as he tried to work out a few of the aches in his body. His dorm room was one of the largest at the base, though that meant he had enough room for a tiny bookcase next to his bed and a chess set. It was not the lap of luxury, but it was enough. And it was right next to the clinic so he could quickly check in on patients. Which was a good thing, since he and Helena had treated nearly half of the base over the last six days, and that was with Helena and Carter doing strict contact tracing and asking everyone to stay in their rooms when not on duty.

They still hadn't identified the initial source of the viral infection—which ran for a little over forty-eight hours. Most of the affected members of the winter team had managed their symptoms in their rooms, with Helena and Carter doing routine checks. But their three clinic beds and two of the cots had patients that required closer monitoring to make sure they stayed hydrated.

The day that Bodhi and Olivia had presented with symptoms, they'd tracked down four additional patients. The next day there'd been eight. Then six members and then three had presented with new symptoms over the next two days. With any luck, they'd continue the downward trend today.

Helena's tired eyes met his as he stepped into the clinic. She offered a weary grin as she gestured to the beds. All their patients were resting comfortably—or as comfortably as one could in the compact clinic. And no additional patients had presented overnight. That was good news. She was looking over Erik—a scientist working with the Event Horizon Telescope. He'd had an IV line of fluid two days ago, and Carter was glad to see that he'd made it through a second day without needing any more. Carter would never deprive his patients of necessary treatment, but he was grateful that the scientist was the only one to need intravenous fluids at this point. Dipping into the limited resources at the start of the season was a terrifying prospect.

Carter's stomach rumbled, the sound echoing in the silent clinic, and Helena's head popped up.

"Are you okay?" A hint of gold sparkled in her eyes as she studied him. Over the course of the last week, she'd been nothing short of amazing. The woman seemed to be able to do anything on limited sleep. It was impressive, and he felt more than a twinge of guilt that he'd doubted her the first two days.

Rationally, he had known she was healthy in her teen years. But Carter could still remember the three weeks she'd spent in the hospital when they were all in the third grade. An upper respiratory infection had turned into pneumonia. Owen had been fearful, enhanced by his parents' constant worry. He and Owen had always looked out for her, and here, at the end of the world, he was doing the same.

Pulling the boxes from her. Trying to lighten her load any way he could. But she'd called him out on the assistance, and he'd nearly broken when she'd asked if she was being treated differently. Of course she was.

His heart raced every time she was near. The sound of her voice was enough to make his lips ache to turn up. He'd never had an issue keeping his distance with his other colleagues, but he wanted to know everything about her. And the way she was with him and the patients over the last week had only heightened the pull he felt around her.

He watched as she rubbed the back of her neck. She was exhausted, but she was born to be a nurse. And he was grateful that it was her who stepped off the LC-130. Happy to be given just a slice of time with her. He didn't want to explore those emotions, but Carter recognized that this winter couldn't be exactly the same as the others.

Not that he planned to do anything different. But even during a stomach flu outbreak, just spending a few hours with Helena lessened the lonely ache in his heart. And that was enough.

*It has to be.*

Helena's eyes roamed over him, assessing him. She cared about everyone. It was a common trait he saw in the healing profession, but Helena was especially gifted in connecting to her patients. She always gathered information from them while also asking personal questions, a typical technique, but Helena was genuinely interested in all the answers that came back.

He'd watched her return to ask further questions when the shift was quiet or a patient was particularly uncomfortable. Her need to help others, to make sure they were all right—to fix them—had not changed.

His stomach rumbled again, and she raised an eyebrow. "Are you okay?" She repeated.

"Just didn't feel hungry when I woke up, so I came straight here." He still didn't feel hungry, but his body felt differently, apparently. The concern washing over her face sent a pang through him.

No one had worried about him since he was eighteen. Even Laura, his ex-fiancée, had simply accepted when he told her he was fine. She'd never probed further. A warning flag that Carter had failed to recognize. But he'd been so lonely at the time, he'd clung to the illusion that everything was all right between them.

But lonely was better than brokenhearted. It was a lesson he wouldn't forget. It was why he couldn't indulge the part of him that wanted Helena to ask after him.

Helena looked over at Erik one more time before she pulled open a drawer, grabbed something and turned to him. Two granola bars dropped into his hands, but it was the brief touch of her fingers that sent tingles racing along his spine.

Over the last few days, there'd been tiny moments where they'd touched. Always for milliseconds when she passed him a tablet or handed something over. But he could remember each one. And he wanted more... not that he had any plans to give in to that desire.

Carter needed to find some control. Since the end of his engagement, he'd worked with countless skilled female colleagues and never felt any pull toward them. The tiny lifelines he'd let himself explore after he graduated from med school had all been cut loose when he'd discovered Laura's infidelity.

With his friend.

That still rubbed. That Brian had lied to him, too. Sat across the table from him at dinners and joked in the break room with him while he was sleeping with Carter's fiancée. He'd been a complete fool.

When he'd caught her lie, Laura had thrown down a newspaper article that she'd printed showing Carter and his father after he'd won a science competition in his final year of high school, claiming she wasn't the only one hiding things.

As though not discussing his family was the same as infidelity.

It was a conversational shift his mother would have appreciated.

He hadn't seen the image in years, and it had torn him up to look at it. His father had looked proud of him, like the proud, supportive father he'd always thought he'd had. Pain he hadn't known for years had torn through his soul as he'd looked at that image. At the happy smile on his dad's face. But that man had disappeared after his mother's lies were exposed.

He'd told Laura he had no interest in discussing things further. She'd broken down, tears streaming down her cheeks as she begged him to forgive her indiscretion. To let her past his walls. To let her in. To let her love all of him, past, present and future.

He'd told her it wasn't an option. She'd been lying for months and had only confessed when he'd confronted her—and then shifted blame to him. They'd separated immediately, dividing the materials they'd accumulated over the last three years, and he'd withdrawn further into his shell. And applied to the polar medical program the next day.

Then he'd buried the pain of the broken relationship and the torn-apart friendship with Brian deep in the recesses of his heart. He'd put himself back together—again. The edges of his soul were more jagged now, and late at night, in his quiet apartment, the loneliness was difficult to ignore, but he wouldn't survive that level of destruction again.

If his mother and Laura could hide their affairs, if his father could turn on the son he'd raised since birth after finding out that he didn't share any of his genetic material, if a man he thought was a friend would carry on an affair with his fiancée, then whatever love was, it was too fleeting to trust.

"If you are still hungry after you finish those, there's a giant box of granola bars in the supply closet. I asked Martha if she could send a few bars over before I reported for the shift last night. Given all the extra time we're spending in the clinic, I think she felt like sending the whole box was a small way the kitchen staff could help. But don't tell anyone—I think she might have smuggled it for me." Helena's quiet words drew him from the ache of memory.

He blinked and looked up from the bars in his hand. "Probably. The supplies are all carefully tracked around here—you scored big." Pride radiated off Helena, and Carter smiled. It felt funny. How long had it been since he smiled organically? Not because it was expected in a situation?

A lifetime.

It didn't surprise Carter that Martha had been willing to help Helena. Helena had always been able to put people at ease, to connect with them. And it meant others were willing to help her, too. It was an admirable trait—as long as one used it for extra granola bars and not for hoodwinking your husband, son and fiancé.

Carter wanted to shake the unkind thoughts from his head. To drill out the pieces of his brain that automatically sought the worst-case scenario. But the routine was buried too far in his core.

"Thank you." He tapped the granola bar against his head, wishing there were a way to put all the emotions that had escaped his carefully constructed walls back in their rightful places.

"You're welcome, Carter. Did you sleep okay? There are circles under your eyes."

He shifted as her gaze assessed him, the nurse checking on a potential patient. That hurt; it shouldn't. The last thing that Carter should want was for Helena to look at him for any other reason. But the tiny voice deep in the recesses of his soul he'd ignored for so long cried out for more of a connection.

"I slept fine." The words sounded gruff as he put the granola bars in his pocket. Helena raised a brow, though she didn't comment further. But he caught her studying him out of the corner of her eye as she wrapped up the final few notes from her shift.

He shifted again, uncomfortable with the watchfulness in her gaze. Helena had known him before his soul crusted over. And her looks and concern swept easily through cracks in his apparently not-so-well-constructed walls.

They'd been too busy over the last few days to have more than a few chats regarding patients' notes, but when this crisis was over... He swallowed the lump in the back of his throat.

In a few days, life would go back to the normal pace of checking a few patients a week. At least Carter prayed it did.

And they'd have hours, perhaps even days, of uninterrupted time together. How would she react when he kept her at a professional distance, encouraged her to engage with the other team members at the base while leaving him to his solitary life? It was what he'd done with the other colleagues he'd worked with, but his heart screamed at the idea of Helena offering him only a brief greeting and cool professional talk in the clinic.

The dull ache in his heart for her and Owen's missed friendships spiked through him as she moved close to him. His stomach twisted again, but he wasn't sure if it was because of Helena or his lack of breakfast.

She yawned, and he wanted to kick himself. He'd been so concerned with how he felt he hadn't reacted to her exhaustion. Forcing his mind away from his tumbling thoughts, he looked at her. Really looked at her.

Deep circles stood out under her brilliant eyes, too. She'd worked each of the night shifts—claiming that she'd come off nights recently and adjusting to the schedule would be easier. The clinic usually only had a staff member on call during the evening, but with their patient load, they'd needed to run the unit full time. He'd accepted her suggestion, never questioning whether it was true, or if it was just Helena trying to make life easier for everyone else.

For him.

"You need to get some sleep." Carter reached for the tablet. Her fingers were warm, and his heart picked up a bit before the brief connection ended.

What was wrong with him?

She covered another yawn with the back of her fist, and her nose scrunched as her eyes closed. "I'm fine."

*Fine*... A word that almost always meant the opposite in his experience. It could be a weapon wielded in an argument. But in his field it was often used to cover the pain underneath the surface. How many times had he heard a patient utter the word while trying to hide their discomfort? It was a common refrain when a nurse or doctor in the emergency room had dealt with a crisis that ended poorly and still had several hours on their shift left.

*Fine* was not a word he wanted to hear on Helena's lips. Particularly when there was evidence to the contrary.

"I just need to finish up the notes, then—"

"No." Carter kept his voice low, not wanting to disturb their sleeping patients. "You need to take care of yourself, too, Helena." She'd spent her childhood making her parents happy, trying to keep their worries at bay. She'd always put Owen's needs before hers, and she'd gone into nursing. A field of healers who often put everyone above themselves.

Who looked after her?

He might not be able to give anyone more of himself, but Carter always made sure his staff had what they needed. And right now, Helena needed rest. "This is a viral infection, and viruses have an easier time if you're exhausted."

Helena's hand pushed against his shoulder as she shook her head. The touch was over before his brain registered the feeling, but his heart had a mind of its own.

"I know my limits, Carter." Her lips turned down for a second before she nodded toward their patients. "When they wake, provided they feel up to it, I think they can weather the rest of the virus in their rooms with water and electrolyte packages. Hopefully we are on the downside of this, and you and I can figure out how we are going to work together. As a true team."

Her cheeks colored as the words hung in the air between them. Her eyes dipped and tiny lines cut across her forehead before they melted away. When her gaze met his again, it was clear. Tired, but clear.

The hint of dissatisfaction, again hidden before most people would notice. "I wasn't doubting your abilities, Helena." His stomach rumbled again, but he ignored it as he tried to get Helena's attention. "I wasn't."

She nodded, but he saw the doubt hovering in her eyes.

How could she doubt herself? Her work was superb.

She'd worked in emergency medicine and done a medical deployment. She would be considered by many employers as one of the top nurses in her field.

Before he could process that thought, his stomach rolled again. And this time Carter knew exactly what was causing it.

"Dear God." He bent over as the pain ripped across his middle.

No wonder so many of their colleagues had stumbled into the clinic. The pain seemed to radiate through his abdomen, and even with all his medical training, he briefly wondered if his middle might explode.

"Carter?" Helena's arms wrapped around his shoulders, steadying him as he tried and failed to stand. "Take a deep breath. It helps."

Her words carried over him, but the pain cutting through him was so deep that he wasn't sure he could follow the instruction. But he tried as she squeezed his shoulders. The pain lessened, but not by much.

"Let's get you back to bed. I think you'll be more comfortable in your room, and it's close enough I can easily check on you."

She needed rest. The argument was on the tip of his tongue, but he bit back the words. He was in no condition to see patients. "Jackson Fatre, a scientist in the Event Horizon program—" His stomach screamed, and the words died on his lips.

"Is a trained medic. I know. I talked to him at the movie night on my first night. I also spoke with him a few days ago in case one or both of us got the virus. I'll call him—as soon as I get you situated."

*Good.*

At least she wouldn't be all on her own and exhausted. His stomach constricted again, and Carter tried to force air through his lungs. Then he was moving, or rather shuffling, toward his room.

Helena helped him into bed and disappeared. She was back in moments with a cup of water and electrolyte powder. "If you can get some rest, the worst of the cramps should be over in a few hours. When you wake, drink half of this. If you manage that for an hour…"

"I know the protocol." He hadn't meant to growl, but he knew what to do.

"Doctors are the worst patients." Helena grabbed the blanket and pulled it over him. "Try to rest, Carter." Her fingers brushed a piece of hair from his eyes. A look floated over her features that Carter couldn't read, then she left.

He closed his eyes and tried to rest, but the image of Helena's eyes, and the desire to do more than ignore the emotions twirling through him, chased him. When he finally rested, it was Helena who came to his dreams.

Helena and hope.

# CHAPTER FOUR

LOCKING UP AT the clinic, Helena rolled her shoulders, trying to pull any of the weariness from her body. She'd made it through the day with no new patients presenting with the virus. *And* she'd been able to discharge the others to finish recuperating in their own rooms.

Overall, it had been a good day. Exhausting...but good. The one slight hiccup had been when Kelly found her napping on her desk. It wasn't ideal, but given the patient load and Carter's illness, she'd needed the catnap.

She flipped the note on the clinic door listing it as closed and then wrote out her room number as the medical staff on call for the night. It felt a little strange to enter the normal routine for the first time since she'd arrived. With any luck, she and Carter could settle into a regular schedule shortly. Maybe she'd even get a few of her questions answered.

Passing Carter's room, Helena paused. She'd checked on him when she'd made her rounds with the other patients this afternoon. He'd been resting comfortably both times.

She crossed her arms as she stared at the door. Carter wouldn't appreciate the extra check. She hadn't exaggerated when she'd told him doctors made the worst patients. But if it was any other patient, she wouldn't hesitate to do one more check during the first full twenty-four hours.

*If it weren't Carter, you'd march in—so go!*

Huffing at her own indecision, she reached for the door handle. The room was nearly pitch-black, but she didn't want to risk waking him. The room's warmth slid through her tired body. The ache of exhaustion was another reason to celebrate that Carter was her last patient. Provided no more stumbled through the clinic door.

Nope. She was going to think positively. No reason to search out the negative.

A yawn broke free, and she had to fight through the fatigue just to move forward. She'd been excited to come to the South Pole, thrilled at the adventure. But she hadn't expected the first week to be so eventful.

*Or to find Carter.*

Her brain still hadn't fully processed that. The man kept her at arm's length. They'd spent most of their first days fighting a stomach bug outbreak, but in the few quiet moments they'd had, she'd seen him look at her. And for just a moment her heart would race. Would twist with what she feared was hope.

Part of her had always hoped he might pop back in. That he'd have a great explanation for his disappearance and ask her on that coffee date. That the boy who'd seen her true self so long ago might return a man who still wanted the Helena she'd been trying to become.

She wasn't the girl she'd been. Her fingers dipped to her hip, the habit she'd developed after her accident. No, she certainly wasn't the same. And the few people she'd shown the physical damage to had all recoiled.

Helena shook herself. None of that mattered at the moment. And it was just exhaustion causing her brain to drift to what-ifs. Fatigue and loneliness were a dangerous combination.

"Look at me, Dad," Carter whimpered. "Please."

The words struck her as she made her way to his bed. He shifted as she laid a hand on his head. "Carter?" He was cool, so this wasn't a fever dream.

She hated to disturb his rest. This virus just had to run its course, but if he was having a nightmare... Dreams rarely affected the quality of sleep, but nightmares certainly did. They could break up an REM cycle as the body tried to force the person awake, and once awake, it often took longer for the brain to slide back into sleep.

"It's not my fault. Please just look at me."

The distress in his voice made the decision for her. Reaching for the lamp on the bedside table, Helena blinked as a soft light filled the room. "Carter." Her voice was stronger this time, but he still didn't wake.

"I didn't know Mom cheated. Look at me. Please. I am still your son."

The shock momentarily stunned her. The sudden dissolution of the Simpson marriage. The quick sale of their house. His father's terrible words about not caring where his son was. The likely reason clicked into place as she saw Carter frown in his sleep.

"Carter!"

His eyes blinked open, and she put a hand on his shoulder before he could sit all the way up. She'd seen the others shift too quickly and the stomach cramps return. "You were having a nightmare, but don't move too fast."

Carter's eyes were unfocused as his gaze landed on hers. "Helena? God, I missed you." The tips of his lips pulled up.

For a moment it was the sweet boy from her past staring at her. Her chest seized as her gaze wandered across Carter's relaxed face. The pangs of what-ifs loosened her tongue. "I missed you, too, Carter."

It was the truth. Helena had missed him. Missed the fun-loving, caring boy who had always had a smile and joke for everyone. The kid who'd transitioned from childhood playmate to confidant…then disappeared.

"You were having a nightmare," she repeated. The spell broke as recognition flew through Carter's eyes. She patted his hand, offering comfort to the man he was now.

Coming out of any dream could be disorienting. Coming out of a nightmare to find someone from the past who'd known the person you were crying out to? She wasn't sure how she'd react. But she doubted Carter would want to rehash any of it.

"How much did I say?" His voice was hoarse.

She raised an eyebrow as she passed him the bottle of water she'd put on his nightstand earlier. "Not much. But you were frowning and calling out for…someone." She hated the half-truth, but watching Carter pull away from her, she felt it was best not to let him know how much she'd guessed from his sleepy words.

Though when he was feeling better, she'd find some way to broach the subject. They had months together, and if he was having nightmares about his family…

She let her thoughts drift away. Her focus right now was making sure that Carter got through the virus that had struck so many others. But after—

"I don't like lies."

Carter's dark eyes bored through her, but Helena didn't flinch. She didn't like lies, either, but sometimes white lies were necessary. Particularly with a prickly patient who needed to focus on getting better, not on what he'd said during his sleep. They'd talk about it later, and she'd find a way to make him understand. This should be an easy enough fix. Besides, she doubted he was going to tell her anything tonight. And punishing himself for a slip of the unconscious tongue wouldn't serve anyone.

"I am not a fan of lies, either, Carter." She took the bottle of water back. He needed to stay hydrated, but too much on his stomach too soon would be a problem, too. "Is anyone?"

"My mother..." He swallowed the rest of that sentence before he continued, "You'd be surprised how many people seem unbothered by them." His flinch sent a bead of sorrow through her.

He'd always known his mother struggled with the truth. Helena remembered him saying that she wished she was acting full time. Maybe she looked at life as a role she was playing, but the character flaw had wounded her son. And it hurt to find out the people you thought you knew were capable of destroying you— even if they hadn't meant to. "I think they bother most people, but once you start spinning a web..." Helena shrugged.

Life was complicated; people were messy, creative, wonderful creatures that could love each other in ways no other species could. But they could also hurt each other in unique ways, too.

Her fingers involuntarily traced the edge of the scar on her belly. Kevin had seemed genuinely appalled by his behavior. By the lies that had destroyed their engagement. By the fact that he couldn't look at the scars that traced across her stomach. By the night he'd spent in another's embrace after she'd returned home weak and broken. It didn't make his actions right. Didn't make the end of what she'd thought was a beginning any easier to handle, but only a true monster lied and felt no consequences. And thankfully, monsters were rare.

"You always tried to find the best in everyone." Carter took another sip of water.

"Of course." Helena nodded. "There is always some good to find. You just have to look."

*Sometimes pretty hard...*

She left that final thought unstated.

"Really? How did that work out? Your parents ever fully accept your career choice? Are they happy you're here? So far from home?" Carter's voice was stronger, but she could hear the bite of bitterness beneath his question.

How she wished she could give the cynic in the bed an answer that would rock his world. But that lie wouldn't be a white lie to make him more comfortable. "Not yet."

"You've been a nurse for years, Helena. I saw your résumé. It's impressive. You've worked in highly accredited critical units. You extended your twelve-month tour with the Department of Defense into an eighteen-month rotation."

"That wasn't..." Her voice died away as her fingers brushed her scar again. The extension on her résumé was accurate, but she hadn't worked at all during that final six months. She'd spent it battling for her life and then in rehab to rebuild her muscles and then in therapy to accept the permanent changes to her body. She'd explained that to the hiring committee when she'd submitted her résumé, but it wasn't listed on the document—and she did not feel like explaining it now.

"You are an amazing nurse. But they still wish you

were home instead of sitting on the edge of a patient's bed at the literal end of the world?"

"That would be their preference." The words sounded detached even to her own ears. But she was far too exhausted to let the pain of those emotions come close to the surface. She might not get them back in the mental drawer where she stored them.

Carter nodded, proud of his assessment. "Sometimes the people who are supposed to care the most about us only care about themselves, and they cover that lapse with lies." His eyes popped as the words poured forth.

The dam of emotions the man had been holding in was faltering. But it was too late, and she was too tired to hash it out now.

"I refuse to focus on past hurts." Her words slid into the quiet, and she wanted to believe they were true. But part of her called the lie to herself. The past chased her, too. It was why she was here, trying to prove herself.

That he was trying to put distance between them with her own pain sent more than a tinge of anger floating through her, but she refused to give in to it. Particularly because she suspected that was what the man lying next to her wanted. Letting out a breath, she pushed a strand of curly dark hair out of his eye.

Why did she feel the urge to touch him—even when he was in such a foul mood?

She needed to get some rest before her feelings tripped any closer to the surface. "I choose to believe the best in people—it's served me well." Helena stood and didn't wait for Carter to find another reply. "I am glad that you seem to have a light case of the virus. But remember, you have to be symptom-free for at least twenty-four hours before you return to the clinic. I'll check in on you tomorrow."

"Helena."

She could hear the regret in his voice. She hated how it was tied to her name. Hated that what had happened in the Simpson household had tainted the sweet boy she'd known. But the past didn't have to drive the future. At least not completely.

"Good night, Carter. Get some more rest." She stepped out before he could say anything else. Before she could beg him to confide in her, to let her hold him. Because that was what Carter needed. But Helena didn't know if that was something she could offer.

*Or should offer.*

Carter's skin prickled as he looked at the entrance to the clinic. It had been twenty-four hours since he'd had any viral symptoms and twelve since he'd last seen Helena.

*And almost forty-eight since she'd found him having a nightmare.*

She'd told him he hadn't said much—and Carter wanted to believe her. But he only ever had one nightmare. It played on repeat through his subconscious. Refusing to let his body rest when he was stressed or sick.

It was always a repeat of the last day he'd spent in Drake Simpson's house. His mother had been grateful that the lies were finally out—and hadn't cared how it affected her son. She'd contacted a divorce lawyer and said she was looking forward to the next stage in her life—and since Carter was technically an adult, she'd believed her parenting role was complete.

He'd never been close to her. She'd always been more interested in the show of parenthood, like it was a role for one of the plays she'd dreamed of being in. Except there was no script, and the director never shouted cut.

It had taken eighteen years for him to realize it was because he was the greatest lie she'd ever told.

But he'd been his father's shadow. Following him to the office, learning the names of all the bones in the body before he was ten. Carter had considered being a surgeon—and if his father hadn't turned his back on him, he probably would have. Just to make his dad proud.

But Drake Simpson hadn't been able to look at him after Carter revealed his mother's deception. And he'd blamed Carter for it. That was the cut that refused to heal. That he'd believe Carter was responsible; that he'd destroyed their family with the truth.

Maybe he had.

Yet the thing a person controlled least in this world was who their parents were. Though that hadn't stopped his father from acting like Carter had chosen to hurt him with a genetic code he'd had no control over. He'd reached out only once in all these years. A short one-line email.

I have something I'd like to discuss.

Carter hadn't bothered to respond. He'd tried to push it from his mind. Whatever it was his father wanted, the one line didn't seem like it was an apology. Carter wasn't sure that was what he wanted...no, he was sure. But finding out reconciliation wasn't what his father was after was a risk Carter couldn't take.

Even with all that baggage, it had been unfair of him to snap at Helena. Or to ask if her parents had accepted her choices. If they were happy she'd ventured so far from home. If she'd said yes, Carter would have been happy for her—he hoped. But part of him wouldn't have believed it.

Most parents wouldn't have seen the decision to become a nurse as a rebellious act. But they'd kept her so sheltered. They'd probably prefer it if their daughter had never spread her wings and discovered her calling.

Which was a shame, because their daughter was an amazing person. Caring, giving, empathetic. All the things that made a wonderful nurse.

*And friend, and...*

He pushed a hand through his hair. This was a crossroads. His heart yearned for him to choose a fresh path. To abandon the isolation he'd clung to since Laura cheated on him. He hadn't experienced the need for companionship in years. And he'd been content—until Helena set foot on the pole.

And it was a set of feelings he didn't particularly enjoy rushing through him now.

Carter shook his head before he let his mind wander any further than thinking of Helena as a friend. He'd sworn off relationships after Laura had cheated on him. The only women he dated were women who wanted short connections with no deep attachments.

And there was no way Helena was capable of such a connection, even if that was what he wanted with her. Helena connected with everyone: patients, the kitchen staff, scientists…even the grumpy doctor. She brought light wherever she went, but the recesses of his soul were too dark.

But that didn't mean they couldn't be friendly—that *he* couldn't be friendlier. Helena had checked on him. She'd kept the clinic functioning while he was ill. She'd done nothing but be an excellent nurse and kind to him.

And he'd pushed her away for reasons that were not her fault.

All because she'd known the person he'd been before, and she'd heard his nightmarish mutterings. People had a tendency to lash out at those who were closest to them. Those who should be the last people they hurt.

It was what his father had done to him. And Carter would not continue the terrible tradition. At the end of this winter rotation, they'd go their own ways, but for now they could be... His brain refused to provide an adequate term.

*Friends* seemed too dangerous. Even if part of his heart yearned for a return to the friendship they'd had once. But friendly...surely he could manage that?

That wouldn't be too difficult, right?

Carter stepped into the clinic before his brain could jump to all the reasons he should erect solid walls between him and Helena. Maybe it was that she'd known the person he used to be, or maybe it was that the hectic first week here had made the walls he'd used to keep everyone else out less effective against Helena. Either way, he owed her an apology and a fresh start.

Her head was bent over a laptop. He took a minute to breathe in the wonder that she was here. He'd run so far from Chicago, but the woman he'd never forgotten had wandered into his frozen clinic. A bit of his spirit lifted as she blew a piece of her short hair out of an eye.

*Helena Mathews...*

He was unable to keep his soul from smiling.

She looked up, and he saw a multitude of emotions pass across her face before she offered him a hesitant grin. He understood the hesitancy—he'd more than earned it.

"How are you feeling?"

"I'm fine." Carter closed the distance between them and took a deep breath. "I owe you an apology. I shouldn't have brought up your parents. That was unfair."

She closed the laptop and set it aside. "It was."

The truth sent an unexpected shot of hope through him. The young woman he'd known before would have offered a platitude…a lie…to make him feel better. It would likely have been done with the best intentions.

*No.* This was Helena Mathews sitting across from him. She only knew good intentions. But lying never led anywhere good.

"I am truly sorry. I just lashed out—I'd like to blame the virus or the fact that it exhausted me. But the truth is, your presence shocked me." He crossed his arms as she spun in the chair towards him. It didn't offer him much protection, but he'd needed the bit of distance it forced him to keep as her jade eyes met his.

She sighed, raised a brow and gestured to him. "Could you be any more walled off? I won't bite, Carter. You're the last person I expected to find at the South Pole. But I am grateful you're here."

He forced himself to unwrap, to loosen his shoulders. Tension radiated through him. This was definitely a crossroads. It felt like his life was tumbling from his carefully orchestrated isolation. And Carter wasn't sure if he liked the dance his heart was doing. But keeping Helena at the professional distance he kept with others wouldn't work.

Even if he thought he could do it, there was no doubt in Carter's mind that the woman before him wouldn't stand for it. So better to set the boundaries between them now. "I don't want to talk about Chicago. Or the reasons I left. Are you okay with that?"

Tiny lines pinched along Helena's forehead as she sized him up. "I think a lot can change over the next nine months. What I promise is that until you're ready, I won't bring it up."

"You can't fix me, Helena." He meant the words, even though part of him wished it wasn't the truth.

"Stubborn is a trait you haven't lost." Helena grinned as she leaned toward him. "I am not the same person I was in Chicago. We've each had a lifetime of experiences." Her fingers drifted to her side.

He saw her run her thumb along her hip before she looked at him. "We can't pretend that we don't have a history, but we don't have to focus on it. In fact—" she opened the laptop and flipped it around "—we can focus on something else. How would you feel about co-authoring a paper?"

"Paper?" He blinked, trying to understand the shift in the subject. Helena bounced in the chair, and her excitement was a balm to his frayed edges. Carter looked at the words on the screen and felt his mouth fall open. Viral Contact Tracing in Arctic Settings.

Under the headline were a bunch of notes and even a graph. How had she gotten so much done with the patient load? "Do you ever sleep?"

"Yes. But there is also a lot of downtime around here when there are no patients." Her cheeks colored as she bit her lip. "I am not complaining about the lack of patients. Promise. But idle hands and all."

That had been her parents' favorite statement. He remembered a cross-stitch of the words hanging in her mother's kitchen. So, the lessons she'd learned at home were still affecting her, too.

"There are only so many times you can do inventory."

Carter chuckled. She was right. "I am more than willing to help with the paper, but not as an author."

Helena's lips turned down, and he reached for a plausible excuse. Most people in their field would have jumped at the prospect to coauthor a paper. Particularly one with a colleague you respected, who'd already compiled some of the initial work. Once it was his greatest desire, even.

But his father read medical journals exclusively. Stacks of them sat in the corners of his childhood home. Articles his dad thought were important hung on the fridge—until his mother forced him to put them somewhere else. Most physicians read journals in their specialties—the field changed too quickly for you to be up-to-date on new procedures without them. But Drake Simpson read as many as he could fit into his life, across all specialties.

Carter had kept a distance between him and his father since he left. It would have been too easy to hope that once his temper cooled, he might regret what happened. A tiny piece of hope that his brain refused to acknowledge, and his heart refused to discard, still hovered deep inside him that one day...

He swallowed the hope pooling in his belly. This was why he never searched for the name Drake Simpson on the internet or looked up the roster of surgeons at Mercy Hospital. Even after years of isolation, it was too easy to give in to hope.

If Helena Mathews's and Carter Simpson's names appeared on a paper, there was a chance his father might see it. And if he looked at the stats on the journal and saw it had been read in Chicago—even with the size of the city, even with the number of physicians operating there—he'd wonder.

*And hope.*

And hope was too dangerous an emotion.

"You've done much of the initial work, Helena." He held up a hand as she frowned, hoping to forestall any interruption. "I will absolutely help. I think it's a brilliant idea, and I can be the first reviewer, of course. But this should be your accomplishment."

Helena bit her lip as she held his gaze. "Let's see if it goes anywhere first. Right now, it's just the initial notes I made while seeing patients and a chart of the infection rate. Nothing may come from it, but…" The words died away as she looked toward the door, then back at him. "We have months to work it all out."

"We do." Carter nodded, trying to ignore the tingle of excitement running along his skin. They had months together. "Do you still play chess?"

Her eyes lit up, and his heart jumped. The feeling stunned him as her lips parted. She stepped from behind the desk and practically danced across the room to her backpack hanging on a peg by the door. It was such a happy motion; it brought back a wave of memories of him and Owen and Helena playing together. Hanging out together…but it wasn't his long-lost best friend radiating through those memories.

How was he supposed to protect himself from her for so long?

He let that thought drift away as Helena held up a travel chess set. "You carry a chessboard with you?"

"It can be relaxing."

She beamed, and another part of the ice coating his soul melted. But Carter didn't worry about its loss.

# CHAPTER FIVE

"I THINK WE need a timeline of the start of the virus up front in the paper. It sets the stage for how quickly it could have gotten out of control if we hadn't instituted contact tracing immediately." Carter's head was close to hers as they stared at the bright laptop screen. Hints of his sandalwood shampoo trickled through her senses, and Helena felt a smile cross her lips.

Many things had changed. But he still used the same shampoo, still leaned close when a topic engrossed him, still pulled at the tip of his chin when he was deep in thought. Heat poured down her spine as his fingers brushed the back of her chair.

It stunned her, and it privately embarrassed her that she still remembered so much about the man standing next to her. It had been so long since they'd seen each other. They'd been friends, but it was Owen who'd held their band together. Owen and Carter had been inseparable, and when none of her friends were available, they usually let her tag along. But she'd been the third wheel.

Until they'd gone to college. And the night she'd shown up at their dorm room with an anatomy book had nearly changed everything.

Why was that memory the strongest one? There were hundreds, thousands of pleasant memories she could pull from her mind that involved Carter Simpson. But her brain only wanted to load the one where she was certain he was going to kiss her...until Owen barged in.

Owen wasn't here now, but Carter wasn't thinking of kissing her, either. Helena pulled at the back of her neck, conscious of how close her fingers were to his skin as he leaned over her shoulder. If he wasn't standing so close, she'd shake herself; she needed to focus on their paper. Even if her body seemed far too inclined to lean toward the tall man behind her. She was not the young woman enthralled by her brother's best friend anymore.

They were only colleagues now. Coresearchers on a paper. Close associates...all those definitions sent a stab through her chest. They were accurate descriptions—though remarkably unsatisfying.

"Helena?" Carter's hand brushed the edge of her shoulder as he shifted next to her. "If you don't like the timeline idea, we don't have to include it." He grinned as he leaned against the desk. "It's your paper, after all."

"Is it?" She chuckled and tapped the top of his thigh with the back of her hand. Sparks ran from the tip of her fingers to the base of her neck, and she prayed the heat in her cheeks hadn't turned into a full-blown blush.

The urge to touch him, to will a bit of the tension from him, had driven her crazy over the last few weeks. He was lonely; whether or not he stated it, she saw the subtle shifts in his body language when patients talked about their families. How he always left the room when the round of limited satellite phone time was being divided among the base staff for the coveted weekly calls. It was clear he hated the reminder that others had loved ones to call.

In those moments, Helena wished there were a way to pull him close. To remind him that no matter what had happened, there were people who cared about him. Owen still regularly searched social media hoping he'd find his friend's profile. Helena always looked over the staff rosters, wanting to find a Carter Simpson.

But there was no tension in Carter now. He was relaxed and grinning—a happy sight, to be sure. And a tap on his thigh was not a hug of comfort. It was...

Well, it was something she would not do again. If she could just get her body to behave.

"Of course it's your paper. I'm just a helper." He offered a mock salute as he leaned closer.

"But you always wanted to coauthor a paper. This is..."

"I think I hear something," Carter interrupted as he pulled away.

It took all her willpower not to frown...or call the statement a lie. She raised a brow, but Carter had already turned toward the door, perhaps hoping a patient might materialize. Anytime she'd brought up the idea that he was truly a coauthor on the paper, he'd redirect the conversation to something inane.

After all, he'd labeled the past off-limits and didn't want to discuss his contributions to the paper, and the South Pole didn't provide many new discussion opportunities when you spent the vast majority of each workday together, anyway.

But this time, Carter got lucky. Letitia walked through the door, her face tearstained.

Helena stood as Carter made his way to the climate scientist, but she looked at Helena, her eyes pleading. "Letitia? What's wrong?"

"I jammed my knuckle six months ago, and it swelled. It never fully went back to normal size." Her lip seized and tears pooled in her eyes again.

Carter lifted the hand she held out, and Helena saw Letitia's eyes flutter to the engagement ring on her finger before she bit her lip—hard.

"It is a little swollen. Sometimes the knuckle never fully returns to its former size. But are you still in pain? After six months, you shouldn't…"

"Carter. Let me," Helena interrupted. She remembered the desperate need to have the ring Kevin had given her off her hand after she'd learned of his infidelity. The metal had felt like it was burning as the truth had spilled from his lips. Her knuckle hadn't been swollen, but she'd still cut the inside of her ring finger with her thumbnail as she pulled the tarnished bauble from her hand.

"Have you tried lotion to get the ring off? Or soap?" She saw Carter shake his head and pinch the bridge of his nose out of the corner of her eye. It was a fair mistake to make; Letitia had looked like she was in pain when she walked through the door. And she was. But this was not a pain that one fixed with bandages or antibiotics.

Only time could lessen the impact of whatever had happened between Letitia and her fiancé.

"Yes." The sound was choked. "I still can't get it past the knuckle. I just want it off." The sob echoed off the clinic walls. "Sorry." Her cheeks colored as she realized how loud her distress was.

Helena reached for Letitia and pulled her into her arms. "It's fine. You have nothing to apologize for. I remember how much I wanted my ring off when my engagement ended." She saw Carter's head pop up on that statement, but Helena didn't let go of Letitia.

She rarely discussed her broken engagement or the dreams that had fallen apart with it, but Letitia needed to know she wasn't on her own. She'd felt desperately alone in those early days, like she'd failed, like there was something wrong with her because she couldn't be what Kevin wanted. Couldn't fix her body.

Broken engagements were far more common than people realized, but it felt like no one ever experienced it because there was no long, drawn-out legal separation like a divorce. You could just part with broken hearts, shattered dreams and a pile of baggage that you had to work hard to not carry around with you.

The woman sobbed into Helena's shoulder, and she rubbed her back and whispered platitudes she knew that Letitia wouldn't remember. The next few days and weeks might be a blur for Letitia, but she'd remember these few moments of comfort. And Helena hoped that would be enough.

It took several minutes, but eventually her cries became less intense. Carter stepped up and held up a box of dental floss. Helena patted the top of Letitia's head and smiled as the tearstained eyes met hers. "I promise, you are going to be all right. I know it doesn't feel that way right now. And it might not for a while, but a day will come when you realize that anyone who could make you weep like this wasn't worth it. Ready to try to get the ring off?"

Letitia's dark gaze hovered on the ring for a few moments before she nodded. "Yes. I want the cheater's cheap trinket off my hand." The brave words ended with a hiccuped sob, but the determination in Letitia's eyes made Helena happy. She'd find her footing without the person who'd caused her so much pain.

"I am so sorry, Letitia. But Helena is right. You're going to be okay, even if it doesn't feel like it now." Carter's voice was soft as he held up the pack of floss he'd shown her a few minutes before. "We're going to try the dental floss method first."

"I thought you would cut it off."

"That's more for the drama in television and movies. Dental floss is not exciting or sexy. Though a dentist might disagree." He offered her a playful wink.

Letitia let out a small chuckle and immediately covered her lips.

Helena knew it felt weird to laugh or smile when your heart was broken. But it was important to know you could. And Carter was giving her that knowledge, with dental floss.

Her lips tipped up as Carter carefully took Letitia's hand in his. For just a moment she wondered what it might be like for him to hold her hand. Then she shook herself. This was not the time or place for such thoughts.

Carter pulled the thread from the container. "I do have a ring cutter, but I would prefer not to use it unless we absolutely have to. While they are called ring cutters, they are really heavy-duty wire cutters, which can injure your finger. So we try this method first."

"If this—" Letitia gestured toward the floss, clearly uncertain this trick would work "—fails?"

"Then we'll cut it off and you can send the pieces back to your ex, if you'd like." Carter offered another wink as he threaded the floss under the ring.

A weepy smile fell across Letitia's face as she stared at the gold band with a giant diamond. "I wouldn't mind sending it back in pieces. That way he couldn't give it to…" Her strong words died away as the tears dripped down her cheeks. "Let's just get it off."

"Right." Carter threaded the end of the string through the band and then wrapped Letitia's finger tightly in dental floss.

"How is your research coming along this season?" His voice was soft as he unwrapped Letitia's finger with the end of the floss under the ring. It was an old trick that doctors often recommended people try at home. As you unwrapped the floss, it pulled the ring up the finger.

When Letitia didn't immediately answer, Carter asked again, "Are you having any luck with the ice core samples you gathered a few weeks ago?"

She shook herself and looked away from the ring just before it got to the base of her knuckle. "Oh, yes." Letitia launched into a scientific speech that flew over Helena's head. Carter nodded along, but she doubted he understood it much better than she did. The point was to get Letitia focused on something other than the ring sliding over her knuckle.

His words were light, completely unfocused on the trauma that Letitia had received. Carter may close himself off to others when he wasn't treating them, but the charming, caring boy she'd known popped through as soon as his patients needed care. Which meant he was still under the shell that Carter had built.

"Here it is." Carter held up the ring, and Letitia's face shifted. "I'm really sorry, Letitia. But I promise this feeling of loss will lessen with time." He dropped the ring in her outstretched hand.

Helena watched Letitia's fingers close around it, and her shoulders shuddered. Television programs often showed the end of the relationship. Then one episode where the hero or heroine ate a bucket of ice cream and cried, then they were magically ready to face the world again. Unfortunately, real-world emotional trauma didn't work like that.

"If you need anything, you let me know." Helena put an arm around her shoulders.

Letitia leaned her head against Helena's for a moment. "Thank you both. I'm going to go back to my room and try to…" Her words died away, but the tears didn't spill from her eyes. "Thank you," she repeated, then she strolled to the door.

Helena watched her go and made a mental note to check in on her over the next few days to see if she needed anything. She could provide a friendly ear to listen to complaints. And make sure that Letitia was handling the days well enough. While they weren't trained therapists, they'd each completed courses in mental health management, and if necessary, they could arrange a videoconference with a trained therapist for any of the base employees.

"That was rough, and it wasn't distinctly medical." Carter leaned against the desk again, his arms crossed as his dark gaze bored through her.

"You've worked in emergency departments, Carter. How many people stumble through there with non-medical emergencies?" He nodded as his eyes drifted away from hers. It wasn't possible to work in this field and not see people at their worst, and often it had little to do with the disease or injury ailing them.

"True." Carter nodded as she moved toward him. "You never know what you might get."

Emergency medicine was a mix of treating patients who were close to death—or sometimes battling to reverse death altogether—and treating injuries that belonged in a regular doctor's office, but the patient didn't have insurance or the office was closed or they just panicked and came to the ER. Then there were those in mental health crisis situations…one never knew what might occur in emergency medicine. You learned to roll with the punches or to find another line of work.

"Shall we get back to the paper?" Carter's eyes were bright as he met hers. His body was so close again, and again the urge to lean toward him pulled at her.

What was wrong with her?

She stared at the closed laptop for a moment, then looked at the clock. An escape hatch appeared, though her heart ached as her brain planned to use it. "Too close to dinnertime to pick it back up tonight. And I doubt we get any more patients before we put up the on-call notice." She grabbed the end-of-day checklist—even though she'd had it memorized since the first week she'd been here. It gave her a purpose. A reason to step away and put a bit of distance between them.

All too quickly they finished the daily chores, and they were at the door. This was the part of the day she hated. When Carter retired to his room and only peeked out for a quick bite of sustenance before reemerging the next morning at the clinic. How did he live such a lonely life...and was there a way for her to draw him out at all?

"Do you have any plans tonight?" He closed the door to the clinic and turned the key before pivoting to look at her.

Carter's words stunned her, and her tongue felt frozen to the roof of her mouth.

*At least it isn't hanging open.*

"Dinner, then maybe read for a bit." She was on call tonight, so no giant parties for her. Not that there were many, or any, massive parties at the South Pole.

"You up for a game of chess after dinner?"

His smile sent a thrill through her. "Sure."

"Then it's a date. See you around seven." Carter tipped his head her direction, then slid into his room next to the clinic.

*Date...* The word wrestled around Helena's brain

as she looked at his closed door. It was only a turn of phrase. A meaningless word. She knew that, but her heart still skipped more than it should. She had an hour to get that pesky organ under control before she showed up at Carter's.

An hour to fix what years hadn't…

*Date…*

The word refused to leave the echo chamber of his brain as Carter looked over the small dorm room one more time. He was an inherently tidy person, but he'd still spent the better part of the last hour picking up the few items he had and dusting. He sighed as he looked at the chess set in the middle of the room.

The chairs were nearly touching, but there was no other way to arrange them. The berth was not really meant for entertaining. If he'd been thinking, he'd have invited her to play in the game room…better yet, left the invitation unstated in his mind.

He'd been thinking the words, and they'd spilled out before he could weigh his options. But once it had been made, Carter hadn't wanted to withdraw the offer. And he certainly hadn't wanted to move the location. Helena was incredibly popular among the staff. Even if she hadn't climbed through a busted window to rescue Kelly on her first day or nursed nearly half of the staff through a stomach virus, she ate with the staff each day, listened to everyone and always made sure she was available. In short, she was the caring, selfless Helena she'd been years ago. Of course everyone enjoyed being around her—and he wasn't willing to share her tonight.

But this was not a date. It was two friends playing a game of chess. Except the more time he spent with Helena, the more he wanted—

*No.* He would not let his brain travel that well-worn path. He was enjoying reconnecting with her. Enjoying seeing her as the woman she was meant to be. The nurse and healer.

And if he looked forward to spending each day with her, to working on their paper together, to being close to her, that was just because…

No words came as he tried to justify his heart's need to be close to Helena. He enjoyed watching her head tilt to the left when she was trying to figure out something important with the paper they were working on. Or the hop that she had mastered to grab the items off the top shelf of the clinic's storage cupboard. How she smelled of something sweet that his brain had yet to place.

The only problem was that he was looking forward to seeing her. On the days when he made it to the clinic before she did—which was a shockingly rare occurrence—he monitored the door until she came. Each new sound, his senses were always on high alert waiting for her.

It was disconcerting. Carter hadn't looked forward to seeing anyone in so long. Hadn't let himself.

Carter wanted to believe that he could just go back to his hermit ways anytime he wanted. But the shift in him seemed to be taking root. It was terrifying. If he was thinking clearly, he should probably ask Helena to reschedule tonight…then not. But that avenue held no appeal at all.

Plus, he wanted to know more about what he'd learned today. They'd both had failed engagements. Both lost a person who they thought, at least at one point, was the one to complete them. He'd retreated even further from the world after Laura had cheated on him, but Helena still seemed open. How did the woman look at the world through such rosy glasses?

When she'd hugged Letitia today, Carter had yearned to feel those arms wrap around him. He'd coveted the hugs she gave whenever someone needed one, even though he had no right. But she never hugged him.

Because they were colleagues. Partners. And he was technically the senior medical professional. Not that it meant much, since the director of the polar staff was who they each reported to. The medical professional with the most polar experience was considered the senior on the team; his first year on the ice, the nurse practitioner had been the senior.

He didn't need the comfort of a hug. But he wanted one.

Wanted to feel connected to others. The seed of hope that his soul hadn't managed to darken was spreading across him. He didn't know how to stop its growth. And even if he did, Carter wasn't sure that he would want to.

That was a truth that he didn't know how to deal with.

A knock echoed on the door, and Carter's stomach rumbled as nervous energy pulsed through him. A quick glance at his watch told him he'd missed dinner. He'd dig up a few of the snacks he had after Helena left. His stomach growled again as his fingers reached for the door.

Or maybe before they played.

Swinging open the door, his breath caught in the back of his throat as he met the jade eyes standing a few feet away. Instead of scrubs, she now wore a pair of jeans and an oversize purple flannel shirt. Her short hair had a small clip in the side. It was simple and mouthwatering.

His stomach let out a loud growl, and heat burned down his neck. What an awkward way to start this evening. But it shouldn't matter, since this was not a date. *It isn't...*

She smiled, shook her head, and her gaze wandered to his stomach. "You didn't come to the canteen for dinner."

"I lost track of time." It was the truth. He'd spent the entire last hour picking up the already-clean room, attempting to convince himself that he wasn't trying to make a good impression despite all the evidence to the contrary. "I have a few granola bars and crackers in here. It'll be enough to keep my stomach from interjecting too much during our game."

"Or—" Helena smiled as she pulled one of the to-go boxes from behind her back "—you could eat a proper dinner before I kick your butt in chess."

The smell of pasta wafted from the paper container, and his mouth watered. "You brought me dinner?" Blood pounded through his ears as he stared at the metal container and pack of silverware on the top. His breath caught at the simple gesture. Carter couldn't remember the last time someone had looked out for him.

His throat closed as he looked at the box. "I can't believe you brought me dinner."

"Of course." She brightened as she stepped into the room. "I enjoy taking care of people." She winked. "Probably one reason I like being a nurse so much."

A bit of the warmth leaked from his core. Helena was a fixer. This was her taking care of others, making sure that they were happy, no matter the cost to herself. And she'd try to fix him. But he couldn't be fixed. He needed to remember that.

Swallowing the lump at the back of his throat, Carter flipped open the box and took out the thick slice of garlic bread. He took a bite. It tasted fantastic, and another piece of his ice shell melted.

*Is it such a bad thing for others to care about you?*

The thought should have sent a river of worry through him, but as Helena's gaze met his, it was impossible for his brain to manifest it. This was just someone caring for a friend. It didn't have to end in heartache. Particularly since they were just playing chess. As colleagues.

*Nothing more.*

He tried to ignore the bead of laughter in the back of his brain at that rationale. He wanted more with Helena. He wasn't sure why, and wasn't going to reach for it, but maybe acknowledging it would help him set it aside.

"Do you prefer to play as white or black?" She was so close in the tight confines that it would be easy to brush against her. Easy to lean over and push the small piece of hair from her forehead. Easy to see if each of the little touches and blushes his brain had registered over the last weeks meant what his heart hoped. If her heart tracked the few times their bodies connected. If she still wondered *what if*? None of those were fair questions, and that wasn't what tonight was. But part of him wished it was.

"Either is fine for me." Carter gestured for her to take whichever seat she wanted at the board. Some players had a preference. He'd worked with a doctor in Boston who swore that he never lost a game when he started as the black player. But Carter had never developed any preference.

She sat behind the white, and he watched her shoulders relax.

"Do you prefer to start the board with the white pieces?"

Pink trailed along her cheekbones as she shrugged. "Owen and I always started our games with him playing the black pieces and me here. I guess I just feel more comfortable..." She let the words die away.

"So, you *do* have a preference." Carter scooped another pile of pasta into his mouth as he watched her.

"I guess." Helena sighed. "But if you had wanted to start here then it's not like I care that much."

But she cared some. The woman before him had stepped away from her family's expectations. Stepped out on her own, but she still wanted to make others happy. Still would put others before herself on even minor things.

"It's okay to state your preferences."

She flinched.

If he could have reeled the words back in, Carter would have. But they weren't wrong.

"I understand that, Carter. But this is a silly thing that my twin and I did when we were growing up. It is not that big a deal." The tip of her nose shifted as her lips pulled to the side. "Sometimes it's okay to make others happy just for the sake of making them happy."

She swallowed, then moved her first piece. "But quarreling is not how either of us wants to spend our evening. So, your turn."

Carter let the pinch of worry slip away as he took up the seat across from her. She was right; he did not want to spend the evening arguing. "Thank you for dinner, Helena."

"Anytime. Though we would love for you to come to the canteen to eat with us."

He moved his piece and hit the clock. "We?" Carter did not appreciate the string of jealousy snaking its way across his back. He had no claim on Helena. In fact, he'd encouraged her to make friends, wanted it to happen only weeks ago. Still wanted it. But part of him also wanted her to himself.

The wrestling between his heart and brain was sending him into a tailspin.

"The support staff." Helena smiled as she moved her next piece.

He studied the board for a moment before looking up at her. "There are around thirty support staff here, Helena."

"Thirty-two, actually. That includes the two of us." She studied the board, tilting her head one way then another before selecting her next move. "And twenty-three scientists for a grand total of fifty-five winter residents."

"I've eaten a meal with every member of the support staff except for you." She raised a brow as he held up the now empty to-go container. "No, that does not count."

"I guess that is true." Carter grinned as he set the container aside. "A meal together has to include dessert."

A chuckle escaped her lips, and Carter felt his heart rate escalate as the beautiful sound echoed through his room. The deep vocals made him happier than he'd been in forever. Happier than he had any right to be. He tried to memorize the notes so that he could replay them the next time he was feeling lonely.

"Funny you should mention that."

As she pulled two cookies with chunks of white chocolate from her shirt pocket, he felt his mouth fall open. The kitchen staff made white chocolate macadamia nut cookies only a handful of times during the winter season.

She passed him both and held up her hand as he handed her one back. "I'm fine. I always check the dessert selection. They are your favorite, and Kelly said she didn't know when the staff would make more. You were the only kid I knew who wanted cookies instead of cake at their birthday." She winked.

"I haven't had a birthday celebration..." He barely caught the words, but he saw recognition fly across Helena's features. Luckily, she said nothing.

Carter looked at the cookies, tiny treasures in the frozen wasteland, and then pushed one across the chessboard to her. "Please share with me. A silly toast with cookies." He held up his, then waited for her to pick up the other.

"To old friends." Carter beamed.

"And new futures," Helena added before taking a bite of her cookie.

"And new futures," Carter repeated before taking a bite of his cookie, too.

*New futures.*

Such loaded words with dozens of meanings. His knee shifted, and it grazed the edge of her leg. He nearly jumped as sparks of need flew across his body.

"Thanks for sharing. I miss easy access to an oven. Not that I ever baked much, but it's funny the things you miss when you can't do it. I felt the same way when I was deployed..."

Her voice trailed off as she studied the chessboard again.

"I always miss swimming." He laughed as her head popped up. "I know. It's something that I ever really did, but the ability to go to a pool and swim a few laps.

Or splash around like we did at the community pool a few minutes from our neighborhood."

His throat closed as the easy reference to their childhood popped from his brain to his mouth. He hadn't meant to bring that up. This was what he worried about with Helena, that it would be too easy to slip into the familiar. Too easy to travel through memories better left in the recesses of his subconscious. Those were the dreams he'd had for years. But now the real woman was before him.

His body leaned forward without conscious thought as he watched her study the chessboard.

"That place closed down two summers ago. I guess too many people now have their own inflatable pools—including Owen. His kids spend all summer in the one in his backyard." She blew a piece of blond bangs from her eyes.

Carter reached over without thinking and pushed the stray lock to the side. Heat tore between them. At least it poured through him as he stared at the beauty before him. The urge to lean even closer, to drop his lips to hers, to see if what had ignited between them all those years ago still smoldered, nearly overtook him. She was so close. So lovely.

The crinkles around her eyes deepened as she grinned at him. It took all his control to hold himself still.

Helena tilted her head, studying him for just a moment.

What was she thinking?

Then her grin expanded to a brilliant smile and the room lit up as she shifted her final piece. "Checkmate."

He blinked as she pulled back from the board. From him.

For a moment he'd thought…well, it didn't matter

what he thought. This was a friendly chess game. Except that he didn't believe that anymore.

Did she feel the electricity bouncing between them?

His eyes wandered to the board; his king was in the smothered mate with her knight in the perfect position. "Nicely done." He tilted his king to its side and leaned closer. "I demand a rematch."

"Of course." Helena closed a little of the distance between them, and Carter's heart twisted as it urged him to bridge the final space between them. He swallowed that urge and shifted away as he reset the board.

"I like your hair." He wanted to hit his head as she put her pieces back in their starting positions. He'd been searching for a safe topic that would adjust the energy between them, but the hair comment was a definite conversational fumble.

"I just mean it's so different. It was always in braids and…" He blew out a breath as he looked at her. "It suits you, Helena."

"Thank you. I fear it was a very clichéd breakup move. When Kevin and I ended our engagement two years ago, I chopped all my hair off. Much to my surprise I loved it, though my mother let me know she didn't share that opinion."

"I'm sorry that they don't seem to accept your choices." It was another phrase that Carter wished he'd kept in his mind, but it was true. It was a shame that the Mathewses couldn't see the amazing woman their daughter was—just as she was.

"They will."

The certainty in her voice sent a wave of emotion passing through him he didn't know how to explain. It was a mix of hope, coupled with the fatalism that had been his constant companion for years.

"If anyone can make them." He grinned. "After all, you're perfect."

"Please don't call me that."

"Why not?" Her features shifted, and Carter wanted to force his brain to stop finding all the wrong words. He hated the frown dancing across her delicate features. Hated that he'd put it there. But she was perfect.

She bit her lip as her gaze held his. "Kevin used to call me that. All the time. Then once I wasn't…" She shook her head. "Perfection is something no one can live up to."

"Helena…"

"It's okay, Carter. You didn't mean anything by it." Her smile was brighter than it should be, and he saw the effort it took her to make it. As much as he hated the frown, he preferred it to the false smile. He never wanted her to feel she had to pretend around him. But he had no idea how to voice that.

He reached for her hand and was grateful when she didn't pull back from his squeeze.

"You always find the best in others. Even if they don't deserve it." Carter sighed as he let his thumb run along the side of her palm.

She shook her head. "That makes me sound like a veritable saint, and it's not true. There are a few people I don't see the best in."

"Hard to believe."

A snort echoed in the room, "My ex-fiancé didn't have a ton of redeeming qualities. Which I did not discover until—" She hiccuped and shook her head. "Well, too late."

He'd found out too late about Laura, too. "My fiancée cheated with my friend Brian. He and I were roommates during residency. I thought…well, I didn't expect my friend and fiancée to betray me. She blamed me for being too distant. Which was partly true."

Her fingers wrapped around his. It was such a simple action, but it felt so much more personal than the loose grip they'd maintained before. "I am so sorry. Even if you were distant, that isn't an excuse."

"Well." Carter shrugged. It had bothered him for so long, but tonight, with Helena's hand resting in his, the wound in his soul felt tiny. "Did your ex have an excuse?"

Her eyes shifted and the fingers on her free hand drifted to her side again. "He did."

What was with his loose tongue tonight?

"I am so sorry, Helena. I shouldn't have asked. I swear, I am not normally this talkative and I never ask probing questions. You just…"

Her face brightened as she wrapped her fingers through his again. "If it helps you come out of your ice shell, Dr. Simpson, I'll take all the personal questions. I just might not answer all of them."

She pulled her hand back, and he hated the loss of her heat, of her touch—even as her words sent a flash of panic down his spine. She was trying to get him to come out of his shell, and it was working.

"Are you ready for me to beat you again?" She moved a pawn.

Pushing the panic, excitement and need to the back of his mind, Carter moved his first piece, too, conscious that she'd shifted her legs, so they tilted away from him. And her free hand was in her lap, too. Out of his reach. Which was fine…better than fine. But it left him feeling oddly bereft.

# CHAPTER SIX

A SOUND ECHOED in the hallway, and Carter spun his chair to face the door of the clinic. He waited, but Helena didn't walk through the door, so he tried to return his focus to the words in Keith's email. Their shift didn't start for another fifteen minutes, but he'd been here for almost an hour.

He'd tossed and turned all night. The few times that he'd fallen asleep, he'd dreamed that he'd leaned forward to kiss Helena. And his dream had ended the same way each time, with him pulling back just before his lips met hers. It was deeply unsatisfying and disconcerting and not conducive to resting at all.

For the millionth time, his brain reminded him that he'd sworn not to get close to Helena—at least not in any way that was more than as a friendly colleague. But his heart wasn't interested in listening to the rationale.

"Good morning, Carter." Helena's voice was bright as she stepped into the clinic carrying a blueberry muffin and a yogurt smoothie. "You're early today." She playfully glanced at the clock as she sipped her smoothie.

"Or you're late." Carter chuckled as she wagged a finger in his direction. It was a motion she'd done so often when they were young. It had always made him and Owen laugh, because she was never cross with anyone. The motion was adorable, and so Helena.

"I am never late." She pulled another yogurt smoothie from her backpack. "I swear I am constantly hungry!"

"It's the pole. Those of us who work in the main building need to up our calorie load by about five hundred just to maintain weight, and the supply runners need to eat around six thousand calories a day."

Carter had to constantly remind people they needed to eat enough calories, particularly the building staff. It was easy to get used to the cooler temps in the building and not realize that your body was working harder to keep you warm.

She leaned against the desk next to him and took another sip of the smoothie. "I remember that from the orientation packet, but you don't realize how true it is until you're on the ice!" She put the lid on the smoothie cup. Her fingers were millimeters from his.

It was ridiculous how much his pinkie ached to close the minuscule distance. His heart longed to throw years of caution away and take a chance. His throat was dry as she leaned closer to look at the screen, then pulled back quickly.

"Sorry, Carter. I thought you might have pulled our research paper off the server. I didn't mean to look at a private email." Her cheeks colored as she straightened. "There was no reason for me to think that. I just…"

"It's fine. Just a note from Keith." Carter grinned and tapped the file where the paper was located. "And it's not like we haven't started each morning with a quick look at it at least."

Carter had found Helena at the computer typing away most mornings when he entered the clinic. They'd spend the first thirty minutes of the day going over her notes, then any time left after they'd completed their regular work. On days when there were few or no patients, they could manage a few hours of work at least. It was his favorite time of the day. Uninterrupted minutes, hours with her.

Sure, had they been anywhere else, the draft would have taken months when combined with patient load, paperwork and the other dozens of tasks that landed in medical professionals' laps outside of Antarctica. But Carter would have worked on anything if it meant spending time with Helena.

"Does the director need anything?" Helena pulled a notepad from the top drawer of the desk and started a to-do list. When he was not on the ice, Carter kept a small list on his phone that he often forgot to check throughout the day—or week. But Helena always made a list first thing in the morning with the tasks for the day.

He often found them on the edge of the desk or on the shelves in the supply closet or saw them sticking out of the back pocket of her scrubs. She carefully arranged little boxes next to each item that had to be done. And the list always started the same way: *Do something good for someone.*

And it was never checked because Helena said you could always do more than one good thing. It was such the perfect Helena response. The perfect human response. The world would be so much better if everyone looked at their to-do list in such a way.

"Keith was making sure that I am playing nice with the nurse practitioner." Carter overemphasized his sigh as he looked at Helena. "Not sure if you've heard, but I've got a bit of a reputation for being grumpy."

"I was warned. I was expecting a nightmare, instead—" She gestured to him, opened her mouth and closed it as she studied him.

Finally, she continued, "Instead I got an old friend I dearly missed."

Carter swallowed the lump lying in his throat as he met her gaze. Such a simple statement. The knowledge that she'd missed him. That someone had cared when he left Chicago knit together another piece of his soul. It had been so much easier to breathe since she'd stepped off the plane, easier to remember the person he'd been. He'd missed her, too. So much.

And he didn't want to hide that fact away. "I missed you, too. I'm glad you're the one who walked off that LC-130." The truth landed between them, and he didn't pull it back. He wanted her to know, needed her to know, that he was happy she was here.

He hadn't known that he wanted a different experience, hadn't known that he craved it. But Carter couldn't imagine anyone else joining him on the ice now.

"You seem to be buttering me up." Her nose twitched as she smiled. "Is there some duty you don't want to do or a favor you need?"

"No." Carter held her gaze, not wanting there to be any room for misunderstanding. "I am thrilled you're here." His fingers itched to push the loose piece of hair away from her eye again. But he resisted. Barely.

"Carter…"

His name on her lips made him want to sing. For the hundredth time, he wished he'd asked to kiss her last night. Wished he'd spent the evening without the chessboard between them. "What are you doing tonight?"

The door to the clinic swung open before she could answer, and Carter pushed back from the desk. He wasn't sure where this path he was on was leading. But he wanted to go down it. At least a little way.

"Letitia?" Helena was by her side quickly as the woman wrapped her arms tightly across her belly.

*Not another round of infections.*

"Have you gotten sick at all?" Carter pulled a tablet from the charger as Helena led Letitia to a bed.

"It's not my stomach." The climate scientist teared up as she rubbed her abdomen. "I think I have an ovarian cyst." Her lip trembled as she closed her eyes. "I felt the pain last night, and this morning, too."

"How many have you had?" Carter kept his voice low, soothing. Letitia had been through so much lately.

"Three." Letitia's gaze floated from Helena's to Carter's, and she nodded for her to keep going.

Carter caught Helena's gaze and quickly held up the tablet to indicate that he'd take notes while she talked to Letitia. It didn't bother him that Letitia was more comfortable talking to Helena. Unfortunately, many male physicians had a history of minimizing female pain or assigning any complaint to hormones.

"Did any of them rupture?" Helena asked as she looked over at the ultrasound machine.

"No."

He let out a sigh of relief as he went to grab the machine. Most cysts disappeared on their own; ruptured cysts often caused pain, sometimes severe. But in rare instances they could cause internal bleeding that needed emergency surgical intervention, an intervention his clinic could not give.

"But I had surgery to remove one." Letitia let out a sob and covered her mouth with her fist. "I got an infection, and the ovary had to be removed. So I only have one left…" Tears rolled down her cheeks as she stared at the ceiling.

She hiccuped and sucked in a deep breath. "My doctor said I should still be able to have children. But Mark said he wasn't sure he wanted to be with someone who wasn't sure they could be a mother. At least that was the excuse he threw out when my sister let me know she'd seen him at a restaurant with another woman."

Carter shook his head. "Letitia, I am so sorry. That was a callous statement in the extreme and almost certainly his way of deflecting blame."

Helena met his gaze and offered a small smile.

"So I'll have children?" Letitia bit her lip as her eyes watered.

As a doctor, he wanted to reassure her that she'd be fine, but the truth was more complicated. The gender gap in the research fields resulted in most studies being focused on males, since most researchers were male. It left an entire landscape of medical unknowns in half the population.

Carter sat on the edge of the bed. "Fertility is an area of medicine with so many unknowns. Women with only one ovary get pregnant routinely, and women with two struggle sometimes."

He handed her a tissue as she sniffled. "Sorry."

"For being emotional during a trying time? There is no need to apologize for that, Letitia. You have gone through a lot, and I wish I could alleviate all your fears, but that wouldn't be honest."

"And there are many routes to parenthood." Helena stated, but there was a shift in her voice as she looked from their patient to the ultrasound machine. "Let's take a look."

Letitia nodded and lifted her shirt. Helena dropped

a dollop of gel along her stomach and rolled the ultrasound over her lower belly.

The ovarian cyst was easy to locate. It measured less than four centimeters. That was excellent news. Cysts four centimeters or larger were more likely to rupture and to need surgical intervention. He heard Helena let out a soft sigh as she looked at the ultrasound measurements, too. Clearly he wasn't the only one feeling relief at the sight of the small cyst.

"You were right—there is a cyst." Carter pointed to the fuzzy object at the base of Letitia's ovary. "It's two and a half centimeters. So your body should reabsorb it. But I want to follow up in three months to make sure that it hasn't gotten any larger. And if you have any concerns or pain, come back. We'll check it again. Any time you want," Carter reassured her.

Their patient dropped her gaze to her abdomen and stroked her belly. "He didn't like the look of my scar." Letitia's words were so quiet, Carter nearly missed them.

The scar was barely noticeable. In fact, if Letitia hadn't dropped her fingers to it, Carter would have missed it completely. In a few years, it would lighten up. "That's nothing." Carter nodded. "Promise. It's not like you have a giant scar across your abdomen."

He saw Helena flinch. He looked over at her, but she didn't meet his gaze. They were with a patient, but something in her body posture sent a tingle down his spine. Her shoulders were straight, and she was blinking quickly.

Was she blinking away tears?

Something was wrong. Her lips were pressed tightly together even as she held Letitia's hand.

"It's a small cyst," Carter added, as he monitored

Helena's reactions, too. "It shouldn't be a problem, but don't lift anything over fifty pounds until we are certain that it has cleared. We'll provide some pain medication for you, too."

Letitia sat up and crossed her legs. "I never really thought about children. I thought maybe one day. Then when I lost the ovary—I don't know. It made me think maybe I really wanted a few mini-mes running around."

"That's only natural," Carter stated. He'd never really thought of kids, either. His mother had always seemed more interested in the role of Mom than actually being a mom. And his father's love...well, it had been contingent on genetics, apparently. He wasn't sure that translated well into him being a good father, but Helena was right. There were many paths to parenthood.

Carter waited until Letitia met his gaze. "Do you think talking to a counselor might help with the stress you're experiencing? Talking about the end of your engagement. Your fertility concerns? You do not have to provide an answer, but think about it."

"Speaking to a professional regarding the end of your relationship and your fears about fertility is a good idea." Helena backed him up, but she still didn't meet his gaze. "And about the body image issues your scar has caused."

*Body image...*

Carter blinked. Over that tiny scar? He would never have considered it a problem, but Helena recognized it. Because she saw what others needed. He offered her a quick smile. If Letitia would benefit from therapy through telemedicine, for whatever reason, he'd support it.

Letitia shrugged, her fingers returning to the small

scar again, even though her shirt now covered it. "I guess talking to someone couldn't hurt."

"Excellent." Carter jotted a quick note in the tablet. Just making the choice to get some help should be celebrated. "It's really easy—I'll send you the link. If there is anything else he needs, Dr. Martinez will let me know so we can help you feel a little more balanced."

She hopped off the bed and took the notes regarding care that Helena had prepped with lightning speed. "Thank you both." Then she was gone.

"I would never have thought that little scar would bother anyone." Carter rolled the ultrasound machine back to the corner.

Helena was bent over a pile of notes when he looked back. She didn't look up as she answered, "Little is in the beholder's eye. Particularly, if the person you care about points it out—as her ex clearly did."

"I guess," he mused. What Helena said was true, but scars were not something Carter usually considered— at least not physical ones. "I mean, if it fully covered her belly or was pucker—"

Helena flinched again, and he caught the last words. *Oh no.* The comment about the tiny mark on her cheek not mattering. The blinking away tears. The failed engagement. The puzzle pieces clicked into place.

"Helena?" She didn't look up, and he didn't know how to bridge this gap. No matter what, she was still Helena, still her caring, smart, wonderfully beautiful self. But what if she didn't think that?

When she said nothing, Carter cleared his throat and started down another path. Maybe a change of subject could lighten the tension he saw pooling through her? He'd do anything to make her more comfortable.

"Do you remember joining Owen and me on our make-believe trips?"

She grinned as she finally met his gaze. "I do. I think alien invasion was your favorite, and Owen preferred ghost hunters."

Grateful to be on steadier ground, Carter laughed. "I did like alien invasions. But I was actually thinking of the pretend kids you made us save all the time."

She bit her lip and her eyes darted away.

They were the wrong words…again. His brain reached for another option. Another way to put her at ease, but it refused to produce any workable ideas.

Helena's bottom lip disappeared as she focused on the papers. Then she grabbed a tablet and nodded. "I am going to handle the weekly inventory."

He didn't remind her that they'd completed that job less than three days ago. The inventory wasn't due for five days. But he knew a brush-off. Heaven knew he'd mastered them. Something was bothering Helena—something that he was nearly certain he'd caused.

Helena had hidden in the supply closet for most of their shift. She wasn't proud of the choice, but she was grateful that Carter hadn't tried to bust her out of the shell she'd retreated behind. Though a tiny part of her had wished he might ask what was going on.

But how did she put into words the tumble of emotions rolling through her? That she'd hoped he would kiss her last night. Actually expected it when he pushed the piece of loose hair from her forehead. That she'd enjoyed their morning banter and hope had poured through her when he'd asked again what she was doing tonight. Like there were a ton of options at the South

Pole base. That she was excited about what might be bubbling under the surface between her and Carter.

*And terrified.*

Standing before the mirror attached to the door of her closet, Helena lifted the top of her shirt. The scar was the first thing she noticed. The first thing anyone would notice—and it wasn't even the full thing. A piece from the vehicle she'd been riding in had torn across her abdomen as the truck had rolled. At least that was what she'd been told.

The day's events, and the weeks after, were a haze of foggy memories. Floating in and out of pain, bright hospital lights, noises she could never quite place. She'd been lucky. Helena knew that deep down, but the look on Kevin's face when he'd seen the damage. The bright red scar puckered around the edges was an image seared into Helena's memory.

When she'd called her parents to explain that her engagement was off, her mother had sobbed and promised she could come home. That they'd help in any way she needed. Then she'd said the damage was not something Helena could fix, not completely. That part of her would always be broken.

*Broken.* That was the word she kept rolling around her mind. Her parents were used to taking care of her. They saw it as part of their commitment to being good parents. It was born of love but suffocating. She didn't want to be taken care of. She wanted to be seen. To be loved for the woman she was now.

Blowing out a breath, she tried to push the feelings away. Usually she could force them into the background. But over the last few weeks, they'd pop in uninvited. Always when she was thinking of Carter.

It was just a scar. Tears coated her eyes as she pulled

the rest of her shirt up. The last bit of the scar was buried under the top of her jeans. Impossible to fully see unless she was naked. Which she almost never was.

He'd told Letitia it shouldn't matter. He'd been so caring and understanding with her fears and backed Helena up when she said there were many paths to parenthood. He was so thoughtful with his patients, so understanding when he let you past the walls life had built around him. But this wasn't a tiny thing. Kevin had said that, and her family had reinforced it.

"You're being ridiculous!" Helena pulled the shirt down and shook herself. It didn't matter that she wasn't perfect. Anyone worthy of her wouldn't mind…except she'd thought her ex-fiancé wouldn't care. That he'd just be happy she survived.

The buzzer on her watch vibrated. Dinnertime. She looked at her door and tried to force her happy self out. But she didn't want to see anyone right now.

Helena shook her head as she met her gaze in the mirror. That was a lie. She wanted to see Carter. To apologize for being so distant today. To tell him why.

*Or maybe not.*

But he wouldn't be in the cafeteria, at least not for long.

Perhaps it was cowardice. She was going to be at the pole for months still; there were going to be days when she didn't feel like the happy, perky Helena that everyone knew. People would understand, but she didn't want to face the team today.

Lying down on the small bed, she grabbed a book and ignored the grumble in her belly. She'd eat a giant breakfast tomorrow morning. And there were granola bars in her closet if she got desperate.

* * *

A knock echoed on her door, and Helena looked at the clock before setting her book aside. Seven thirty. She wasn't the medical staff person on call tonight, but if Letitia had questions, she might feel more comfortable coming to her. For a second, she hoped it might be Carter. That he'd noticed she wasn't at dinner and sought her out.

It was ridiculous, particularly because she still hadn't coaxed him out of his own room at mealtimes. Though she hoped he might join the team in a week or two. His ice wall was melting. And she loved seeing each piece fall away.

Pulling the door open, she felt her eyes widen as Carter stood before her. "What are you doing here?"

She barely caught herself before she slapped her forehead. After mentally running through the reasons it wouldn't be Carter, but hoping that it was, she was being rude. "Sorry. I just thought it might be Letitia, or someone looking for medical care."

"You aren't the medic on call, but I have the walkie-talkie in case anyone comes looking for me."

"Why are you here?" She hadn't meant to let that question slip out, either. Letitia's worry about her scars and fertility were cutting too close to Helena's own issues. Her confidence was shaken, and she needed time to put herself back together.

At least as much as she could.

"You skipped dinner." Carter held up a to-go box from the cafeteria, identical to the one she'd brought him just one night before.

*Isn't time supposed to slow at the South Pole?*

She'd been on the ice for about a month now, and it had all seemed to race by.

Reaching for the food, Helena's mouth watered as she lifted the lid and stared at the pork chop, salad and fruit cup. It smelled heavenly. "Thank you, but how did you know?"

"We all waited for you to come down, but around seven, I explained that you'd had a long day and perhaps were hibernating."

"You went to dinner?" Helena was stunned, thrilled and frustrated she'd let her sullenness win. This was why she did her best to ignore the pain her past caused. It could make you miss so much. "I'm sorry I was weird this afternoon. I just…" She blew out a breath and gestured into oblivion, unsure how to explain. Carter slid into her desk chair as she crossed her legs on the bed and started eating.

"It's fine." He grinned as he looked at her. "I am usually the standoffish one. It's nice to be on the fixing side of things."

She raised an eyebrow as she took a sip of water.

He tapped his arms on his knees. "Don't pretend you don't fix things. I've known you since we were six. You make others happy, and you're excellent at it. You're perfect, even if you don't like the word."

*Perfect.*

A lump rose in her throat as the word echoed in the room. *Perfect*…she hated that word. Hated that it was the first descriptor people had used for her. Perfect, flawless Helena who was so pretty…until a piece of a truck's window destroyed her abdomen. Perfect Helena, who never disobeyed her parents…until she did. *Perfect* was not an adjective that could be ascribed to her, at least not anymore.

"I'm far from perfect, Carter." She bit her lip before she forced herself to take a drink of water. "No more flawless Helena." God, that was the whiniest statement ever. She needed to get it together.

Carter sat still in the corner of the room, quiet as his eyes raked over her. "Where is your scar?"

The fork fell from her fingers as his question hammered through her. "I…" No words came as he slid in front of her.

He lifted the empty dinner plate from her lap and placed the dirty fork on it before he put it on the tiny nightstand. "I saw your reaction to Letitia's scar, how you recognized the way it made her feel. Because you felt…feel that way." He took a deep breath as he pulled her to her feet. "You flinched when I mentioned how little her scar was, barely noticeable. I'm guessing that's because yours isn't."

Carter's fingers were warm as they traced the healed cut on her cheek. "You said the first day that this wouldn't be your first scar." He stepped back and shook his head. "I know how much emphasis your family put on your appearance. How your mom called you delicate and ethereal. But no scar changes your perfection, Helena. Because it has nothing to do with how you look."

Her heart hammered as he pulled her into a hug. His arms were tight around her as she let the comfort flow through her. How long had it been since someone had hugged her? She hugged people all the time, offered comfort, but it was always her giving.

Laying her head against Carter's shoulder, she let out a giant sigh. She could stay in this embrace for forever. "I was in an accident in Iraq. A car crossed a road median and my driver overcorrected. So normal, an all-too-regular occurrence every day all over the world. The vehicle rolled and glass cut across my abdomen. It's…" She stepped out of his arms and took a step back.

She lifted the top of her shirt just enough so he could see some of it. She heard his breath hitch, but Helena kept her face turned to the floor. Her ex-fiancé's reaction had torn her to pieces. She didn't want to watch Carter's face. Couldn't.

"How far does it go?" His voice was soft, but the words were heavy.

She drew a line from just below her pelvic bone on her left to under her rib cage on the right. "The wound got infected, and I had multiple surgeries while the doctors worked to save my life. Including a complete hysterectomy."

Helena raised her chin as she finally met his gaze. "My ex couldn't look at me after. He, well, he used it as a reason for his infidelity—while I was still in physical therapy. I moved back in with my parents, so I had help while I rebuilt all the muscle I lost during the months in the hospital. So, no, Carter, I am not perfect. I'm broken."

The words tore through her, but it felt cathartic to say them. *Out loud.*

Her entire life she'd been groomed to be the pretty, sheltered face of the Mathews family. Even after she'd broken with her family's expectations, her mother and father had hoped that she'd come around. That she'd move next door, marry and have a few grandkids for them to chase around the backyard.

And part of her had wanted that, too. Not next door, and maybe a yard full of puppies instead of kids. But someone to grow old with. Someone to love her.

After the accident, she'd tried dating. The men she'd

gotten close to hadn't wanted her either when they'd learned about the accident. She'd learned to ignore the hurt, to hide it away. But she didn't want to hide it from Carter. He'd almost kissed her last night. And she'd wanted to kiss him. To hold him. To see where the heat between them led.

But before whatever was boiling between them went further, she needed Carter to know. Needed to make sure he understood what she was now. She could fix others, help them on their path, but part of her was forever gone.

Anger floated in his eyes. There was no reason to be angry with her, not really. But then there'd been no reason for Kevin to be angry with her when she'd returned home and showed him the aftermath. The death of beauty's fantasy brought out strange reactions in men.

"I know you're angry." She crossed her arms as she mentally reached for a way to fix the dynamic shift here. Maybe she should have lied and said she didn't have a scar, but he'd always hated lies. He'd even brought it up when he was sick.

And she didn't want to lie. Not about this. This was too important. He needed to know the truth.

She wanted him to understand. Wanted to still see the hunger boiling in his eyes—for her. But if this was too much for Carter, it was better to know now.

"I am furious." Carter took a deep breath. "But not with you." He took a step toward her. "I am angry that anyone could look at that and think that you were anything less than one of the strongest people they'd ever met." He offered her a smile as he reached for one of her hands. "Angry that anyone could make you feel you're broken."

His finger traced a line along her chin, burning her as his gaze gripped hers. "You are gorgeous, Helena, and not broken. *Never broken.*"

She let her gaze linger on his face. Drinking in the soft look of his eyes, the roughness of the stubble on his cheeks and the fullness of his lips.

"Kiss me." Her demand poured from the depth of her soul. These were the words she wanted to say all those years ago, the words she wished she'd stated last night.

Carter's fingers slipped to the base of her neck as he pulled her close. The little distance between them evaporating as his lips met hers. The kiss was firm, not demanding, as one hand pulled her hips tighter.

Wrapping her arms around Carter's neck, Helena deepened the kiss. She'd waited far too long to know how Carter Simpson kissed, and she would not waste this moment. The world tumbled as his tongue dipped along her bottom lip.

"Carter." Her head fell back as he traced lines of kisses first along her jaw and then down her neck. But as his fingers slipped along the edge of her shirt, Helena froze.

He pulled back immediately and smiled as he dropped a light kiss on the tip of her nose. "I want you, Helena. I've wanted you for weeks. Years, if I'm being honest. But this goes only as far as you want it to." He swallowed and held her close.

Blood pounded in her ears as Carter gripped her. His fingers skimming across her back in soothing motions. She wanted him. He'd seen her scar—at least part of it—and hadn't recoiled. Swallowing the last bit of fear, Helena looked up and kissed him.

"I want you, too…"

# CHAPTER SEVEN

BEFORE SHE COULD let any doubt grow in her heart, Helena lifted the flannel shirt over her head. A shiver ran across her body despite the heat pumping into the room. She watched Carter's eyes closely, looking, waiting for the moment when he might second-guess his choice.

But the only thing she saw in his dark depths was passion.

"God, you're gorgeous."

"Carter—" His mouth captured the argument her mind prepared to make. Need poured through her, pushing the uncertainties nearly from her mind.

He broke the kiss and let his finger run along her stomach. "All of you is gorgeous—perfect." Carter's gaze never left hers as his thumb traced the outer edge of her breast before dipping lower.

She bit her lip as his hand caressed her side. His fingers never lingered on her scar; they moved as though it wasn't there. Like it didn't matter. It was the response she needed, and her heart soared.

"Helena." Carter's voice was ragged as his lips dipped to the top of her chest. "If you want me to leave for the night, tell me now."

"Leave?" Her voice sounded dreamy as her hands slipped under his shirt. "I want you to stay, Carter."

Her bra dropped to the floor, and Carter smiled.

The grin on his face made Helena smile, too. This should be awkward. They'd been childhood friends, then he'd disappeared, and she hadn't stood fully naked before another person in almost two years. But as he looked at her, really looked at her, it was impossible for Helena to feel anything other than peace.

And a desperate need.

Before she could articulate any of that, Carter feathered kisses along the top of her breasts before wandering down her body. Her legs were weak as he slid to his knees and undid the top of her pants.

She pushed the pants down her hips and quickly stepped from them. For the first time in forever, Helena didn't worry about the long scar stretched across her abdomen.

He kissed his way from her belly button to the top of her lace panties, then looked up at her as he slipped them down her hips. His fingers trailed along the insides of her thighs as he held her gaze. Then his lips followed the same path, edging ever closer to her core. But never quite reaching it.

"Carter," Helena pleaded.

"For fifteen years, you've moved in and out of my dreams, Helena Mathews."

Her eyes flew open, but before she could ask the dozens of burning questions that statement brought to her mind, Carter pressed his thumb against her mound, rolling the bead gently before capturing her with his mouth.

All thoughts evaporated as Carter pushed her closer and closer to the edge with his tongue. When she thought she might not be able to take anymore, he slid a finger inside her. Sparks flew across her body as Carter drove her to the edge of oblivion, but never quite over.

"Carter, I... I..." Words were beyond her as she tried to make him understand.

She felt him smile as he finally let her crest into passion. His name echoing on her lips.

Listening to Helena's sounds of pleasure was nearly enough to drive Carter over desire's cliff. As her moans echoed in the room, he lifted her, enjoying the blissful look on her face.

*Helena.*

Her name reverberated around his mind as he gently laid her on the bed.

Her eyes shifted as the change of position seemed to break through the bliss of her climax. The tip of her tongue ran along her lower lips as she shifted onto her knees. "It seems unfair that I have lost all my clothes, while you—"

He let her pull his shirt off, but Carter grabbed her hands as they slid lower. He wanted her.

*Desperately.*

But as soon as they were both naked, he was going to lose the limited control he was maintaining. And he still had plans for tonight.

*So many plans.*

"Not yet, honey." The endearment slipped from his lips as he ran a finger along her chin, then dipped it lower, dragging it across the top of her breasts, enjoying each tiny hitch in her breath. Rolling a taut nipple between his fingers, he dipped his head and captured the bud with his lips.

He could spend all night worshiping the beauty before him. Laying her back on the bed, Carter hovered over her. "You are so beautiful."

Carter's fingers dipped along her belly as he kissed

the sensitive skin at the base of her neck. His fingers skimmed the tight skin of the long scar, but he was careful not to linger. That part of Helena was just as lovely as the rest of her. But he was not going to acknowledge it directly while he was pleasuring her.

It was just one piece of the smart, loving, beautiful woman. Others had made it her defining feature, and Carter knew she worried he would, too. He was determined that she would experience as much pleasure as possible tonight.

His lips slid down her belly, and his fingers traced her inner thighs. She gripped the sheets, and Carter smiled as her back arched in another wave of pleasure. This was the best place in the world to be!

"Carter!" Helena's cry carried through him as he dipped his head lower, enjoying the taste of her on his lips. The feel of her under his fingers, the knowledge that he was here, with Helena in this moment. He wanted to remember everything.

"I want you, all of you." Helena pulled the top drawer of her dresser open and drew out a condom. She kissed him as her fingers slid down his stomach to the top of his jeans.

Her eyes brightened as she pushed his pants down. Her hand grazed the bulge in his boxers. She grinned as she traced his manhood. "Now, Carter!"

Her touch was too much and not enough all at once. Between her kisses and demands, Carter nearly lost himself.

"Helena." He kissed her and pulled her hand away. "If you want me at all—" he sighed as she pulled his boxers down, too "—then you can't touch me like that. I don't think I have ever been this turned on."

She opened the condom, her gaze never leaving his

as she slid it down his length. "Carter." She captured his lips as she pulled him down onto the bed with her.

Wrapped in her arms, Carter lost himself completely.

The rays of the timed sunlamp turned on as Carter enjoyed the soft sounds of Helena breathing. The bed wasn't truly made for two people, but Carter didn't care that he'd had to hold Helena through the night. This was his happy place.

The thought ricocheted through his skull as he ran his fingers down her back. She grinned in her sleep, and Carter's heart thudded with joy. His happy place.

He had so many memories with the Mathews twins. He and Owen had been best friends for so long. But as the memories ran through his mind, it was the moments with Helena that popped in most easily. The three of them swimming at the community pool, chasing imaginary aliens through the backyard, playing chess together.

The private conversations they'd shared over breakfast in college... He and Owen had been roommates, but he and Helena had spent so much time together that semester. It had seemed so natural, and he'd enjoyed each moment, not realizing just how precious they truly were.

What if he hadn't left all those years ago? Would their friendship have taken this course sooner?

Yes. They'd been nearly there. If Owen hadn't interrupted them, he'd have kissed her the night she showed up at his door. How different would his life look if a lie hadn't blown up his family? If he hadn't destroyed it?

He swallowed the lump of pain that train of thought brought. This seemed right, but he hadn't told her about the past. In fact, he'd barred her from asking. And being Helena, she'd respected his wish—at least for now.

His fingers traced the line of her scar. He was a physician, not a surgeon. But he'd grown up listening to his father discuss surgical trends and started reading medical journals in high school—discussing them with the man he'd admired so much. Carter knew this mark resulted from so much trauma it was a miracle that Helena had survived.

The world had nearly lost a beautiful soul, and he'd been completely unaware of it. All those unsent messages, all that lost time. He'd rationalized away the reasons he hadn't reached out. But the truth was he'd never regretted his choice to leave. He'd needed to protect himself. No regret…until Helena had walked off that LC-130.

Kissing the top of her head, Carter breathed in her scent. They hadn't spoken of what this meant. She'd fallen asleep in his arms so quickly, but as he stared at her, Carter knew he didn't want to lose her. Couldn't…

He wasn't sure what that meant. But it was a truth that settled deep within him.

Carter dropped a kiss on Helena's cheek. He let his fingers roam her body, enjoying the feel of her skin.

His happy place.

She stirred, her eyes meeting his in the early-morning lamplight as a slow smile spread across her face. "Good morning, Carter." Her gaze burned with passion and a touch of uncertainty.

He squeezed her close, enjoying how she molded to him. Nothing had ever felt this perfect. A twist of worry spread through him. *Perfect* was a term he never applied to anything after learning about his mother's deceptions. The bar was too high, the damage too great when illusions shattered.

*Except you've used it with Helena multiple times.*

And the term felt right as her lips skimmed his and her fingers wandered along his hip. He was not going to let fear drive him. He wasn't.

"Good morning, honey." He captured her lips, losing himself in the sensations that she'd awakened in him.

Carter kissed the top of Helena's head as she sat at the small desk in the main portion of the clinic, studiously rereading the conclusion of the paper they'd written about the virus that had broken out four weeks ago. It seemed like a lifetime since then, and in many ways it was.

In four short weeks, Helena had turned his life upside down.

*Or maybe she flipped it right side up.*

Either way, Carter felt happy, truly happy for the first time in forever. It was intoxicating.

"If you stare any harder at that screen, your eyes will cross, honey." He kissed her cheek, enjoying the feel of her skin.

Helena nodded as she deleted a few words, then added them back in. "I know, I just feel like a few more tweaks and it will be ready."

"Always the fixer." Carter pulled her hands from the keyboard and closed the laptop. "Let it rest for a few days, then we can do the final edits and pick a journal to submit to."

Her eyes brightened as her lips turned up.

Would he ever tire of seeing her smile? He hoped not.

"*We* can." Her gaze held his as her not-so-subtle emphasis on the word *we* hit him. "Which journal should *we* submit too?"

He shook his head. Carter knew she wanted him to fully step into the role of coauthor; he wasn't going to, but he was enjoying this moment too much to dampen her mood. It didn't hurt to let the disagreement slide away for now.

"I was thinking *Preventive Medical Journal*. It makes the most sense and certainly falls in their field." He felt himself grin as she leaned against him.

"That sounds like the perfect first place to start. And if they tell *us* no?" She stared up at him.

Rejection was a normal process. He felt *Preventive Medical* was their best bet, but there were always others. Shrugging, he leaned forward and kissed the tip of her nose. "Then we, my dear, shall just have to find another journal."

Helena patted his knees. "That is what I was hoping you'd say." She rose from the chair and kissed his cheek. "You and me, coauthors. Who'd have thought it when we were making mud pies all those years ago?"

The word *coauthor* sent a shiver through him, but Carter didn't want to argue. So he redirected the conversation with a laugh, "I don't think you ever really made mud pies."

Helena sighed. "True. Maybe when we aren't surrounded by ice."

Carter nodded. "Maybe." Uncertainty wrapped through his belly. Such a simple statement—with so much meaning. Would Helena want to go home to Chicago?

*Yes.*

His brain supplied the answer. Mentally he shook the thought away. He had a few more months of bliss before they had to figure out what came next, and Carter planned to savor them.

Carter's chest constricted, and his need to do something, anything, besides let his brain wander gripped him. "I am going to grab some pain meds from the secondary supply closet in the warehouse. We are a little low in here."

"It seems like nearly everyone on the post has had a headache or joint ache this week." Helena rested her head in her hands, seemingly unaware of the anxiety pulsing through him.

"It's the most common complaint we get," Carter confirmed. "And it will only get worse." As the months of darkness and confinement in the small South Pole post lengthened, the body reacted differently. Headaches and general achiness were common, but usually easily managed.

"I'll be back in a few." Carter waved and winked. Then chuckled to himself as he closed the clinic door. He'd never waved or winked to a colleague; so much had changed.

*So much.*

"Are you sure you can make a small batch of cookies for him?" Helena whispered to Elle, the main cook for the base. "I don't want to put you in a bind."

"Of course I can." Elle grinned. "And why are we whispering?" She raised a brow as she looked around Helena at the empty clinic.

Helena covered her mouth as she looked at the clinic entrance. Carter had left twenty minutes ago. He'd be back with the pain medications any minute and she really wanted to surprise him. His birthday was still almost two months away, but planning took extra time here.

"I always order enough supplies for a small celebration for everyone. The base is sparse during the primary season. During the winter it can be dismal, so the food budget for the winter staff is pretty high. One of the few perks. This will be the first time I've made something for Carter. He's usually..."

Elle coughed, and her cheeks brightened. "I just meant that he's kept to himself the past two winters. It's nice that you've drawn him out."

Helena's soul lifted a bit before it deflated. "I didn't actually ask him about this. I mean for it to be a surprise."

*Is that okay?*

A surprise wasn't a lie.

Carter had mentioned that he hadn't had a birthday celebration in years when she'd first gotten to the base. It was an offhand comment, a fleeting moment, but in Helena's experience those comments usually hid real wants and desires.

"A surprise." Elle clapped her hands with excitement. "How fun."

"What surprise?" Carter asked as he stepped into the clinic carrying the small case of pain medicines.

Once more Elle's cheeks erupted into bright pink splotches. "Oh." She looked from Helena to Carter, and then shrugged. "I guess it's okay if you're in on it too, right, Helena?"

Helena opened her mouth but didn't know what to say. She'd just said the celebration was a surprise. But she felt herself nod. There was no way to avoid it now.

"Helena is planning a midway celebration for the base." Elle smiled as she started toward the door.

"A midway celebration?" Carter raised his brow as he looked at her.

Helena nodded. "Yep." The lie was tiny, minuscule, but it still cut through the air as she held Carter's gaze.

Unless she put a celebration together, too.

Her heart lifted with the thought. That was the fix here. And a midway party would be fun, particularly since Carter was participating in base activities this year. It might even make up for his years of missed events.

Carter's eyes narrowed as he looked at her. "Really?"

"Yes. It will be fun." Helena brightened. It would be fun.

"It will." Carter nodded to the boxes in his hands and started for the supply closest.

Helena felt more confident as she watched his easy steps. Returning her attention to Elle, she grinned as Elle offered a playful salute. She'd have to find some time to talk to Elle about planning another celebration.

But that was a worry for another day.

# CHAPTER EIGHT

CARTER'S FINGERS TRAILED along her wrist as he looked over the final draft of the paper. Her body shuddered with desire as he dropped a light kiss on her cheek before sliding back. The last month and a half of dating Carter had been a blissful mix of fun and escape.

But there was still an undercurrent of uncertainty between them. They'd spent each night together since the first time they'd slept together. She'd loved discovering what made him shake with need. And enjoyed the nights they'd just spent lying together talking. But never about the past.

He still hadn't talked about why he had uprooted himself all those years ago. What had caused the dynamic shift between the boy she'd known and the man she cared for now? The few times she'd tried to bring up the words he'd cried in his sleep, Carter had redirected it. Sometimes not so subtly.

She'd promised him she wouldn't push until he was ready. But that was before they started dating, before he'd seen the damage done to her body and the wounds her ex-fiancé had inflicted on her soul. The things about herself that she could never fix. She'd bared all to him.

It was hard to accept that he didn't want to share with her. That he was withholding part of himself.

A big part of himself.

She didn't know if it was something she could help fix, but just telling others your pain could be cathartic.

"You're frowning. Are we missing a comma or something?"

Helena mentally shook off the unease traveling through her soul as she leaned forward. "Nope. There are no missing commas. Well, there probably are, but the tech editor will have to alert us to those. I've reread this so many times that I can't see them anymore. I'll send it for review later today." She tried to smile, but the motion felt false, and his eyes narrowed.

*So much for trying to seem unbothered.*

"What's going on?" Carter crossed his arms as he leaned against the desk. Closing himself off.

She tried not to let the posture hurt. The feelings between them were new...mostly. Part of her heart had instantly recognized his, and hope for the future had bloomed the moment he kissed her. They'd both had lives and serious partners since their young flirtation, but if he hadn't left would this have developed all those years ago?

It didn't really matter. She was glad he was here now. Besides, life was too short not to grab for what you wanted.

And needed.

"You can tell me, no lies between us."

*No lies.*

There was his fixation on honesty again. He'd always been honest. She appreciated the trait, but full 100 percent honesty was a tough life to live without hurting others. Sometimes a small white lie helped.

She'd told friends she liked an outfit they were wearing and clearly loved, even when it wasn't something

Helena liked. If they were comfortable and happy with their choice, who was she to doubt that? There'd been more than one patient she'd calmed with words that a procedure wouldn't hurt too bad. Everyone's pain tolerance was different, and what was minor to one might really hurt someone else. But it made them feel better and usually resulted in less fear and pain.

"Every time I bring up Chicago, you shut down." His face shifted, and she saw the walls that had fallen since her arrival slam back into place. "Carter."

"I told you weeks ago that I would not discuss what happened, and you promised not to ask." His voice was tight, and he pulled back as she reached her hand out.

Pulling on her reserves, Helena shook her head. "That is not what I promised. I promised not to push until you were ready."

"I am never going to be ready, Helena." His jaw set as he crossed his arms.

"Never is a long time." She held his gaze, willing him to open up.

"It is," Carter confirmed as he shrugged.

What had happened that made him push this hard against it?

"You left. Full stop. Owen and I looked for you. If I hadn't stepped off that plane, would you have ever reached back out?" Helena saw the hurt flash in his eyes. She hated pushing this, but she needed to know if this was a winter flirtation or maybe something more.

"No. And I have no intention of ever returning to Chicago or discussing it. I have moved past it—that is all you need to know."

Except he hadn't moved past it. Maybe he thought he had, but whatever had happened still coated his heart, still hung heavy on his soul and created a barrier between him and everyone else. Including her.

"Then what future do we have, Carter?" The question hovered between them, and part of her wished she could drag it back. They'd been together a little over a month and a half, but her heart wanted to believe that Carter belonged in her life for longer than one winter at the end of the world.

*Maybe even forever.*

But pushing him wasn't the answer, either. As his eyes looked anywhere but at her, Helena wrapped her arms around herself. Maybe she just needed to give him more time. She'd given her parents a decade and a half without giving up on them. Why couldn't she give Carter more than a few weeks?

She let out a heavy breath. "I just…"

*I just want to love all of you.*

She caught those words before they escaped. She loved him. Had loved him as a friend for so long, even in the years of silence. Was it any surprise that her heart had leaped to love when he'd looked at her and truly seen her?

But what was love without trust? She bit her lip before sighing. "You'll tell me when you're ready."

And if he didn't? Her heart refused to consider that option.

"Helena—"

The clinic door opened before Carter could say whatever thoughts were racing through his mind. "Dr. Simpson. Helena?"

Pietro Faelks, one of the supply runners, was holding his arm covered in a bloody towel.

"He slipped on the ice while doing a silly dance."

Niel Hurst shook his head, clearly unimpressed with the reason for the injury.

"My son won first place in the state archery contest. You'd celebrate, too." Pietro's grin was more of a grimace, but Helena could see the pride radiating off him.

"Stepson," Niel stated.

Pietro's eyes narrowed as he stared at the man who'd helped him into the clinic. "Matteo is my son. And I don't need you rehashing old news."

"I spent all last winter listening to you complain. How you forgave—" Niel raised his hands, but Helena could see the frustration in them.

"Why don't we take over from here," Carter announced as he stepped to Pietro's side.

Following his lead, Helena nodded to Niel. "We have it under control. We'll let you know if we need anything."

"Sorry about that, Doc." Pietro sucked in a deep breath as Helena and Carter quickly washed up.

"It's fine, Pietro. I remember last winter." Carter nodded as he dried his hands and pulled on a pair of gloves.

Helena wasn't sure what was going on, but she focused on carefully unwrapping the towel. She knew that when the bleeding started, the towel was likely the closest thing the shop had had on hand to stem the bleeding. But she worried how much bacteria it had added to the wound.

Closing his eyes, Pietro shook his head. "I know last winter I was pretty ticked at my ex, but you don't take it out on the kids. It wasn't his fault his mother had an affair and never told me. Should have figured something was off when he was nearly a foot taller than both of us and loads smarter than me, too."

The pieces clicked into place as she started flushing

the large cut. It was going to need dozens of stitches and leave a nasty scar. And based on how they were bent, he'd broken at least two of his fingers, too.

"You did quite a job on yourself celebrating." Helena patted his good arm as she moved to let Carter get a look.

"Matteo has been taking archery since he was six. I bought him his first bow." Pietro shuddered as Carter lifted his arm slightly. "I wish I could have been there, but the pay to winter over is just too good, and the divorce…

"Well, I am just so proud of him." He bit his lip and glanced at Helena. "Do injuries usually make your patients talkative?"

"Sometimes," she answered honestly. When patients were rattled, they talked about all sorts of things. She'd heard some of her patients' darkest secrets over the course of her career.

"But I hear silly things, too. I once had a little girl explain how her mother had thousands of teacups. So many teacups. The mother was so embarrassed. She made sure I knew she had a side business as a miniature dollhouse decorator and that there were less than a hundred mini teacups in her house. She was not a teacup hoarder!"

Pietro laughed.

"What about you, Dr. Simpson? Any silly teacup stories?" Helena looked at him, wondering what thoughts or memories were rolling around his brain.

"None that come to mind," Carter answered as he gestured to the wound. "We are going to need two finger splints and sutures." He met her gaze, but he looked away quickly.

It stunned her; Carter was always smooth with his

patients, friendly and easygoing. But something was bothering him.

*You cornered him less than ten minutes ago, Helena. Of course something is bothering him.*

Gathering her tattered reserves, she nodded to Pietro and went to gather the supplies. She'd thrown Carter off, pushed him about the past and hit a wall that she should have anticipated. But she had hoped the few weeks they'd spent relishing each other would have broken his refusal to discuss what had happened.

And she hated that it hadn't.

But he had silly stories. Every medical professional had a stash of funny tales from their time in the trenches. The light events were the anecdotes that got passed around the break rooms on nights when the job's darkness threatened. She laid out the suture material, then did her best to ignore the twist of nerves in her belly.

"You must have something like the teacups." She winked at Pietro before looking at Carter. He was entirely focused on Pietro's arm.

An awkwardness seemed to hover in the area as Carter measured the lidocaine to numb Pietro's arm. She'd caused this with her questions, but Helena could fix it. Make Carter and Pietro comfortable.

This procedure was going to take some time, and it would pass faster for all of them if at least Pietro and she were talking. And upbeat stories were best in these situations.

"What is your favorite memory of your son?" He was so proud. It would be an easy topic while they repaired his arm.

Carter's hand slipped, and he dropped the needle with the numbing solution on the floor. "Slippery thing." He let out a false chuckle. "Reminds me of an ice storm we had in Boston one night. Seems incredible after wintering here three times that I thought that night was the coldest I would ever experience. The entire floor was slippery with melted snow and ice. The cleaning crew couldn't keep up with it. When there were no patients, a few of the interns pretended to ice-skate down the hall. One even broke his ring finger like you did."

She felt her mouth fall open and quickly closed it. Carter had just said he couldn't recall anything, then he'd mentioned a great memory. What was going on?

He quickly filled another syringe and offered a grin to Pietro. "This might sting. So, tell me about the dance you did. It must have been something to result in this." Carter kept his attention focused on their patient.

"I got the video from my ex-wife showing Matteo's winning shot. It was straight into the bull's-eye. The kid…" Pietro smiled with such pride that it made Helena's heart swell.

She'd never seen that look from her father. Every glance was tinged with worry, with the pain that she might slip away from them. But she still dreamed that one day…

"He's so talented. After the video ended, I might have done a little twirl on the ice."

"A twirl." Helena made a tsking sound and playfully wagged a finger. "It's almost as if you were asking to fall."

He grimaced as Carter started placing the stitches. It wouldn't hurt after the lidocaine, but the feel of the needle and the tightening of the skin bothered many people. "I'm just so proud of the boy. Even if he doesn't share my actual DNA."

Helena saw the little muscles around Carter's eyes twitch. This wasn't just her question about their future bothering him. At least she didn't think so.

Something about Pietro's injury had upset Carter. And she did not know why. But that was a question for when this procedure was over.

Assuming he would tell her.

She tried to push the bubble of doubt away, but it refused to accept its banishment.

"I think I am going to spend the night in my room." Helena's voice shook as she grabbed the backpack she always carried to the clinic. It had a few journals and a book. Though over the last month and a half all their free time had been spent finishing the draft of the paper. But she'd sent their paper off to a few journals for consideration this afternoon.

*Her* paper, he reminded himself, because he wasn't a coauthor. She'd promised that. It was a ridiculous request. One that barely made sense in his own head. He doubted there'd be any interest from his father in the piece, doubted he'd reach out even if he saw it. And even if he did, it would be weeks, maybe months, before Helena heard anything from the journals she'd queried... they might be off the ice by then.

*The future*...

It was still nearly half a year away, but it seemed to be rushing toward him. He wanted Helena in his life. She belonged there, but she wanted to know about what had happened years ago. And she deserved an answer. But he didn't know how to provide it.

And after watching Pietro's response today... Carter pushed his palms into his eyes as a host of unwelcome emotions floated through him. Pietro had been so angry last year, furious. He'd railed for nearly the entire winter. His wife had had an affair and then convinced him Matteo was his child. It was only when the boy had needed knee surgery that he'd discovered it wasn't possible that Matteo was his.

*Through blood-typing.*

The similarities to his own situation had nearly driven him mad then. He'd ached for Matteo. Ached for himself, watching the horror play out again. But he'd understood Pietro's fury, too. After Laura had cheated on him, he'd been so shell-shocked and heartbroken. He could finally understand the sense of betrayal his father had felt—something he hadn't understood in his youth.

But even in all that anger Pietro had never blamed Matteo. Carter had let him use the clinic link a few times when the boy was desperately sad. His bottom lip trembled as he remembered Pietro's calls reassuring him that he still loved him.

He was glad he'd been able to help, but privately, Carter had ached each time Pietro had discussed the boy he would always consider his child. And a year later, seeing how happy the man was over the archery contest. How much he still loved Matteo.

His son.

God, he was jealous. Of a boy he'd never met.

Why couldn't his father have done the same?

That was a question there was no way for Carter to answer…no matter how much his soul craved it.

"Carter?" Helena's voice echoed in the quiet room, and Carter realized he hadn't said anything for several minutes. "I won't push you again today, but you aren't past whatever happened. You're lying to yourself. If hearing that angers you—" She swallowed and closed her eyes.

Helena rocked back on her feet, distraught, but he was frozen in place. He needed to say something, anything. But his brain refused to supply the words. Refused to help his heart at all.

She looked at him, her eyes shining with hope and pain. After a few seconds she nodded. "See you tomorrow."

She was gone before he could force words to his lips.

"Helena…" Her name, too little and far too late, finally broke through, and Carter fell into the chair.

*You're lying to yourself.*

Her words echoed in the quiet clinic. He closed his eyes and let that truth wash through him. If he wanted a future with Helena, he was going to need to open up. His heart seized on the thought, but he forced himself to take a deep breath. Helena was part of his future.

He was falling in love with her. That was a truth he couldn't ignore. She was easy to care for, easy to love. The woman put others before herself, but she called him out when he needed to hear it, too. And he'd let her walk away rather than reach out to her.

Let her walk out hurt, rather than open himself to the truth. Rather than bare his soul.

*Like she did.*

She'd shown him her deepest pain. Bared her soul, and he hadn't reciprocated. In fact, he'd barred her from even asking him.

Once more the image of a crossroad reverberated through his brain. This was another waypoint. He could protect his story or be with Helena. But those paths did not converge.

And suddenly the answer was simple.

He grabbed the walkie-talkie, set the note on the front of the clinic and went to find Helena.

Blood pounded in his ears as he raced down the corridor to her room. Nerves, grief and a weird form of excitement pulsed through him. This was the right path, he knew it.

Helena crossed the small space within her room for what felt like the hundredth time in the last twenty minutes. It was only ten paces between the door and the back wall, but sitting still wasn't possible and leaving the room wasn't an option until she got herself together.

The base carried a real small-town energy, and everyone knew most people's business. People would notice the nervousness echoing through her. Notice that she kept looking for Carter. The winter-over crew hadn't asked about their relationship, but there were few real secrets in the tiny community.

There was no way to tell anyone about their...her brain couldn't find the right word. It hadn't felt like a fight—at least not like the ones she'd witnessed in her parents' home. There was no screaming, no crying, no threats.

But Helena had drawn a line, even if she'd done it quietly. She was right; Carter was lying to himself. But she'd expected him to disagree or to reach out for her. To do *something*.

Instead, he'd let her walk away without a word.

Part of her mind reached for a way to fix the divide she'd forced open between them. But her heart refused to let it wander through any options. Could she accept Carter never opening up about why he'd disappeared from her life?

*No.*

She scraped at the tear that had escaped. That was a truth she needed to accept. If she and Carter had a future, she needed him to tell her. Maybe it was better to push early, before her heart was so entangled that it would destroy her if she lost him.

Helena let out a bitter chuckle. That point had passed the moment she'd shown him her scars, and he'd said nothing. When he'd traced the lines of her body as though it wasn't there, as though she was whole. He'd done what her family, her ex-fiancé and the few men she'd dated after Kevin could not.

But she wanted all of him. Settling for less wasn't an option.

"Helena!" Carter knocked and called out again, "Helena!"

She wiped her palm against her cheeks. They came away wet. If he was here to end things, there'd be more tears. So many more. But she didn't want Carter to see them.

"Helena!" His voice cracked. "Please let me in, honey."

*Honey.*

She reined in the hope spreading through her at the endearment. Whatever was about to happen would happen. Taking a deep breath, she stepped back to let him in.

"My mother had an affair. My biological father was some business associate of hers. I was conceived on a business trip. I found out through the blood-typing exercise in anatomy lab. My dad told both of us to leave. Said he never wanted to see either of us again. Mom refused, but I… My mother blamed me. Actually, they both did."

The words fell from his lips, and Helena felt her eyes widen as Carter stepped into the room.

He pushed a hand through his hair as the story

poured forth. Like he was terrified of not getting them out. "My mother always told little lies. And she blew them off like they were just part of a role she was playing. Like her whole life was an acting studio where she could just call 'cut' and retell the story if it didn't work right."

Helena nodded. But he was talking so fast that she didn't know if he was even seeing her.

"I was her greatest lie, and she hated that I uncovered it." Forcing his hands into his pockets, Carter looked at her and sucked in a deep breath. "That was a lot of words to say I blew up my family."

He let out a ragged breath and tilted his head toward the ceiling. "And...

"And..." Again, his words died away. His teeth bit into his lower lip, and for a moment she worried he might be tasting blood.

"And my dad hasn't spoken to me since." He sighed as tension leaked from his shoulders. "So...that's why I left." He hiccuped as his eyes finally met hers. "I blew up my family. Tore it to shreds."

The weight of what he'd carried made her ache, but he was wrong.

*So very wrong.*

"*You* did not blow up your family." Helena's fist shook as she saw the pain he'd been covering. "*You* did nothing wrong. If your parents blamed you, then that is their failing, not yours."

She wrapped her arms around him, holding him tight. He let out a sob as she tightened her grip.

"I spent my entire childhood—" Carter sucked in another breath as he laid his head on hers "—trying to make my father proud. And I succeeded."

Helena rubbed his back as the waterfall of words

poured around her again. Finally free from the lock he'd created.

"But after… He couldn't even look at me." Carter choked and tightened his grip on her waist. "I didn't know how to tell Owen or you what I'd found out. I didn't know who I was. So I packed up. Boston University was my second-choice university. I reached out to Admissions, and they accepted me and the scholarship I had. I floated between jobs while I was in med school. But…

"My father refused to speak to me, and my mother figured I was an adult under the law, so her job was done. I was lost. Maybe I still am."

His words finally tapered off, and Helena kissed his cheek. "You are Carter Simpson. Dr. Carter Simpson. A skilled physician, a wonderful man, a good chess player—though not good enough to beat me." Her soul lightened a little as he let out a small laugh.

"You are the person you always were. Even if it didn't feel that way." She couldn't process what he'd experienced. Her family hadn't celebrated her choice. But when she called, someone always answered the phone. They hadn't hesitated when she'd needed to move home for her physical therapy. They still worried too much… constantly. But that worry was from love, even if what she wanted was for them to be proud. To realize she was strong…not broken.

"I am so sorry that your father kicked you out. That you felt lost. But part of me wants to throttle you, too, Carter Simpson."

She saw his mouth open, and she kissed his cheek. They'd lost years when they hadn't had to. When he'd run from the truth, he'd run from her and Owen and their other friends. She kissed his cheek again and held him tightly. "I could have told you who you were—you could have stayed with us. You didn't have to be alone."

That was the part that tore through her the most. That he'd suffered alone when there were those who would have held him while he grieved. Helped him carve a new path, reminded him who he was.

He ran a finger along her chin as he kissed the tip of her nose. "I'm not alone now." His mouth captured hers as he pulled her close.

Her heart soared as he deepened the kiss. No, he wasn't alone, and he'd trusted her with the past. They had a future off the ice. They did.

His fingers ran along the top of her pants before popping the button. "Helena."

There was still more to discuss, but they had time. *Time.*

What a beautiful word.

She let her mind drift into pleasure as his kisses trailed down her neck.

"Helena?" Carter laughed as she held out a bandanna folded to look like a blindfold.

"Put it on." She smiled. "Tonight's a surprise."

"Surprise…" Carter raised an eyebrow as he took the cloth from her hand. Tonight was the midway point for the winter staff.

And his birthday.

But he hadn't celebrated it in years. Helena wishing him a happy birthday this morning was the most recognition the day had had since he'd left his parents' home. Still, spending the day with her was the best way to celebrate.

Helena had started planning a midway celebration weeks ago. It wasn't something that they'd done before.

At least he didn't think so. He'd kept to the clinic the other two winter-overs he'd been here. But Helena had changed all that.

They ate all their meals with the other support staff now. Occasionally a few of the scientists joined them, though many of them ate around whatever schedule their lab requirements permitted. He'd gotten to know several people, and they stopped in the clinic now to say hello instead of only seeking him out for medical care.

And Carter liked the change. That still surprised him. After keeping to himself for so long, he felt like he was reemerging. Rediscovering who he'd been.

"Trust me, Carter." Helena's bright eyes held his.

"That is not a problem." His lips dipped to hers. Since admitting to her what had happened with his parents a few weeks ago, his body felt lighter. He hadn't realized how much his soul had carried, though after unburdening himself he'd wanted to kick himself for not seeing the weight he lugged with him.

"I trust you with everything." Those were words he never thought he'd utter, but Helena had changed that, too. One more thing to the growing list of wonders she'd fixed.

"Good. Then put on the blindfold."

Pulling the cloth tight over his eyes, Carter shook his head. "Happy?"

"Blissfully."

Her lips grazed his jaw, and he shivered. Reaching for her heat, Carter pulled her close. "Helena…"

She deepened the kiss, then stepped out of his arms, and with the blindfold, he couldn't easily pull her back. "As much as I would love to see where those kisses go, I did actually plan to surprise you outside of the bedroom."

"Later," Carter mused as her hand slipped into his.

"Absolutely!" Helena breathed before leading him into the corridor.

As they approached the cafeteria, Carter smiled. She might have him blindfolded, but he'd spent three winters in this base and knew each turn. His mouth started watering as the odors of roast beef and potatoes drifted forth.

His favorite. His parents hadn't been big cooks, but his mother made an excellent pot roast and his father's mashed potatoes were the best part of holiday meals. Dinner was still a few hours away, but he was looking more forward to it now.

Leading him a few steps into the room, Helena kissed his cheek. "I probably didn't need this." Helena lifted the blindfold and grinned. "But it seemed more fun this way."

The long tables the staff ate at were all pushed to the side and a small table sat in the middle of the room. A homemade sign read Happy Birthday, Carter, and two chairs sat around it with dinner laid on them.

"Midway celebration?" Carter looked at the small sign and felt his insides bloom, though a twitch of unease passed through him, too. It was a small untruth. Something that people did all the time.

*But she promised no lies. None.*

"I wanted to surprise you. If I had mentioned an intimate birthday celebration, you would have told me this wasn't necessary. And luckily your birthday is right around the midway point." Helena shrugged. "Tiny white lie. Are you upset?"

He hesitated. Could he really be upset about something she'd done to give him a treat? Except lies grew.

"So there is no midway celebration? We've talked about it at dinner with the crew for weeks."

*Did everyone lie?*

Helena bit her lip. "There is, but it's Friday. And in the game room. The team was willing to help me surprise you, but…" She looked at him. "I…"

He hated the pain passing over her features. Hated causing her worry. "This is wonderful. Thank you." Carter pulled her close. He meant it, he did. He valued truthfulness, but even thinking over the last few weeks, he remembered her redirecting questions about the celebration. But she'd never actually said when it was. "Though I am stunned you pulled this off with no one giving the secret away."

She pulled him toward the chairs, her body bouncing with excitement. "It was quite the project. And we have to eat dinner early for the privacy, but it's just good practice for when we're old and gray and getting senior spe—"

Helena's cheeks colored as the words echoed. "I… I just mean that…" She took a deep breath and put her hands on her hips. "Forget it. I love you, Carter Simpson, and I hope this is just practice for when we are old with gray hair and searching out the best deals for senior specials. And that is the truth."

"That's the best birthday present I've ever gotten." He swept her into his arms and kissed her deeply. "I love you, too." The words made his soul lift. He loved Helena, and she was right: this was worth the small mistruth.

It was.

# CHAPTER NINE

THE EMAIL SENT chills through her as Helena tried to make sense of it. She'd read the missive three times. The four lines didn't amount to more than fifty words. Four lines that could radically shift Carter's world.

And their relationship.

His father wanted to talk, wanted to know how he was. And he'd found Carter because Helena had put his name on the paper they'd coauthored. Which Carter didn't know about.

Her nerves scattered as she tried to force air through her lungs. It was meant to be a surprise, if it was ever even published. They'd written it together, and Carter had talked about seeing his name in a medical journal for as long as she'd known him.

But would he see this as a lie?

Helena hadn't meant it that way. But after his initial hesitation over the surprise birthday celebration she'd thrown, she was more than a little nervous.

They'd had a wonderful early evening. Yet when they'd originally stepped into the room, he'd hesitated. And the initial flash in his eyes hadn't been excitement. She'd nearly panicked, but that had been an easy fix for her to smooth over.

*This...*

The email from Drake Simpson had arrived less than an hour after the *Preventive Medical Journal* got in touch, saying they would like to publish the article. She'd forwarded the publication note to Owen, excitement pulsing through her.

Owen had responded almost immediately. Her twin seemed chained to his email box, but it was hard for her to hate the fact that he'd sent such a quick congratulations with a request for a copy of the article. She'd forwarded it and then done a little dance in the clinic. When her email box pinged again, she'd planned to joke with her brother that he needed to look at something other than his email box.

All her elation had crashed as she read the name attached to the new email. She wasn't sure how Drake Simpson had found out about a piece that wouldn't be published until she and Carter were off the ice. But that hardly mattered at the moment.

What was she going to do?

Carter had told her that Drake didn't care where his son had gone. It was harsh and cruel. But fifteen years had passed. What if Drake wanted to apologize? What if he wanted a relationship with the boy he'd tossed away? What would Carter do?

"Good morning, honey." Carter grinned as he stepped through the clinic door.

"You saw me less than an hour ago." She kept her voice light, hoping it didn't betray the rampaging questions bubbling through her mind. She closed the laptop, not wanting him to see the screen until she'd worked through the problem.

The last thing she wanted was to hurt Carter. He'd been through enough with his family. *But...*

He kissed her cheek before leaning against the desk. "You disappeared after breakfast."

"No." She stood and gripped his hand. "I ate my breakfast and came to open the clinic while you chatted away with Holden Summers." She bounced her finger off his nose and winked. "You've become quite the Chatty Cathy lately."

Her stomach rumbled with pride. She'd watched him bloom over the last few months. He no longer took meals alone, and when the base had movie night or some other special event, Carter was there. He was different from the closed-off man she'd met when she stepped off the plane.

But how would he react to his father's email?

She needed to tell him. Helena just couldn't figure out the right words.

"I have. I guess I didn't realize how much I missed connecting with people. Until you forced me to."

He tapped her shoulder as she picked up the tablet chart. "Thank you, Helena. Not sure I've said that."

She gave a playful salute. "Meddling to the rescue."

"I thought you preferred the terms *helping* and *fixing*."

"I do." Holding the tablet to her chest, Helena steadied herself. "Carter—" His dark eyes held hers and sparks danced along her body. Time wouldn't change the bomb lurking in her email. "I got an email this—"

"I can't breathe..." Joseph Bales stumbled into the clinic. His hand covering his heart as he tried to catch his breath. "I can't breathe."

Carter raced toward their patient. Helena darted to the EKG machine and made sure she knew where the electrical cardioversion paddles were in case Joseph's heart stopped.

"Breathe…" Carter stood in front of Joseph as he sat on the bed. Inhaling in a slow pattern that he was trying to get Joseph to follow.

"I can't." Joseph pleaded as his breaths came in rapid succession. "I want to go home."

He was breathing, but his body felt like it wasn't getting air because he was close to hyperventilating. It was a classic symptom of a panic attack. The body seized with anxiety. Many people who'd never experienced one felt like they were having a heart attack. But if they couldn't get Joseph to breathe evenly, he could pass out.

Carter's gaze caught Helena's briefly, and he nodded as she rolled the EKG toward Joseph. "Joseph, I think this is a panic attack. I know it feels scary. But breathe with me, if you can, while Helena sets up the EKG to check your heart."

"I want to go home," he repeated, but he started to follow Carter's breaths.

"I miss home, too." Helena offered a smile as she carefully threaded the electrodes under Joseph's shirt. "Have you ever been to Chicago?" She kept her voice calm as she attached the machine to make sure that Carter's initial diagnosis was correct.

Carter was focused on maintaining the breathing pattern that was drawing some anxiety from Joseph.

When Joseph shook his head no, Helena continued. "The buildings are so tall and it's windy. Not like the winds here, but…" She tried to think of the best way to describe the feel of the heavy winds darting around the buildings. The upturned umbrellas that tourists often thought would provide protection while the hardened residents just lowered their heads and pushed forward.

"It's heavy and forces you forward, then disappears in the blink of an eye before seeming to knock you in the opposite direction. What's your home like?" She leaned back as the EKG machine registered Joseph's heartbeat. Faster than normal, but Carter was right. This wasn't a heart attack.

"Flat." Joseph let out a soft laugh. "I'm from Ohio originally. My parents still live there. I haven't been home in years. Not a ton of work for astrophysicists in Troy, Ohio. It's best known for its yearly strawberry festival. With strawberry doughnuts that are doughy and sugary. They sell them warm at the football stadium."

His body released some tension, and Helena saw Carter relax, too.

"I haven't thought of those doughnuts for years. I just…" He put his hand to his head. "I feel a little dumb. I really thought I might die. Sorry."

"There is nothing to be sorry about." Carter shook his head and waited for Joseph to look at him. "If you are fortunate to have never experienced one, a panic attack can mimic a heart attack. Any time you feel like you can't breathe, you need to seek medical attention. And those strawberry doughnuts sound delicious. There is a pretzel place that I used to visit all the time in my hometown. Sometimes I still crave their salted onion pretzel. It made your breath stink, but…" Carter kissed his fingers and laughed.

*Home.*

Did he miss it as much as she did? He was an excellent physician. But what were his plans when their rotation ended in four months? They'd joked about eating dinner early and growing old when she'd surprised him last week. But they'd never actually discussed what happened next.

They were in an enclosed bubble, a brief respite from

the world at large. But this was a temporary space. Not a place to build a home.

Helena let those questions drift away as she watched him take care of Joseph. Carter patiently explained how to identify stress levels and recommended that Joseph report to him or Helena every day for the next week so they could check in on his symptoms and reevaluate any of his needs.

This had worked out all right...but would everything else?

Panic twisted through her as she tried to figure out how to tell him about his father's email. How would he react? So much had changed in the last few months.

They loved each other. That was a feeling she didn't doubt. Her eyes darted toward the laptop again. Swallowing, she forced the pinch of panic away as she refocused on their patient. It would all work out.

*It will.*

"I miss Oliver's Pretzels, too." Helena squeezed his hand as they closed the clinic door. "Though how you and Owen could eat the salted onion ones was always beyond me."

She giggled as he wrapped his arms around her waist. "I seem to remember you preferred the cinnamon sugar pretzels." He kissed the base of her neck, relishing the light sigh that escaped her lips.

"Was that sigh for the kiss or the memory of the pretzels?" Carter let his fingers run along her back, loving how she leaned against him.

"Maybe both!" She chuckled again and turned in his arms. Her lips met his, but before he could deepen the kiss, Helena pulled back.

"We need to make a pilgrimage to Oliver's." Her

eyes widened and her mouth fell into a perfect O. "And Stan's Pizzeria, too. I still haven't found a deep-dish pizza that is better than their double cheese." Her eyes sparkled, but there was something in them that sent a shiver along his spine. A question he saw hovering in the depths of her soul, one that he didn't want to answer. One he dreaded.

*Chicago...home.*

His throat was tight with memories, with longing—with pain. He'd sworn he wouldn't return to the city. Maybe he dreamed of the skyline, maybe he still woke hoping that things were different, particularly when he was holding Helena. But Chicago was not a place he'd set foot in again.

Clearing his throat, Carter shook his head. "You'll have to go without me." Maybe it was better to get this out now. So she understood.

She blinked, and he saw the hurt pooling in her gaze. He hated causing her pain, but this was nonnegotiable. It truly was.

Carter would always miss Chicago—but returning was not an option.

"Because of your parents?" Her fingers traced along his chin. "Carter—"

He interrupted. This wasn't really a conversation that he wanted to have, but it was something he needed to ensure she understood. He was not returning to Chicago, even for a quick visit. No matter how many times he dreamed of the place. He would not risk running into his father. Even in a city of over two million people.

"My mother lives in New York now. I got a change of address letter with a short note when I was living in Boston. Not really an apology, but..." He shrugged. "I guess she's happier there and she wanted me to know.

She grew up there and always resented Dad for starting his private practice in Chicago."

"It's nice she reached out."

"I suppose. It was more than I expected of her." That was true. He'd been a burden to his mom. That was unfair to him, but she'd been forced to play the role of Mom, a role she'd never really wanted. Her brief handwritten note had said he could visit if he wanted and left her email address.

"What if your father contacted you?" Helena's fingers twisted in his palms.

He hadn't told her that he'd reached out once. Carter hadn't responded to the brief overture, just like he hadn't responded to his mom's. At least hers had been an apology, but he wasn't sure that it was an apology his father had wanted to offer. The email had only asked him to contact him. That there was something he wanted to discuss.

If he'd wanted to apologize, well, the note had been perfunctory. Even if it was closure he was looking for, his father had lost the right to his life when he'd sent him away.

*And if it wasn't an apology he sought...*

Carter ignored the seizing in his chest. If he wanted to rail at him some more or ask for the things that Carter had taken from the house... He closed his eyes as the inventory of mementos that he'd stored in a box and never looked at, but couldn't bring himself to toss out, ran through his mind. Shaking himself, Carter forced the unwelcome thoughts away. He had no reason to have a talk with the man. No reason to risk the pain of it.

Helena was tied to the city. But she'd left several times—surely she'd want to continue this adventure with him? "There are great pretzels in Boston, too. And

I spent a few months working in Michigan on the Great Lakes. The snowfall was so intense. And the Texans always brag about their tacos—maybe we should try those." He'd go nearly anywhere with her—but not back to Chicago.

She shrugged as she opened the door to her room. "I'm sure those are great places. With food that would make us drool, like strawberry doughnuts. But they aren't home. I figured that maybe after we are off the ice it might be nice to go back." She swallowed before continuing. "At least for a brief visit. Show my parents that this…"

"If they haven't accepted that you are a whole unbroken person, then maybe it's time you realized it's possible they never will." He regretted the words as soon as they exited his lips. "Helena…" Carter pushed his hands through his hair, wishing he could kick himself.

"I'm sorry," he muttered. "But I am not sure that anything you do will make them see you the way you want to be seen. Chicago…" He sucked in a deep breath. "No amount of meddling…"

"I get it, Carter." She shook her head. "You don't need to keep digging a hole." Her fingers shook as she looked at him. "You don't think my parents will ever see me for me, and you have no interest in going back to Chicago with me. Even for a short visit. Is that right?"

He wanted to deny it. Wanted to rewind time and start this entire episode over. Taking a deep breath, he reached for her and tried to ignore the bolt of pain tearing through him as she stepped away. "Maybe your parents will come around. Who knows? But my father will not."

"But what if he did?" Helena's voice shook as her gaze held his. "What if?"

"Then I would ignore it." He released the words even as the blip of hope pressed against him. "I have no interest in hearing from Drake Simpson after he turned me out." His heart clenched as the falsehood fell from his lips, but Carter didn't want to let the pinch of optimism touch him. He'd put his life back on track without his father, and he didn't need him now. Even if a small part of him would always wonder, *what if*?

"So you wouldn't want to even know what he wanted?" Her brows were knit together as she watched him.

"No. I wouldn't."

"Okay." Helena nodded, then she straightened her shoulders.

What was going on?

A twinge at the back of his neck sent a prick of uncertainty down his spine. He almost felt like Helena was holding something back.

*Lying...*

He wanted to shake himself. He'd already insulted her several times in the last twenty minutes. He was not going to let his paranoia overrule him now. "Why are we even talking about Chicago? It's just a city, after all." They could live anywhere. And she could visit her family whenever she wanted. It just wouldn't be with him...

Desire to go home warred with the need to protect himself. He'd sworn when he left that he'd never return. But then he'd never expected to see Helena again, either. Life changed.

*But not this. Never this.*

He would never open himself to that pain again.

"I always saw myself settled in Chicago." Helena's voice was small. "It's home."

The statement didn't surprise him. They'd talked

about a life off the ice. But only in vague, "I see you in my future" ways when they'd first said they loved each other. This was another crossroads. Maybe the most important one. But for the first time since she stepped off the plane months ago, Carter couldn't easily select a path.

He wanted Helena, but he wasn't going home. So he settled for the one thing he knew without a doubt. "I love you, Helena."

"I love you, too, Carter." She offered a smile, but it didn't quite reach her eyes. "We have time to make these decisions."

"We do." He kissed her cheek before she settled against his chest. "We do," he repeated as he grasped her waist—willing time to stop. Wishing he could drag out the months here with her.

A little hiccup echoed from her lips, and her bright eyes met his. "I forgot to tell you. The *Preventive Medical Journal* emailed today. They accepted our article for submission."

"Yay!" Carter picked her up and swung her around. "That is excellent. But it's your article."

"Ours," Helena started. "Actually—"

Before she could say anything else, Carter kissed her. "Let's go snag some ice cream to celebrate."

"That sounds great, but Carter—"

"No buts!" he interrupted. Helena had always wanted to fix things. To fix people, and she'd helped him more than he'd ever thought possible. But his relationship with his father was irreparably broken. He knew she wanted to discuss it more, knew they'd have to at some point. But, as the crossroads crystallized in his mind, he didn't want to choose a new path.

Not yet.

# CHAPTER TEN

HELENA LOOKED AT the email from Drake Simpson for the hundredth time. Three days and she still hadn't deleted it. Or told Carter that his father had reached out. And she was torn about whether she should. Would it only hurt him further?

Carter had made it clear that he had no intention of talking to his father again. Made it clear that if he reached out, Carter wouldn't reply. Part of Helena could understand his decision, even if she didn't agree with him.

*People change.*

She had to believe that. If she didn't…

Helena pushed a piece of hair out of her eyes as she looked at the note that had popped in her inbox this morning. Her mother had emailed a job advertisement. The local pediatrician's office was hiring—an entry-level nurse. Even if she were interested in pediatric care, she was a nurse practitioner. She held an advanced degree in nursing and had an extensive emergency-focused résumé. All things her mother knew.

She'd hoped her mother might come around. Might see this assignment as different. But after asking after her health…again, she'd pleaded with Helena not to take another dangerous assignment.

Helena twisted her necklace.

*Dangerous assignment.*

She'd only taken one assignment that was truly dangerous. And she had a permanent reminder of that time, but that car accident could have happened anywhere.

In Chicago she'd treated crash fatalities daily; the busy highways and constant traffic were nightmares waiting to happen for far too many people. Her accident hadn't truly broken her. Hadn't this assignment proven that?

Besides, she had good memories of her deployment, too. Of the people she'd met, the soldiers and locals that she'd treated. It was part of her, a part she wouldn't throw away despite the pain. Plus, it had led her here. She'd never regret that.

And any assignment that wasn't in a local doctor's office with Helena living close by was going to seem risky to her parents. That was a truth that she was going to have to accept. Part of her parents would always see her as the tiny baby trapped in the NICU for months, worried she'd never come home.

But she wasn't that breakable. Her time in the NICU and in Iraq should have shown her parents that she was a fighter, a survivor. But even with all their suffocating worries, they were still her parents.

And Chicago was still home. She could be happy elsewhere. If that was what Carter needed.

But could she strip her family of joint holiday celebrations, require that if they wanted to see her and the person she wanted to spend her life with, that they had to do it outside of Chicago? Strip herself of that?

Carter had said he wasn't going home. And that he wouldn't even entertain visiting with her. Could she live with that?

Part of Helena wanted to say yes, but her heart clenched each time she tried to find the words to tell him it would be fine. Family was important to her. Her family might still worry over her in ways that she hated, but they loved her. She never doubted that.

And they'd love Carter, as a full member of the family. *If he just gave them the chance*. He'd have a family that treasured him again. She didn't need the cute row house in downtown Chicago or the busy city streets and deep-dish pizza places on each corner all the time. But to cut it away from her soul completely...

Carter strolled into the clinic and raised a hand before gesturing to the supply closet. No quick kiss or brief hello before getting the day's deeds done. The energy had shifted between them. His walls weren't back up, but she felt like they were hovering, waiting for her to do something wrong.

She nodded and tried not to let the bite of uncertainty make her follow him. Wednesday was supply day. The current list of everything needed to be delivered to Keith by the end of the day. He'd teleconference with them at the end of the week and go over everything in the sheets. There were no deliveries during the winter, but they needed to keep careful track so that the first shipment allowed through had the most needed items on it.

And they were already planning for the next winter. Trying to make sure that the next staffers had what they needed.

*The next staffers.*

Another twist of uncertainty pooled through her as she looked at the closed supply door. This was Carter's third winter on the ice. Did he want a fourth? And if he did, would he want a fifth? A sixth?

This had been a fun assignment. More than fun. But it felt like an ending point for her.

She let out a deep breath as certainty consumed her. She'd spent the last two years rebuilding herself, trying to find herself after her accident and failed engagement. But she knew who she was…had always known who she was. She was a survivor.

And Carter had helped her remember that.

But it was time to put down roots. She dreamed of Chicago more now. And she wanted to see her nieces and nephews grow up. Wanted to have family picnics and settle herself. Looking around the cool walls of the clinic, tears she refused to let fall danced in her eyes.

This was not a home. It was a waypoint, as Carter liked to say. And it had done exactly what she needed it to. She'd proven herself in another remote location. The *remotest*. But it was time to settle down, even if that place wasn't Chicago.

Stepping out of the supply closet, Carter held up the tablet and smiled. But there was a distant look in his eyes. One she remembered from the first days she'd landed. He was retreating. That stung.

Would he retreat completely? How could she fix this?

The second question rumbled around her brain, and she shook herself. She'd done nothing wrong asking him to come with her to visit her parents. There was nothing for her to fix. For perhaps the first time in her life she recognized that there was no meddling to be done.

"There wasn't much that needed to be checked. Outside of the first week, it's been a light winter season." He playfully rapped his knuckles on the desk. "Knock on wood, it stays that way."

She nodded as she looked around the blissfully quiet clinic. She'd never worked somewhere with so much downtime. She would miss this when she left the ice. Though the fast pace of the ER made time speed by, too.

"You should know that Keith is going to do his best to convince you to join me next winter when we chat at the end of the week." Carter grinned as he leaned toward her.

*Join him?*

She pulled back before his lips reached hers and she saw the frown dip along his face. "You are coming back?" She'd worried about this, but figured he would at least discuss the options with her.

"Helena?"

Standing, she put more distance between them. "Have you already agreed to a contract?"

Carter rubbed the back of his neck, and the reality struck her. She couldn't believe it. Couldn't believe that he wouldn't at least talk to her about this decision. Why not tell her last night when she was talking about moving home? Or at least visiting?

"Not officially."

"Not officially." Her heart clenched as she stared at him. "Were we going to discuss it? Do you want to know what I think?" She pushed a hand through her short hair. "This is a nine-month rotation, at least!"

"I really enjoy the work." Carter blew out a breath. His head popped back as he looked at her. "Nine months and the pay is good enough that you can take the other months off. Think of all the travel we could do. All the places we could visit."

"But not Chicago."

Carter tilted his head. "Helena—"

*Dear God, had she been fooling herself?*

"You like it here, too. And the pay is great," he repeated, as though she cared about the pay. They'd never discussed finances, and she hadn't taken this rotation for the boost to her bank account.

Her parents had tried to outline her life. Made decisions with the belief that they were protecting her. She'd sworn that she would carve her own path when she'd gone into nursing. Sworn that she'd be true to herself. And she wanted a home. A permanent place to call her own.

"What do you want out of life?" The question slipped between them. She held up a hand before he could answer. "Don't answer right now. Think about it. Really think about it."

She gestured to the clinic. "Because we do not have a future here." She closed her eyes as pain washed through her.

"We could," Carter pleaded. "Think about it, Helena, a few months off in whatever location we choose, and then we winter here. What a life."

"Carter." Helena could see the desire pulsing through him, how much he wanted her to say yes. To agree to spend her life on the ice with him. But that wasn't what she wanted, not forever. "This is a good rotation. I've enjoyed nearly every moment. But it's not a home."

"Home," he scoffed before pulling his hand over his face. "That word doesn't mean to me what it means to you. But I love you."

"I know." Helena put her hand on his chest. "The word doesn't have to have the same meaning to us. But if what we want out of life is so different…"

*Then love won't be enough.*

She let her voice die away. She could barely think the words, and there was no way for her to utter them without breaking.

"We don't have to decide anything right now." His eyes held hers—pleading.

"No. We don't." She swallowed the pain pooling in her soul. She could wait a few more days, but her heart clenched as though it was certain of the outcome. And she didn't want to accept it. Not yet.

*What do you want out of life?*

The question floated through his mind as he made the final notes for their meeting with Keith. It had been forty-eight hours since she'd asked it, and he still didn't have an answer. Still didn't know what he wanted.

He'd only planned winter to winter for the last three years. It had taken all the unknowns out of his life. And made it so he didn't have to focus on what he didn't have.

Carter blinked as that truth settled through him. Was he hiding here?

*No. Yes.*

He swallowed as his brain and heart warred over the decision. He should have discussed next winter's contract with Helena. Particularly after they'd talked about the future, except they hadn't, really. Because he'd made sure of that.

He'd pushed the conversation off. Hoping that he wouldn't have to make a choice. So what did he want out of life?

Still, his mind drew a blank. He hit his forehead with his palm several times, trying to force an answer out. This shouldn't be that difficult. Except the last time he'd had a plan for his life, his ex's affair had blown everything to pieces. Plans were so fragile if you let yourself hope for the future. When it collapsed, the results were devastating.

*But what if it doesn't collapse?*

It always had before, but what if it was different this time? With Helena?

Carter hit his forehead again, trying to force some steady thoughts through them. To find an answer.

"If you keep that up, you're going to give yourself a headache. And they aren't any fun." Helena pulled his hands away from his face as she kissed the top of his head.

The patch of worries eased as she touched him. It had been a long day without her after she'd complained of a headache yesterday and asked for the day off. Since he was almost certain that he was at least partially responsible for the headache, he'd told her it was fine. And given her space.

It gave him more time to think over her question, but not seeing her for a full day had sent a sense of longing through him he hadn't felt in forever, if ever.

She felt like his other half. And Helena wanted to go back to Chicago. Wanted to settle down.

*And she should get what she wants.*

He knew that, even if he couldn't give it to her. All his roots had been severed the day he asked about his parentage and imploded his family. Except the ones tied to Helena.

Those were still strong, still grounding him. If that connection was severed…

Pain washed through him as he tried to imagine life without Helena.

"Good afternoon." Carter grinned as Helena sat on the other side of the desk. She was here now. Here with him. How could she not want to stay with him?

He refused to voice that question. Instead, he asked, "Are you feeling any better?"

She nodded, "I'm doing better. Are we ready for the meeting?"

Their meeting with Keith was due to start in just a few minutes, but Carter didn't want to discuss it. He wanted to pull her into his arms, to pretend that the walls building between them were easy to tear down. Easy to hurdle. That her desire to put down roots, to live in Chicago, and his need to avoid the place at all costs weren't insurmountable.

Because at the moment they felt like they were far too high to climb.

"Does it have to be Chicago?" The question popped out of his mouth, and Helena smiled. The first genuine smile he'd seen in days. It made his heart soar.

"No." She reached for his hand. Her smile was bright, but there was still a touch of pain in her eyes.

He'd seen that pain before. It was the look his mother always wore when she talked about New York. Carter blinked. His mother was not a perfect woman, that was an understatement, but he'd never realized how much it hurt her to live away from her family.

It had never bothered his father. They visited his grandparents at least once a year, but his mother always cried when they left. Always clung to her parents before they parted and promised she'd visit soon. She'd even taken a few trips on her own.

Carter had always been excited for those boys' weekends with his father—though part of him had wished that she might want to take him with her. But as close as she was with her parents, his mother had never been overly motherly with him.

Would it have been different if his father had settled his practice in New York?

Maybe. But then Carter wouldn't have been born.

He sighed as that truth worked through him. His parents might have had a more successful union if his father had set aside his wants for his wife. But would that have made his father miserable?

Were Helena's and his dreams just too far apart? Why were there no simple answers?

"Carter?" Her eyes were full of hope, and he felt the pressure in his chest relax a little. There had to be a pathway they could travel together. But before he could compose any words, the teleconference system beeped.

"We have time." Helena squeezed his hand, and for the first time in days Carter felt at peace.

"Dr. Simpson and Helena!" Keith's voice boomed through the computer.

Carter sighed as Helena slid into place beside him. Beside her was where he wanted to be. They'd find a way to work through everything else.

"Hello, Keith." Helena leaned across him and waved. "It's good to see you."

"Good to see you two, as well. I've looked over the supply numbers and the recommendations you both sent for next winter. I think most things are in order. We can outline more for the summer rotation next month. Nice work."

Helena let out a soft chuckle as she looked at the screen. "Not that we don't enjoy seeing you, as it is—" she gestured toward the computer "—but since we don't know what the weather will be next month or if we will have any issues connecting, is there anything you want to go over with us?"

Keith smiled and held up a small stack of papers. "Honestly, I had planned to cancel this meeting, but I wanted to congratulate the two of you on the acceptance of your paper."

Carter grinned at the notes in the director's hands. They weren't the first to publish a scientific article based on what they'd learned here. Papers routinely came out of the base, but they were the first medical personnel to draft, submit and have a paper accepted while still at the facility. It was exciting. He almost wished he'd let Helena put his name on the paper.

"Helena did great work on it." Carter beamed and squeezed her hand.

"Then it's good she's listed as the lead author," Keith stated.

"Lead author…" Carter shook his head. "Wait." He looked to Helena. Her cheeks were nearly the color of apples. "No—"

"I tried to tell you," Helena whispered.

Carter swallowed and kept his attention focused on Keith. There was nothing to be done about the issue at this point. It hadn't published yet. He could request that his name be retracted. But that would likely mean that the journal wouldn't publish it out of fear that he disagreed with the substance. He couldn't do that.

"It's nice work. Maybe you can do another when you're on the ice next winter, Carter. Though preferably not about a virus outbreak." Keith chuckled, unaware of the crackle of energy in the polar clinic.

"What? I thought you were just thinking about it?"

Helena's questions slapped him. He hadn't officially signed a contract. But when Keith had asked a few weeks ago, he'd instinctively said he would return. When Helena had asked him about it, he'd left that part out. He should have told her, but they were already teetering on an edge. And he'd cowardly not wanted to cross it.

"I'd love it if you could winter with us again, too,

Helena." Keith's voice echoed in the clinic, but Carter wasn't sure that Helena heard him.

"I… I don't know what to say." She didn't even look at their director as she answered. Then she stood and grabbed a tablet off the counter. Placing the electronic between her and Carter, like a shield.

He blew out a breath as he looked back to the screen. "We'll get back to you on our intentions." Carter forced out the words while looking at Helena. He hadn't signed a contract; nothing was truly set in stone. He hadn't lied to her…but he hadn't been fully truthful, either. Carter wanted to kick himself. Wanted to apologize to find some way to fix this. But not with Keith watching.

"Anything else?"

"Um." Keith's voice wavered as he looked from where Helena had been sitting to where Carter was. Apparently news of their relationship had not traveled off the base, though it was clear now.

"Actually, there is one thing. A Dr. Drake Simpson reached out to me this morning to ask for your contact email."

Helena let out a small cry, but she didn't move toward him.

Carter's insides chilled as he tried to process the words.

His father had reached out to him through Keith. Why now?

"Normally I forward an email address with little thought, but Dr. Simpson indicated that he'd reached out to Helena, and she hadn't returned his contact."

Ice poured through his veins. Not only had she not told him he was a coauthor, but she'd also kept the fact that his father had reached out a secret.

*What other secrets is she holding?*

He hated the thought, hated the rush of emotions that were ripping through him.

Keith coughed. "Uh, I thought maybe…" He took a deep breath. "Simpson is a common name but—"

"It's my father, and I would prefer you not send my contact information to him." Carter nodded toward the screen, careful to keep his gaze away from Helena.

"Okay, but Carter." Keith waited until Carter met his gaze through the screen. "If he searches the website, we list everyone's emails."

"Understood. Anything else?"

"Nope. You two know how to reach me, otherwise I'll speak with you next month."

The phone clicked off and Carter turned to face Helena. "This is over."

*Over…*

Her heart screamed as her brain registered his bitter words. "Carter…" Helena breathed out, her soul crying. Grief warred with confusion and anger as she stared at the man she loved. They'd both made mistakes in the last week, both kept things from the other that they should have discussed. They'd let fear rule them, but that didn't have to mean that they were over. Just that they needed to have the painful discussions they'd put off.

"You lied to me, Helena."

"I did not." Her palms shook as she let anger take over. She should have told him about putting him as a coauthor on the paper and found a way to tell him about his father reaching out. But each time she'd tried, he'd changed the subject. "I told you when we started the paper that I would list you if you earned it, and you more than did. I should have told you, but every time I brought it up you redirected the conversation. If I had left your name off, it would have been dishonest. You coauthored it with me whether or not you wanted that recognition."

She pushed a hand through her hair as she tried to figure out how this had fallen apart so quickly. "And I will admit to being a coward. I should have told you what I'd done rather than hope that seeing your name on a journal article—something that you talked about as a seventeen-year-old kid—I mean what teenager does that besides you…"

She took a deep breath as the rambling words spilled out. "I wanted to surprise you. I thought it would make you happy."

"And my father?" His eyes flashed as he raised his eyebrow.

"Another cowardly move." Helena raised her chin. She'd spent her life trying to make others happy, pleasing them, and it was backfiring horribly now. "I asked the other day what would happen if he reached out, if he wanted something different, and you said he'd lost the right to contact you."

Carter flinched as she threw back his words. But Helena didn't stop. "I was trying to help. Trying to keep you from getting hurt."

"Lies of omission are still lies. I don't need your meddling, Helena. I don't want it."

*Meddling…*

The word cut across her heart as she pushed the tear away from her cheek. "Fine. If you see my help as meddling, my caring about you as meddling, my trying to make you happy as meddling, then you're right, we are over."

She closed her eyes and rocked back on her feet.

The world was collapsing around her. All the hopes and dreams she'd given in to over the last few months evaporated as the walls around Carter's heart rebuilt before her.

*But they were never really gone.*

She hiccuped as pain radiated between them, "But—" Helena swallowed "—I was not the only one keeping secrets. When were you going to tell me you'd already agreed to come back next year?"

Carter opened his mouth, but no words escaped.

"Lies of omission are still lies." She shook her head. "You use the truth to keep people out, Carter. No one can live up to the standard you've set. I promised never to lie about the important things, but you don't want to talk about certain topics and when I drop them, then I commit a lie of omission. And I think you're okay with that. It means you won't have to worry about getting hurt later."

Rather than address her concerns, Carter shook his head. "And your need to please is so you don't have to figure out exactly what you want, Helena. The few times in your life that you've broken away, your career, the medical tour in Iraq and here, have all been adventures you've enjoyed. You make others happy, but what do you really want?"

She pursed her lips as his words flayed her. She'd come here to prove to her parents that she wasn't the broken child they'd always seen. And her mother's latest email showed that nothing had changed. But she didn't want to examine those feelings now. And not in front of Carter.

"You're right." She nodded, a small part of her taking pleasure in the shock radiating off his face. "But running from home hasn't made you any happier, either. You're hiding here, and hiding is one thing I will not do. Goodbye, Carter."

She grabbed her bag, fully aware that they'd still have to see each other every day for the next several months. But it wouldn't be the same, never the same. The tears started a few steps from the clinic, but she let them flow.

She didn't know how to fix this. And for the first time in her memory, Helena wasn't sure that she wanted to repair the damage. Maybe some things were better left broken.

# CHAPTER ELEVEN

CARTER TAPPED HIS fingers against the desk and sighed as the sound reverberated around the empty clinic. Over the last two days, Helena had reported for her assigned shift and left as soon as it ended. Just like every other nurse practitioner he'd wintered with.

Silence had never bothered him before.

No, that was a lie.

He'd been used to the silence, but he hadn't really enjoyed it. If he had, it wouldn't have been so easy for Helena to pull him from it. She hadn't had to try at all—because part of him wanted to join the world. And look what had happened when he did.

Rolling his head from side to side, he let his gaze wander to the door, knowing that no one would come through it. The walls he'd built around his heart wobbled as the image of Helena danced before his eyes. For a moment, he'd thought he'd found it all—then she'd lied.

*Because you wouldn't let her discuss coauthorship or your father.*

His conscience had been ruthless in the last few days. And his subconscious had played more than a few dreams where Carter had done something different and saved his relationship. His email dinged, and he sighed as he opened the email from Keith. His contract for next winter was attached.

Carter opened it and glanced at it. It was the same contract he'd signed three times before. Scrolling the mouse down, he clicked on the digital signature button. The pop-up window asking him if he was sure he wanted to sign hovered in his gaze. The little reminder that his signature was binding blinked.

And Carter hesitated.

He tried to force his hand to move, but his heart refused to let his brain finish the gesture. He'd discussed this contract despite dating Helena. Despite knowing she wanted to go home.

To protect himself. What did he want?

Helena had asked him that. Told him to really think about it, but Carter hadn't done it—at least not successfully. Pulling up a blank document on the computer, he stared as the cursor blinked. Why was this so hard?

Blowing out a breath, he typed out: *Because what I want more than anything is to go home to Chicago. To be accepted.*

But that wasn't possible.

Except it had been within his grasp. Carter shook with pain as he stared at the words he'd typed out. There was no mention of his parents in those words. He wanted to be accepted.

And he had been.

And he'd thrown it away on a flimsy excuse. Accused the woman he loved of lying. Called her helping, generous nature *meddling*. Told her he didn't need it. Didn't need her.

*The biggest lie of all.*

The computer chimed as another email popped in. Carter closed the contract. He'd let Keith know he wasn't going to winter on the ice again. He'd enjoyed this adventure, but Helena was right. He was hiding here. The nine-month contract kept him from having to find a permanent place, from having to examine that what he wanted was to go home.

*Chicago.*

His breath caught as he stared at the new email.

Please read this, Carter.

His father's subject line was short and to the point. He moused over the delete button out of habit, then shook his head. He'd spent fifteen years running from this. Fifteen years building walls to keep everyone out because his father had tossed him aside. But Carter was done running.

Carter,

I hope you read this. Several years ago, I contacted multiple journal editors and asked them to keep an eye out in case you ever wrote a paper. When Richard sent me the article you wrote with Helena, and I found your picture on the Polar Medicine website, I jumped for joy.

This email is not the way I wanted to tell you how sorry I am. A few years ago, when I sent my last email, I hoped you'd respond so I could do this in person. However, I will accept it if you never wish to see me again. I earned that by lashing out at you.

Those days were dark for so many reasons, but I will never forgive myself for telling you to leave and not stopping you when you did. But I need you to know that I love you, and I am so proud of you.

If you ever wish to visit, please know my door will always be open.

Love you,
Dad

Carter blinked away the tears as he reread the missive. *Helena would be so excited...*

The thought floated into his mind, and tears of a different kind settled in his eyes. She'd done this, unintentionally, but it was her determination that he receive credit for his work, her doggedness that he didn't need to keep to himself, that had made this possible. Without her...

But he could right this. He could. He pushed back from the desk, then he halted. Helena would understand if he responded to his father first.

Then maybe his mother...

He sucked in a deep breath. He might not have sent her a note or followed up her missive, but he'd memorized the email address she'd sent.

He glanced at the clock. Dinner had started a few minutes ago. But what was one more missed dinner? He'd make it to all the rest.

That was a promise he was keeping.

Helena looked at the cafeteria door for the fourth time and sighed before turning her eyes to the dull tiles on the wall. Carter hadn't eaten any meals in the cafeteria since they'd broken up. And it looked like tonight wouldn't be any different. Over the last couple of days, he'd said less than fifteen words to her.

And Helena hated that she'd counted. And that she hadn't initiated any additional talks, either. He'd told her not to meddle, not to placate him, and she was obliging.

At least that was what she kept telling herself.

But the truth was that she was punishing herself. Helena spun the fork around on her plate as she huffed out another breath.

Carter had called her out on her meddling. Part of him was right. She had added his name without asking, believing that he'd be okay with it after. She still wasn't sure the exact reason he didn't want to be listed, though she suspected it had something to do with his father. The man had carried medical journals around like many people carried books when they were growing up.

If she'd known why Carter had shifted his childhood dream to be published in a journal his father read, she wouldn't have... Helena let that thought drift away. Would she have left it alone?

*No.*

That was a hard truth to face. She bit her lip as the seats around her emptied. She'd maintained their regular schedule of eating with the rest of the support staff. Not that she said much.

She would have tried to force Carter to accept his role in the paper. She'd spent her life trying to make others happy. But she hadn't considered what Carter wanted, just what she wanted for him. And he'd called her on it.

The irony was that she'd gotten the thing she thought she wanted most. She'd spoken to her parents over the satellite phone this afternoon after getting an email from Owen saying they wanted to chat.

It had been short, because time was limited in the poles, but they'd told her how proud they were. Owen had sent them a copy of their paper. They'd spent the few minutes they had praising her and never once asked how she was feeling or after her health. It was everything she'd wanted for so long, but the sweetness of the victory was absent.

*What do you want, Helena?*

She sighed as the memory of his question pushed around her brain. She'd spent so much time making others happy, trying to prove herself. Did she actually know what she wanted? *Yes.*

The answer was simple and devastating. She wanted Carter. And rather than accepting him where he was at, she'd tried to force him out of the shell that he'd hidden behind for so long. Her parents had spent her life treating her like the sick baby that had nearly died the week she was born, and she'd given them grace for her entire adult life.

She'd told Carter it didn't have to be Chicago before they'd argued, but her heart hadn't been fully in it. Her smile hadn't been true.

She wanted to go home. Wanted to put roots down, but without Carter, her chest heaved at the thought. Without Carter, those roots were pointless. Carter was home. She looked at the dull cafeteria tiles again. She'd never noticed that they needed a good buffing, never noticed the small size of the base, never noticed the multitude of things that drove some winter-over personnel mad.

Because she'd been happy here.

*With Carter.*

It had felt like home. She was right, this wasn't a place to put down roots, but it didn't have to be all or nothing. Love took compromise.

Given time, she was sure he'd be willing to visit Chicago. She'd seen the longing in his gaze at the mention of pretzels. And he still referred to it as home. But it didn't have to be his first stop when their tour ended.

Standing, she picked up her plate as Joseph let out a shriek. "That is not what I said!"

A clatter of dishes echoed in the nearly deserted cafeteria. Helena looked around and caught Kelly's gaze. "Go get Dr. Simpson. Now. Tell him to bring a sedative."

Another scream, and a few more broken dishes crashed to the floor.

"And then get security," Helena added as Kelly ran from the room.

Winter-over syndrome could cause aggression, and they'd all been here for nearly half a year. Sunlamps helped, but not everyone could handle the stress of a South Pole rotation. She didn't want to involve security unless absolutely necessary, but they needed to control the situation.

Moving cautiously, Helena approached Joseph with her hands in the air so he could see that she wasn't a threat. "Joseph." She kept her voice light. He had a steak knife in his hand, and his glazed eyes shifted from her to the plates he'd thrown to the floor.

During her deployment, she'd seen people break. Stress did weird things to the mind. She heard the cafeteria door slam behind her and watched Joseph flinch. Helena didn't turn to see if it was Carter, the security personnel or the few people left in the cafeteria exiting the premises.

She thought Joseph was more of a threat to himself than he was to anyone else, but the fewer people here, the better. "Can you tell me what happened?"

"Dr. Englewood said my idea was flawed." Joseph's lower lip shook as he closed his eyes.

Helena took a step forward before he opened them. The door to the cafeteria clicked again, and Helena heard Carter's quick intake of breath. A bit of the tension eased from her knowing he was here. He'd dealt with winter-over syndrome before. And he was a calming presence, at least for her.

"Dr. Simpson, don't come closer. Please." Joseph's eyes widened, and Helena glimpsed Carter in her peripheral vision.

"What's going on?" Carter redirected the conversation, his voice soft and soothing, too. He'd made sure not to agree to Joseph's demand that he stop his advance. But he didn't move any closer.

Joseph's eyes narrowed.

"He and Dr. Englewood disagreed about a scientific experiment," Helena offered.

"Exactly." Joseph nodded, the motion tight as anxiety pulsed through him.

Helena looked to Carter and gestured to herself before taking another step forward, hoping that Carter would understand that she was trying to keep Joseph's attention on her while Carter moved closer to administer the sedative she saw in his left hand.

"What was the disagreement about?" Helena asked, and then listened as Joseph rattled off numbers and figures she didn't understand. Whether that was because he was speaking nonsense or the astrophysics was beyond her, she didn't know. And it didn't matter. Carter was within three steps now.

Joseph started to turn his head, and Helena took a giant step forward, trying to keep his attention. "Tell me more, Joseph."

The diversion didn't work. The world slowed as she watched him raise the blade in his hand. "No!" Helena shouted.

Carter plunged the syringe into Joseph's upper arm,

pressed the plunger and stepped back. But he hadn't been quick enough. A slip of red bloomed on Carter's abdomen as he held his arms up.

"Carter?" She sucked in a breath as she forced her feet to stay where they were. This was still a dangerous situation.

He held up a hand and placed his other over the wound as he looked at Helena. "I'm fine, Helena."

The blood spreading along his shirt made her suspect otherwise, but she held her position.

"Doc, I'm sorry." Joseph's words were slurred. "I didn't mean to."

The doors of the cafeteria flew open as the small security team stepped through the door.

"Doc?"

"It's under control, Hal," Carter offered.

"I feel woozy." The knife slipped from Joseph's hand.

Helena moved fast, kicking the knife toward Hal and his security team. She slid to Joseph's side, though she kept a close eye on Carter, too.

"Joseph, that was droperidol I administered in your arm." Carter's voice was steady, but Helena suspected he was operating on mostly adrenaline at the moment. Knife attacks were notoriously fatal, but Joseph had swiped at Carter rather than stabbing him.

"You're going to go to sleep here in a few minutes, but I promise we will take care of you." Helena rubbed Joseph's arm as he slid to the floor. Carter motioned for one of the security team to grab a gurney for Joseph as his eyes started to close and Helena leaned him back.

"And for Carter," Helena added. She held up a hand before he could argue. "I am taking care of you. End of discussion." She slid to his side and took a quick look at the wound along his right side. It was going to need at least a dozen stitches to close, and it might need more than one layer of sutures, but he was going to be fine.

Carter smiled, but she could see the pain finally hitting him. "I love you, Helena. I know it's not the best time, but I needed to say it."

"I love you, too." She offered him a smile. "But if you attempt to help us lift Joseph on that gurney—" she nodded as Hal parked it before them "—I will sedate you, too. You've been heroic enough for today."

"Just gotta keep up with you." Carter tapped her hand as another security guard brought in a second gurney. "But I can walk to the clinic."

He was probably right, but until Helena could get a full look at his wound, she wasn't going to take any chances. "Humor my meddling." She winked, then immediately regretted her choice of phrase. "I just meant…"

"I'll humor it any time." Carter squeezed her hand as he slid onto the second gurney. "Any time."

"You're going to have a scar," Helena whispered as she pulled the last stitch along Carter's wound. Not that there was much chance that her words would wake the heavily sedated Joseph. It had taken nearly thirty stitches in two layers of the epidermis to close the injury.

She laid the needle to the side and noticed her hands shaking. At least her body had waited an hour before finally crashing. Before she could think, Carter pulled her into the bed with him, careful to avoid his right side.

"I am so sorry, Helena. For so many things." He kissed the top of her head. "I've spent the last fifteen years hiding but wishing for acceptance. And then when you gave it, I looked for reasons why it wouldn't stay.

And I started looking for reasons long before I found out about the article. I am sorry, Helena."

"Wow," she breathed out. "That was quite the apology." She kissed his cheek and snuggled closer.

"Say you forgive me. Please."

"Of course." This was an easy apology to accept. "But you were right about some things. I do always try to please people. To do what I think will make them happy. I thought your name on that article would make you happy. Thought I was protecting you by not telling you your father had reached out. But it was like the protection my parents always gave me. *Unneeded.* I should have told you, and I promise I will in the future. That is a mistake I won't make again."

She let her gaze wander his. "Can you forgive me?"

"Yes. Easily." He laid his head against hers. "But there is still the issue of home."

Helena sighed. "Home is wherever you are, Carter." She felt him smile against her forehead. She took a deep breath. "I know you want to do another winter here. If it's what you need, we can do one more. But just one more. I do want to put down roots, even if it isn't Chicago." She held her breath. She loved him, but this was not a point she was willing to compromise further on.

"I emailed Keith this afternoon to let him know I was going to pass on the contract. It's time to give someone else this adventure."

"What?" Helena shifted next to him, afraid she'd misheard his words. "Carter, you didn't have to do that."

"I know." Carter shrugged. "But I wanted to. It surprised me, too." He winked. "I have another surprise as well. When I think of home, it's always been Chicago, Helena. I can go anywhere, even home, just so long as you are by my side."

She thought her heart might burst from her chest. If a knife hadn't sliced his stomach less than three hours ago, she might spin him around. "I love you, Carter Simpson. I vote we let you get some rest and then make plans tomorrow or the next day. We have time."

"As much as we want." Carter grinned.

"Forever?" Helena kissed his cheek.

"Forever is just my starting point, Helena."

# EPILOGUE

THE SOLD SIGN in front of the redbrick row house made Helena want to scream. It was really hers and Carter's. Or it would be after they signed the papers later this afternoon.

She already had plans to put some annual flowers in the decorative planters she and Carter had seen when they walked through the hardware store last night. They'd only meant to look at paint swatches, so Helena could update the small half bath by the entryway. But they'd spent nearly two hours roaming the store, discussing projects. Reveling in their home.

*Home.*

They were really home. She rocked back on her feet and looked around for Carter. He'd had a shift at the hospital and said he wanted to meet her here before they headed to sign the final papers. She looked at her watch and pulled her phone from her pocket.

"I'm here!" Carter raced up the side of the house, a smile covering his face. He'd made peace with his parents. Their relationships would never be the same, but with time, who knew what healing might happen.

"Finally." Helena laughed as he spun her around. "We should get going."

"One sec." Carter took her hand and kissed her fingers. "There's one thing that needs to happen first."

The wind raced around them, and Helena pulled her coat tight. "Well, what is it? 'Cause it's windy and those clouds look like rain."

He slid to one knee and Helena put her hands to her lips as Carter pulled a ring box from his pocket. "I love you, Helena Mathews. Say you'll be my wife."

She bounced with excitement as she stared at him. Her throat closed as all the emotions poured through her.

"Are you going to answer? That wind is a might nippy."

She laughed as she nodded yes. "You're my home, Carter. Always."

\* \* \* \* \*

# COMING SOON!

We really hope you enjoyed reading this book.
If you're looking for more romance, be sure to
head to the shops when new books are
available on

# Thursday 28th October

To see which titles are coming soon, please visit

**millsandboon.co.uk/nextmonth**

# MILLS & BOON

## THE HEART OF ROMANCE

## A ROMANCE FOR EVERY READER

**MODERN**
Prepare to be swept off your feet by sophisticated, sexy and seductive heroes, in some of the world's most glamourous and romantic locations, where power and passion collide.

**HISTORICAL**
Escape with historical heroes from time gone by. Whether your passion is for wicked Regency Rakes, muscled Vikings or rugged Highlanders, awaken the romance of the past.

**MEDICAL**
Set your pulse racing with dedicated, delectable doctors in the high-pressure world of medicine, where emotions run high and passion, comfort and love are the best medicine.

**True Love**
Celebrate true love with tender stories of heartfelt romance, from the rush of falling in love to the joy a new baby can bring, and a focus on the emotional heart of a relationship.

**Desire**
Indulge in secrets and scandal, intense drama and plenty of sizzling hot action with powerful and passionate heroes who have it all: wealth, status, good looks…everything but the right woman.

**HEROES**
Experience all the excitement of a gripping thriller, with an intense romance at its heart. Resourceful, true-to-life women and strong, fearless men face danger and desire - a killer combination!

# MILLS & BOON

## Coming next month

### CHRISTMAS MIRACLE IN JAMAICA
### Ann McIntosh

Chloe took a deep, audible breath and then said, "I'm pregnant."

The words made no sense to him. And yet they must have, because his heart stumbled and an icy pit opened up in his stomach.

"And before you ask, yes, the baby is yours. If it isn't, then we'll need to contact the Vatican about a miracle, because you're the only man I've been with since I left my husband two years ago."

Her words came at him as though from a distance. The frigid sensation had spread from his belly to form a band around his chest, causing the fleeting thought that perhaps he was having a myocardial infarction.

Then Chloe's face softened into an expression so beatific, all other thoughts flew from his head at the sight.

"It's actually a true miracle to me," she said, her voice low and so full of joy it melted the ice in his torso. "I was told I wasn't able to conceive because of endometriosis. So—" She paused, her chin tilting up to that pugnacious angle he'd come to know so well. "So what I wanted you to know is that I'm keeping this baby, and if you don't want to be involved in his or her life, I can assure you my child will lack for nothing."

He knew he should say something, but try as he might, nothing came out. And it felt as though he'd been turned to stone. All he could do was watch as Chloe gave him a small smile and stood up.

"I'll let you get on with your afternoon," she said, and then she was gone.

Pregnant? With my child?

Sam's brain couldn't seem to grasp the concept, and he finally staggered to his feet, not knowing where exactly he planned to go.

Endometriosis…

His heart stopped, and a wave of nausea had him swallowing against the thickness rising in his throat.

Chloe's pregnancy was high-risk.

His legs gave way again, and he plopped back into his chair, momentarily overcome by fear so strong it dulled the edges of his sight to darkness.

What would be worse, he wondered dully: losing a child you never knew existed until it was gone or a second one you suddenly realized you wanted almost too much?

Because, just then, Sam realized the baby growing in Chloe Bailey's womb meant more to him than he'd have ever expected.

That baby—his child—was as much a miracle for him as it was for its mother.

*Continue reading*
CHRISTMAS MIRACLE IN JAMAICA
Ann McIntosh

*Available next month*
www.millsandboon.co.uk